THE SEEDS OF CHAOS

IN THE SHADOW OF SIN:
BOOK TWO

BY
ALAN HARRISON

This is a work of fiction. Names, characters, places, and incidents either are the product of the author's imagination or are used fictitiously. Any resemblance to actual persons, living or dead, events, or locales is entirely coincidental.

Cover design by MiblArt
Map by Cornelia Yoder

ISBN 9781838132828 (paperback)
ISBN: 9781838132835 (ebook)

For those who know they are not

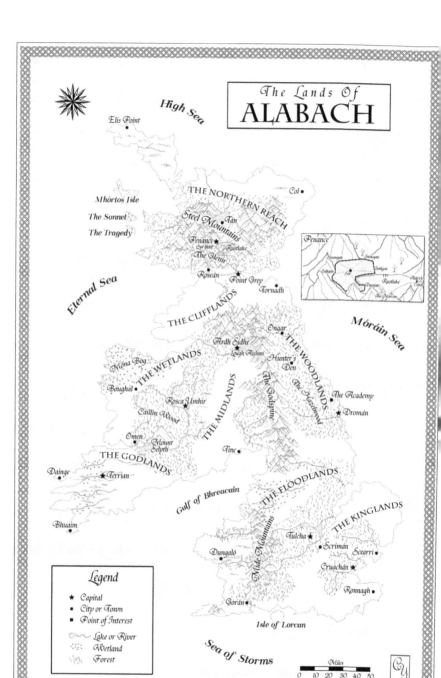

CONTENTS

CHAPTER 1: THE CLIMB

Alone and afraid, the young mage tried to move, but his body refused to comply. With no eyes to see or mouth to scream, he could do nothing but succumb to the terror that came upon him.

***

The rising sun burst over the horizon of the Eternal Sea, spilling golden light over the Clifflands of Alabach. Fiery rays licked the Teeth of the Glenn, but little heat reached the poisonous valley beyond. The tide, now gilded under the morning's influence, crashed against the cracked cliffs of the country's western coast. On the beach lay a dying Simian, desperately trying to remember who he was.

Saltwater filled his lungs, cast out again by a spluttering cough and a barrage of retches. The taste of vomit stung his throat.

Somewhere between the throbbing ache inside his head and the sharp pain at the back of his skull, the Simian remembered a time when he was young, running through the dusty streets of Penance. He saw himself as if a spectator, watching the child weave between the crowds, a coin-purse too large to be his own clutched against his chest.

Two men dressed in the scarlet robes of the Churchguard gave chase, but the young thief was too fast for them.

Swift. They used to call me Farris the Swift.

Then Farris saw himself treating with criminals, led by a Simian with greying hair across his face and shoulders. Next, he was in Cruachan, capital city of Alabach, telling lies to King Diarmuid the Third and Nineteenth.

He held a knife held against a drunken Simian's stomach. He boarded an airship larger than the Basilica itself. He fled from a pack of beadhbhs, then from a mountain troll. Farris remembered it all, along with the dozens of names he took throughout his life.

Another wave, stronger than the first, washed over Farris's body. As he closed his eyes to keep the water out, a woman's face appeared before him. A young, beautiful woman dressed all in white. Or blue. Or both. The image was transient, threatening to vanish at any minute.

After a moment, he recognised her as Sláine the White, the healer he had travelled across the Glenn with, but she was gone before he could be sure. A voice, fainter than the water washing against his ears, spoke to him.

"Because the gods have willed it, Chester."

He remembered. Sláine had told him about destiny and fate, though she believed his name was Chester at the time. The healer had described her own struggles in a world without free will, and how every moment in Farris's life would lead to this final one.

But the gods didn't send me here. A deranged king did.

Even with the last of his life slipping away, Farris smiled. Before he left the capital, King Diarmuid had given him instructions to destroy the Simian skyfleet harboured at the ruins of the Tower of Sin, in Penance. The king claimed he was attacked by the Silverback and the other Simian dissidents, but Farris knew this could not be true; he himself was allied with the separatists.

So why did King Diarmuid lie about the Silverback? Why did he think attacking Penance was the best solution? Farris had never known, but the answer was clearer now than ever.

King Diarmuid has lost his mind.

The tide rolled back, and Farris struggled for another breath. The next wave would kill him. That was the only thing he was certain of now.

But the king's madness left a bitter taste, worse than the salt and sand, for Farris was now the only living person to know of his plans. Soon, there would be nobody left.

The woman flashed before his eyes once more, with a terrible smile spread across her face. In an instant of clarity,

Farris saw that this was not Sláine the White. Before he could put another name to her, she was gone, and the tide came creeping back.

My time has finally come.

His lungs exhaled his last breath, his heart thundered out one final beat, and each muscle in his body began to relax. The wave passed over his face once more.

No!

A maddening desperation took hold of him. He pushed his lips out over the surface of the water for another breath of air. His heart gave another beat, and he slowly tilted his head forward. For what seemed like an eternity, the tide remained over him, but Farris fought the thousand voices in his head that begged him to lie back and die. It almost seemed as if they sang to him, telling him that his pain would cease if he just lay his head back into the sand.

But another voice cast them aside. A voice that roared 'No!'

He balled the fingers of his left hand into a fist, shifting the weight of his body onto his arm. As the tide retreated, he pushed himself up, agony in every movement.

He slowly sat upright, the water now only up to his waist. Through blurred vision, he saw the face of the cliffs bathing in the morning sun.

A shrill shriek cut through the air, and Farris looked up. The cliffs were perhaps thirty feet tall, but the distance did little to dampen the sound of the troll's slaughter. The troll he and his companions had brought to the fields by the cliffs.

Farris shook the memory from his head.

More will die worse deaths if the king goes to war.

He tried to stand, but his left leg buckled under his weight, sending him splashing forward into the water once more. With salt upon his tongue, he pulled himself up and crawled towards the cliff-face, dragging one useless leg behind him.

Don't stop.

His hands found the rough rock of the cliff, fingers groping against the prickly beachgrass jutting out.

Don't look up.

He reached one hand up and clenched an overhead rock in his fist. The stone grazed against his knuckles, and his wounds stung with salt, but he tore his attention away from his pain. With a muffled roar he pulled himself upwards and reached up with another hand.

Don't give up.

Soil and loose sand trickled over his head, and Farris shut his eyes. His leg throbbed, but he pulled himself upwards again, dangling both feet over the ground.

I'm their last hope. Only I can warn them.

He reached upwards, struggling to find another grappling point. Instead of solid rock, his fingers grasped a handful of beachgrass in the cracks of the cliff. He held them tightly by the roots.

If I stop now, everyone's death will be for nothing.

First there was Chester, the Simian navigator Farris had impersonated to board the ship. Chester's death was a necessity to make up for the Crown's lack of preparation for the mission. The king had just as much a hand in killing him as Farris did.

The beachgrass took Farris's weight well. A strong breeze caressed the fur on his shoulders as he reached up again. His arms ached with fatigue, but he turned his thoughts back to his mission.

If I fall now, Penance will follow.

He was the one who caused the fight aboard *The Glory of Penance*. He was the one who caused the ship to crash into the Glenn. He was just as guilty as the beadhbhs that picked off the survivors.

But it'll only be justified if I make it home...

His fingers found solid stone again, but their grip failed for a fraction of a second. He slipped, barely catching himself with his other hand. The muscles in his shoulders cried out in protest, and his mind almost submitted to their pleas.

Fionn the Red. Sir Bearrach. Sláine the White. The crewmen, the labourers in the field, all dead to save the Simians of Penance.

The scene of the troll's killing field resurfaced again in his mind. The death didn't bother him; he had seen plenty of that since he first left Penance...but one memory from that morning stuck harder than the rest.

The girl.

He pulled himself upwards again, almost losing his grip.

Chester may understand. Reasonable people like Sir Bearrach and Sláine the White would surely accept that sacrifices must be made in times of war. Their lives could secure the well-being of thousands of Simians in Penance, or hundreds of thousands of Humans across Alabach. They'd understand...

But how could that reasoning apply to a child who watched her mother die?

His grip failed, and Farris felt weightless for the instant his hands fell away from the Cliffside.

Just a child.

Farris braced himself for a long plummet to the ground, but he fell no further. Something strong wrapped itself around his wrist. For the first time since he set his hands against the stone, he looked up.

A large Human leaned over the edge of the cliff, his mouth open in shock.

"Yarlaith!" he cried. "There's another one here. Alive! And a Simian!"

***

Farris woke up drunk, not quite sure where he was. At least he felt drunk. His memory was hazy, his thoughts seemed slower than usual, and he certainly didn't know where he was.

He raised his head. He was on a bed in a small room, with one window opening out to the east. The Teeth of the Glenn were barely visible through the dusty glass.

Farris sat bolt upright, suddenly aware that the pain in his leg was gone. His muscles no longer ached, and even the grazing across his knuckles had vanished. Apart from a slight sense of light-headedness, he felt perfectly healthy.

A wooden shelf bolted into the adjacent wall gave him a hint to where he was, with glassware and alchemical solutions racked neatly on its surface. Translucent screens separated his bed from the rest of the room, but a moving shadow on the other side told him that he was not alone.

Farris was about to call out, but a sharp scream cut him off.

The cry went on until the voice went hoarse. It was a man, a young man, by the sound of it. After a short breath he called out again, more agony in every note than before.

Then he went silent.

Farris tentatively removed himself from the bed, spotting his few belongings folded neatly by his feet. He pulled a plain vest over his head – what had once been an attempt to dress as Chester. After he put the rest of his clothes on, he checked his leather shoulder-pack. Its contents were still inside, undisturbed.

"Ah, you're awake. I'm sorry about that racket."

Farris turned to face a man in white robes speckled with blood. He was short, even for a Human, with wiry strands of dark, grey hair in tufts across a balding head.

"What did he do to deserve that?" asked Farris, nodding towards the other bed.

"Ah," said the man, rubbing his hands together and casting his gaze to the floor. "Another patient, a mage, from the field. He...lost an arm."

"Fionn..." whispered Farris. "How is he doing?"

The man shook his head. "Not well. Not well at all. Did you travel with him and the others?"

Farris quickly played out a dozen scenarios in his mind. To tell the truth could put the Crown one step closer to figuring out his role in the ship's crash. Assuming the king's men were looking for an answer, or even had any influence in this town, or settlement, or wherever it was he had landed himself.

"Where am I?" he asked instead, stepping past the man to take a closer look at his surroundings. It was indeed a clinic, the man clearly a white mage. However, a portrait of a woman hanging against the opposite wall held Farris's attention while the healer spoke.

"This is Roseán, a village in the Clifflands. We're about half a day on foot from Point Grey to the east. My name is Yarlaith the White, and I am the one who has tended to your wounds. Are you feeling well enough to walk?"

"Who is she?" Farris asked, pointing up at the picture. His arm was trembling, not from fatigue.

"Ah, Lady Meadhbh of the Trinity," said Yarlaith. A flash of confusion appeared in his eyes.

No...no, it can't be.

"I need to clear my head," said Farris, slipping past Yarlaith towards the door. "How much do I owe you for the treatment?"

"Free..." muttered Yarlaith. "Free to all who walk in the Light of the Lady."

"Thank you," said Farris, bowing ever so slightly to his saviour.

Though I'd rather be free of Her light entirely.

As he walked out through the old cottage into the fresh autumn air, Farris tried to recall the vision he had seen at the bottom of the cliff. The beautiful woman with the terrible smile.

No, it can't be Her. She doesn't exist. By Sin's stones, She can't possibly exist.

CHAPTER 2:
THE BEAR AND THE
BEADHBH

Fear had claimed the young mage many times before, but it rarely strayed from his dreams. Hours had passed since he last saw light, and he could no longer tell if he was asleep or awake. He prayed to the Gods that he would not dream, but when sleep eventually took him, it was clear that the Lord had not listened.

***

The road from Yarlaith's clinic followed an irregular path, meandering through the village as if its buildings were rocks in a river's path. To the east, the sun had begun to set over the Móráin Sea, casting long shadows that seemed to grope the land below. Farris set his sights southwards, where the road opened up to a wide cobblestone square, with large buildings of red brick and black slate contrasting with the houses of wattle and daub he passed.

Maybe there'll be a tavern, thought Farris, some excitement rising in his chest. *I could do with a drink.*

One of the buildings towards the centre of the square was large enough to be an inn. Farris squinted to make out its name, barely noticing the bottleneck of villagers outside the chapel to his left.

He picked up his pace, careful not to make eye-contact with those leaving the church.

How many died, four? Five? He tried to shake the thought from his mind, but the image of little girl alone in the field remained. *Skies above! What where they doing there before sunrise?*

Regardless of why they were there, it certainly wasn't the peasants who brought doom to the Clifflands. Only one man could take the real blame for that.

"King Diarmuid Móráin," Farris whispered, a vain attempt to drown out the voice in his head that roared, '*Me!*'

"Look at that! There's that Simian fella ye saved from the cliffs!"

Before Farris had a chance to make sense of the words, he found himself confronted by two young men in black tunics, both thick with muscle and perfect mirror images of one another. One reached out to grab Farris's hand, and shook it vigorously with little effort on the Simian's part.

"Good to see you're well! Gods, I've never seen one of your kind before."

"He's always been afraid of Simians," the other said, taking Farris's hand in an equally firm grip. "Good thing he didn't balk at the sight of ye, else we'd be scraping you off those rocks!"

Farris faked a smile. "You have all the thanks I've got to give."

"Tell us about the troll!" said the first man. "What were ye doing in the Glenn, of all places!"

"Please," said Farris, emphasising the weariness in his voice. "I'm in no state to be telling tales right now. I need to be alone."

Before either of the men had a chance to object, Farris produced a coin-purse from his shoulder-pack. Unsure which had been the one to save him, he shoved a handful of gold into each of their hands.

"Take this as my thanks," said Farris. "Buy yourselves a pint on me."

"A p-pint?" stammered the first stranger. "We could buy a barrel with this much! Come on, Cillian. We've gotta pay the cider house a visit!"

The other man nodded curtly towards Farris before both ran off together. Sure, their reward had indeed been excessive, but it was important to keep people from prying into the events that led him to the village.

Farris went on into the inn. The common room was wide with a high ceiling supported by thick, wooden beams. Cold limestone rock formed the floor and walls, but an array of torches and a roaring fire ensured the room remained warm. The tavern was mostly empty, except for the lone bard tuning his lute in the corner, and the bar staff outnumbering the patrons.

"So, what'll it be for you, sir?"

Farris carefully considered the barman standing before him. There had been only a slight hint of hesitation in his voice, as if he too had never seen a Simian before but was trying hard not to be rude.

"You don't happen to serve thainol here, do you?" said Farris.

The innkeeper smiled. "Ah, the Simian stuff was never popular with the locals. We had a batch of it before, but it took us months to sell the whole—"

"A pint of pale will do," interrupted Farris.

"Aye." The innkeeper deftly pulled a pint glass out from under the counter. "You arrived here in good time. The funeral crowd will come pouring in here any minute, and most will spend the night standing. You were lucky to get a seat."

"Lucky, yes," muttered Farris. From the way the innkeeper nodded in agreement, Farris guessed that he missed the bitterness in his tone.

He did feel fortunate, however, for the innkeeper left as soon as the pint had been poured and paid for.

The ale tasted just as well as those served back in the capital, though a little thicker than what Farris was used to.

The first few mouthfuls were bliss, but he was barely halfway through when the doors to the inn slammed open, admitting a flood of villagers.

Most took seats at the tables throughout the room, but the few that sat at the bar gave a wide berth to the solitary Simian. The bard at the corner of the room began singing, and those sitting nearby seemed to immediately forget about the stranger in their tavern. The people clapped along to the sweet melody of the bard's song. There was some discord in the air, however. The two brothers that had saved Farris were now singing by the door of the inn, though their song was far less musical than the bard's.

Luck and fate. One threw me off the edge of a cliff, and the other put those men in the right place at the right time. Perhaps both played a role in saving him.

Farris shook the thought from his head. The will of the Gods would need to wait. There was work to be done.

Point Grey is half a day away. The ferry from there to Penance would be the quickest way to bring word to the Silverback. I could catch one early in the morning if I leave here tonight....

But where would that leave him? It might already be too late to unravel the king's plot. For all he knew, Diarmuid may have already planned a second pre-emptive strike as soon as news of the crash reached him.

Would it be in the Silverback's best interest to fight back now?

No, there was no use in speculating. Without the full story about what really happened down in the railway with Santos and the king and their supposed attackers, it would be futile to plan ahead.

Farris drank deeply from his pint, the bitter ale helping relieve some of his pain. The healer had done well to repair his injuries so quickly, but a dull ache still remained at the back of his head. He was grateful, of course, for even an inch from death, a few hours' worth of white magic was enough to bring him back to his feet. With that kind of power on the side of the Crown, what hope did the Silverback have in a war?

Someone took a seat beside Farris, but he didn't turn to see who it was. He muttered as they sat, and to his relief, they didn't try to strike a conversation. Everyone else was happy to be distracted by the bard, who sang rude, boisterous songs, poking fun at the nobility.

Wasn't this supposed to be a funeral? Humans had a strange way of dealing with the dead. For all the sanctity of their ceremony, it was all forgotten once the mourners reached the bar. He couldn't blame them, of course. The Simians had a similar way of dealing with grief. They just didn't try to disguise it with piousness. When a Simian was cremated in Penance, it was customary for family and friends—not some local druid—to say a few words.

The night went on, and Farris found it quite easy to pay for the pints coming his way. The men from earlier had it right: a handful of gold was more than enough to pay for a barrel of ale this far from the capital. With what little money he had left, Farris could have purchased most of what the bar had to offer.

As he took another drink, Farris paused; something in the air had changed. The music still went on—a slow and valorous marching song this time—but now everyone was standing, and in silence. Worse still, they were all staring right at him.

Oh, it seems they've noticed the Simian in their midst.

The song ended, and the bard held an upturned hat towards the crowd. But none paid him any mind. One man spoke up.

"Excuse me, sir, you should show more respect!"

Farris glared at the speaker, an elderly farmhand with a hunched back.

Is he talking to me?

The Simian slammed his near-empty glass on the table, perhaps a little harder than he meant to. But when everyone around him recoiled in response, Farris suppressed a smile.

Skies above, they're terrified.

"And what have I done to offend you, little man?" said Farris, in a voice as cold and commanding as he could manage.

"You've disrespected your hosts," the stranger began. "The least you could do is stand for our Ballad, but you lot are all alike: ignorant of everything the Trinity has done for you."

Ignorant? You don't know the half of it.

Farris stood slowly, keeping his intimidating glare locked on the farmhand as he rose above him.

"You should read a book, Human, instead of listening to jesters for your history lessons." Rage shook his chest as he spoke. He pointed towards the bard. "This one seems to have left out the verses where your people slaughtered mine...how they used their magic to enslave us."

Another voice cried out from the crowd. "It was not our choice! We gave your kind a chance to live alongside us!"

"You gave us a choice between giving our lives to your Gods or to your swords," he snarled.

"And you chose neither," called a third voice. "You've done nothing but spit in the face of the Trinity ever since we let you rats live!"

Is he serious? He can't possibly be serious. The slur 'rats' reminded Farris of a conversation he had with the Chester, who spoke of the subjugation of the Simian people by the Human Church and Crown. That was before Farris killed him. The memory caused Farris's heartbeat to accelerate. All he wanted to do now was leave.

But before he could, the first villager spoke again. He pointed at the person sitting adjacent to Farris.

"This girl lost her mother today! You deny our Gods, so tell her what you believe! Tell her the fate of her mother was nothing but bad luck!"

It was only now that Farris who was sitting beside him: the girl from the field. She looked up at him, with bright green eyes that seemed to have seen too much. Sorrow lined every feature of her face.

If the Gods are true, they are as sure as Sin not good.

But no, there was no use in blaming the Gods, or the king, or the weavings of fate for what happened back by the cliffs. If this girl wanted someone to blame, these townsfolk had found the right person.

In silence, the girl stared deep into his eyes, a spark of curiosity in her expression.

"I have nothing to tell you, little one," he started, not quite sure where he was going with it. "My words are as empty as the prayers of these fools. Listen to them, and they'll blind you to the truth: your mother will not live forever in Paradise. Instead, she will live on in your memories."

His words were met with silence. A hundred eyes stared at him, as if he had committed a sin far worse than murder. Before anyone had a chance to react, Farris quickly finished the last of his ale and stormed towards the tavern door. Before leaving, he paused and glanced back at the girl.

"Cherish the moments you had together," he said. "Instead of praying for those that will never come."

Something between anger and anxiety tore through him as he left the tavern, as if every ounce of blood in his body had been set to boil. He strode through the cobblestone square as he tried to cast the memory of the girl from his mind. By the time he reached the edge of the town, he realised that his eyes were filled with tears.

CHAPTER 3:
ANOTHER SEED

Even as he lay in the darkness, writhing with pain, the Pyromancer dreamt the same dream that had haunted him all his life. He found himself entombed once more in that terrible coffin made from flesh, gradually filling with blood. He knew that crying for help would do no good, so Fionn the Red simply waited until he was fully submerged. Then he drowned again just as he had done so many times before.

***

The road took Farris eastwards from Roseán, through a dying countryside. Dark trees flanked the path, with leaves in decay at their roots, and little life left upon their branches.

There was certainly a strange sort of peace in this side of the country, far from the politics of Cruachan and the steam of Penance. Life must be so simple, with only the weather and crops to worry about.

Except when the occasional troll comes lumbering out from the Glenn.

Farris attempted to shake the thought from his mind, but it wouldn't leave him. How often would smallfolk be forced to deal with a death as brutal as that child's mother's? And even if the Silverback did go to war, how badly could a conflict between Man and Simian affect a life as simple as this?

No, I cannot trivialise the threat of a civil war. This madness must be stopped before the first seed is sown.

Even in the silver light of the crescent moon, Farris barely noticed that the trees had grown more numerous around him as the path continued into a forest. Tufts of grass now speckled the ground, growing upwards between cracks in the stone.

The king had another spy stationed in Penance. We were supposed to meet him once the ship docked at Sin. Perhaps it wouldn't be too late to track him down. Indeed, the king had said that he would be disguised as a druid—that alone was a very uncommon sight in the City of Steam.

As his mind rolled through the possible scenarios involving the Silverback's men and the false preacher, it took Farris longer than usual to feel that something was not right. The forest was absent of life, with no sound but the wind rustling through bare branches. The hair across Farris's shoulders stood on end, and gooseflesh emerged on his forearms.

He paused and quickly examined his surroundings. The ground on either side of the path sloped upwards, like the sides of a valley. The trees were thickest along the tops of the hills and would make for a perfect spot for an ambush.

Farris cursed under his breath. Although he had a small dagger concealed inside his pack, it certainly wouldn't help if he was already being watched.

I should have been more prepared.

"I know you're there," he called out. "If its gold you want, I have plenty. But I cannot give you any if you stay hidden."

In an instant, the forest came to life. Three men emerged from a hedgerow just beyond the path, and two more armed with crossbows appeared from atop a hill.

"There's no need to hurt yourself," said one of the three men as he approached. He held an iron spear in both hands, the tip pointing towards Farris's chest. "Hand over whatever you've got, and we'll be on our way."

"Of course," said Farris. He slowly took the pack off his shoulder. "I have no reason to start any trouble." His eyes remained fixed on the spear.

Intimidating, yes, but not very practical for close combat.

The other two, although also armed, were far from intimidating. One held an iron dagger with the blade pointing upwards as if it were a butter knife. The other wielded a longsword, but his grip was far too tight for complex manoeuvring. The only foes that gave Farris pause were the two crossbow men on the hill, but even they would only have one shot apiece. Not counting reloading, of course.

"Your armour is fine for a highwayman," said Farris to the first bandit. "Have you been stealing from Simian soldiers lately?"

"That's none of your damn business, rat! Just hand over the bag and we'll let you go on your way." He thrusted the spear dangerously near Farris's face.

"You're using your weapon wrong," said Farris, keeping his voice clear and calm. "A spear has little use outside of a phalanx." He fastened his grip on his pack. "Good for hunting, perhaps, but you'd need a fairly good throwing arm. Have you thrown a javelin before?"

Before the bandit had a chance to react, Farris shoved the spear downwards. It took little effort to force it to drop, and its momentum caused his attacker to lose balance. Farris leapt forward and grabbed the spearman by the throat. As soon as he heard the sound of bolts being loosed, Farris shoved the bandit towards the direction of the crossbowmen. One bolt caught the rogue between the shoulder blades, the other went whizzing over Farris's head.

He dropped the spearman and faced the other two. They came at him together, from either side. The first swung his sword towards Farris, but he hopped backwards to avoid it. As the sword's weight carried the bandit through its arc, Farris hurled his pack into the bandit's face. Though not heavy enough to do damage, it did loosen the bandit's grip on the sword. With a quick strike of Farris's open palm against his chest, the bandit's weapon fell to the ground.

The third attacker thrusted towards Farris with the dagger, swinging it too widely to be of any threat. Farris evaded one swing easily and anticipated the next before it came. When it did, Farris grabbed the bandit's wrist and struck his forearm. The sound of snapping bone was enough to give the two crossbowmen pause in their reloading.

"Do you think your next bolt will reach me before I reach you?" called Farris. He moved forward, deftly picking the spear from the ground as he went. The two marksmen fled at the sight, not looking back at the comrades they abandoned.

"You should visit Penance," Farris said to the others on the ground. "There is some honour amongst the thieves there."

Only the bandit armed with the longsword seemed to hear him, for the spearman lay dead, and the other was more concerned with the bloodied bone jutting out from his skin.

"What makes you any different than us?" stammered the swordsman. He reached out for his dropped weapon, but Farris drove the spear's head into his wrist. The Simian leaned in towards the bandit, who howled in pain.

"I fight for a better cause," Farris whispered, twisting the spear.

Farris fetched his pack, and deftly threw it over his shoulder.

"Best to keep your voices down," he called out as he left. "If the wolves aren't drawn in by your scent, they'll sure as Sin hear your squealing."

***

The night had deepened by the time Farris reached Point Grey. Dark clouds blanketed the sky, blocking out the light of the moon. Still, the town's huge stone wall was easily visible, with torches burning by the gates. Two guards stood at its base and regarded Farris with caution as he approached. Farris switched his stride to a limp.

"Bandits," Farris rasped, letting more pain than he felt linger in his words. "Highwaymen on the Sandy Road attacked me as I travelled."

"And what has you walking the Sandy Road so late in the first place?" said one guard.

Farris groaned. He held a hand against his waist, as if nursing a wound. "Can't you see that I'm in dire need of medical attention? What danger do you think I could cause your people in this state?"

The second guard remained silent but signalled up to a watchtower overhead. Before Farris could press the matter further, the gates began to open slowly, creaking with every inch.

"There's a healer living down beside the Earl's manor," said the guard. "He'll tend to your wounds if you can wake him."

"Thank you," said Farris. "The bandits were on the road about five miles back. They didn't look like they were in a hurry to leave."

"I'll send a patrol as soon as possible," replied the second guard. "Many thanks, citizen."

Farris walked through the gates, careful not to move too deftly.

As one of Alabach's seven capital cities, Point Grey was almost identical to Cruachan in its architecture. Red-bricked buildings with low thatched roofs leaned over the road, as if threatening to fall forward at a moment's notice. Cobblestones of uneven shapes and innumerable shades of grey formed the streets, which extended out in each direction from the gates. One wound up a hill towards the Earl's manor, another stretched out to the west towards the harbour. Farris took the second path, bracing himself against the cool wind from the sea.

He walked by more taverns than he'd typically prefer to pass in an evening, but he dared not stop. With Point Grey being a major port town so close to Penance, it was likely that he'd be forced to meet some familiar faces before the night was through.

Eventually the street opened up to the harbour, but the stench of shellfish reached Farris before he could see the water. He quickened his pace once the grey pier that gave the town its name came into view. There, the ferry to Penance swayed alone on the water.

On approach, it became clear that something was amiss. It had been three years since Farris had been to Point Grey, but he was positive there had always been plenty of activity at the dock, even this late at night.

Farris frantically searched for another soul, eventually spotting a solitary Simian looking out at the sea. He wore a large, yellow raincoat brightly buttoned against the wind, with a bacum cigar held between his lips.

"You haven't heard, have you?" the stranger said, his voice thick with the brogue of the Dustworks of Penance. "No ships or trains leaving here till this business with the king blows over. Though the stones of Sin would be quicker to sway in the wind."

"The king?" asked Farris, letting a slight look of confusion cross his face. "What happened?"

"War, friend." His voice was grave. "He's getting ready to invade Penance. A dozen battalions of mages landed here earlier today. Fifty or so 'mancers in each. Hundreds of soldiers, and they're all marching out tomorrow. Where, I don't know. But we'd be in trouble if they choose to head towards Penance."

Farris considered the stranger for a moment, choosing his next words wisely.

"Surely the Silverback would be a prime candidate to stop them," he said. "Not to mention the Triad."

"Ha!" laughed the Simian, pulling his cigar out to let a smile stretch across his face. "The Silverback has less control of the city than a sailor has over the sea. And all the Triad have done is put an embargo on the city, shutting down this port and plunging Penance into chaos in one blundering move."

"An embargo?" Farris almost spat the words. "I need to get there by the morning. Is there no other way there?"

"Not unless you're up for a swim." The Simian grinned. He was enjoying this far too much.

Farris pressed a hand against his forehead as a familiar pressure built up in his skull, as though his brain was threatening to break through. A single pang of terror shot down his spine, slowly spreading out into his limbs. A breath caught in his throat.

I could walk. Take the railway line around the Glenn and under the Steel mountains...but if I'm caught in a tunnel when a train comes...

Another wave of anxiety gripped Farris, and it took every ounce of strength for him not to fall to the ground. If his bones could scream, they'd surely be doing so now.

Farris threw his gaze up to the sky and was almost tempted to say a prayer to make the madness end, when a smile spread across his face instead.

A moonless night, without a single star to spoil it.

The other Simian was staring now, the whites of his eyes shining out in the dark.

"Are you okay, friend?" he said, a little more concerned than before.

"You're a sailor, right?" said Farris, regarding the Simian's attire once more. "Are you familiar with the waterfront?"

"No and yes. I'm a fisherman, but I know the ports as well as the sea knows them Herself."

"I'm looking for a...sailor," said Farris, almost tripping over his words. "Goes by the name of Jacob the Blind."

"Ah, the smuggler!" The Simian smiled again, but this time it seemed as if he meant it. "Only the Silverback's men call him that. Why didn't you just tell me you were part of the Movement?"

***

Farris didn't need to travel far to find the residence of Jacob the Blind. He lived in one of the wattle-and-daub hovels facing the sea, all crowded along the pier with their backs against the cliffs. Fortunately, the Simian fisherman had been able to give Farris exactly the directions he needed.

Farris knocked on the door as per his instructions: three quick taps, a brief pause, then four more. The door swung open almost immediately, revealing a rather large Simian in its frame.

"As the tower still stands!" he bellowed, thrusting his giant arms around Farris. "The Silvertongue has returned!"

"I knew there was never anything wrong with your vision," said Farris, patting a hand against one of Jacob's massive shoulders. "We have lots of catching up to do, friend, but plenty of time to do it. I need you to take me to Penance."

Jacob paused, taking a step back as if to consider Farris once again. "I was sure you heard. Penance is closed. Not a soul can go in or out."

"I know about the situation. That's why I've come to you. Have you got your sails ready for a job?"

"Tonight?" stammered Jacob. "It's been a long time since I've worked, but tonight's not a good night."

"Of course it is! Look at how dark the sky is. 'A moonless night, without a single star to spoil it,' isn't that what you used to say?"

"Goes to show how much you know about smuggling. There's cloud coverage, sure, but the crescent moon of Macha is as bright as they come, and she's almost blowing a gale tonight. With wind like that, the clouds could pass at a moment's notice."

Farris smiled. "Right you may be, Jacob, but you'd be shocked to hear how much I learned about smuggling during my work with the Crown's intelligence network. Are you familiar with the Black Sail of Cruachan?"

"Familiar? Ha! The bastards only put me out business once they took the crystal trade. What do you know about them?"

"For the past three years, I was investigating their operations between Dromán and Cruachan under the king's orders. I have information on their suppliers, their routes, and their figures."

Jacob looked as if his jaw might have fallen to the floor if it hadn't been so tightly attached to his face.

"Well, that kind of information could very well put me back in the game. I'd be eternally grateful if you'd share even a fraction of it."

Farris patted Jacob on the shoulder. "Better than that. I'll tell you all about them on the way to Penance."

CHAPTER 4:
THE STONES OF SIN

As the blood filled his lungs, Fionn woke with fright. The details of the dream faded from his memory, but the fear still remained. In darkness, he waited once more, unable to move.

Gods, what is this place?! *roared a voice from inside his head.* Why have you forsaken me?!

The words alone may have been enough to frighten the mage, but there was something more unsettling about the voice: it was not his own.

***

"Ruadh's wind!" cursed Farris, holding a hand up to his eyes. "It's darker than pitch out here. How can you see?"

Jacob howled with laughter behind him. The smuggler tended to the great black sail of the tiny skiff; his movements surprisingly deft in the darkness.

"You'll get used to it," he said. "And someday your eyes will see better in the dark than they can in the light. Then maybe they'll start calling *you* blind!"

"Smuggling may suit me," Farris said. "I've learned enough from the Black Sail to start my own venture."

Jacob howled with laughter again. "Sure, but if all you've told me is true, you'd be looking at the wrong crew to learn the ropes. Why is it that they haven't been caught yet?"

"Corruption," said Farris. "The captain of Cruachan's City Guard is being paid to turn a blind eye."

"That's Padraig Tuathil, isn't it? Wasn't he the one who tried to topple the Guild?"

"Aye, it's the same fool, alright. He wouldn't have gotten as close as he did if we hadn't been stringing him along. It was all carefully planned and perfectly executed by Argyll."

"Ah now, Farris," said Jacob. "You're far too modest for a liar as talented as yourself. Way I heard it, that was mainly *your* doing. The false informants, the setups...and what was that about scapegoats?"

"Traitors of the Guild we would have executed anyway," said Farris dryly. "Two beadhbhs, one boulder, as they say. Now the king thinks the Guild has been dismantled, and I've gained some valuable work experience in the Crown's spy network."

"The Silverback would do well to have you back by his side," muttered Jacob. "Things have really been going to shit lately."

They sailed on in silence, eastwards towards a horizon invisible in the dark. Farris wore a spare black cloak Jacob happened to have at hand, which he became more and more grateful for as the cold night went on. After a few hours, Jacob adjusted the sail and the skiff changed its course, curving northwards, then westwards, back towards the shores of Alabach.

"We need to give Moray's Head a wide berth," said Jacob. "We could have made the journey in half the time if we hugged the coast, but with the Crown's battlemages patrolling these lands now, we can't take any chances."

Farris didn't immediately realise that the darkness was beginning to fade. It was only when he could partially see his hands again that it was apparent that morning was approaching.

"Don't worry about that," said Jacob, apparently aware of Farris's concern. "We'll be docking deep in Heretic's Bay soon. There's a path through the Steel Mountains that'll take us around the Rustlake into Penance. We're past the worst of it, trust me."

"We're not taking the canal?" asked Farris.

"Ha!" laughed Jacob. "Of course not. The main trade route is far too risky for smuggling, even with the city locked down. We'll be making most of this journey by foot."

"Of course." Farris's voice quivered slightly. "And how confident are you we won't be seen?"

Jacob eyed him. "Farris Silvertongue! Are you frightened? Skies above and below! That's one for the history books."

He doesn't know the half of it. Nobody does.

Farris had first fallen victim to what he called 'the fear' when he began his work with the Crown. Only when the *Glory of Penance* had crashed into the Glenn, did he really feel that it had left him. But now, away from the bears and the beadhbhs and the trolls of the Glenn, the anxiety had begun creeping back. Wild carnivorous animals were less terrifying to him than kings and politicians.

Neither of the Simians spoke as the skiff approached the Steel Mountains. Farris was more sceptical of Jacob's talent than he let on, but when the broken remains of Sin came into view far above those shimmering peaks in the waxing morning light, it was clear that the smuggler was a master of his craft. The vessel had been expertly steered through a very long course, with few stars or landmarks to guide the way.

"Is it as lovely as you remember?" asked Jacob.

"No. It's far better."

He meant it. There, a few dozen miles away, was the remains of the Tower of Sin, jutting out from the mountains. Legend had it that the tower had once pierced the sky, built by heathen Simians that wished to usurp the Gods themselves. But when the tower reached a height greater than the sacred Mount Selyth to the south, Lord Seletoth appeared before the Simian builders and cursed their deeds. He tore the tower from the sky, and left its ruins for all to see, as a reminder of the greatest Sin of the Simian people. He then banished every Simian in Alabach to live in the tower's foundations, claiming that to be their Penance.

Even at only a fraction of the height it had once been, the remains of Sin were still a wonderous sight to behold. Amongst the uneven edges of the mountains, the tower shot straight upwards like an iron shaft. Only the peak showed any sign of ruin, with a gaping hole now taking the place where the rest of the structure once stood.

"There's a cave not ten minutes away," said Jacob. "That'll take us towards the city unseen."

"Yes," said Farris, barely hearing Jacob's words. The rising sun had finally burst over the mountains. The skiff continued onwards, towards the long shadows cast by the mountains.

Once they reached the jagged cliffs of Penance, Jacob began deftly dismantling the sail. Farris watched with interest as the smuggler went to work, folding the sailcloth until it was small enough to fit into a coat pocket, and taking the mast apart until he was left with two short poles identical in length. It was only when Jacob handed one to Farris that he noticed that they were actually oars.

"The current will pull us through," said Jacob. "Just use these to keep the rocks away from my boat."

The skiff rocked gently under their feet as they navigated towards the cliffs. Jacob peered forward through squinting eyes, as if searching for something.

"Are we docking anywhere near here?" ventured Farris. Dwarfed by the sheer scale of the mountains, it seemed reasonable to question if they were going the right way. Jacob remained silent, however, re-enforcing his proficiency a master smuggler.

As if the cliffs themselves had listened, a yawning cave appeared ahead of them. Amidst white waves of foam crashing against the walls, the skiff drifted towards the opening. Jacob changed his grip on the oar, now forcing it straight down under the water, pushing the boat onwards by pressing against the rocks beneath the surface.

"I'll take it from here," said Jacob, right as Farris was about to do the same. The smuggler navigated the ship through the cave with precision and agility as if he had full control of every inch of the hull. In the dim light, the damp cave walls glistened with moisture, dripping with wet mud and sand. Farris ducked his head as the ceiling dipped lower.

It was only then that he noticed Jacob lying flat and forward on the skiff.

"It's usually tighter than this on a high tide," he whispered back. "Be grateful that we don't have a greater load."

"A greater load? Surely I'm the most valuable cargo you've smuggled into Penance."

"You've obviously never sold white crystals on the black market." Jacob let out a roaring laugh that caused the boat to quiver. "If they were worth their weight in gold, I'd be selling them at loss."

The cave's walls widened to reveal a tiny grotto with sharp stalactites hanging low from the ceiling. Jacob manoeuvred the skiff against one of the cave walls, gesturing to a ledge slightly overhead.

"We'll climb up and carry on through the cave," he said, producing a length of rope from the side of the skiff. He reached out and found an iron ring bound to the rock, then quickly looped the rope though it, punctuating each pull with an abrupt knot. When he was satisfied, he stood and hoisted himself upwards onto the ledge.

"Do you need a hand?" he asked. "It's probably been a while since you did any second-story work."

"I'll be fine," said Farris, stubbornly. He rapidly scaled the wall up toward Jacob, displaying less effort than he gave.

"I'll lead the way then." Jacob ignored Farris's exasperated breaths. "It's not far to the Rustlake."

Farris followed for some time through those winding caves, hoping each corned they took would reveal the full splendour of the City of Steam, but to his disappointment, each turn led to more dark tunnels.

Just as he was about to complain, however, the cave levelled out and formed a straight path. Up ahead was an entrance. Morning had fully broke, and Farris heard the faint sounds of wildlife up ahead. The last time he had emerged from a cave like this, he had been chased by a mountain troll. Today, with his old ally, returning to the city he so dearly missed, was certainly an improvement.

"Here we are," said Jacob. "The walk around the Rustlake is lovely this time of the morning."

Farris emerged from the cave immediately after Jacob, and welcomed the fresh air, blended with the faint scent of soot. Across the lake, the city of Penance was in full view: huge buildings and spires peering over great stone walls, all surrounding the remnants of Sin. The details of the broken tower were visible in the morning light now; Farris could even spot a few individual airships docked at its upper levels.

The sight was marred by a peculiar movement across the Rustlake. The lake itself was as still as the surrounding rocks, but there, on its north bank, a number of distant figures were moving towards them, with startling speed. Some moments later, their forms came into view.

"Jacob?" asked Farris, pointing to the north. "Are you sure we weren't seen?"

The smuggler was tending to his equipment, folding a rope in loops around one hand. "Seen? No, of course not, I—"

The sound of hooves thundering on stone cut him off. Farris met Jacob's eyes, and nodded towards the source: a group of elk cavalry came galloping along the lake, only close enough now for Farris to appreciate their speed, and to realise there was likely no use in fleeing.

"Quick," said Farris. "Who else knows of this passage?"

"Nobody. Just me and the Silverback!"

"Perfect. Just leave everything to me."

They stood still as the elk riders approached. Farris had figured they were likely scouting for the Triad, based on their lightly armoured bodies and steeds. If the Silverback's bid to curry favour with the Triad was going according to plan, it was possible he informed them to monitor this passageway.

Over the course of several more seconds, Farris found the optimal line of questions and answers that would lead him straight to the Silverback if his previous assumptions were true. As the riders approached, one mounted Simian took the lead, slowing to a halt in front of Farris. The elk towered over the Simian, with two great antlers emerging from its hulking mass.

Its rider wielded a long halberd with an axe-head of green-tinted steel. He pointed it at Farris, then spoke. "The city is closed for trading and travel at this time. State your business."

Once Farris heard the rider's voice, all his alibis and answers vanished.

"Come now, Garth," he said, reaching out to push the weapon aside. "That's no way to be speaking to me. What would Mother think?"

CHAPTER 5:
THE CHILDREN OF
PENANCE

Penance is one of the largest settlements on Alabach, and the oldest by a significant margin. Before the Fall of Sin in AC 88, Penance was the focal point of trade for Simians across the Northern Reach. However, following the Fall of Sin, Simians were forbidden to leave Penance's walls. This led to the migration of natives from the other Simian settlements of the Northern Reach, leaving Col, Tán, and Elis Point mere ghost towns today.

Although restricted to Penance, the Simian people forged significant scientific advances in the years following the Fall. The building of Aldrich Canal brought unprecedented growth to the city in the following years, essentially forcing the Seachtú of Alabach to trade with the Simian city.

Today, Penance is made up of five districts, built around the remnants of the Tower of Sin. The area immediately surrounding the Tower is known as the Shadow of Sin. The other districts extend out from the Shadow. Starting with the most northernmost and going clockwise, they are: The Stoneworks, the Goldworks, the Dustworks, the Saltworks, and the Steamworks.

Guide to the City of Penance, Benedict the Blessed, AC388.

***

The walls of Penance loomed ahead as they made their way around the Rustlake. Farris walked alongside Garth and his mount, accompanied by Jacob. The other riders lingered behind. Whatever urgency brought them to the caves had vanished now as they took a slower pace towards the city.

"We've been keeping eyes on Moray Head," said Garth. "Can't be too careful with battlemages crawling through the Clifflands now."

"Indeed," said Farris, throwing a glance at Jacob. Either he had vastly overestimated the smuggler's prowess, or the Triad was just being extremely cautious. The scowl on Jacob's face alluded to the latter.

"Are we're under arrest then?" asked Jacob. "Why not put us in chains and be done with it?"

Garth smirked. "We may hold the banners of the Triad, but I have another chain of command that takes priority."

"What?" cried Farris. "Are you—" He lowered his voice to a growl. "You're with the Silverback now?"

Garth nodded.

"Skies above, brother. You've been berating me for years about mixing up with 'those types.' Kept at me to get a nice safe job with the Triad. What changed?"

"Not too much," said Garth. "I just realised that the storm is coming whether we like it or not. And I fancy Argyll's chances a lot more now."

Farris sighed. "I can't blame you for that. I just thought one of us could stay on the right side of the law."

"What do you mean?" Garth shrugged. "All I do is tell him about what I see in these parts and keep him informed on the Triad's scouting. Nothing illegal."

"That's how I started, too. Just a quick job here, some information there...then when the gold comes in and he starts talking about taking back this land for us, it gets harder and harder to say 'no.'"

Garth smiled. "Ah, Farris. Are you trying to look out for your little brother? I know exactly what I've gotten myself into."

"Are you sure? Five years into this, and I'm still not entirely sure myself."

Garth didn't have an answer for that. The path rose abruptly as they approached the Rustlake. The sounds of the city rose above the great stone wall up ahead: an amalgamation of people shouting and chattering as engines gushed and whirred among them. They passed the harbour on the north side of the lake, great vessels moored against its bank.

Eventually, the trail came upon a road. But this wasn't the roads of loose gravel Farris had grown accustomed during his time in the Seachtú to the south. This was a proper Simian road. Huge slabs of basalt flattened and precisely positioned for the even distribution of the weight of heavy machinery. Unlike the cobblestone streets of Cruachan, the roads of Penance didn't bend to whim of the landscape; they cut through the earth with the sole purpose of connecting one location to the other via the shortest possible route. Although he had yet to step through the gates of Penance, Farris was already home.

"I'll take my leave here then," said Jacob. "I've a few people to track down at the harbour. People who would like to know what you've told me about the Black Sail. I'll find you in the city before I leave again."

Jacob patted Farris on the shoulder. "Thanks, Farris. We've needed someone like you here for some time now."

"Aye," said Farris with a nod, not quite sure what else to say.

Do they really think I'm going to turn all this around?

It was already starting to get too much for him. Sure, he succeeded in his mission in Cruachan, but he still had no idea why the Silverback wanted from King Diarmuid in the long-term...not to mention whatever happened down in the railway with Santos.

But now, he couldn't dwell on that. He still had work to do.

***

Farris and Garth approached to the Goldgate of Penance on foot; Garth had left his mount with the other riders by the lake. Apparently, there were many winding paths through the Steel Mountains, and the Triad had scouts crawling through most of them.

And most of those riders were bought by the Silverback.

"How much power does Argyll have now?" asked Farris as they approached the gate: a steel archway embedded in the thick stone of the city walls. At this hour of the morning, the road between it and the harbour would have been teeming with activity, but now it just housed a small crowd of labourers and merchants waiting to enter

"Almost all of it," said Garth, choosing his words carefully as he nodded at a guard by the gate. The guard barely gave Farris a second glance as he ushered them both through, much to the dismay of those still waiting.

"Let me see," he continued. "The City Guard are ours, and we're working on the merchants of the Goldworks; the embargo isn't helping. Myself and the Triad's scouts give us eyes outside the city, and we've curried the favour of Humans aligned with the Sons of Seletoth."

"Of course," muttered Farris, moving aside as two Simian children pushed past. One held a red ribbon that streamed behind her as she ran.

"You have a problem with the Sons?" asked Garth.

"I was close to Derelith, back in Cruachan; we had a decent working relationship as long as he didn't talk about religion."

"Well, nothing much else you can expect from the fanatics. Funny how it's the fringe religious sects that always take their faith far more seriously than those who follow the traditional creed."

"That's because these particular fanatics have spoken to their god."

"Allegedly, you mean?"

"Of course," said Farris. "Allegedly."

The two emerged in the business precinct of Penance, on the northern side of the Goldworks. Empty wooden stalls lined the walls either side, with only a handful of Simian merchants carrying meagre cargo between then. Up ahead, a contingent of red-robed Simian Guards marched through the street, armed with spears held over their shoulders. Their boots clapped against the road in unison as they went.

"The Churchguard," sneered Farris. "Presumably they still stand against us."

"Of course," said Garth. "But not for want of trying. They've been refusing to meet with Argyll for some time now."

"They're probably too busy licking the boots that walk all over us." Farris spat. "Traitors, the lot of them."

"Can you blame them? A well-paying job with steady income..."

"Some things are more important than income."

Garth laughed. "Easy for you to say; you don't have any little mouths to feed. Unless you have a little secret over in Cruachan."

"If so, it's a secret to me too."

"Well, the Churchguard are the least of our worries. Argyll reckons we could wind up fighting Wraiths at some point."

Farris cursed under his breath. In his three years working in Cruachan, he had learned a great deal about the mysterious hooded figures known as the Wraiths of Seletoth. Rumoured to be risen spirits, Farris knew they were merely men who answered directly to Seletoth Himself, often tasked to carry out the more unsavoury actions of the Church.

"Just men in robes," said Farris. "They'll fall like any other."

"Aye," said Garth. "But we'd struggle to convince the rest of the city that."

Eventually, they approached the Shadow of Sin: the district in the immediate surroundings of the great tower. There stood one of the most prominent buildings of the city: The Triad. Great marble steps led to a huge triangular portico, held up by a dozen thick columns. A large crowd of people had gathered at the foot of the steps, Humans and Simians, men and women, all calling out to the soldiers of the City Guard keeping them away from the entrance. A thickset Simian guard raised his arms overhead—perhaps a feeble attempt to calm the crowd, but it did nothing to quell the cries of the citizens.

Garth led Farris through the crowd, pushing his way past the rabble. As he went, Farris caught the occasional racial slur directed towards the guards. He couldn't help but draw his gaze downwards, inspecting the exposed purses and wallets of the distracted protesters.

When they emerged from the crowd, Garth saluted the Simian guards at the door. With a curt nod they opened the door, and the two Simians went inside. The shouts and cries from outside where silenced with the slammed shut of the door.

A brilliantly clear, clean room now presented itself to Farris and Garth. White marble floors stretched out before them, with huge paintings and portraits lining the walls.

"We got news about Santos two days ago," Garth said, leading Farris down a hallway flanked with clay busts of old

Simian leaders. "As Chief Engineer of Penance, his death is a significant loss. Not to mention how many of our preparations were undone in an instant."

"What happened to 'just doing some favours' for Argyll? Now they're *our* preparations?"

Garth waved a dismissive hand. "Fine. You can lecture me later, but we've more pressing matters to deal with first. We were scrambling to react to Santos's sudden death, when we got a crystal wave in from Cruachan. King Diarmuid is accusing us of having a hand in it, while also claiming that we attacked him, too. Argyll has alibis to prove otherwise, but the Triad panicked and closed the ports. Now the Crown sees that as an admission of guilt."

"I see," said Farris. "So, Argyll had absolutely no role in the ambush down in the railway?"

Garth paused as they approached a huge white door. He pressed a dark, hairy hand against it. "Why don't you ask him yourself?"

The door swung open, revealing a small, quaint meeting room adorned with a large oaken table and a marble hearth with a great fire crackling inside. The room had two occupants. The first, a Human, wore a loose-fitting shirt draped over a slim frame. His top three buttons were undone, revealing a bare chest and an extravagant pendant for the world to see. The pendant bore a symbol similar to that of the Holy Trinity, but with warped, crooked shapes replacing the perfect circles usually associated with the Church. Farris recognised it immediately as a mark of the Sons of Seletoth.

The second occupant was a Simian, and his presence alone roared louder than the blazing fire. With broad shoulders and thick, muscular arms, someone unfamiliar with his people's anatomy might mistake him for a youth, but the colour of his coat told a different story. Every inch of his body was covered in dark, grey hair that usually only comes with frail old age. This Simian was anything but frail, however. His followers called him the Silverback, although his fur was not silver, and it covered more than his back.

"Welcome, Farris," he said. "I'm sure only dire need would take you away from your post." His voice remained calm through every word he spoke, and his expression showed not a fragment of surprise, despite his thinking Farris was on the other side of the kingdom.

"Thank you, Argyll," said Farris, trying to keep his voice from quivering. Something about the way the Silverback spoke made Farris feel like a child again. "I bring news from the capital. News that I believe you should hear from my own lips, and not from a letter or a wave."

"Then speak it," said Argyll.

Farris paused, throwing a quick glance to the human standing next to the fire, then back to the Silverback.

"This is Ruairí Ó Críodáin," he said, as if reading Farris's thoughts. "He's a representative of the Sons."

"I thought as much," said Farris, struggling to keep the contempt from his voice. "But this is a highly sensitive matter, it concerns—"

Garth placed a hand on Farris's shoulder. "You can trust him. He's as much one of us as you are. Things have changed around here quite a lot since you left."

"Indeed, he's right," said Ruairí, holding a hand to Farris. "It's a shame we didn't meet under more peaceful circumstances."

Farris ignored the human and turned his attention back to Argyll. "If you are certain, I'll continue. While working in the Crown's intelligence network, I learned that there was an attack on the king, leaving him wounded and Santos dead. Diarmuid seemed convinced that you had a role in this."

"This is not news to us," said Argyll. He stared at Farris with pale, cold eyes that could have seen his soul if Simians had been born with one.

"True," continued Farris, "but it was what he told me next that should concern all of us. He sent me and four other spies on a mission to Penance in order to carry out a pre-emptive strike on the skyfleet. We were placed on an airship named *The Glory of Penance* and ordered to rendezvous with a preacher at Sin."

Argyll's stone-like face appeared suddenly animated in response. It was Ruairí, however, who broke the silence first.

"*The Glory of Penance?* It was supposed to arrive two days ago, but it never turned up. The skyfleet has since dispatched a search party, but they haven't found anything yet."

"The wreckage is in the Glenn," said Farris. "I was left with no choice but to ensure the ship never reached its destination. I was one of the only survivors of the crash."

"And you came here on foot?" asked Garth with amazement. "Through the Glenn?"

"Aye, brother. I used some of what you taught me to find my way home."

"Well, I'm surprised you listened."

"Enough," said the Silverback. He barely had to raise his voice to silence the Simians. "What can you tell us about this rendezvous?"

Farris grinned openly. "He's dressed as a druid. Giving a sermon in Sin, of all places. He shouldn't be too difficult to find. The Crown would have had better luck hiding a beadhbh in a brothel."

The others didn't seem to find the humour in this. Garth averted his gaze while Argyll looked on in silence. Ruairí chuckled softly, then cleared his throat to speak.

"It seems as if your brother had it right," he said. "Things are not the same here as you had left them. Those in the city who follow the teachings of the One True God are more numerous than they were three years ago. The Tower of Sin hosts scores of preachers now, spreading the Good Word of the Lord."

Shocked, Farris glanced at Argyll. He nodded ever so slightly.

"So, it's the Sons who preach there?" asked Farris. "We were told to meet with a druid spreading the word of the Trinity. We were given a passcode, to ask about the king's health, which should produce the response, 'The Lord and Lady protect him.' Surely someone like this would stand out amongst the...Sons, correct?"

Ruairí nodded. "This is true. I'll go ask about the tower. If your druid was a regular preacher, there still may be a chance to track him down."

"Do what you must," said Argyll. "If that's all, Farris, I have an embargo to break."

"That's the full of it," said Farris. "I was left in the dark concerning the king's plan, and only this druid knows the rest."

"True." The Silverback made his way to the door. "And once we find him, he'll wish he knew nothing."

CHAPTER 6:
THE FALSE PREACHER

EMBARGO BROKEN: SILVERBACK SPEAKS OUT AGAINST KING
The Daily Penance
14th Day under the Moon of Macha, AC403

A two-day-long trade embargo on Penance was broken yesterday after Argyll the Silverback addressed the people at the steps of the Triad.

"King Diarmuid has accused us of crimes we have not committed," said the Silverback, "just as the Gods accused our ancestors of the sin of striving to be better than Man."

Earlier this week, the Crown claimed that the Silverback and his followers – campaigning for a separate state of Old Simia – murdered Santos, chief engineer of Penance. In yesterday's speech, Argyll vehemently denied such allegations.

"Diarmuid makes these claims from the safety of the Grey Keep of Cruachan, but he does not dare to put me on trial, for he knows

his accusations are baseless. I have a thousand alibis placing me in this city on the day of the attack, but evidence and reason do not concern the King of Alabach. If he wishes to bring this issue to the rest of the Triad, I'll be more than willing to oblige."

The Triad rules Penance in parallel to the Crown. Comprising a human (Cathal Carríga), a Simian (Borris Blackhand), and a king (King Diarmuid Third and Nineteenth), the governing body was formed to represent the voice of the people, but Argyll disagrees.

"Having Diarmuid on the Triad does a grave disservice to its original intent. Yesterday, the other two members were pressured into closing our ports, purposely making us appear guilty and weak to the rest of the kingdom. As of this moment, the gates of Penance are open once again. And rest assured, the Crown will no longer interfere with our city."

***

The Tower of Sin was exactly as Farris had remembered it. The huge stone monument to Simian ingenuity defined the city of Penance, with each district spanning out from it like spokes on a wheel. The tower itself loomed a hundred feet over Farris's head, but one could only guess at how high it once been before it was ruined. Each stone block was as large a mammoth, arranged with precise cyclopean masonry. The other buildings of Penance were constructed using more recent advances in Simian engineering, but none came close to sheer scale and fortitude of the old, broken tower.

Indeed, even the Lord Himself could not finish the job of tearing it down.

Garth stood beside Farris, taking in the sight of the Tower.

"Sure," said Garth. "On the outside it looks as fine as it did before you left, but you're in for a shock when we go in. Don't say I didn't warn you."

"I won't," said Farris. They made their way up the cracked stone steps which led to double-wide iron doors at the tower's base. Human men and Simians loitered around the entrance, some huddled in groups, others standing alone. Sin had been a common meeting place for as long as Farris could remember. The upper levels housed the airships of the skyfleet, while tradesmen and merchants sold their wares closer to the ground.

At least that's how it used to be, Farris reminded himself, eyeing a woman walking by who wore the symbol of the Sons of Seletoth.

The doors of the tower were set open as the two Simians approached. A thick, twisting staircase stood on either side of the entrance, winding clockwise and anti-clockwise all the way to the top of the tower.

"Ruairí says that the preachers occupy the second floor," said Garth, gesturing to the staircase on the left. "And we have no way of recognising the druid, other than the passcode King Diarmuid gave you, correct?"

"Yes," said Farris. "If the ship had arrived as scheduled, then he would have met us on the quay. If what Ruairí told us is right, it's possible he's a regular here."

Garth smiled. "You don't trust Ruairí."

"I've always had an aversion to the religious types."

"Apart from Derelith, right?"

"True, but I knew him from before he had his..." Farris trailed off, trying to find the right word.

"They call them 'Seeings,'" finished Garth. "The Sons say that Seletoth contacts them directly, and they learn of truths that the Church has hidden from the world."

"Truths..." mused Farris. "What kind of things do they see?"

Garth shrugged. "Very few Sons like to talk about their own Seeings. From what I gather, each Seeing differs from person to person. Most go on to dedicate their lives to Seletoth afterwards, while some feel the need to climb Mount Selyth and confront Him themselves. Those are the ones we never hear from again."

Farris suppressed a shudder. He could relate, and that frightened him. Back when he first left for Cruachan, he didn't believe in the innate power of the Móráin bloodline, but the evidence he found supporting Divine Penetrance changed his mind on that. Then, before he left Cruachan, he had believed he was in control of his own destiny, and all of his choices were his own. Then he met Sláine the White, and her story about a little girl with a head injury...

And the Sons...were they just normal Humans before? A single vision away from giving their lives to their god?

He recalled the image of the woman he had seen at the bottom of the cliff at Roseán, but he dared not name her.

Farris shook his head as they reached the first floor. Stalls and stands were set up all around, selling everything from jewellery and rugs to Simian-made arms and armour. On a good day, one could have found a black-market dealer selling crystals for healing or other minor spells. But those days were long gone now, with the Crown clamping down on smuggling from the Seachtú.

"Derelith told me that some Sons go mad after their Seeing," said Farris as they continued on up the steps. "Have you heard of anything like that?"

"Well, one could argue that you'd have to be mad to even consider climbing Mount Selyth, but there have been some incidents. I met a Son once who claimed he saw Seletoth with his own eyes. He went blind immediately afterwards. Even the healers couldn't explain what happened. Others lose their ability to think straight, as if their minds broke upon learning what they call *the Truth*."

"Maybe they learned that their whole religion doesn't make an ounce of sense."

Garth did not laugh. "There was a Human navigator on a ship called *The Rising Sun,* who had a Seeing. Like most of his Simian colleagues, he didn't care much for the Trinity. Then he became a Son. After that, he was obsessed with the stars of the firmament."

"Sounds like normal behaviour for a navigator," said Farris. "Aren't they all well-versed in astronomy?"

"Not like this. When he became a Son, he left his job and spent every waking hour observing the stars. Not for any practical purposes, no. He just studied them for the sake of it. He was found dead in his lab after a week, from dehydration. He never left to eat or drink or defecate."

"Is this a true story?" ventured Farris.

Garth nodded. "The City Guard seized his notes, and some were published in the Daily Penance. Pages upon pages of absolute gibberish."

"Gibberish he felt was worth more to him than his life," said Farris. "That's why I don't like dealing with these fanatics. With a worldview as warped as that, how can any of them be trusted?"

Garth surprised Farris with a smile. "Now you're thinking like the Silverback."

Farris's eyes widened. "I knew it! I fucking knew it! He's just using them, isn't he?"

"Well," said Garth. "Let's hope it's not the other way around."

Farris snorted, right as they reached the top of the second staircase. *The Silverback is a master of lies and subterfuge. These zealots would find it easier to recruit Arch-Canon Cathbad to their cause.*

When the open landing of Sin's second floor came into view, Farris's glee turned sour. Far more people were crowded into this area than the previous, all clustered around a dozen or so speakers, who were raised above the rest on wooden platforms. And there were Simians there too. Farris quickly scanned the crowds, and when he saw that his people actually outnumbered the Humans, a slow, creeping panic began to set in.

"Don't worry about them," said Garth, obviously noticing the dread that was taking hold of Farris. "The numbers here prove that the Sons are not alone in their hatred of the Church."

Farris inhaled deeply. "But both Simians and Humans are equal in their love for the Lord?"

"Aye," said Garth, his voice cool and calm. "That's another way of looking at it." He gestured towards the first cluster of worshipers. "Come, let's find our druid."

The first preacher they came across was an elderly Human man, dressed in loose, flowing robes. He raised feeble hands over his head as he spoke, but his voice was as strong and as powerful as any youth.

"The Lord's light should benefit all men and should not be used for selfish means. But there are some in this city who profit—yes, profit!—from his teachings. They call themselves druids and cardinals, canons and arch-canons, all claiming tithes for spreading the word our Lord is perfectly capable of spreading Himself."

A muttering of agreement ran through the crowd as the preacher paused, his sharp eyes meeting those of each person who stood before him. His gaze fell upon Farris for a half a second. A shot of terror tore through Farris's body.

"And what about King Diarmuid?" cried Garth, immediately taking the preacher's attention away from Farris. "Does the light not shine upon him?"

"A holy abomination and a fraud!" cried the preacher. "He is the face of the institute known as the Church, founded for no purpose but to keep us from knowing the Truth! There can be no salvation under Seletoth's light as long as Diarmuid rules this country!"

"Not our guy," whispered Garth. "He's a Son through and through."

"And a damn fine speaker," muttered Farris. "There's got to be an easier way. Wouldn't this bring more attention to us?"

"True," said Garth. "We should split up and try to be more subtle." He nodded towards a female Human standing on the next podium. "I'll start with her."

"There are women in the Sons, too?" asked Farris. "That doesn't make much sense."

"Well, they also believe that Seletoth bore no sons. Nobody said any of this had to make sense."

He disappeared into the crowd, leaving Farris to decide for himself who to pose the passcode to next. A younger man gave a sermon to a handful of people across the way, and he seemed to be far less animated than the first. When Farris approached, however, the preacher's words gave him pause.

"Nothing frightens the Lord more than chaos, for even if fate dictates His own demise, Seletoth shall gladly see Himself through to the end."

A woman from the crowd spoke up. "But what of the Lady Meadhbh, is she not the weaver of fate?"

"Of course not," said the preacher with a soft smile. "For surely fate has existed long before the supposed Apotheosis of the Trinity. If she was the master of fate before the Final Conquest of Alabach, then what led the Human armies to this sacred country? Seletoth is the beginning and the end, but He does not have control over fate. More proof that the Trinity is founded upon lies."

No use asking him.

Farris worked his way through the crowd, catching a few words from each speaker before moving on. The people who had come to hear the sermons moved from preacher to preacher too, some exchanging questions and comments with those on the pedestals.

Farris spotted Garth talking with another preacher. The Human gestured wildly as he spoke, moving his arms in wide, looping circles, possibly mimicking the three crooked rings of the Sons. Garth turned and caught Farris's gaze, then shook his head in disappointment. He bid farewell to the preacher and began hurrying towards Farris. Farris moved forward, too, but right as they were about to confront one another, an arm appeared from the crowd and grabbed Garth on the shoulder. A bearded face leaned towards him, with eyes mad with fear.

"Where the fuck *were* you?" he rasped. Garth turned as Farris approached, and both faced the preacher. "I was waiting here for *hours!*" he said. "Then I got word that the ship crashed, and nobody told me what to do if that happened. You're lucky everything is still in place." He eyed Farris cautiously. "Is it just you two? I was expecting five."

"Will two be enough?" asked Farris, careful not to let on he knew less than he should.

"The timing may be off," said the preacher, "But we'd do a fair share of damage anyway. The first load is on the first floor. Follow me."

The preacher led the way towards the stairway. Garth followed closely behind, fumbling through his pockets as he went. He pulled out a piece of fabric with one hand, and a tiny glass vial in another. He deftly uncapped the vial, pouring its contents onto the cloth, all without missing a step behind the preacher. At the top of the staircase, Garth lunged forward, shoving the damp cloth against the old man's face. In an instant, the man's body went limp, and Garth was left holding on to him. Some people stopped to look on, but neither the cloth nor the bottle were anywhere in sight.

"Edgar!" cried Garth to Farris. "Edgar, come quickly! Aonghus has gone and passed out again. Help me bring him home!"

***

The false preacher awoke no less than an hour later, just as Garth had predicted. That alchemical mixture had given them enough time to carry the old man down to *The Ferryman*, an old tavern deep within the Dustworks of Penance. It had also given Farris plenty of time to tie the preacher up, while Garth went off to fetch the Silverback. To Farris's dismay, Argyll arrived with Ruairí at his side.

Has he found himself a new right-hand man? He didn't have a chance to voice his opinion, as the preacher began to stir moments after the two arrived.

"What has he told you?" asked Argyll, careful to keep his voice low. "Is there anything we should know before we begin?"

"Not much," whispered Farris. "He seemed to be working alone, expecting five of us to come off the ship. He overheard Garth use the passcode and confronted him directly." He rummaged through a coat pocket. "We also found these on his person." He held five flint-rings before Argyll. "The same kind that Pyromancers use to create a spark for their spells."

"I'm...familiar with them," said Argyll. Farris wondered if the Silverback implied more than what he said.

The old preacher slowly raised his head, his weary eyes falling upon Ruairí first, then Argyll. A look of confusion crossed his face as he noticed Garth and Farris standing side by side.

"You...you're from... Sin? No...I can't remember."

"We'll help jog your memory," said Garth, stepping forward. "Whether you want to or not."

"Where...where am I?"

Garth stuck the preacher across the face with a sickening crack. "You're in a bad place, friend. Tell us everything you know."

A flash of realisation shook the preacher awake. The weariness left his face immediately, his mouth opened in shock, his lip quivering in fear.

"I have nothing to tell you. I swore not to—"

Garth cut the old man off with another right hook, faster and harder than the last. A spray of blood followed the arc of his fist; Farris was sure he heard something break with the impact.

The Human's eyes met Garth's, then he spat a bloodied tooth onto the floor.

"I'll never betray the king!" he cried, his words as strong and proud as they had been back in Sin. "The light of the Trinity protects me!"

Garth raised his hand but paused instead of bringing it down again. "Edgar," he said, turning to Farris. "What was it you used before, to make those smugglers talk when you were in the capital?"

Farris suppressed a smile. The memory was not a fond one, but he enjoyed the game all the same.

"I'll need a pillowcase and a pale of water," he said, shooting a glance at the preacher. "It won't take long."

"No!" cried the captive. "Not that, please no!"

Farris turned to Ruairí. "We'll need to lay him flat on his back. first. Micheál, can you grab what I need from upstairs?"

Ruairí did not respond, doing nothing to hide the sheer confusion from his face. *A shame. Though, Humans have never been good at this game anyway.*

"I'll talk!" cried the preacher, looking up at Garth. "I'll do whatever you want, just keep *him* away from me!"

"Then speak," said Argyll, practically spitting the words.

"I was contacted by the king himself," said the preacher. It was as if the words couldn't leave his lips quickly enough. "I've been keeping an eye on the Sons here, for the Crown, but I got a crystal wave in from the king. He told me to meet five spies at Sin, and that I'd confirm their identities with a passcode."

The preacher looked on expectantly at his captors, as if he hoped he had said enough. The four said nothing. It didn't take long for their captive to continue again.

"Before they were supposed to arrive, I hid...barrels of Simian black-powder in different positions around the tower. I was to give the spies a flint-ring each to light their fuses. The instructions I was given said that it would be enough to take the tower down. And with the gas in the ships, the skyfleet would be wiped out, too."

The Silverback took a step towards the preacher. "Is that all?"

"Yes, yes, please. It is. I was told nothing else. It was supposed to take just the six of us."

"Does the Crown have any other spies in Penance?" asked the Silverback, towering over the little man.

"No...no, it's just me. Please, I told you everything you need to know. Please, don't let him do what he said, with the water and—"

"Go to Sin," interrupted Argyll, turning to Farris, Garth, and Ruairí. "Find these caches and remove them from the tower. Immediately."

Garth and Ruairí nodded curtly and went to leave. Before Farris had a chance to follow, the Silverback placed a hand on his shoulder.

"You have experience working with the Crown's network," he whispered, barely loud enough to be heard, even by Farris. "Will he be missed?"

Farris looked at the preacher. The old man was still shaking, his eyes cast upwards, his lips moving frantically in prayer.

"No," said Farris, with a sigh. "Probably not."

CHAPTER 7:
CHORUS OF THE SOUL

My latest experiment has yielded results quite unexpected but intriguing in their own right. I'll record my findings here as I come across them, but I dare not put their conclusions down on paper right now. The implications are most worrying.

First Entry of a journal entitled "*On the Manipulation of the Flesh*" by Yarlaith the White.

***

Fionn's eyes shot open abruptly and a gurgled gasp escaped his throat. He panted, trying to make sense of his surroundings. The room was dim, with little light coming in past the dark, thick curtains covering a nearby window. White cotton sheets were wrapped tight against his body, restricting his movement. Not that he could move if he wanted to. With little feeling below his waist, it seemed to Fionn that he would not leave this strange place for a long time.

He closed his eyes tight, trying to recall the dreams that had plagued his sleep. He remembered a feeling of being trapped alone in the dark. It was a familiar dream, one that had haunted him since he was a boy. He was accustomed to every detail now, from the coffin made from flesh to the blood slowly drowning him.

Gods above and below, where am I now?

Other details resurfaced in his mind, though it was difficult to tell which were real and which were from the dreams. He was aboard an airship, sailing through the sky, when a fight broke out and....

"Fire," Fionn muttered, as a pang of realisation caused his heartbeat to quicken. "I caused it."

The rest of the details came flooding back: a burning airship falling from the sky, its survivors running through the Glenn.

And the troll, said a voice. *You forgot about the troll.*

Fionn sat upright, ignoring the dull ache in his hips protesting his sudden movement. He pressed his left hand against the mattress to support himself, but when he tried to do the same with his right, the limb was clumsier than usual. This was of little concern to the red mage, however, for there was a more pressing matter: the voice that spoke was not his own.

"Who's there?" he called out, twisting his head to look around the room. It appeared to be a quaint little clinic, similar, yet far simpler than those he was used to back in the Academy. The shelves were full of ointments and potions, only some he could recognise, but apart from himself, the room was void of life.

But that voice, it sounded so familiar.

You half-witted fool! cried another, louder than the first. Hatred burned in every word as it spoke. *I should have fucking wrung your neck when I had the chance. I should have stabbed you in your sleep. You've taken everything away from me. Everything!*

Fionn gasped with fear.

What is happening to me?

Alone! cried a third voice. *All alone, without a single soul to save me. This truly is a fate worse than death.*

The speakers went silent. Fionn tried to focus on their source, searching through his own memories for any sort of clue. Without warning, a thousand cries all began calling in unison, blocking out Fionn's train of thought. Their words were mostly unintelligible, though Fionn was able to pick out a few.

Don't go there! You won't like what you find!

They've torn me apart, and they've bound me to a dead man!

I'll kill them. I'll fucking kill them all if it's the last thing I do.

He hasn't noticed yet. He hasn't noticed his arm! I told you he was a fucking fool!

Fionn glanced down at the bed. Hidden beneath the sheets, his right arm was indeed numb, as if he hadn't moved it in a while. He wriggled his fingers and feeling returned to his hand. He slowly moved the arm from under the sheets, but something felt peculiar. At first, he thought his arm had been wrapped in a cast, for the sheets seemed to barely graze his skin as he pulled it out. But when he did, the sight caused a shrill whimper to catch in his throat.

Where his right arm had once been, a great, muscular limb now sprouted from his shoulder. There, the arm was bound to Fionn's own flesh with black thread, thick and ropey, criss-crossing all the way around his shoulder. The arm was almost twice as large as his left, with biceps like boulders wrapped beneath skin. Forked blue lightning veins extended down towards his wrists, crooked and cord-like.

He raised the hand up to his face, marvelling at every alien detail of its digits. He made a fist, curling each thick finger inwards. For a moment he kept it tense, watching as the knuckles whited and the muscles in the forearm spasmed with effort.

Darkness, oh Darkness! cried one of the voices. *The void has consumed me whole. There is no light, no light!*

The rest of the voices responded in a cacophony that shook Fionn's skull. Some roared obscenities, others muttered incoherent nonsense. Here and there, Fionn caught a few words of prayer, with whispered mentions of names like "Father," "Mother," "Aislinn," "Cathal," though the names of the gods—Seletoth, Meadhbh, and Móráin—were repeated the most.

"Shut up!" cried Fionn. He closed his eyes and pressed his hands against his ears—the hand on the right almost big enough to cover his head. "Shut up, shut up, *shut up!*"

"Ah, is everything alright?"

The voices went silent immediately. Fionn turned to see an old man standing by his bed. Fionn supposed he was a healer, for he wore loose white robes, tied at the waist. A pair of eyeglasses rested on a sharp, pointed nose.

"How are you faring?" asked the stranger, resting a hand on Fionn's forehead. "You've been out for a long while, but your recovery has been steady. It's a miracle you're still alive. You've lost enough blood to kill three men!"

"What's this?" demanded Fionn, raising the muscular arm before the healer. "What happened to my arm?"

The healer's expression darkened. "You came from the Glenn, with a mountain troll in pursuit. It chased you to the outskirts of this village."

Whereas the man's words had once been soft and warm, he now spoke with an almost clinical precision, as if he were reading from a textbook.

"You are your companions tried to fight it off," he continued. "The troll killed all but two. The Simian was knocked over the edge of the cliffs. He made a full recovery.

The troll tore your arm off, leaving you for dead. Yet here you are."

"I won't be here for much longer," said Fionn, swinging his legs from the bed. The horrific details of the encounter with the troll came back to him, and they gave him pause. The blood. The screams. The pain.

Sláine, Sir Bearach. Dead...

"You must rest," said the healer, pressing a hand on Fionn's shoulder. "You've been through so much, and the procedures I've used are highly un–"

Fionn suddenly grabbed the man's wrist, using the strange, muscular hand.

"You said I was out for a long time," Fionn said, sternly. "How long has it been?"

The healer's lips quivered, his eyes not moving from his wrist, enveloped by the thick fingers.

"Just over three weeks," he whispered.

Fionn slowly released the healer's hand. Words failed to escape his lips.

Three weeks...Gods above and below. Has it been that long?

"I must insist," said the healer, more strength in his voice than before. "I have tests to run and plenty of questions to ask." He pulled out a small notepad and pen from his cloak. "Now, my name is Yarlaith the White. Your companion told me your name is Fionn. Is this correct?"

"Y-yes," stammered Fionn. His frustration retreated, leaving a hollow feeling of hopelessness in its wake.

"Where were you born?"

"I was born in the Academy of Dromán."

Yarlaith raised an eyebrow. "Is that so?"

"My mother came to the brothers of the Academy when she was about to have me. It was a complicated birthing, and she died on the table. I was supposed to be sent to an orphanage, but when they saw I had latent ability for magic, they kept me there as a student, even though I was well under-age."

"Curious," said Yarlaith. "So, what brought you across the Glenn?"

Fionn sighed deeply. "Both Sláine and I were being transferred to the Penance Chapter. I'm going to study become a master Pyromancer. She was supposed to..."

Fionn's voice trailed off to a whimper before he could stop himself. His eyes went wet with tears.

"It's okay," said Yarlaith, closing the notebook and placing it back inside his cloak. "We can continue this another time. Please, get some rest. I'll bring you something to eat."

As soon as Yarlaith stood, a door from across the room slammed shut, followed by a quick pitter-patter of footsteps against a wooden floor.

"What was that?" asked Fionn, craning his neck to see behind Yarlaith. The healer turned to look back at the closed door.

"That's just my niece," he said. "She must have been eavesdropping." He smiled at Fionn, eyes twinkling in the dim light. "Her name is Morrígan. I'm sure she'd love to meet you."

***

The next few days passed by in a blur. Fionn could barely keep track of the time between Yarlaith's medical procedures, with his strange salves and poultices. Whenever the old healer came to Fionn's bedside, he either had another alchemical brew to try, or a salvo of tests to carry out on the arm.

My *arm,* Fionn tried to remind himself when Yarlaith first came poking it with needles to test for sensitivity to pain. Each sharp prick was another reminder that this was indeed *his* arm, and he would have to get used to it.

After Yarlaith's first set of examinations, his niece, Morrígan, came into the room. She was a strange girl, with a perpetual dark expression and eyes that never quite met his own.

"Why were you travelling through the Glenn?" she asked, approaching Fionn with hardly a 'hello.'

"It's a long story," said Fionn, nursing the numb ache that still ran through his arm. "I'd rather not elaborate right now."

Before he had a chance to change the subject, she was gone, rushing through the clinic door, her black feathered cloak flowing behind her.

She was there in the field. The troll almost killed her, too.

Yarlaith had told Fionn that Morrigan's mother died in the attack, leaving the girl an orphan. Her father had fled the scene, and he hadn't been heard of since. He was Yarlaith's brother, but if the old healer was upset over his disappearance, he certainly didn't show it.

The voices had been silent since Fionn had first awakened; he hesitated to tell Yarlaith about them at first. Eventually, he did, and although the white mage listened intently as Fionn described the words each voice said, it was clear that it wasn't a medical concern.

"Just a side effect of being asleep for so long," he had said, clearly trying not to sound too dismissive. "Sometimes our dreams can leak into our waking minds in the morning, as we re-adjust to reality."

But Fionn insisted they were real, that the voices stopped talking when he told them to 'shut up.' Yarlaith shook his head on hearing this, and reassured Fionn that it was nothing to worry about. Fionn had heard enough stories about people being locked up for claiming to hear things that weren't there, so he left the topic alone after that.

On the morning of the Harvest Moon, Yarlaith strolled into the clinic as he always did and made the same routine checks of Fionn's condition.

"You seem to have made a full recovery," said the healer, examining the stiches that bound the muscular arm to Fionn's shoulder. "Have you adjusted to your new limb?"

"I guess so," said Fionn. He had asked Yarlaith many times where the arm had come from, but the healer always dodged the question, assuring Fionn that everything would be all right, and that this was a perfectly normal medical procedure.

"You can reach Penance by tonight if you leave now," said Yarlaith, gathering Fionn's few belongings. "It's half a day's walk to Point Grey, and there's a regular trains and ferries from there."

"Sure," muttered Fionn, staring at the clothes Yarlaith had set out before him. The Pyromancer hadn't carried much when he left Dromán, as he assumed his needs would be tended to once he arrived. All he brought aboard the airship was a pair of boar-hide travelling boots and an old red travelling cloak, which Yarlaith had apparently washed thoroughly, for the stains of blood and mud he had gathered from the Glenn were nowhere to be seen. Fionn always made sure he was wearing flint-rings wherever he went, of course. But those had been on his right hand; the one he lost out by the cliffs.

"Come," said Yarlaith, offering Fionn an arm. "I'll see you to edge of the village."

They walked out through the clinic, down a narrow hallway leading to the entrance to the house. At the front door stood Morrígan, dressed in the same black cloak as before. Her arms were folded, her face contorted into a frown.

"He can't leave yet," said Morrígan to Yarlaith, as if Fionn wasn't there. "He hasn't told me about the Glenn!"

"Fionn is in a hurry, Morry," said Yarlaith. "He has important business in Penance. Business that is certainly none of yours."

The two passed the young girl and made their way towards the town square via a winding, dusty road leading downhill.

"Come back!" cried Morrígan, following Fionn and Yarlaith. "I need to know about the troll!"

"Please," said Fionn, trying to force the memory from resurfacing. "I don't want to talk about it."

"But you must!" said Morrígan, catching up to his side. "I need to know about the troll that killed my mother!"

Your mother wasn't the only one the troll killed, you little brat!

Fionn gasped in terror, holding a hand up to his mouth. That thought was not his own.

"I told you," he whispered. "I don't want to talk about it." He realised he was shaking, so folded his arms

"Leave him be," said Yarlaith.

Desperately wanting to be alone, Fionn told the girl that he was in a hurry and needed to reach Penance soon. But this didn't satiate her curiosity. Morrigan narrowed her eyes and studied Fionn for some time.

Eventually, she asked, "Why are you going to Penance?"

Where do I begin? I just wanted to be a Pyromaster, but now I need to bring news of Sir Bearach and Sláine...

"That's enough, Morry!" cut in Yarlaith, before Fionn had a chance to speak. The girl protested, but Yarlaith insisted that she leave his patient alone. Fionn didn't hear the words, for another voice began speaking into his ear.

If I were alive, I'd teach her some manners. The back of a gauntleted fist speaks louder than words!

Fionn shook his head.

"Yarlaith?" he asked, voice quivering. "The voices...will they ever stop?"

"Quiet," whispered the healer, urging Fionn onwards. "You're going to be okay."

The healer led Fionn to the edge of the town, to a winding road leading straight to Point Grey. Yarlaith told him what it was called, but Fionn didn't listen. He searched through his memory for a person whose voice matched the one that spoke earlier. He felt close, so close to remembering, but the answer was tantalisingly beyond his reach.

The healer bid him farewell. Fionn began walking eastwards, his back to the morning sun. It was only after Roseán vanished in the distance behind him that Fionn realised he had never thanked the old mage.

He's an odd one anyway, said one of the voices. *I doubt he'll notice you're gone.*

Oh, how the strange ones are always best at their trade, said another. *I was only half the knight my sister was.*

Darkness and solitude! roared another. *Darkness and solitude until the end of days!*

"Stop it!" cried Fionn, turning his stride into a run. He shut his eyes tight as he went, but it did nothing to hush the sounds. "Leave me alone!"

A dozen voices called out, too, moaning and crying, begging for mercy, singing like a choir out of key. As more joined the chorus, the cacophony almost became too much to bear.

Halfwit! You left me for dead!

Alone and dead!

No light, no light! No lighter than the Holy Hell!

The Holy Hell would be a paradise compared to this fate.

Pain! Pain! Pain! Pain!

Fionn stopped in his tracks, opening his eyes to see that he had strayed from the path. He stood alone, in an empty forest of decaying browns and blacks.

Now he is as lost as I am!

Now he knows what he brought upon me!

The last two voices were clearer than the others, speaking as if they were people, real people, standing next to him. With these voices clearer than the last, one thing became apparent: The voices all belonged to the same person.

Fionn took a moment to focus on the rest of the discordance. Deep in concentration, he picked out one voice, moaning incoherently. But when the Pyromancer touched upon the fire in his soul—the source of his magic— the voice became clear.

Light! I have found light! it cried. *The pit is not so black after all!*

He focused on another speaker, one that roared obscenities, and it too became coherent. The voice joined the other two, and they became one, like notes forming a single chord.

One by one, Fionn used his power to pick out the voices, adding them to the ones that had calmed. The others went quiet too, as if they realised what was happening. Indeed, one frantically whispered, *He's doing it. He's bringing us back together.*

Like a musician tuning an off-key lute, the disjointed sounds eventually blended into one another, forming one voice, stronger than the rest.

Fionn? it asked. *Is that you?*

"Yes," whispered Fionn, bracing himself for another barrage of insults. When they didn't come, he asked, "Who are you?"

The voice laughed heartily. It was a familiar sound, like an old friend long forgotten.

Why, it's only your most formidable companion, Sir Bearach of Keep Carriga! How is that old arm of mine serving you?

CHAPTER 8:
THE NECROMANCER AND
THE KNIGHT

Perhaps I was too quick to send Fionn on his way. The success of the procedure opens up some interesting new avenues of research. What was once thought impossible may be made possible if I can recreate the conditions of that fateful night. It wasn't healing that attached the knight's arm to the boy's body, but something else. There are some records of those who practiced dark magic, but the Church made sure their techniques could never be passed on to others. A smart move, for what use would there be for an afterlife if the dead can be brought back with magic?

Journal of Yarlaith the White, 15th Day Under the Moon of Nes.

***

"No," muttered Fionn, shaking his head. "It cannot be. You're dead."

I was, said Sir Bearach. *I was dead, and free of my pain and suffering for a short time. Then that fucking heretic came along with his twisted magics.*

"Yarlaith?" asked Fionn, turning back to face the west. He had managed to stray far from the path, and the town of Roseán had long since vanished from the distance. From where he stood in the forest, even the road was out of sight. "He's the town healer. What makes him a heretic?"

Fool! roared the knight. *You of all people should know. I was at the gates of Tierna Meall when I felt something grasp at my being. Before I knew it, my soul was dragged from the heavens, and shoved into your dying body.*

"That's impossible," said Fionn. He pressed a hand against his head. Sir Bearach's words made him recall a memory from long ago. The young mage had spent many lonely hours in the library of the Academy, reading whatever he could find. Old accounts of dead mages, of healers describing methods long made obsolete by advancements in the field.

Necromancy! The manipulation of the flesh!

Not quite, said Sir Bearach. *It was as if he reached into my very soul, gripping it with his filthy hands.*

Fionn gasped. "You...you can read my thoughts?"

I can see everything, said Sir Bearach. *I know more about you now than I ever cared to. I see your memories, of a lonely boy raised by old wizards. Of a recurring dream, of a child drowning in blood.*

"Get out!" cried Fionn. He began walking briskly back towards the road. "Get out of my head!"

Your first crush was a girl named Síle Ní Mháirtín. You were twelve years old, and she was twelve years your senior. You asked her to marry you in front of her friends, and they laughed. But none laughed as loud as she did.

"Why are you doing this?" said Fionn, pushing his way through the trees out onto the road. "What have you to gain?"

I want to learn more about the Necromancer that trapped me here.

"Yarlaith? I don't know much about him, he—"

No, you fool. You!

Fionn stopped abruptly.

"Me?" he whimpered. "But I didn't do it. It was all him!"

The healer tore me down from heaven, yes. But my soul was still free, even when he stuffed it into your body. Every aspect of my being had a voice, and I understood myself more than I ever could before. We observed you for a time, like an audience, until we felt the touch of dark magic again.

"No," said Fionn. "You don't mean..."

You used the same magic as the Necromancer. You bound each part of my soul to yours. Now I am one with your being, just as my arm is part of your body. And I am here to stay.

"I...I didn't know. I didn't know what I was doing."

But deep down, Fionn knew that he had done *something* when he had quelled each of the voices. He invoked his flame, the power of his soul, and manipulated something that wasn't flesh, or fire, or any other aspect of Nature.

He used his power to manipulate another man's soul.

Ah, the copper drops! jeered Sir Bearach. *You've read about those practising Necromancy. The Church hunted them down, burned them, hanged them, erased their memories from history. Will you be next?*

"I'm not like them," said Fionn. "The Druids of Rosca Umhir were graverobbers. Callaghan the Black was a murderer. We're not the same."

How can you be sure? Everyone has to start somewhere. Whether you mean it or not, you deprived me of paradise, and I'll never forgive you for it.

"I'm sorry," whispered Fionn. "Maybe I can undo it. I'll find a way."

Would you kill yourself to save me? said Sir Bearach. *The only way I'm going to Tierna Meall now is if we go together. Would you be willing to make that sacrifice?*

"No!" cried Fionn. "I won't."

"Halt! State your business, in the name of the King!"

Fionn turned to face a dozen soldiers. He had barely heard them approach. They stood before him, clad in grey, weathered armour, with spears raised to the sky. The one who spoke stepped forward. His armour was identical to that of the others, but a spotless white cloak draped over his shoulders set him apart.

"As captain of the Point Grey City Watch, I suggest you find your tongue, boy."

Go on, taunted Sir Bearach. *Tell them that you're a Necromancer now. Tell them that you've stolen a soul from the shores of paradise.*

"My name is Fionn the Red. I come travelling from Cruachan to Penance."

The captain's eyes narrowed. "You've strayed far from your route, then. What brings you to this part of the Clifflands?"

Ha! roared Sir Bearach. *Tell them about how you burned the airship from the sky, killing most of its crew and stranding the rest in the Glenn. That'll make for a fine tale.*

"I... I..." stuttered Fionn. He quickly considered his options. Was it wise to tell the truth, about the ship? Or perhaps there was another way.

The captain raised a gauntleted fist, and with a clatter of chains and armour, the rest of the guards lowered their spears towards Fionn.

Gods, prayed Fionn. *What am I supposed to say?*

Tell them you're running an errand for the Church, whispered Sir Bearach. He spoke with more urgency than before, the sarcasm absent from his voice. *Mention High-*

Cardinal Maeleachlainn Ó'Brian of Ard Sidhe and say no more. They won't question you further.

Fionn took a breath. Beads of sweat formed on his forehead. He chose his words carefully.

"My business is of a precious nature," he began, speaking slowly. "The Church has advised me to keep the details to myself. If you must know more, feel free to contact His Holiness Ó'Brian of Ard Sidhe."

The captain's expression changed. For a second, Fionn was sure he saw a flash of fear in the man's eyes. The captain gestured to his men again, and a dozen spears were raised back safely over shoulders.

"My apologies," said the captain. "We have had a report of bandits in this area. Have you seen anything of note on the road so far?"

Fionn scanned his memory. He couldn't remember much after leaving Roseán. After all, he was far too distracted to notice anything other than the voices.

"No," he said. "I saw nothing." The mage considered his position with the guards. "Is there anything I should know?"

"We found a bandit dead on the road some weeks ago, two more wounded," said the captain, an ounce of pride in his voice. "In-fighting, we believe. These outlaws would gut their own mothers if they thought it profitable. We found a camp, not too far from here, and raided it, taking many prisoners. There may be some stragglers left in the area, though. That is, if they haven't fled south." The captain spoke as if he was delivering a report to a superior.

"Good work," said Fionn, adapting an air of authority.

"We'll let you be on your way," said the captain, bowing slightly. "May the road rise to your feet."

"And may the stars follow yours," replied Fionn. The guards left, leaving Fionn and Sir Bearach alone on the road.

"Who was that?" asked the mage. "The High-Cardinal you had me mention?"

A person no sane man would want to cross, replied the knight. *And there's no need to speak out loud for me to hear. You don't want people thinking you're crazy.*

Sir Bearach didn't speak much more after that. A few hours of walking took Fionn to the gates of Point Grey, where a score of caravans and horse-drawn carts stood waiting by the walls, their owners lingering nearby. Fionn glimpsed into one of the carts as he passed. It was full of leafy greens and freshly picked vegetables. An array of earthly aromas hit him all at once, with the scent of tomato vines strongest amongst them.

"Have you come with any cargo?" asked a guard as Fionn approached the gate. The mage shook his head.

"No," said Fionn. "I'm travelling to Penance. Is the ferry still running?"

"Aye, but it'll be you who'll have to do the running. It's preparing to leave now."

Fionn immediately sprang into a sprint, straight through the gates into the city. He wasn't sure which direction to take, but he followed the path through the cobblestone square, northwards. The scent of salt was in the air, and Fionn followed it, assuming it would lead to the port.

He used his arms to gain momentum, throwing them up and down with each stride, his hands flat and tense, chopping through the air. His cloak fluttered out behind him, leaving both arms exposed. Some people gasped as he passed, but Fionn just assumed they were shocked at the speed at which he was running; the Pyromancer certainly didn't look like the athletic type.

Fool, whispered Sir Bearach. *You think they never saw a lad run before? It's the arm they're looking at.*

With a pang of realisation, Fionn slowed to a stop.

"Syl!" slurred a burly looking fellow. "Come look at this young lad. He's got an arm like a leg!"

The Simian named Syl wasn't the only one to come look. A dozen Simians and Humans all came to the window of the tavern, their faces pressed against the glass.

"Would you look at that!" called a voice. "It's almost as big as he is!"

"Ha! That's what me ma' said would happen if I spent too much time riggin' me mast. I guess she was right after all!"

There was a roar of laughter at that, and Fionn turned away from the crowd.

"Ah, he looks like a mage," said another patron. "I wouldn't upset him if I were you."

"A mage?" said the first. "Aren't they celibate? I suppose *that* explains it!"

Another wave of laughter, larger than the first, rose out from the tavern as Fionn turned a corner away from the street.

Imbeciles, he thought, picking up his pace again. *A fool with half a brain would know mages can't be celibate. How else could the Gift be passed on to another?*

They have a point though, said Sir Bearach. *If you even think of using my arm for that, I swear I'll–*

"You swear you'll what?" snapped Fionn. This outburst caused a few heads along the street to turn, but he ignored them. "What could you possibly threaten me with?"

The dead knight had no response for once.

When he reached the waterfront, Fionn was relieved to see that the ferry had yet to leave. The ship was almost full, with just a few passengers waiting to board. The mage jogged up to join them, his breath running short.

As he waited in line, he began fumbling through his pockets. It had been a while since he last needed to produce his purse.

They'll let you on for free if you show them your flint-rings, said Sir Bearach. *Just don't burn the ship down in the process.*

The rings were on my right hand, replied Fionn. *They were lost with the arm.*

Oh...I didn't realise.

"Three stags a head," called a voice. Fionn looked up to see that he was now at the top of the queue. A young lad stood at the entrance, dressed in a plain white vest and black trousers. He looked barely ten years old.

Fionn pulled out his purse and counted out three silver coins. He handed them over and stepped aboard.

The ship was wide and flat, with a low-ceilinged cabin to house its passengers. The benches were arranged perpendicular to the ship's hull, a gap running through the middle of each row like seats in a chapel. The benches were filled for the most part; Simians vastly outnumbered the Humans. Some passengers chatted quietly to one another, but most sat facing forward, eyes locked ahead. Fionn sat down beside a lone Simian.

It certainly wasn't as exciting as the airship back in Penance, but this was Fionn's first time travelling by sea. In fact, this was his first time travelling at all. He'd never had a reason to leave the Academy until now.

A sudden thought occurred.

Sir Bearach, he asked. *Why are you travelling to Penance?*

Cause I don't have a fucking choice in the matter, you thick-skulled idiot!

Fionn swore under his breath. *I'm sorry. I just–*

You just, what, forgot that I was dead? Forgot that I've had my soul molested by two Necromancers under the same moon?

The mage went silent as the ship began to move. A crewman strode up along the pier, removing ropes from its bollards. The waterfront slowly slid from view, until there was nothing but blue seas in every direction.

My brother is sick, said Sir Bearach, eventually. *He took ill almost a year back. The healers say there's not much they can do, and his time is running out. I was supposed to visit him, while I still could.*

You still can, replied Fionn. *What if I brought you to him, and spoke to him using your words?*

That'll never happen, said the knight. *They'll never let you in.*

Fionn had no reply to that. He considered telling the healers the truth, but that would probably land him in a prison cell for heresy. For how else could he be speaking a dead man's words, other than through profane magic?

You're right, they would arrest you on the spot, said Sir Bearach. His words caught Fionn off guard. It would take a while to get used to having the knight listen in on all his thoughts.

Couldn't I claim to be a relative? I'm sure I could get in somehow. Where would I find him?

In the most secure building of Penance, said the knight. *Under the care of the kingdom's most talented healers and protected by the city's best guards.*

Fionn paused, wondering who this man could possibly be. Of course, Sir Bearach heard that too.

His name is Cathal Carríga. The Human representative of the Triad.

CHAPTER 9:
THE BROKEN TRIAD

We are here because we have seen too much yet learned so little. Only by sharing the sights of our Seeings can we truly know the way of the Lord. Some of our brothers and sisters have gone mad from their revelations, but it is they who should feel sorry for us, for only they have seen the face of God.

Sermon of the Sons of Seletoth, from *God's Blood*, 4:21.

***

"How long has he been like this?" asked Farris, taking a step closer to the patient's bed.

"Eleven moons have come and gone since he first started showing signs," said Ruairí, idly touching his pendant as he spoke. "But he didn't seek medical attention until last spring. By then, it was too late."

"Yet he still lives?"

Ruairí gestured towards the bed. "Would you consider this living?"

Farris shook his head. The bedside of Cathal Carriga was a morbid place. The Human had once been a strong youth, besting many of Alabach's greatest knights at tourneys. Cathal was the youngest person—Simian or Human—to be elected to the Triad and was well loved by those he governed. Now, he was reduced to a life at the frontier of death, barely conscious, capable only of breathing.

"Can the healers do nothing for him now?" asked Farris, tilting his head as he considered the features of the dying lad. Cathal's face was drained of colour, his skin like a layer of thin film, clinging to deflated cheekbones. Dark circles surrounded his eyes, as if they were threatening to sink back into his head. Every strand of hair from his head and face had long since gone, leaving a shadow of the man who had once shared rule over Penance.

"Coal tumours," muttered Ruairí. "Quite common amongst those in the Steamworks. Treatable with surgery if caught early, but—"

"I'm familiar with the condition, Human," spat Farris. For the past moon, Argyll had assigned Farris to be Ruairí's shadow, apparently to learn about how things worked in Penance.

Fools, the pair of them. It's as if they've forgotten I was born here.

Despite his protests, Farris was forced to accompany the Human on all his business throughout Penance. From overlooking the operations of Jacob's re-established smuggling ring, to attending sermons of the Sons of Seletoth, Ruairí was never without his new shadow. The sermons had been the strangest, with their vague, riddled verses and rambling prayers. Farris had never seen men speak so much while saying so little.

At the very least, he had hoped to learn more about Seeings, but the Sons rarely spoke about them directly. Many alluded to serving some sort of higher purpose, and Farris had only caught brief mentions of the so-called "Truth" they had all learned about. He, of course, was intrigued from an investigational perspective; collecting information was a skill he prided himself on. But on another level, part of him needed to know what it is that could cause a Human, or even a Simian, to shift their perspective of the world so quickly.

I need to know...I need to know to make sure it doesn't happen to me.

"Why are we here?" asked Farris, abruptly. He stepped aside as a white mage tended to Cathal, fussing over a long, twisting tube connected to the patient's wrist.

"Cathal Carríga is an honourable man," said Ruairí. Even as he spoke, his eyes never left the hands of the healer. "Do we need a reason to visit the sick?"

Farris had no answer to that. He watched in silence as the healer went to work. With a shock, Farris realised that the tube connected to Cathal's wrist *beneath* the skin, though no blood was present at the site of the wound.

"Come," said Ruairí. "There's something else you should see." He turned to go, and Farris followed, stealing a glance back at the patient.

No need to say goodbye. He probably didn't even notice we were here.

The two exited Cathal's quarters out into a long hallway, with a bright, red rug stretched straight down the middle. Portraits of old Triad representatives hung on the walls, Humans to the left and Simians to the right.

"Why is the Silverback concerned with his condition?" asked Farris, catching up with Ruairí. "Why have you been ordered to monitor him?"

"The white mages of the Church are obliged to help the sick no matter what," said the Human. He led the way down the hall towards a curving marble staircase to the ground floor. "As long as a patient lives, they must do everything within their power to keep them alive."

"They're doing a fine job of that," said Farris. "Too good a job, if you ask me."

"True," said Ruairí. "The Silverback has seen that Cathal receives the greatest care possible, using the most recent advances in medicine. His treatment combines Human alchemy with Simian chemistry. The Penance Guild of Chemists have invested all of their resources into treating Cathal's condition."

"The Silverback requires him to recover?" asked Farris. "Because Cathal is in favour of the movement?"

"No," said Ruairí. He let the word hang in the silence, giving Farris time to consider its weight. The Human didn't speak again until both he and Farris had left the building.

"The laws of Penance state that all members of the Triad must keep their position until death," he continued, taking Farris down the stone steps of the House of the Triad. A cool breeze met them as they descended, its frigid kiss hinting towards a long, cold winter ahead of them. "Cathal Carríga will remain as the Human representative until the day he dies."

"If your Lord is just, that day will come soon," said Farris.

"These laws were written long ago," continued the Human, not taking note of Farris's interjection. "When our ancestors founded the Triad, they did not consider the possibility of a man being able to be kept so close to death's door, with a heart that still beats."

"So, the Humans are without a seat on the Triad. Can't the law be changed?"

"Yes," said Ruairí, letting a slight smile escape his lips. "Old Borris Blackhand has been trying to have the law changed, but such a treaty would need three signatures."

"The three points of the Triad," said Farris. "So, Borris and King Diarmuid will be the only active rulers as long as Cathal remains in this condition?"

The Human didn't respond. They made their way to the Dustworks of Penance, the poorest of the five districts and the place Farris had been born. Old wooden shacks lined the streets, one stacked upon the other, with chipped and broken staircases connecting the highest levels to the ground. As a child, Farris had seldom used those stairs; it was often quicker—and safer—to climb the buildings themselves.

Children ran to and fro, playing in the dusty streets, wearing little to no clothing. They were all Simians, of course. Only wealthier Humans chose to live in the City of Steam.

Amidst the rotting wooden buildings and the streets paved with dirt, one structure stood out. A stone wall rose up further down the street, with massive, iron gates facing the slums. The walls formed a perfect circle in the heart of the Dustworks, and inside lay the Great Basilica of Penance. The centre of the Church of Alabach.

"I've never once been inside," said Farris, in an attempt to break the silence. "I grew up on these streets, always hearing stories of the beauty that lay behind those walls. Marble arches and buildings made from solid gold. A great fountain in the centre, with silver statues dedicated to the Trinity, all manner of gemstones embroidering their forms. We tried to climb the walls to steal one, once. A single gem would be enough to feed a whole family here for a year. But that was before the Guild, and before we—"

"You have no need to convince me of the Church's injustices," interrupted Ruairí. "This is one belief you share with the Sons."

"One and only," said Farris. "Where are we going now?"

He had asked the Human this question many times, but rarely got an answer. Ruairí was the type of person who preferred to show Farris his intentions, rather than explaining them. To Farris's surprise, however, this time he got an answer.

"This shall be your last day as my shadow," he said, taking Farris between two wooden hovels adjacent to the Basilica walls. "From this day forward, you will be assigned to the Chief Engineer of Penance. There is plenty here for you to learn."

Ruairí halted abruptly and squatted down to examine the lower section of the hovel's wall. Only when the Human reached out to it, did Farris notice that there was a narrow door at its base. Ruairí carefully opened it, revealing a descending passageway inside.

"This used to be a warehouse for the Guild of Engineers," said Ruairí, gesturing to Farris to go inside. "The building has been long since abandoned, and the doors haven't been opened since." Farris ducked inside, shimmying through the gap. He carefully slipped down the slope, skidding on the back of his heels as he went. Some light illuminated the chamber from the entrance, revealing stacks of chests and crates with bars of iron and copper discarded on the ground. The light vanished as Ruairí closed the door, consuming both himself and Farris in darkness.

"Carry on forward," said Ruairí, somewhere behind. "There's a door a little further on. There should be light inside."

Farris shuffled through the darkness, careful not to trip over on anything on the floor. His feet met obstacles here and there, but he moved over them cautiously.

"Skies above," he cursed. "Would it have killed you to bring a torch?"

"No," said the Human. "It would have killed both of us."

Before Farris knew it, they had reached the door. Ruairí fumbled at its lock, eventually pulling it open, spilling a dim, red light over both of them. The hue seemed somewhat unnatural, like something between a torch candle and an oil lamp.

Ruairí led Farris into the room. It was a large chamber, certainly larger than what the warehouse above seemed capable of holding. The light emanated from dozens of red crystals hanging from the ceiling. Along the walls stood huge barrels, their lids sealed and re-enforced with sheets of thick steel.

"Black Powder," muttered Ruairí as they went. "That's why we can't have torches in here. The fire crystals will have to do for now."

Farris suppressed a smile, remembering his time on board the *Glory of Penance*. "I understand the risks," he said.

"No, you do not," said a voice. "You understand far less than you let on."

Both Farris and Ruairí turned to see a female Simian walking through the shadows. The faint, crimson light illuminated her in a way that brought attention to her curved hips and sleek, muscular arms. Farris fought to keep his eyes level with hers. She was of height with him, and with shoulders almost as wide, which wasn't uncommon for females familiar with hard labour.

"Pleased to meet you," said Farris, extending a hand. She didn't react, and barely looked at Farris as she spoke.

"Now there are two in the city who shouldn't know about this place," she said, arms folded, glaring at Ruairí.

"Nicole," said Ruairí. "This is Farris Silvertongue, an old acquaintance of Argyll. He—"

"I know all about what he has done," said Nicole. "And I know all about what he believes." The features of her face stood out now: a thin mouth between raised cheekbones, and eyes sharp enough to cut steel.

"Ah," said Farris. "So, my reputation precedes me?"

"If you could call it that," she replied. "Three years, they said you spent, living in the capital, cup bearer for the king. Tell me, how was it he didn't notice you were a Simian? Have you spent so much time amongst the Humans that even they can no longer tell the difference?"

Farris smiled. "Well, Cruachan is a diverse city. There are many Simians in the king's Royal Guard, and even more in the Crown's intelligence network. We dissidents are an unfortunate minority."

"We?" spat Nicole. "You leave us during our greatest period of growth, and you return, years later, singing of the might of the Human king like a court bard."

Farris took a step towards Nicole. Her frame was almost as thick as his own; if it came to blows, it would be impossible to predict who would come out on top.

"Your father was a very intelligent man," said Farris. "I never had the pleasure of meeting him, but every Simian who met Santos would speak of his flawless, immutable logic. I expect you to hold rationality to the same esteem as he, yes?"

Nicole nodded, not breaking eye-contact.

"I was as shocked as any free-thinking Simian," he continued, "when I found solid, empirical proof of Diarmuid's immortality. Only those influenced by petty beliefs would deny the king's power had they seen what I have seen." Farris let his eyes drop, considering the curves of Nicole's hips once more. "It would take me a long time to convince you, but I'd appreciate it if you could someday give me the chance."

Nicole rolled her eyes. "You are as pathetic as you are blind, Farris Silvertongue."

"Nicole," said Ruairí. "Farris will be liaising with you in my stead. He'll be paying your laboratory a visit every fortnight until your work is complete."

"And the Silverback," said Nicole. "Does he understand that it takes time, accomplishing the impossible?"

"Argyll is confident that you will succeed where your ancestors have failed." Ruairí glanced around the room, at the stacks of crates and barrels piled up to the ceiling. "The supplies for Dromán," he said. "Are they ready?"

Nicole turned and disappeared into the darkness without saying a word. Before Farris had a chance to ask Ruairí what exactly was going on, Nicole emerged from the shadows, with a wooden crate cradled in her arms.

"Ten prototypes here," she said, presenting the box to Ruairí. "Loaded and ready."

The Human slowly cracked open the lid, cautious, as if expecting something to jump out at him. Farris craned his neck over Ruairí's shoulder to see what lay inside, but the darkness obscured his view.

"Good work," said Ruairí, reaching inside. "These are far better quality than the first batch I've seen."

"Yet they are far from perfect," said Nicole, irritably. "The task at hand is more challenging than anticipated."

"True," said Ruairí, pulling an object out from the crate. "But if it were easy, it wouldn't be worth doing."

He handed the item to Farris. It was a strange shape, like a short length of steel tubing, bent and embroidered. It fit into Farris's hand neatly, with the long end of the shaft pointing out over his knuckles. His index finger found a trigger, like that of a crossbow, right on the inside of the curve. He dared not go near it.

"It's...some sort of weapon?" asked Farris, moving his hand up and down to discern the item's weight. "What's it for?"

"For killing Humans," said Nicole, throwing Ruairí a sly smile. "Present company excluded."

"They're called firearms," said Ruairí, tentatively taking the object from Farris's hand. "Nicole has been making them for years, supplying the Silverback's people with them for skirmishes. Mass production has only begun recently."

"How does it work?" Farris caught a glance at the other firearms in the crate. With ten or so in that one, there could easily be a hundred more stored where they stood.

"I borrowed a concept from Pyromancy," said Nicole. "Like a red mage using flint-rings, the trigger is used to create a spark. But instead of amplifying its strength with magic, we use black powder to cause an explosion inside the chamber. This forces whatever is inside to shoot towards an enemy. Faster than a speeding arrow."

"No knight in the kingdom could fight against a man armed with this," said Ruairí. "A score of men—or Simians— could take on an *army* with the right training."

Farris's eyes widened. How could such a simple device, so easily smuggled, cause so much damage? "You," he said to Nicole. "You invented this?"

"No. It was my father's invention. I'm trying to improve on it."

"Improve?" asked Farris. "Sin's shadow! What is there to improve on?"

"The material," interjected Ruairí. "A Geomancer could bend it out of shape in seconds, rendering it useless. The projectiles could be stopped and sent back to the marksmen."

"Of course," said Farris. "What do you propose we do?"

"There he goes again!" cried Nicole. "There is nobody working on this but *me*. I alone am labouring day and night to achieve what no other Simian engineer could: to create a new type of material, stronger than Simian-steel, and completely resistant to Human magic."

"Imagine," said Ruairí. "Arms and armour made from something not even a battalion of Geomancers could touch. When the time comes to march, there'll be no stopping us."

Farris suppressed a shiver. He always knew it would take *some* violence to bring the Crown to its knees, but he never expected the conflict to be so one-sided.

"And there's more," continued Ruairí, some excitement entering his voice. "Nicole is working on her own invention, something that will change the way wars are waged for centuries. Something to—"

"Enough," said Nicole. "I wish not to have conjectures made about my work at this early stage. Nor do I want King Diarmuid's bootlicker knowing more than he should. Tell me, Farris, have you proved your loyalty to the Movement since you returned to Penance?"

"Well, I did prevent a tactical strike on our fine city. The Crown was trying to disable the sky-fleet before a civil war could begin. I've saved the fleet, and the hundreds living in the Shadow of Sin."

"The skyfleet would have been no loss," said Nicole, "not with my work on our side. And more than a thousand will die if we go to war. Would that bother you, Farris

Silvertongue? Would that make you reconsider calling yourself one of us?"

Skies above. She's beautiful when she's furious.

"No," he said eventually. "I'll prove my worth in the coming months, you'll see."

"You've seen too much already," she said. "I must ask you two to leave. I've work to do."

Farris and Ruairí began making their way back out through the darkness, the latter with the crate of firearms held tightly to his chest.

"There's fire in her," whispered Ruairí, right when they were out of earshot. "I'd reckon she hates the king more than the Silverback himself."

"Aye," said Farris, trying to catch a glance back at her. "I hope she doesn't hate me half as much as that."

Chapter 10:
Rings of Fire

Let us consider the sexual habits of the Simian. With the absence of a soul, one is incapable of the strongest Human emotions, including love and hope. To accommodate for a lack of the former, the typical Simian resorts to a life of promiscuity and perversion. Couplings of more than two individuals at once are not uncommon, and it seems that many have no preference for a particular gender. Life-long unions are as absurd a notion to them as their atheistic beliefs are to us. Indeed, the seed of a Simian does not quicken in the belly of a female as easily as a Human's would inside a wife, so little care is given to the selection of a mate. The term 'rat' is often used as a derogatory term for the Simian, but this comparison is a poor one. The natives of Alabach do not breed as quickly as rodents. If they did, then their numbers should surely outnumber our own.

Excerpt from Between Penance and Sin: A Study of Simian Biology, King Eoghain Móráin, First of his Name, Third Incarnate of Seletoth, AC101.

***

Face it, you have no idea where you're going, said Sir Bearach. *I see no Academy around here.*

Fionn sighed, turning back to face the way he came. The straight streets of Penance's Saltworks were identical in every direction, with terraced buildings either side of the road like clay walls enclosing a black river. Even the ground felt strange, for Fionn's feet were more accustomed to cobblestones than this city's flat surfaces.

Still, he continued in the direction he initially intended, ignoring the taunts of the knight inside his head.

The directions I was given in Dromán brought me here, thought Fionn. *And I doubt the brothers of the Academy would be wrong about something as important as this.*

The mage felt Sir Bearach snort at the back of his mind. Or *their* mind. Lately, Fionn wasn't quite sure. The knight had opened up to him a little on the ferry, but once the Tower of Sin appeared on the coastline, Sir Bearach went quiet, only to speak again once Fionn realised he was lost.

Do you even know what you're looking for? asked the knight. *I'd expect the Academy Chapter of Penance to be on a busier street than this.*

Fionn agreed. The Saltworks were the residential epicentre of Penance. Despite its name, this district didn't smell at all like the sea. The streets were also void of life, with the buildings either side of Fionn almost derelict in their stature.

We're definitely at the right address, Fionn reassured himself, yet he still felt unsure. The streets of Penance had been nameless since the Fall of Sin, so they could be only identified by numbers. The Academy Chapter was supposed to be located in the fourteenth building on the eighth street of the Saltworks.

Are you sure it wasn't the eight building of fourteenth street? asked Sir Bearach. *That area seemed far livelier–*

"No!" said Fionn, out loud. He immediately felt grateful that there was nobody around to hear him. He closed his eyes and inhaled deeply. *It is supposed to be right here!*

He half hoped to see the Academy building before him when he opened his eyes, but was instead confronted with the same plain, clay-terraced building as before. A stained wooden door hung in its frame, splintered and cracked throughout. Although he had passed it a dozen times, only now did Fionn notice the number "14" chalked out on the ground before it. As he went to take a closer look, Sir Bearach spoke again.

Don't tell me it was here all along. Gods, tell me anything but that!

Fionn's gaze caught a tiny metal sign next to the door, roughly the size of an envelope, with thin letters scratched into its surface: *Conleth the Red*.

Who's that? asked Sir Bearach. *He sounds like a Pyromancer.*

Fionn frowned. *He's the one we were looking for.* He stood back and looked up at the tenement building, two stories tall and box-like, identical to the hundreds of others in the Salt-works. *This is the Penance Chapter of the Academy.*

I was expecting more, said Sir Bearach. *The Academy of Dromán is a sight to behold. This is the type of house a dozen commoners would share.*

Fionn ignored the knight's remarks—at least, he ignored them as best as he could. His oversized hand rapped upon the wooden door with more force than the mage had intended, causing it to open slightly.

Unlocked, said Sir Bearach. *I'd put money on the place being looted long ago.*

That brought a smile to Fionn's face. From what he was told, Conleth the Red was one of the greatest living Pyromancers, a Master of Fire for longer than most of Fionn's tutors in Dromán had been alive. No sane person would dare attempt to burgle the home of someone capable of turning the city to cinders.

"Firemaster Conleth?" called Fionn, slowly pushing the door inwards. "I was told you'd be expecting me?"

The door immediately slammed shut, causing Fionn to jump away from it in fright. He had been sure there was nobody on the other end.

"Expecting you, so I was!" cried someone from inside the house. "I was expecting you a bloody moon ago, and I was about to give up expecting altogether!"

The voice was shrill and sharp, speaking quick words that cut through the air, like daggers against a chalkboard.

"I was delayed," said Fionn. "There was an accident on our journey here. I was wounded and healed before I could continue here on foot."

There was silence. Fionn considered repeating himself for fear that he wasn't heard, until the door slowly creaked open.

The inside of the tenement's hall was visible, with wooden floors and stone walls holding empty torches at eye-level with Fionn. It took a moment for the mage to realise that the house's occupant was standing before him, less than half the height of the door.

Conleth the Red leaned in against the door, as if standing alone was an effort. Thick-rimmed glasses hid most of his face, his pale mouth thinned into a shrewd line. He wore loose, grey rags that Fionn supposed must have once been red, before the passage of time had removed whatever colour they had.

The man himself stood little over four feet tall, his height stunted by a hunched back. In fact, more of the mage's body seemed to be leaning forward than was standing straight, indicating that he could have once been a tall fellow.

"There was supposed to be another one," said the mage, leering up at Fionn. "Sláine something-or-other."

"She didn't make it," said Fionn, making a special effort to keep his voice from quivering. "I'm the only one who did."

Conleth grunted and beckoned Fionn inside. He led the young mage through a narrow hall toward a room at the back of the building.

"Seán got fed up waiting for her," said the Firemaster. "He's gone back to Dromán now. He never did like it here."

"So, it's just you?" asked Fionn as they stepped through the remnants of a kitchen, with an old stove against the back wall and a round, wooden table in the centre. Every other surface of the room was covered in books and loose pages. On the floor stood piles of leather-bound tomes, some stacked taller the Firemaster himself.

"Aye," said Conleth. "All the others left. They call this a *Chapter* of the Academy, but it's more a footnote than anything." He gestured absent-mindedly around the room. "Everything you need to study is here. You'll be sleeping on the top floor. There's a bed up there, I think. It's been a while since I used the stairs. Now, if you'll excuse me."

Conleth pushed past Fionn and made his way to a three-legged stool in the corner of the kitchen. He sat and picked a book from the ground, and began reading, ignoring the bewildered Fionn standing in the centre of the room.

"Is that it?" he asked. "Aren't you supposed to teach me how to master the element of fire?"

The old mage lowered his head and gazed back at Fionn. "You're not ready yet," he said, and returned to his book.

"How do you know that?" said Fionn, his voice rising only slightly.

"Because you lot never are. Come, conjure some fire for me here. Show me what you learned in all your years at the Academy."

Fionn narrowed his eyes with frustration. *I'll show him alright*, he thought, raising his right arm to click his fingers together.

With a pang of embarrassment, Fionn realised that the flint-rings he once wore on his arm were no longer in his possession. This didn't seem to be the concern of Conleth, however.

"Curious," he said, slowly rising to his feet. "I hadn't noticed that until now. My eyes are not what they once were." He took a step towards the young mage, eyes focused on his over-sized arm. "Such a curious monstrosity. How did it happen?"

Fionn swallowed deeply. "I don't see why you should know. Put me on the course to be a Firemaster, and I'll share some of my story."

"Curious indeed..." muttered Conleth to himself. He pulled two flint-rings off his own fingers and handed them to Fionn. "Here, show me that you are ready. I fear they may not fit."

He's right about that, said Sir Bearach. *Those little things would never fit me.*

Fionn placed both rings on the middle and fourth finger of his own hand. The movement immediately felt strange, for he had never worn flint-rings on his left hand before. He attempted to click them together—something that would have once come as easily as breathing—but he failed to produce a spark. Again, he tried, and again, until fatigue began to set into his wrist.

Conleth looked on without a word. Fionn was relieved at this much; anything the old man could say now would only frustrate him further.

Come on, he told himself, flicking his wrist again. *It's the same as before, but with the fingers facing the other way. Why can't I—*

A spark appeared in mid-air as the rings successfully rubbed off one another for the first time. It had disappeared before Fionn could grab it, but this did not deter him.

Again, said Sir Bearach. *You had it there!*

Fionn couldn't help but smirk. If he hadn't known better, he supposed that the knight was rooting for him.

With more confidence than before, Fionn raised his left hand and brought the flint-rings together. When the spark appeared, he searched inward, pulling at the power of his soul.

The spark immediately burst into a ball of flame. Fionn tugged at the fire flaring in his own heart, and adjusted the ball's heat, decreasing it to not burn the surroundings. He focused on the ball, enclosing both his over-sized and under-sized hands around it, and moulding it between his fingers.

He turned his attention back to the power of his soul, fuelling the embers in his heart, which in turn strengthened the fire in his hands. The flames around him expanded and enveloped his whole body, but they burned nothing he did not command them to.

For the first time in weeks, Fionn felt like there was a soul inside him. Its power fed the flames, the flames fed his confidence, and the fire in his heart flared with might. His whole life, he had felt the power of his soul that way, like flames inside his chest. When it came time to choose a discipline back in the Academy, the School of Pyromancy made the most sense.

But things were different now. No, not only was it the rings on his left hand, or the massive arm attached to his right shoulder, but there was something else *inside*. He turned his focus away from the flames, and looked inward, more closely than he had before. The fire in his heart was there as it had always been, but it was no longer alone. No, beside it, there was something else. Another spark that had yet to be touched.

"I've seen enough," cut in Conleth, suddenly.

Fionn immediately extinguished the flame. It felt like an eternity had just passed, for he had almost forgotten where he was standing.

"So," said Fionn. "Does this mean I am ready?"

Conleth let out a laugh. "Sure, you're ready to start, but I can't promise anything beyond that. Give me a moment…"

He disappeared from the kitchen, leaving Fionn with the hundreds of books littering the floor. He was no stranger to tomes written about magic or history, but he didn't recognise any of these particular texts.

One book did catch his eye, however. The book that Conleth had been reading was left discarded on the floor beside the stool. Fionn walked over to get a closer look. When he did, he chuckled softly to himself.

What's so funny? asked Sir Bearach, his voice a little more irate than normal.

This book, said Fionn, bending down to pick it up. It was bound in black leather, with tiny, golden letters written across the spine, as if the scholar who had made the manuscript was ashamed of its contents. *'Between Penance and Sin: a study of Simian Biology, by King Eoghain I, third incarnate.' Have you heard of King Eoghain?*

I have not, said Sir Bearach. *If he was the third incarnate of Seletoth, he died long before I was born.*

That's right, said Fionn. *He ruled during the Fall of Sin, some three hundred years ago, but he hated Simians even before they defied the gods. He fancied himself a bit of a scholar, and he attempted to explain why Simians are the way they are, based on their physiology. His own prejudices came out in his writings Now he's remembered as a bigot and a fool.*

Interesting, said Sir Bearach. *Why would an old mage living alone in a city full of Simians be reading such a text?*

Before he had a chance to response, Conleth the Red returned, a tome as large as himself clutched tightly against his chest.

"Take this," he wheezed, forcing the book into Fionn's hands. "Your parlour tricks with fire won't make you a great mage. Studying the right material, *this* material, will."

Fionn took the tome in his hands and leafed through it. Numbers and symbols flashed by his eyes, with barely a full word in sight. Some figures he recognised, but most he had never seen before.

"Gods above and below, what is this?" he asked, not attempting to hide the shock in his voice. "This is...mathematics. Sums and equations, like those studied by Simian engineers."

"And studied by Firemasters," said Conleth, curtly. "Any child descended from the Firstborn can learn to use magic. Any fool that can afford tuition and four years of their life can study in the Academy. But you came here because you want more. The path before you is not as simple as the one you left behind."

The Firemaster raised a pale, crooked finger and pointed to one of the pages before Fionn.

"Mastering the School of Pyromancy is easy. Even children can do it. But if you want to master fire itself, then you need to understand it. You need to blur the lines between your soul and the flames."

"Where does *this* come into it?" asked Fionn, holding the book before the old mage.

"The Simians are not the only ones to use mathematics to study the world. This volume covers everything a trainee Firemaster needs to know about the nature of fire and the energies that dictate its movement through the air. You are adept at manipulating the flames, but can you command their heat? How much does it take to turn wood to ash? To turn water to steam? To melt iron and stone? These are things you must learn to calculate before they can be attempted and mastered. These equations must fill your mind and possess your soul. Rionach's Twelve Theorems of Heat Transfer must be on the tip of your tongue at all times, as familiar as your own name."

Fionn glanced down at the textbook.

"I am to read all this? Over the course of my year here?"

"No," said Conleth, removing the glasses from his face. No longer magnified by the thick lenses, his eyes now seemed like little black beads. "You must memorize it, cover to cover, and be capable of producing it blind within four moons."

You were right, said Sir Bearach. *He's mad. The Academy left him alone too long, and he's been driven insane by the solitude. We should leave. We better–*

"I'll do it," said Fionn. He closed the book and tucked it under his massive arm. "I'll do whatever it takes."

CHAPTER 11:
THE BEGGAR'S FLAME

What was created by the Lord cannot be undone by Man, for magic lets one only manipulate the earth and Her fruits. The extent to which one can take control over an element is proportional only to the power of one's soul, or whatever fraction can be accessed.

These are the limits that Seletoth has set upon His Gift to us, lest those with as much hubris as the Simian try to usurp the Lord Himself.

An abridged version of Rionach's Twelve Theorems of Heat Transfer, transcribed by Foalín the Grey, AC344.

***

The air of the Steamworks was every bit as thick as its name suggested, with pillars of dense smoke billowing from factory chimneys up towards a blanketed grey sky. Farris walked slowly between the huge buildings, taking in the strange splendour of their forms. They appeared like twisted,

Simian-made monstrosities against a backdrop of chaos, with plumes of swirling steam in constant motion against eruptions of flame.

No wonder the Humans rarely come here. If I were a little more credulous, I'd believe I was walking along the shores of the Holy Hell itself.

In truth, Farris had seldom come to this sector of the city. Those who worked in the mills had long since become adjusted to the smog-filled air, but Farris had to make special effort to stop his lungs from convulsing as they took in soot. Like a traveller in a storm, he went onwards with a forearm raised over his eyes. The few other solitary Simians who shared the streets walked without such apparent effort, as if they were strolling through the countryside. Often, the Humans who conquered Alabach would complain about the Simians of Penance, who were apparently poisoning the land Seletoth promised His children. But the Simian people rarely paid much mind to the waste that Penance produced.

As sure as Sin, this is our land, not theirs. We can do with it whatever we wish.

He carried on, taking a swig of thainol from his pocket flask. The liquid singed his tongue, but he welcomed the taste: back in the Human capital, Farris had often been forced to be content with their stouts and ales. His own supply of thainol had been running low when King Diarmuid forced him to leave.

Perhaps the Lord does look over me. Another week in Cruachan, and I would have run dry.

The footpath carried Farris towards his destination, a huge square building nestled in an obscure corner of the Steamworks. The surrounding structures dwarfed the Simian, but he never felt intimidated by their size. As unsightly as it was, the skyline of the Steamworks was every bit as Simian as he. Whereas Humans looked upon the pollution of Penance with disgust, many Simian artists and poets created wonderful works inspired by the steel behemoths, and the pillars of fire they threw into the sky.

The square building came closer. Farris hesitated. This was to be his first trip of many into the depths of the Steamworks, at the behest of the Silverback. It was a welcome change from accompanying Ruairí on his business for the Sons of Seletoth, but at least the Human didn't balk at the sight of Farris.

The great building stood before him, its huge, shuttered door as high as the walls themselves. Only one Simian invention would require an entrance as grand as that: an airship.

At the bottom of the gargantuan steel shutter was a smaller door, large enough for a Simian to enter. Its outline was almost invisible against the steel, and perhaps would have gone unnoticed by someone not looking out for it.

Farris pulled an iron key from a coat pocket. As long as a finger and as slender as a needle, the key slid easily into a thick lock holding the door's cross-bolt in place. Farris would have expected a building as old as this to be stiff with rust and negligence, but the mechanics of the lock worked with little effort. Once unlocked, Farris pushed the door open and stepped in, hesitantly.

"Hello?" he called, not quite sure what else to say. He found himself inside a huge room, as large as the building itself, with a ceiling a hundred feet overhead. Once used to manufacture airships, the factory had since been cleared out, and its contents replaced with several smaller workstations scattered throughout an empty floor. At the far side of the floor, Farris saw two figures standing very close to one another. He began walking towards them, his footsteps echoing throughout the large, empty building.

"Ah Farris!" cried one of the Simians as he approached. "I was hoping to see you before I left!"

It took Farris another few steps for him to recognise Garth, standing with his arms stretched outwards. The second figure was Nicole, kneeling with one knee on the floor as she fussed with something at Garth's hips.

"Glad to see you, too, brother," said Farris. "I hope I didn't catch you at a bad time."

"Not at all," said Garth, nodding towards the female Simian at his hips. "Nicole's just taking a few more measurements before I head out to the Clifflands. She's hoping to be finished with the Reaper by—"

"You speak as much as your brother," said Nicole, standing, and rolling a stretch of measuring tape about her wrist. "I don't wish for everyone to know about our work before it's complete."

"Ahh," said Garth, glancing at the floor. "I take it that this is all you need?"

"Yes. Your brother requires my attention, too, apparently."

Garth turned to Farris. "This will just be a routine scouting. It shouldn't take too long, and I'm sure I'll come to no harm."

"Ah now," said Farris. "You were never quite as good a liar as I was. I know well that Argyll has you spying on mages to the south now. Boars and beadhbhs won't compare to a battalion of Geomancers in a fight."

"Relax," said Garth. "I'll be armed with one of Nicole's little gifts, and I'll be sure not to be seen. We need to know their numbers, and I'm the best Simian for the job."

"Sure," said Farris. "Just, be careful out there."

Garth snorted and patted Farris on the shoulder. "You worry too much, just like Mother did. I'll be *fine*."

With that he strolled away, leaving Farris and Nicole alone in the empty factory floor. Farris's heartbeat quickened, ever so slightly.

"What was that about?" he asked, ignoring the excitement rising in his stomach. "Something about a... Reaper?"

"Argyll sent you here to help, not learn," said Nicole. "Though I doubt there's anything you can help with. What do you know about the basics of metallurgy?"

"Absolutely nothing," said Farris. "But I'm sure you could use the extra hands."

Nicole laughed abruptly, revealing a set of perfectly white teeth, with sharp fangs framing her smile.

"Extra hands you have, sure," she said. "But they'd be likely to do more harm than good if they were put to use. Have you ever operated a blast furnace? Have you ever alloyed steel from iron? Skies above, do you even know what that means?"

Farris did not respond straight away. He knew very little of the science of material, and Nicole certainly didn't seem like the type of person one would lie to. Of course, Farris was well used to lying to females just as attractive as her. When he spoke to tell the truth, the words felt strange on his tongue.

"I know as much as a Simian child would," he said, "and no more. Carbon and iron make steel, and it takes a blast furnace to make it so. That is the full extent of my knowledge of metallurgy. I'm in the dark just as much as you are as to why the Silverback assigned me to work with you."

Nicole smiled, and for once it didn't seem to be at anyone's expense. "I may not like it," she said, "but at least now we have a starting point. I guess Argyll didn't give either of us a choice."

She walked past Farris and beckoned him to follow. Long wooden tables stood in the centre of the room, with an assortment of twisted steel and iron-ore laid upon their surfaces along with some scatterings of paper.

"Geomancy is the manipulation of the earth and Her fruits," said Nicole, gesturing to the metals on the tables. "So, a green mage can only manipulate what nature produces itself: sand, soil, stone, iron."

"But not steel?" Farris knew it was important that he make Nicole stop speaking to him like a child.

"Wrong. It takes a little more effort, but a well-trained Geomancer *can* manipulate steel. Other alloys even further removed from natural metals are harder, with Simian-steel amongst the most difficult. Unfortunately, our own legendary metal is still within the reach of a well-trained Geomancer. Twisting Simian-steel is even the last rite of passage for green mages wishing to graduate from the Academy.

"But you're trying to make one that's stronger than Simian-steel? One that even the best Geomancers cannot touch?"

"Yes," said Nicole with a sigh. "Argyll feels convinced that this war cannot be won otherwise. Even with a thousand Simians carrying firearms, we'd be quickly overwhelmed by handful of Geomancers."

"How goes the progress?" asked Farris, eying a particularly strange mass of steel upon the tabletop. It glimmered green and blue, with red veins streaking throughout. It certainly seemed far from *natural*.

"Not well," she said. "I must have tried a hundred combinations by now. I've tested some with a master Geomancer, and while many are indeed more difficult to grasp than Simian-steel, it seems like making one that's invulnerable from Geomantic interference is...impossible."

"How so?" asked Farris, careful to put only a little sincerity in his voice. Nicole seemed like the type who wouldn't appreciate sympathy from strangers.

The engineer paused, as if carefully considering the words. Eventually she shook her head. "It would be impossible to describe," she said. "There's a mathematical equation that dictates the relationship between a Geomancer's capacity to manipulate an alloy, but without a way of understanding those terms, you'd never comprehend it."

"Can't it be described in words?" chanced Farris.

Nicole wrinkled her nose, deep in thought. A slight hint of a smile appeared at the corner of her lips, as if she had found a suitable way to describe what she was meaning to say. When she spoke, it was with greater enthusiasm than before.

"Consider a plank of wood," she said, raising her hands to indicate its length. "Let's pretend it's four foot long. If you were to cut it in half, how much would you be left with?"

"Two," said Farris, without hesitation. The last thing he needed was to appear slow when it came to basic arithmetic.

"Okay," she said, bringing her hands closer together, at a distance that seemed like two feet apart. "And what if you were to do the same again?"

"I'd be left with one," said Farris. He was half-tempted grab her hands and embrace her, there and then, but decided against it. She was speaking to him like an equal now, and it seemed wise to let her continue uninterrupted.

"Correct," she said. "We are left with one foot, or twelve inches. Now, what would happen if we were to cut this in half three more times?"

Farris thought about it for a moment. "We'd have six inches, then three inches, then one and a half."

Nicole brought her hands together until they were barely touching.

"And if we were to continue with this pattern," she said, "we'd end up with three-quarters, then three-eights, then three-sixteenths, and so forth."

"Until we end up with nothing?" asked Farris.

"Incorrect," said Nicole, sternly. "What remains would get smaller and smaller, but it will *never* reach zero. As I said, this relationship can be described with a mathematical equation, and it too describes the relationship I've found between Geomancy and Simian-steel. I can produce compounds that eventually become more and more difficult to manipulate, but it never becomes impossible."

"I see," said Farris. Nicole began walking again, and Farris followed, deep in thought.

Could it really be impossible? There must be a way. Although he truly knew little about the sciences of which Nicole spoke, something did stir at the back of his head. Something he had seen before, recently, even. Something that didn't abide by the laws Nicole had described.

Farris barely noticed that he walked through the shadow of something hanging on the ceiling, blocking out the little light that entered the chamber. When he looked up to examine it, he gasped with awe.

Skies above and below. How did I miss this?

Held up by thick cables and wooden beams was something shaped like an airship, but much smaller than the one that had carried Farris to Penance. It had just a single ballonet about the size of a mountain sloth, though it was painted black and almost invisible against the dark ceiling. A single engine almost as large as the gondola itself hung at its back, with thick propellers extending outwards.

"Ah," said Nicole, appearing at Farris's side. "That's *Skirmisher*. I helped my father build it when I was a girl. He claimed it could travel from Elis Point to Cruachan and back within a day, but he never had the chance to test it."

"It hasn't been used since?" asked Farris. It was such a strange sight, an airship only capable of carrying a handful of supplies. "That's certainly a shame."

"My father didn't think so," she said. "Once King Diarmuid commissioned him to build that damned railway tunnel, nothing else mattered to my father. Not even his family."

"I'm sorry. It's said that Santos was one of our age's great minds."

"He was," said Nicole. "Until King Diarmuid killed him down in the tunnels they built together, and framed Argyll for it."

Farris frowned. "That's what you believe happened down there?"

"That's what I know happened!" snapped Nicole. "If Argyll had been planning anything of the sort, I would have found out about it. And what would the Movement possibly have to gain by killing someone like Santos?"

"Perhaps you're right," said Farris. It seemed as if Nicole didn't know, or chose not to mention, that the King's Royal

Simian Guard was also killed in the supposed attack. If what Nicole believed was true, King Diarmuid would have had to kill the six Simians himself. The Silverback lying to Nicole and the other dissidents seemed a more likely explanation than that.

They continued in silence. Farris's mind returned to the events that followed the death of Santos. The King's attempt to destroy the Skyfleet of Sin. The other spies aboard the airship. The smell of the flowers of the Glenn.

I'll have to tell Garth about my own experiences with beadhbhs once he gets back, he realised, fighting back a smile.

Of course, Farris had seen first-hand that mages could hold their own against the predators of the Glenn. Sláine the White with her healing powers. Fionn the Red with his fires. And—

"Nicole!" cried Farris. "I've got it!"

"What are you talking about?"

Farris paced quickly towards one of the tables, gathering some scattered papers and notes that lay upon them.

"Are these important?" he asked. As soon as Nicole shook her head, he tossed them on the floor.

"Farris, what's going on?" She watched as Farris took out his flask of thainol and poured the liquid onto the papers. He knelt down and pulled a line of flint from his pocket.

"There's none of that black powder here, is there?"

"No, but – what are you doing? she yelled, stepping forward. She paused as Farris produced sparks from the line of flint, which fell onto the damp paper, immediately producing a bright, blue flame.

"We called these beggar's flames back in the Dustworks," said Farris, ignoring the fright in Nicole's eyes. "Thainol is flammable, and often the best way to keep warm at night."

"You better start making sense soon."

"I travelled with a Pyromancer on my way here," continued Farris. "When I created a beggar's flame, he claimed that he was unable to touch it with his magic."

Nicole looked away from the flames, into Farris's eyes. It was as if she had forgotten for just a moment that there was a fire raging at her feet.

"No," she said. "It can't be. He must have been a novice, or untrained in red magic."

"I didn't know him very well. But I think he was graduated from the Academy. His name was Fionn the Red. Does that title imply he was better than a novice?"

"It means he earned his red-cloak at least," she said. "And lower only than a Firemaster, in the eyes of the Church."

"Then it stands to reason, that if there is a type of flame untouchable by a well-trained Pyromancer, the same could be said with steel and Geomancy?"

"Yes. Yes, that's a possibility. This Pyromancer, where is he now? Is it possible that he could be of use to us?"

The image of the troll in the field flashed through Farris's mind. The screams of the red mage as he was picked up by the beast. The blood that sprayed through the air as his arm was torn off. The way Yarlaith the White had shaken his head when Farris asked how the lad was doing.

"No," said Farris, stamping on the blue flames until they went out. "He died with the rest of them."

CHAPTER 12:
THE SECOND SPARK

E.S.,

We note that you have collected the payment, and trust that it was sufficient. Please find ten more compounds enclosed in this package. As before, score the ease of manipulation for each (one for easy, ten for impossible), and return your results to the agreed location. As before, we encourage utmost discretion in your actions.

Yours in the Shadow,

N

***

Fionn's arm ached as he wrote, its muscles bulging with effort. The letters and symbols he put upon the parchment grew more and more illegible with each line, but he dared not pause to correct them.

Sir Bearach's voice growled at the back of the mage's mind, but Fionn had long since given up on trying to reason with it. The knight still felt the need to protest against

Fionn's studies, even after four weeks at the Penance Chapter of the Academy.

In truth, this was no real branch of the Academy. There was little reason for mages to operate in Penance, other than the single 'arcane advisor' to the Triad. And even that was not a full-time position. That role belonged to Earthmaster Seán, the landlord of their tenement building in the Saltworks.

"You're losing focus, lad,' said Seán from across the kitchen. The Earthmaster sometimes supervised Fionn's studies into the intricacies of Pyromancy, yet he seldom had any constructive feedback.

"I know little of fire magic," said Seán, stroking the wiry chestnut beard adorning his square jawline. "But I know when a student is day-dreaming when he should be concentrating on his sums." The Earthmaster let out a short roar of laughter. "Go on, tell us her name then!"

Fionn shook his head and continued with his scribbling. Experience had taught him it was usually best to ignore the Earthmaster's comments. Although Fionn often wondered if Firemaster Conleth was completely sane, he much preferred his company over Seán's.

The Earthmaster leaned in towards Fionn, his massive frame casting a shadow over the three tomes laid open on the desk.

"Ah, Rionach's theorems on the air's currents," he read aloud. "Seems like something a Windmaster would read. Why are you wasting your time with that?"

Fionn threw down his quill. "My time is my own. What constitutes a waste is for me to decide, not you."

That's it, said Sir Bearach. *If I still had that arm, I'd strangle the fool where he stands.*

Seán raised an eyebrow.

"I meant no offence, lad. Just curious. Conleth tells me you have a lot of work to do and little time to do it. What has you reading outside the recommended material?"

Fionn sighed. "It's still relevant. The nature of air. Fire requires it to burn, and flames need to travel through it. Knowing how the tides of air work will help me with my own studies, too."

"Is that so?" asked Seán. "Show me what you've learned, then."

Fionn cast a glance at the scattered parchments around him. He had been working through those equations for most of the day now, and even the slightest distraction could ruin his train of thought.

Still, he welcomed a break, and it was a while now since he had actually practised Pyromancy.

"I'll conjure a flame," Fionn said, idly rubbing the flint-rings on his finger. "Instead of it swaying with whatever tides of air are moving throughout this room, I can hold it as still as stone."

Before the Earthmaster had a chance to respond, Fionn artfully brought the two flint-rings together. With a snap, the spark appeared, and during that same instant, Fionn reached into the power of his soul.

The fire of his heart was there, as it always was, ready to be amplified. With a gentle touch of its heat, the spark before him turned to a flame, burning in mid-air.

Fionn quickly ran through the calculations of Rionach's theorems, balancing equations to fit the forces of air that would typically inhabit a room of this size and ventilation. These were all estimates, of course, and only by feeling the sway of each of the fire's tongues could he allocate the correct influence to bring the flame to a halt.

It would be easier if I could use some Aeromancy, too. Of course, only one of the Six Schools could be attempted at a time, since that alone required the full power of one's soul.

But as the fire raged in Fionn's heart, it seemed large enough to hold more than one spell at a time. It was a common mistake among novice mages: overestimating their own strength. From many past experiences back at the Academy, Fionn knew well that even attempting to split his power in such a way would be a waste of effort.

He turned his attention back to the flame, now losing its movement and slowly becoming a motionless mass of heat.

The fire in Fionn's heart reacted the same way, calming, quenching, fading…

But something else did not fade. Deep within, there was something separate: a second set of embers, never touched by his soul.

Fionn paused. He had never felt those other sparks before the incident with the troll. But back when he first showed his Pyromantic abilities to Conleth, they had been there, lying dormant.

Cautiously, the mage turned his attention towards the new sparks. He pushed his power against them, and they too ignited, as if part of his own being.

Wait, said Sir Bearach. *I felt that. What did you–*

"Stop," said Seán abruptly. "I've seen enough."

Fionn let go of the two flames in his heart, and the fire before him vanished. Seán was standing now and looking at something over Fionn's shoulder.

"Someone's at the door," he said. The red mage turned to look back toward the hall door at the opposite end of the kitchen. If there had been a knock, it certainly hadn't been very loud.

But Earthmaster Seán bounded towards the door with more urgency than Fionn thought necessary for an unexpected visitor. He watched as Seán opened the front door, waiting to hear him greet whoever had called.

After a moment's silence, Seán quickly bent down towards the ground.

Conleth's bedroom door halfway down the hall opened, and the Firemaster stepped out into the hall, discoloured robes trailing behind him.

"Seán," he said, his voice wearier than usual. "Was there someone at the door?"

"No," said the Earthmaster. He slammed the door shut and turned to face Conleth, keeping one hand hidden behind his back. "It must have been the wind."

"Curse the wind, then," said Conleth with a yawn. "I was having the most wonderful dream. I was standing at the peak of—"

"I must leave," said Seán. "I have urgent work for the Triad to attend to."

The door to the tenement building opened and shut before Conleth had a chance to respond. With Seán gone, Conleth sighed and began making his way back to his bedroom.

"What was that all about?" called Fionn from the kitchen. A second distraction from his work would be as welcome as the first.

"Nothing," said Conleth. "Just Seán being as strange as he always is. I tell you, with the amount of time he spends with those rats, I'm surprised he hasn't turned into one yet.

Though, between the stench of his breath and the hair on his face, he could easily pass for one already."

CHAPTER 13:
SEVEN STAGS

Humans live with the belief that everything in life happens for a reason, or "Under the Light of the Lady," as the Church puts it. This worldview takes on the assumption that all of one's choices have been determined before they were made, which seems wholly illogical to those who favour reason. Even more absurd is the Human concept of luck. We Simians would equate luck with chance, chaos, or stochasticity. The random events that make up life can be fortuitous or tragic. Good luck or bad luck. However, if these actions have been destined since Creation, then why do some Humans hang horse-hoofs over their bed, or avoid eating hog's meat at night? How could one attempt to influence what fate has already decided?

Excerpt from A Hundred and One Logical Fallacies Concerning the Trinity, Volume Four, by Samuel the Iconoclast.

***

Argyll the Silverback remained motionless as Garth relayed the details of his skirmishes into the Clifflands. The old Simian's eyes seemed to stare through the scout as he spoke, and Farris couldn't help but wonder how his brother kept a calm composure under that gaze.

He's getting better at this. He's become almost as good as I was back then.

Back then they wouldn't have shared a meeting as important as this with a Human. Ruairí sat next to Farris, sharing one of the more wood-rotted benches of *The White Rose*—a small brothel deep in the Dustworks. Nicole and Garth were on either side of the Silverback; Argyll sat forward with one arm on the table, twisted to face Garth for the duration of the report.

Farris considered the party for a moment. A scout, a thief, an engineer, and a fanatic. If the Silverback chose to assemble a team eclectic enough to inspire a bard's song, he had done a pretty good job.

But for capitulating a dynasty descended from a God, headed by an invincible king...we could do with more muscle.

When Garth finished, Argyll waited a moment before responding. He'd always done this, even back when he ran the Guild, just to make sure there was nothing left to be said. From the way Garth's bottom lip quivered during the silence, Farris reckoned there was indeed more to be told.

Thunder roared outside, and the pelting of rain against the tavern's walls indicated that Autumn was well and truly passed, with the depths of winter soon to come.

"That is all?" asked Argyll. "A regiment of battlemages in Point Grey, and battalions in five of the surrounding settlements. Did you see anything else?"

"No," said Garth. "Other than the details on their patrols I've already described, there is nothing more to report."

"So, it went smoothly? You weren't seen?"

Garth hesitated for a fraction of a breath before delivering a second "No." Farris threw a quick glance around the table. It seemed like nobody else picked up on it.

"That will do," said Argyll. He slowly turned in his seat to face Nicole. He leaned in towards her, with the same intimidating stature as before.

He didn't even need to ask for Nicole's progress, as she quickly began discussing the work she and Farris had been carrying out.

She never mentioned Farris's input with the beggar's flame, but no other detail was omitted. Compounds that worked, combinations and quantifications of metals that could be candidates to replace Simian-made steel. One experiment she explained with such enthusiasm, the outcome wasn't lost on Farris, even though he understood little of the technical jargon.

If only she could be this animated when we're alone, he thought. Eight weeks had gone by since Ruairí passed Farris onto Nicole, but they had spoken little to one another outside of what the job required. He helped with the processes when he could, whenever an extra pair of hands was needed, but the real work, the work she was telling the Silverback about, was all her own.

There's almost no need for me to be here at all.

Even as Argyll leered on, Nicole's voice didn't quiver, and she didn't sink back into her seat as Garth had.

Perhaps he sees her as an equal. Skies above. Knowing her, it could just as well be the other way around. Her courage was admirable, that couldn't be denied, but Farris felt a tinge of sorrow as she spoke.

This is all I need. Another reason to be infatuated with her.

That was always the case with him: cursed to be severely attracted to the most strong-willed of Simian women, while they were always the only ones who'd see him for what he really was.

"The Reaper project," said Argyll, suddenly. "How is the progress on that?"

As if the Silverback had just announced he was the Lady Herself, the others jerked in their seats, sitting up to listen with a newfound eagerness.

By Sin's stones, am I the only one in Penance who doesn't know what that means?

Nicole's composure wavered for a moment. Her mouth fell slightly ajar, and she cast her eyes down to the ground. Then she looked over at Garth, and threw him a quick smile so subtle, so secretive, that Farris would have considered himself the luckiest Simian in Alabach had it been shared with him instead.

"It's nearing completion," she said, regaining the resilience she had shown earlier. "Once the right material is found, we can start field tests right away."

"And how long will that be?" asked Argyll, raising his voice. Whatever enthusiasm Garth and Nicole shared seemed to dissipate as soon as the question was asked.

"Soon," muttered Nicole. "In this moon's batch of compounds, I'm almost certain that one of them is what we've been looking for."

"That will be all," said Argyll. He glanced at the others around the table, implying the words were meant for them too. "Continue as you were but remember this. The day we strike back is almost upon us, and we are woefully unprepared as we are. Once the time comes, there'll be no room for being 'almost certain.'"

Nicole flinched as Argyll stood. The old Simian moved with more agility than one would have expected from a frame so broad. Nobody else spoke when he left through the front door of the tavern into the storm outside.

"I'll go fetch Madam Bruna," said Garth. "She'll be eager to open her business to the public again."

"And she'll open it to me, too," said Ruairí, clasping his hands together. "I could do with a stiff drink and a loose woman."

Nicole snorted. "She only caters for Simians where the latter is concerned, you know."

"Don't worry," said Farris. "I've seen Humans drink thainol before. After half a glass, I doubt he'll be able to tell the difference."

Garth howled with laughter at the jape, while the Human shook his head meekly. But Farris was paying more attention to Nicole's response. She smiled, as if to herself, but it was every bit as genuine as Garth's gaudiness.

"Either way," said Nicole, "I'll leave you to it. I've work to attend to up in the Steamworks."

"And I need some rest," said Garth with a stretch. "The beasts of the Glenn know how to sap one's stamina."

The two turned to leave, Nicole exiting through the front door, Garth going behind the bar to find Bruna to tell her she could open the doors to customers again. Though, given the state of the weather outside, Farris reckoned it wouldn't make much of a difference.

Still, the publican emerged, a frilly red gown flowing behind her, followed by two young barmaids dressed simply. One made her way straight towards Ruairí and Farris.

"What'll it be?" she asked. She was one of the prettier of Bruna's girls, and short for a Simian.

"None of that Simian stuff," said Ruairí, reaching for a coin-purse from an inside pocket of his shirt. "A pint of pale will do."

"And for you?" she asked Farris. He noticed the change in her tone now that she was speaking to a potential client. He glanced at her figure once more.

Her waist is certainly slenderer than Nicole's....

"The same for me," he said, shaking his head. The barmaid turned and left without saying more. Over by the bar, Garth appeared to be in a quiet, yet very vigorous debate with the proprietor.

"I knew this day would come," said Ruairí. "A night on the town with Farris Silvertongue. Are you going to tell me how you got that name?"

"Only if you tell me what you saw in your Seeing of Seletoth." That quickly wiped the smile from the Human's face.

The barmaid returned with their drinks, which Farris paid for despite Ruairí having already laid the coins out on the table. Previous experience had dictated that paying for the first round brought more success when it came to extracting information.

"You know what Nicole was talking about, then?" he asked, once the waitress was out of earshot. "Something about a field test?"

"I know enough to know not to share anything," said Ruairí, putting his pale Human lips to the tankard of ale. "And that's little enough as it is."

"But Garth seems to know," said Farris. He took a gulp of his own. If it wasn't for all the foam, he could have mistaken it for water. He suppressed a grimace. "Are they working on it together?"

"If you're sure of that, then you'd know more than I do."

Never a straight answer. He took another drink. *One thing's for sure. Next round, I'm switching to thainol.*

They spoke only of idle goings-on after that. The storm outside grew stronger as the glasses neared empty. Supposedly it was going to last all winter.

"You know what they say," said Ruairí. "Rain on the first day of winter means no sun 'til Spring."

"And who says that?" asked Farris, beckoning the barmaid over for a second round.

"People!" said Ruairí, almost spitting the word. "Look, I'll ask her."

"Please, don't."

"Excuse me!" said Ruairí once the barmaid approached. "What is it they say about a storm on the first day of winter?"

The girl laughed as she collected the glasses. "I know that it's only fools who claim they can predict the patterns of weather," she said, smiling at Farris. "My father once told me that. He used to work aboard an airship, and he saw his fair share of storms."

"Is that so?" asked Farris, though he cared little for the answer.

"Yes, he told me a great many things before he left," she said. "Same as before?"

Same as before is right. Why is it so many of them have runaway fathers?

"Of course," said Ruairí, starting to slur already. "We'll both have thainol now, and this time I'll pay for it."

Little time passed between the second and third round of drinks, with Ruairí paying for both. The Human's drunkenness grew more and more visible—he now lay slouched forward across the table.

"Why is it," he said, "that your lot can drink so much of that, yet still stay standing?"

Farris took a long, deep swig of the thainol. In truth, he felt a slight delay in his movements, a sure sign that he was well on his way to Ruairí's state, but he gave no indication that this was the case.

Because we hide it better, came to Farris's mind first. Instead, he said, "For the same reason the Tower still stands.

It's made of stronger stuff than anything down in the Human capital."

"Ah, Cruachan," said Ruairí, closing his eyes as if to imagine the city itself. "I've never been interested in seeing it. It's the same as any other capitals, really. Just a little larger than the rest."

"There's some truth in that," said Farris. "The only thing that sets it apart from the likes of Terrían or Ardh Sidhe is the Grey Keep, and that's as dull as any other keep in the kingdom. Except for Dromán, of course. They say the Academy is the largest building in the kingdom, built in a style entirely different to that of the rest of the Seachtú."

"Dromán?" interrupted the Simian barmaid, appearing by the table again. "I'm going to work there some day. I've heard so many stories about the lords and ladies of the Seachtú. To see them would be a treat, but to live amongst them? That would be a dream come true!"

Her words echoed at the back of Farris's memory, as if he had heard such naivety from a Simian before...but his current thainol-induced state hindered the process that aided recollection.

"It's not as glamorous as the bards make it out, you know," he said, looking up at her. She was standing closer to him now, closer than any ordinary barmaid would an ordinary customer. Farris sighed deeply and shook his head.

"I'm sure you could earn ten times here what any servant would down south."

The waitress playfully slapped Farris on the shoulder. "You're about as subtle as a mountain sloth! Business is slower than usual, because of the storm and all."

"Is there anything I can do to help?"

The waitress leaned in and whispered in Farris's ear. "Upstairs in ten minutes. Ask for Lucy."

He watched as she went, letting the sight of the movement of her hips remove the last ounce of doubt in his mind.

Ruairí still lay slouched over the table, apparently completely oblivious to what had just transpired.

I may never see a Son this drunk again. Farris took one last gulp from his cup of thainol and eyed the Human. The subtle approach certainly wasn't going to work on a mind as addled as his.

"Tell me, Ruairí," he said, allowing his companion a moment to reorient himself in the tavern. "What was it exactly that you...saw?"

"What do you mean?" he said, rubbing his eyes. "Just now?"

"No," said Farris, making sure to enunciate each word. "What did you see, in your Seeing of Seletoth?"

The hazed look vanished from Ruairí's gaze; the slouch moved from his shoulders. If one could sober a man with words alone, Farris had just stumbled upon them.

Ruairí cleared his throat and narrowed his eyes. "Farris, when was the first time you masturbated?"

"Excuse me?"

"You heard what I said."

The memory came back to Farris immediately, but the Tower would fall again before he'd ever retell that story. Especially to a Human. Especially to a zealot.

"I don't see how that concerns you," said Farris, choosing his words carefully.

"That would be the same answer I'd give to your question. A Son's Seeing is his own. It's an intimate experience between a man and the Lord. What He allowed me to See is for my own eyes only."

The Human sat back after that, with his arms folded and his head lulling to the side. Farris smiled.

He's still drunk out of his mind. Sure, he probably won't recall this night anyway. What harm could it do?

"I was fifteen years old," he began, taking a long drink from his cup, even though it was empty. "I'm one year older than my brother and was older than most of the other Simians we ran with in the Dustworks. They'd often ask me about what it meant to mature, about the changes that occur when a Simian reaches a certain age."

He paused, allowing Ruairí a moment to realise what he was actually telling him. From the way he sat forward again, it was clear the Human had.

"Things changed gradually. So gradually, I didn't even notice. Soon, all the other boys began talking about...that. You know how ones that age can be. Bravado, and all that comes with it. They'd all brag about where they'd do it, and how often they did it, and the girls they thought about during it. I swear, some of them were telling tall tales just to outdo each other."

He paused with a sigh. "What am I saying? My tales were the tallest of them all. Of course, I was older, I had to let on that I was the most experienced. There was no way they could ever learn the truth."

"And what was that?" asked Ruairí, his voice calmer than before.

"I just...never figured how. Nobody ever told me what to do. 'Was it something they read about in a book?' I'd ask myself. 'Does it just come as natural as breathing to others?' I was so sure that I was just missing a tiny piece of information, but I was far too embarrassed to go asking about for it. So, I did what any young pickpocket in the Dustworks would do."

He gestured towards the bar.

"I came here."

"*The White Rose?*" asked Ruairí.

"Well, back then it was called *The Sailor's Rest*, but still owned by 'friends' of the Guild. Anyway, I took my earnings from a whole moon's span—made up entirely of counted coppers— then I approached one of the whores and asked her to teach me."

Ruairí stared back at Farris for a moment. "What happened next?"

"She taught me. She was sympathetic, and that was that."

"I see..." said Ruairí, allowing a sip of thainol to remove the need to fill the silence with a better response.

"So, your vision," asked Farris. "What did you see?"

"I'm still not going to tell you," said Ruairí. "Even if I did, you wouldn't understand anyway."

"OH, FUCK OFF!" roared Farris, his mind clouded with rage and alcohol. He barely heard the cup of thainol smash as he leapt out of his chair and towered over the Human. "You fucking fanatics, you all walk around this city now like you built it. Just because you all had the same stupid dream about a bearded man in the clouds. You claim to know all these secrets of the Lord, but you don't. You fucking know nothing, but you hide it by acting all mysterious, pretending that the Lord would never want us to know about it. What kind of sense is that supposed to make? If He created all of us, what makes you bastards so special? If He's supposed to love each and every one of us, why did He create fucking dunces like you?"

If it was possible, the almost-empty brothel went even quieter than before. Even the rain outside seemed to go silent.

The Human stared straight into his drink, as if the thainol inside would provide him with an answer.

More likely than getting a response from his god, for sure.

"If you have nothing to say," said Farris. "Then I'll be going upstairs. Good night!"

He turned to go, hoping to make an exit as dramatic as his speech, but a voice interrupted him. A voice that spoke with a whimper, with words barely audible over the silence.

"You're wrong," it said, the syllables shaking as they were spoken. "He doesn't love us."

Farris expected to see someone else—a frightened child or a sickly crone—sitting in Ruairí's seat when he looked back, but the Human was still there, his head buried in his hands.

"That's what I saw," he croaked, avoiding Farris's gaze. "Though there was nothing to see. We call them Seeings, but there's nothing to see. I just felt Him."

Farris took a step closer, not daring to interrupt.

"I felt Him. I felt every inch of His body. I felt every ounce of His impossible strength. His thoughts blended with mine for what felt like an eternity, but there was nothing I could truly comprehend. He exists in every corner of the world, yet His body never leaves Mount Selyth. He has seen what preceded existence, and He knows what will come after everything disintegrates back into emptiness. We ourselves are nothing to Him: Human, Simians, animals, plants, it doesn't matter. This world floats alone through infinite darkness, in the space that separates the stars...and that darkness has no end. We are less than a drop in the vast oceans of Seletoth's experience."

He looked up at Farris, eyes red as if they had been rubbed raw.

"The Church insists that He loves His children, that He wants what's best for everyone, but how could something like *that* possibly love us? Why would He even care about anything as trivial, as transient, as meaningless as...life?"

Farris paused, not quite sure what to make of the Human's words.

"Is this true?" he said.

"Yes," replied Ruairí. "I've seen a glimpse of the Truth, but it was enough to frighten me into faith. Most of the other Sons are like this, too. They worship Seletoth because there is no other reasonable thing to do after what they saw."

"And the others," said Farris. "The ones who go to the mountain to see the Lord Himself. What happens to them?"

"Nothing," said Ruairí, staring down into his drink. "They never come back."

Farris frowned, and glanced back at the stairway.

It must have been at least ten minutes by now...

It would be a shame, he knew, to leave the Human alone, with his mind in such a frail state, with so much thainol in his blood, but...

But I can't keep a lady waiting.

He left the silence of the bar, taking the wooden staircase two steps at a time to the second-floor landing. The planks creaked as he went, even under the stained, yellow rug laid out across the floor. Three doors faced him, guarded by a particularly burly Simian with arms folded.

He'll be fine, thought Farris, stealing a glance down at the bar. *He's just drunk. He doesn't know what he's saying.*

"I'm looking for Lucy," said Farris, attempting an air of defiance before the Simian bouncer. "I was told to ask for her."

"Door behind me," he said, his voice barely more than a grunt. "That'll be seven stags."

Farris counted out the silver coins, leaving an extra one in the Simian's hand, as was customary.

The guard didn't seem to notice the gratuity. "Do what she says," he said. "And nothing else. One wrong move —"

"I know, I know," said Farris, reaching for the door behind the other Simian.

The second-story bedroom was as grubby as expected, but that didn't bother Farris in the slightest. A frigid draft came down from somewhere amongst the rafters overhead, bringing a hint of condensation to his breath. A thick candle stood tall on a bedside table, tears of wax running down its sides as it burned.

Lucy was already laid out upon the bed, naked as the day she was born. That day wasn't all that long ago, but Farris tried not to focus on that minor detail.

She's young enough to be your daughter, said a voice from somewhere at the back of his mind, but he ignored it. He focused instead on the dark nipples on the centre of Lucy's supple breasts, covered in silky fur gilded under the candlelight.

"Do you always keep girls like me waiting?" she asked, shifting amongst the sheets to drape her legs over the bed, the manoeuvre as smooth and rehearsed as a gymnast's act. She smiled and leaned her head to the side.

"No," said Farris, promptly pulling his shirt off. "There aren't many like you."

She laughed, doing a rather convincing job of making it sound genuine, but Farris hadn't meant it as a compliment.

There are none as green as her, or as naive to the way the world works. She'd mistake a mercenary for a knight if she ever went to Cruachan.

That same, strange thought from before began to form in his mind, but Lucy was walking towards him now, one step right in front of the other.

"None like me?" she said, reaching out towards Farris's waist. "But we haven't even begun…"

She fumbled at the knots holding up his trousers, clumsily undoing them one at a time, digging her nails into each loop as she went.

Nicole probably would have figured that out in seconds, he thought, just as the last knot was undone and the trousers fell bundled to the floor. Only as Lucy put her hands against his smallclothes, did he realise how strange a thought that was.

He shook his head, trying to vanquish the memory of Nicole's smile.

Skies above, it was only a smile. A firm hand grabbed hold of his exposed member, quickly bringing him back to reality.

"Is something…wrong?" asked Lucy. She took another step closer to Farris; something he wouldn't have thought possible. "We can take more time to—"

"It's fine," said Farris, taking one of her dainty little hands in his. He gritted his teeth in frustration, and his heartbeat quickened.

Don't think about it. Just focus on this now.

He stooped his head closer to hers, and planted a quick kiss on her lips, though he couldn't taste much over the thainol on his breath.

Lucy pressed her mouth against his with a surprising force for Simian of her size. Both of her hands grasped at the nape of his neck, pulling him towards her. He loosened his body and let her spin him round until his back was facing the bed.

"Relax," she whispered, gently pushing him down onto the mattress. "I'll take it all from here."

He landed on the bed softly, and Lucy was on top straight away, both legs straddled over his own. She leaned forward, palms stretched out against his chest, and shifted herself towards his hips.

A slight look of confusion crossed her face, but she quickly resorted back to her calming, seductive expression.

"Don't worry about that," she said sitting straight up, giving Farris a full view of her naked torso. "We'll take all the time you need."

Farris closed his eyes, but flashes of images from the meeting kept interrupting his attempt at tranquillity. The way Nicole looked up to the Silverback, the way she and Garth seemed to share some secret between them...

Lucy. Focus on Lucy.

But even as he let his eyes roll over her body, he couldn't help but wonder what sort of life choices would cause a girl so young to turn to whoring.

What was it she said about her father? he thought, placing his hands on her waist and idly stroking her fur. *He wasn't around. Yes. That's one thing they all have in common.*

Lucy pressed her lips against his again now and moved her hands beneath his small-clothes.

He was a traveller, or a sailor. Someone who told her all about the Seachtú, distilling false tales of the wealth and wonder of the aristocracy.

She brought her lips to his neck, then slowly worked her way towards his chest.

Such a shame, he thought, looking back up at the ceiling. *She'd probably be proud to work in the Grey Keep, emptying chamber-pots for the lords and ladies of–*

A pang of realisation struck his chest. He breathed in deeply, but Lucy mistook it for a reaction to her, and began working even more enthusiastically with her hands.

"Your father, what was his name?"

Lucy looked up at him, something between horror and confusion in her eyes.

"What?"

His heart pounded as he felt his chest constrict. The images from that night long past came flooding back. The waterfront. The canal. The tavern.

"You said your father worked on an airship. What was his name?"

He barely noticed that he had grabbed her arm now, pulling her towards him, desperate for her to say a name, any name, that wasn't the one he was thinking of.

Terror struck her face, and instead of answering, she screamed.

It was only now that Farris realised how tight his grip was. He let go, and the door to the room slammed open. The Simian bouncer came thundering across the room, grabbing Farris beneath both arms and shoving him off the bed.

Farris didn't give a fight as he let the bouncer pull him out the door and down the stairs.

I deserve this, he thought, watching his legs being dragged across the tavern floor. A lump formed in his throat, and he fought back tears. *No, I deserve far more than this.* Only the lowest of scum ever raised a hand against a whore, for there were few crimes worse than hurting someone so vulnerable.

Such as murdering a drunkard on the streets of Cruachan...

The next thing he felt was the barrage of freezing raindrops cutting against his naked body. He flew through the air for a moment, collapsing in a heap on the soaking street. Farris looked up to see the bouncer shut the tavern door.

She didn't need to tell me his name, he realised, lying back on the stone road. He looked up to the sky, dark clouds blocking out the moon and the stars. No light illuminated the drenched streets of Penance.

"Chester," Farris rasped. "His name was Chester, and I killed him. I killed him because I'm..."

His voice broke off, the words unable to leave his lips. His face was soaked now, but from rain or tears, he could no longer tell.

Because I'm a coward, he thought, wiping his eyes with even wetter hands. *Because I've always been a coward.*

Right as he lay there, ready and willing to never get up again, something heavy, dry, and warm, fell over his shoulders.

No. Just let me freeze. Just let me die.

"Come on friend," said a voice, slurred and familiar. "You'll catch the death of a cold out here."

Farris looked up to see the blurred Human standing against the rain, but all he could make out was a rough shape of a pendant against his chest: three crooked, interlocking circles.

"Come on," said Ruairí. "I'll take you home."

CHAPTER 14:
THE SEEDS THRIVE

We are the eyes that have seen too much,
The knees that bend, the souls you touch,
Our hands, we raise,
To Seletoth.

***

After the final scratch of chalk, Fionn took a step back to admire his work. Wild markings covered the blackboard, filling every square inch with the material he had memorised over the previous three moons.

Three moons to the day, said Sir Bearach. *Gods, let there not be one more.*

Fionn ignored the dead knight's words, just as he had during all those hours of revising and reciting. The task that Conleth had set for the young Pyromancer had been near impossible, and it had taken every ounce of Fionn's determination to see it through to the end.

And every minute of my time, whispered Sir Bearach.

Fionn scanned the blackboard once more. Rionach's Theorems came first, all twelve scrawled with the smallest writing Fionn could manage. Next came the Three Laws of Thermal Equilibrium, expressed from first principles just as the Firemaster had demanded. Those had been more challenging, and Fionn still wasn't sure if he had gotten it completely right.

Maybe I'll start it again, he thought, reaching for the stick of chalk once more. *This final clause seems a bit off–*

Gods above and below, swore Sir Bearach. *Just call him out to start the exam already. Being trapped in you is far worse when you're trapped in this room!*

It was true: Fionn had rarely stepped outside the grimy old kitchen since his studying began. With food and drink delivered to the tenement house daily by Earthmaster Seán, Fionn had little reason to leave.

Perhaps you're right, he replied. *I've always been one to overthink exams before sitting them...*

"Conleth!" he called over his shoulder toward the hallways. "I'm ready to start whenever you are!"

Fionn waited in silence, anticipating the familiar rustle from Conleth's bedroom that came whenever the old Firemaster awoke. Experience had taught Fionn that it was best to simply wait for Conleth to arrive, no matter how long it took.

But the faint sounds of movement did not come as Fionn expected. A loud *thud* answered the call instead, followed by a slow, repeated noise, like clothes being dragged across carpet.

"Conleth?" asked Fionn, taking a step forward. "Is everything all right?"

No voice answered, just the same sounds as before: one muffled movement following another, and another. Gradually, they grew louder, until Fionn was sure Conleth was just beyond the kitchen door.

"Are you there?" called Fionn. "Is something the matter with—"

The door swung open, revealing the old Firemaster. Fionn immediately averted his eyes, for Conleth's grey robes were discarded on the ground, caught amongst his feet. Pale, leathery skin hung from every crooked bone of his body, with blotchy dark spots spread across a swollen stomach. Thin, frail arms held up his frame. He leaned against the opened door.

"Chaos!" shrieked Conleth, his already shrill voice an octave higher than usual. "Disorder has been sewn once more by those who...who..."

"Conleth?" whimpered Fionn, still not quite sure where to look. "What's wrong?"

The Firemaster's bulging eyes locked onto Fionn, then his head lolled to the side, and his bottom lip quivered.

"Animals!" he cried. "No different than animals! For I have seen the Truth as He has intended it to be!"

He's gone mad, whispered Sir Bearach. *He needs a healer, or a Druid. Or both.*

"Calm down, Conleth," said Fionn, raising both arms in a stance of submission. "It's going to be all right. I'll find someone to—"

The old mage gasped suddenly and pointed a finger at Fionn.

"You should not be here!" he roared. "You were never supposed to make it! A fate worse than death was meant for you, for you, for you..."

His voice trailed off, and a shiver ran through his body.

"The disorder..." he whispered. "The disorder is worse than He could have known. Worse than He can stand. Worse than..."

He cocked his head to the side, as if he suddenly heard something nearby.

"No..." he said. "This one is not like the others. This one...this one..."

"Conleth, please," said Fionn. "You need help. Come with me, we'll make you better, I'll find you a healer."

"No!" roared Conleth. He raised his hand and clicked his flint-rings together with a flourish. A ball of fire filled his hands. "This one cannot live untouched by fate! He is far too important to be free!"

A dozen streams of fire shot towards Fionn. He held up his own hands in defence, igniting the fire in his heart, summoning his own power. Rionach's Theorems, the Laws of Thermal Equilibrium, every equation, every figure, every number faded from Fionn's mind as the heat intensified around him.

Hold it back! roared Sir Bearach. *Push it, lad, push it!*

Fionn flared the power in his heart, taking a step back to bring both hands over his head. The tongues of the fire tumbled inwards, spitting forth embers. Fionn narrowly avoided them, stepping to the side as he forced Conleth's fires away. Wood crackled and burned behind him, but Fionn did not turn to see what work had been destroyed.

Conleth stood up right now, taller than he had ever been before. His hands ignited once more.

"Oh, His eyes! His eyes! They bored through my being, melting my soul until there was nothing left but pain!"

The fires roared again, tearing towards Fionn like lightning bolts. He braced himself once more, calling upon the power of his soul to hold them back, but that was already starting to wane. When the fires collided with Fionn's power, the young mage was almost knocked from his feet.

You can't fight his fire with your own! said Sir Bearach. *You must flee. It's our only chance.*

Perhaps.... He quickly shifted his weight to the side, sending the fire soaring towards a stack of papers against the kitchen wall.

Fionn's whole body convulsed with exhaustion, each breath a strain. Beads of sweat poured down his face, rolling into his eyes and blurring his vision. But Conleth seemed unburdened, though there was no longer fire in his hands.

"He has shown me too much!" he cried, covering his eyes. "His voice! I can't comprehend His words, but they hurt. Oh, they hurt!"

There was no need for flint-rings, for the wood and papers of the kitchen burned all around the two Pyromancers. Fionn ignited the power of his soul, barely an ember left.

I need rest, he thought, furiously trying to flare it further. *I can't hold him off any longer.*

Fortunately, Conleth seemed unconcerned with the fires now. He walked slowly toward Fionn, his naked body glistening under the heat.

"This city...this city of Penance is a cancer upon the Tapestry of Fate. Every day it sows seeds of chaos, and they threaten to unravel the threads that hold this world together."

Fionn reached within once more, but the fire inside was too weak to even grasp at a flame. He shut his eyes tight, groping through his soul, searching for something he had found before, something he had failed to understand....

And there! The second spark. The power in his heart that had never been touched. He reached for it, kindling it with his soul.

What are you doing? asked Sir Bearach. *That feels...strange.*

You can feel that? Do you know what this is?

The answer immediately came to Fionn before the knight could respond, but there was little time to explain. The old mage raised his hands above his head, and the heat around them intensified. He looked right at Fionn, with those eyes, wide open with fright.

"You have no idea, do you?" asked Conleth, saliva foaming at the corner of his mouth. "You have no idea what you are..."

The Firemaster threw his hands down, and the flames of the room surrounded Fionn. At the same instant, Fionn flared the spark of Sir Bearach's soul, and blended that power with his own.

The Firemaster's flames bore down upon Fionn, but he pushed back, with the weight of two souls behind him. The flames went still, for barely a moment, then moved away from Fionn. With another push, they erupted out, consuming Conleth where he stood.

The Firemaster did not scream as he burned to death.

***

"And what has the Crown's response been to these events?"

"Silence," said Argyll, hands clasped together and resting upon the oaken table. Lips pursed, he stared coolly at Borris Blackhand. "King Diarmuid has not retracted the accusations linking me to the death of Santos, nor has he denied involvement with the attempted attack on Sin."

Borris wiped sweat from his brow. The Simian representative of the Triad seemed to have aged dramatically over the past few months. Even though Farris would have put his age at six and sixty when they first met, Borris always carried his age well. But now, he seemed as close to death as Cathal Carríga himself.

What if both pass away together? What if Diarmuid is the only person left on the Triad?

Indeed, this was a legitimate worry, for Argyll had demanded this meeting with the remaining representatives of the Triad in order to discuss King Diarmuid's position with Penance.

"I agree that His Grace no longer holds the citizens of this city in high priority," said Borris, struggling with the words. "But he cannot be removed from the Triad unless we have irrefutable evidence."

The Silverback didn't react immediately, for this was presumably the response he had expected. Ruairí sat next to him, his eyes avoiding those of everyone else at the table. He seemed to be avoiding Farris the most, as neither had spoken about what happened at *The White Rose* that night.

Farris cringed at the recollection. For the past few weeks, he had performed all sorts of mental acrobatics to try and justify his actions. He had drunk too much; he had eaten too little...but nothing could excuse him for what he done.

"I have something to add," said a gruff voice. A bearded, thickset man clad in layers of green spoke, leaning back in his seat as if he were lounging before a fireplace. He was a Geomancer, and a particularly good one, apparently, but Farris didn't know much more about him.

"Enlighten us, Earthmaster Seán," said Borris with a nod.

"In all my years counselling the Triad," he began, "I have not spoken directly to our king once. Yet he has a vote equal to Borris and to Cathal, along with the right to veto either of theirs. The Triad was founded to bring Humans and Simians together, under the rule of the Crown, but it seems King Diarmuid would rather we do that ourselves."

He sat forward, gesturing towards Argyll. "With all due respect," he said, "the accusations you bring here to us today are irrelevant to this issue. Regardless of the king's actions over the past few moons, removing him from the Triad was always a considered course of action."

"Considered for one moment and dismissed the next," snapped Borris. "Taking the king out of this government is not a decision we can make on our own. The Triad would need to be in agreement, and we'd need a majority vote from the earls of Alabach before ..."

Farris's attention waned as the argument went on. It seemed that he had been demoted back to the position of Ruairí's shadow again, for he was no longer needed in Nicole's laboratory. Even without the sound of her voice and the scent of her fur, Farris would have easily chosen the lab over this meeting room. But Nicole needed no further help; she had finally stumbled upon a material stronger than Simian steel. She claimed that it was well beyond the reach of any Geomancer, but how she came to that conclusion, Farris had no idea.

No fucking idea, he thought, balling a hand into a fist beneath the table. *I used to be in the Silverback's inner circle. I used to help with the Movement's most important work. Now I sit and watch like a child, while the adults make all the decisions.*

Since Garth had returned from his skirmish, he had spent more and more time with Nicole, providing aid for the Reaper Project, whatever that was. *Why couldn't I have helped her with that instead?*

But that was nearing completion, too, all without any input from Farris.

Fuck them. If they want to free our people on their own, they're more than welcome.

The debate steadily grew more heated. Seán was standing now, arguing vigorously with Borris, but Farris must have missed a point from earlier that would have allowed him to understand what they were talking about. Still, he pretended to listen, nodding idly as each person made their points.

Skies above. What's the point in me even being here?

The door to the meeting room slammed opened, and a guard strode in. He was a Simian, armoured in steel tinted blue. He walked straight towards Seán, barely paying any mind to anyone else in the room.

"Apologies for the interruption, Earthmaster," he said, bowing his head slightly. "But there is a young lad here to see you. He says it's urgent."

Seán waved a hand. "Bah! It bloody well better be. Send him up."

The guard left, leaving the room in silence. Farris wasn't quite sure where to look. Seán had taken his seat again, fidgeting uncomfortably with his hands. Argyll remained still, as if there hadn't been an interruption at all.

Moments later, the door opened again, and there stood the strangest sight Farris had ever seen. A young lad wearing a red cape, draped over a torn shirt and dusty breeches. The edges of the cape were charred black, and the lad's thick black curls were mottled with soot.

But the strangest thing about the young lad's appearance was his arm. One arm was twice as large as the other, with a shoulder as thick as a leg. As he limped into the room, he leaned to one side, as if the weight of the arm was too much to bear.

"Earthmaster Seán!" cried the lad. "It's Conleth. He's dead, I..."

Seán stood up abruptly. "What happened? Are you hurt?"

The young man paused, his eyes widening with fear. Farris had seen fear like that before, in a Pyromancer he had travelled through the Glenn with...

No. It couldn't be. Fionn lost his arm in the Clifflands. I watched as the troll tore it from his body. The healer said there was little chance of surviving.

"Who is this, Seán?" asked Borris, sceptically. "Is this Firemaster Conleth he speaks of? It's tragic news, but Conleth lived a long life. He was ill with old age and—"

"I killed him!" cried the mage in red. "He went mad and attacked me, I...I..."

"Sit down, Fionn," said Seán, offering a seat by the table. "Take as much time as you need and tell us exactly what happened."

It is Fionn. But how did he survive...

"Now," said Seán. "In your own time, and in your own words, tell us what happened."

"Here," said Ruairí, offering Fionn a Simian-made pocket-flask. "The Simian stuff tastes vile, but it'll help with the shock."

Vile? If he believes that, why would he carry a bottle of it around with him? Farris supressed a smile. *Perhaps he's becoming more like one of us.*

Fionn took a mouthful of thainol, cringing as he swallowed it. He wiped his lips with the sleeve of his over-sized arm. Its skin was scratched and abraded, and it too was dark with soot.

"I was about to take an exam," he began, after a moment. "Conleth was training me to become a Firemaster. He was sleeping in his quarters, and I called him into the study. When he came, he was acting strange. He was talking gibberish, and then he attacked me. With fire. We fought and...the fire. It was everywhere."

"When did this happen?" asked Borris. "Did you report the fire?"

"About half an hour ago," said Fionn. "I informed the guards. They're fighting the flames now, but I didn't tell them about Conleth."

"You were alone?" asked Borris, raising an eyebrow. "Have you any proof that he attacked first?"

Before Fionn could respond, Seán raised his voice.

"Gods above and below, Borris. Can you not see the state he's in? Does this look like the time for an interrogation?"

Borris paused, considering the young mage once more. "You're right," he said, eventually. "We can investigate this another time."

"I'll vouch for his character in the meantime," said Seán, patting Fionn on the shoulder—his normal sized one. "Is there anything else you need?"

Fionn nodded slowly, his unblinking eyes far away.

"I best return to Dromán," announced Seán. "Better they hear this ill news from me than a wave."

"I better follow up on this fire," said Borris, standing as he spoke. "Argyll, we'll need to continue this another time. Apologies for the inconvenience."

Argyll nodded solemnly without saying a word, his eyes locked on Fionn's arm.

At least I'm not the only one to notice that. I'm sure there's another story there too.

"Excuse me, Fionn, is it?" asked Ruairí, rolling the sleeves of his white shirt up to his elbows. "How was Conleth's mind before this happened? Had he shown signs of illness before?"

"No," said Fionn, taking another sip of thainol. "I mean, he was always a little eccentric, but when he stepped out of his room, he seemed like a different person. He...changed."

"And the words," asked Ruairí. "You said he wasn't making sense, but what did he say?"

Fionn closed his eyes. "He said something about chaos. I think he was talking about Simians. Saying they were wrong, or bad, or something."

"Pah!" said Seán. "That's not new. He always was a fucking bigot."

"No. This was different. He also said something about Seletoth. He said that he saw Him."

"It sounds like he had a Seeing," said Ruairí, solemnly. He idly fingered the pendant around his neck. "The Lord came to Conleth, and the vision crippled his mind. There are some things living men are not meant to see."

"Sloth-shit!" cursed Seán. "Don't be using this man's death as an excuse to preach about your cult. I wouldn't care if he saw Lady Meadhbh sucking off the Arch-Canon himself. All that matters is that Conleth is gone, and we must deal with the consequences now."

"And what do you suggest we do from here, Seán?" asked Borris. "You can't just fly off to Dromán with no notice. The Triad needs you now more than ever."

"The Academy needs me even more," said Seán. "I'm not as valuable to you as you think."

A slight smile crept slowly across Seán's lips. He stroked his beard, as if deep in thought. "You know," he began. "Back in the early days of the Academy, students reserved the right to challenge any master to a duel, taking the title from them if they won. Few were actually foolish enough to request a duel, and none were ever successful..."

"For the love of Sin," swore Borris. "Are you suggesting we make this lad a Firemaster because he defeated Conleth? Don't be absurd!"

"It's a decision only the Academy can make," said Seán. "Fionn, if you take my place here while I'm gone, I'll pull a few strings down in Dromán. Next time we meet, I may be calling you Firemaster."

"Oh..." said Fionn. "I don't think I can. I don't know anything about politics."

"That never stopped Seán," said Borris. "We'll call it a temporary solution. Now, I must meet with the city guard. I sure as Sin hope they have this fire under control."

"I'll make my preparations to leave tonight," said Seán. "Fionn, come with me. I'll show you your chambers and fill you in with what you need to know."

"Thank you," mumbled Fionn. Farris almost felt sorry for the lad. The Triad hadn't exactly left him with a choice.

Ruairí and the Silverback both stood together. Argyll went to leave without saying a word, but Ruairí crouched down beside Fionn, and whispered something into his ear. Fionn nodded after a moment, then Ruairí followed the Silverback out into the hallway.

Another waste of a day, thought Farris, about to follow the two out. *What will they have me observe next?*

"Excuse me," said Fionn, just as Farris stood to leave. "Have we met before? Is your name Chester?"

Sorrow panged in Farris's heart. What was he to do? Humans often confused Simians with one another, but if Fionn was working with the Triad, surely their paths would be crossing again and again...

"Yes," he said, eventually. "But I don't go by that name anymore. Call me Farris."

A smile flashed past Fionn's lips. "I was told another Simian survived the attack. I knew you were still alive."

"Ah. I can't say I believed the same of you. The old healer in Roseán said that there was little hope you'd live much longer."

"That was true," said Fionn, the joy leaving his voice. "But things have changed since then. A great many things have changed since then."

CHAPTER 15:
WHAT HAS ALREADY
BEEN SOWN

To those it concerns most,
It is complete. Arrive at midnight.
N

***

Farris clutched the tiny parchment in his fist, not caring if he obscured its ink. Although barely a dozen words long, Farris had read through the message near a hundred times by the time he reached Nicole's workshop deep in the Steamworks.

Darkness had long since fallen, with dawn further off still. With the factories and mills closed and their labourers retired for the evening, the silence of the night was as thick as the smoggy sky of the day. Still, Farris caught the occasional glimpse of lingering steam in the corners of his vision as he went, though he paid little attention to them.

Surely, I'm not the only one she summoned, he thought, recalling the opening words of the letter. 'To those it concerns most,' it said, emphasising the plural. But nothing other than the spectral, smoky remnants the day's work accompanied the lone Simian through the murky streets.

Eventually, the familiar hangar came into view, its colossal stature even more foreboding than usual in the dark. A chill ran down Farris's spine, tingling each vertebra. A more superstitious person would have hesitated on that alone, but Farris pressed on, thinking only of the words presently being smudged in his clammy hands.

They've finished it. Whatever it is, they've finished it.

The pedestrian door to the hangar was slightly ajar. However, the gap could have been as wide as the Endless Sea to Farris, who was accustomed to the door being bolted and locked.

She invited those without keys, he realised, slipping his fingers between the door and frame. A slight tug was all it took to give him enough room to slither inside without making a sound. But as he moved to return the door to its initial position, a rough, male voice called out to him.

"Lock it behind you," it said. "You're the last one here."

Farris peered through the dim hangar as he let the door click shut behind him. Several figures stood a fair distance off, huddled around a shapeless silhouette. A sliver of moonlight from a window far overhead caught one of those standing in the dark, accentuating the distinctive grey hair of Argyll the Silverback.

The other shadowy figures resolved themselves as Farris approached. Ruairí stood next to Argyll, his arms crossed over a puffed-out chest.

The rest were Simians whom Farris had never met before. He counted eleven in total, which came a surprise given that they outnumbered those in the Silverback's inner circle.

'To those it concerns most.' Is it possible that these strangers know more about what's going on here than I do?

Another glance at each of the Simians confirmed that they did not. One of them was a young fellow, glancing this way and that as they waited. Another held his arms behind his back in a stance as patient as a Simian Churchguard, but as forced as one true to his heritage.

They're all frightened, he realised, noting how a particularly dark-furred Simian idly shifted his weight from leg to leg while another curled his fingers in and out of a fist. None dared to speak out of turn while in the company of the Silverback. His overbearing presence of authority still seemed to manifest even with his face barely visible.

The object which the Simians had all gathered around was even less discernible than their purpose. Where once it seemed like a shapeless mound of steel, now there appeared to be something more solid hidden beneath a draped cloth.

I expected Garth to be here. Farris craned his neck over his shoulder to observe the rest of the bare hangar. *Surely, he's the one this concerns most.*

Nicole's absence also came to mind, but he forced the thought away before he could consider it fully. It had been almost three weeks since he had last dwelled on her, and he had hoped his feelings would dissipate as quickly as they had first overcome him.

But that was before he had found that parchment on his doorstep, written by her hand, signed with her mark.

He heard Nicole's footsteps first, echoing through the hangar with a rhythm of one walking with confidence and urgency. She appeared at a far corner of the room, coming from what seemed to be a small cabin tucked away from plain view. Farris realised that he had never seen her enter or leave that building, back when they worked together. Only now did the thought that she also lived there cross his mind.

She always said that she was working day and night. But I never thought she could have meant that literally...

"I had a speech prepared," she said, walking up to the side of the strange object. She reached a hand to one if its upper corners, barely reaching the creased fabric.

"From the early days of this project, I dreamt of this day, fantasising about what I'd say. I was going to refer to the Simians who build Sin only to witness it fall, or quote Elis

Highwind, who built the first airship only to have it grounded by the Church. Words, however, are easily forgotten. This is something that will be remembered for eternity."

With a flourish, she revealed what was hidden beneath the shroud.

It looked like a suit of armour, standing tall and proud in the characteristic blue-tainted steel of Old Simia. But as the others took a step back, Farris compared its proportions to the Simian who had built it.

It was more than twice as tall as an average Simian, with broad shoulders supporting a heavy helm with no features other than thin slits for eye holes. On legs as thick as a Human's body, it stood in a position so natural that it seemed able to spring to life at any moment.

Then it did just that, abruptly stepping forward with a thud of metal against stone. A shrill gasp escaped Farris's lips.

Despite its apparent weight, its movement was agile and quick. Its legs worked like ones made from flesh, bending at a knee covered with plates of steel.

The monstrosity raised two hulking arms over its head. One was longer than the other, gradually tapering off to a sharp tip like a lance used by a knight. The shorter one ended at the elbow —if such a word could be applied to something so abnormal—and instead held a thick tube, like something Farris had seen before.

A *firearm*. His feet took him several paces away from the steel beast before his brain fully processed the revelation. As the mechanism went into action, Farris learned that this observation was false, and the truth was far more unsettling.

With a hideous roar, a massive burst of fire erupted from the arm. Blue flames brought sudden illumination to the room, immediately casting away every inch of darkness from the hanger. The plumes extended upwards, almost singeing the rafters overhead.

All around Farris, the others cowered in fear, covering their faces from the sight before them. He too was shaking, with the familiar fingers of anxiety groping at his heart.

But as quickly as they appeared, the cobalt flames vanished, leaving those who had witnessed them in darkness.

None spoke as the steel beast returned to its initial position. Faint sounds of movement came from within, then the helm began to shift slowly backwards, smoothly and silently, until it hung open. From the hole emerged Garth's head, beads of sweat running down his brow.

"It gets too hot in there," he said, casually hoisting himself out of the huge frame. "We'll need to troubleshoot that ventilation system a little more before we move forward." Softly, he landed on the ground. "The mechanisms of the limbs feel more natural now. The legs could have passed for my own!"

He delivered the last line like a jape, but the smirk vanished from his face once he realised that the others were in no humour to laugh. The youngest Simian wore an expression of terror, petrified like a sculpture. The tallest of the group held his head in his massive hands. Ruairí stared only at the ground, his lips moving silently, his head shaking back and forth.

Only the Silverback smiled. The grin seemed out of place on the old Simian's face, so much so that Farris could have mistaken him for another. Argyll's features were no longer stern and solid, rigid with determination. The whites of his eyes seemed to shine through the dark, his face beaming at the monstrosity that had unfolded before him.

"Nicole," he said, his tone different to how it had ever been before. "Is it true that not a single component of the Reaper is made from material that can be manipulated by a mage?"

"Yes," said Nicole, her voice barely a whisper. Although she gazed straight at the Reaper, her eyes didn't seem focused. "The flames, too."

"Ah!" said the Silverback, giving Farris a very uncharacteristic pat on the back. "I believe we have Farris to thank for that. Beggar's flames, fuelled by two tanks of thainol, correct?"

"Yes," said Nicole, in the same flat tone as before. Her lips moved after that, but nothing came out. Her stance was no longer as confident as it had once been, for now she stood with her shoulders hunched forward. Her eyes were wider than usual, and some colour was lost from her cheeks. Garth and Argyll didn't seem to notice.

"One alone could take on a battalion of mages," said Garth. "And once the other eleven are built, not even the gods themselves could stop us."

"The recruits," asked Argyll. "How long will it take to train them?"

"Not long at all. The mechanisms of its movement are complex, but once you're inside, it feels just like an over-sized suit of armour."

"W-wait," stammered the youngest Simian. "I'm just a soldier. I don't know the first thing about working with...that."

"You were not chosen for your skill," said Argyll. He threw a glance over each of the other Simians. "None of you were. Garth was chosen to be the first Simian to pilot one of these because he has the passion to put his life on the line for our cause. You were all chosen for the same reason. It will not be skill or finesse that will win us this war, but technology. As I speak, Humans faithful to the One True God are arming themselves with weapons we built, ready to help us in this struggle. These Humans who call themselves the Sons of Seletoth are willing to give their lives to win our war, but can the same be said for you?"

"Of...of course," said the young Simian. He stood slightly taller now. "The Movement comes first. It always has."

"Then follow Garth, and march across Alabach armoured in the steel of Simian ingenuity." He made a grand gesture to Ruairí. "The Sons of Seletoth will be joined by the Sons of Old Simia, united by a common cause. War is almost upon us, but there is much to do before then."

Without a word of farewell, the Silverback turned to leave. The other Simians meekly followed, with Garth in the rear. He whispered frantically to the youngest Simian as he went, wrapping a fraternal arm around his shoulders.

"Seletoth," muttered Ruairí, in the monotonous voice he reserved only for prayer. He held a fisted hand against his chest. "Guide us through the darkness with your light and grant us the strength to never stray from your path."

Ruairí followed the others, his stride not as quick as it usually would be. Farris's focus then fell on Nicole, who had not moved since the Reaper was revealed.

"Are you okay?" asked Farris. "Is there anything I can help with before I go?"

"I will not pray for the Gods to forgive me," she said, still staring ahead. "Not because I don't believe they exist, but because even if they did, they would never forgive this."

"This is a Reaper, then?" asked Farris, gesturing to the machination. "Weren't you and Garth working on this for a long time? Isn't this what you wanted?"

"No," she said, her eyes glistening with tears. "When I designed the firearms, and the new alloy of Simian Steel, I told myself that they would protect us during a Holy War. If Argyll plans to separate Penance from the kingdom, surely the Church would send its mages against us. I was ensuring we would be ready."

"It seems like we are. You've achieved what most learned Simians thought impossible. The steel, the firearms. The Reaper. None would dare start a war against a side armed in such a manner."

"They won't have a choice," said Nicole. "The Silverback wishes to march first. Raids on the Clifflands, to draw the mages out from the Academy. The Sons of Seletoth armed with my weapons, clad in my armour, with twelve Simians piloting Reapers amongst them.... They could wipe a city off the face of the earth before the Church or the Crown could even respond. It was never supposed to be this way, Farris. It was never supposed to be this strong."

"What do you mean?"

"It feels like it was pure chance that led to its creation. I was struggling with the material just as you were assigned to work with me, and you helped me put right pieces together, even if you didn't understand the shape they would form.

Argyll initially only wanted me to work on the firearms but put me on the Reaper Project long before you came to Penance. After my father died, I threw myself at the task, focusing all my energy and my time on it. I let it consume me, further than it should have, and this is the result. This...this twisted perversion of science!" She raised her voice with that, the final words caught by a sob. "Now it has grown to something I can no longer control. The seeds have already been sown, and now the Silverback wields the scythe. It was never supposed to be like this."

She succumbed to a barrage of tears, wiping them as they poured silently down her cheeks.

"I don't know what to say," said Farris. "If there is anything I can do to help, I'll do it."

With that, Nicole abruptly threw her arms around Farris, burying her face into his shoulders. Guilt bubbled deep within him, as he realised how much he was relishing their embrace. He fought the urge to hold her even tighter.

"Don't leave me here alone with it," she said, her voice muffled by Farris's damp fur. "Please."

"Of course," said Farris, not quite sure what to do with his hands. He placed one gently on the back of her head. "I'm not going anywhere."

CHAPTER 16:
THE TRIAD BREAKS

E.S

I must commend your quick thinking on the day Firemaster Fionn joined the council. Your abrupt flight to Dromán provided the best excuse to keep him nearer. Without Conleth keeping him in Penance, he could have fled, too. Now, he will be right where we need him when the time comes.

A.

***

A cold midnight breeze rolled through a window of the Triad's North Wing, caressing the hairs on the back of Fionn's neck. They immediately stood on end, responding to the whisper of the wind.

Fionn shrugged off a shiver that ran through his body, not paying much mind to the healer who closed the window shut.

"You shouldn't be here, you know," she said, nodding towards the patient on the bed. "In his state, he'd barely know the difference between being awake and asleep, and he's very far from acknowledging the visitors who come here."

"Then what difference does it make if we stay?" asked Fionn. He had been vague about his intentions to see Cathal Carríga, but the mage's new position amongst the Triad obliged the staff to accommodate his needs. Or the needs of Sir Bearach.

"Well," said the healer, holding her hands over her hips. "You've got five minutes while I give him his dose. Say whatever prayers you need to say."

Fionn nodded, clutching the cheap Trinity emblem to his chest. He had purchased it at a reasonable price from the Penance markets earlier that day. Claiming to be a devout representative from the Church seemed to be the best course of action to lie his way into Cathal Carríga's private chambers.

He took a step towards the dying man. Well, it was said that he was dying, but it was certainly taking him a long time. He seemed as if he could have been a strong youth not so long ago, for a pair of broad shoulders with frail arms suggested the latter were once round with muscle.

Fionn flexed the fingers of his right arm. Even though he hadn't done an ounce of the training that Sir Bearach did, the muscle mass in his new limb hadn't deteriorated an inch.

Necromancy, mused Fionn. *Gods, we don't know the first thing about how it works.*

Sir Bearach didn't say a word. In fact, the dead knight hadn't said anything since Fionn started hatching the plan to re-unite the Carríga brothers. He spent three weeks sitting in on Triad meetings, giving the occasional counsel regarding the ways of the arcane—things trivial by any well-read mage's standards. All he had to do was claim he wished to give Cathal Carríga some 'holy blessing' from the cathedral of Dromán, and he was granted access. The patient was only able to receive visitors twice a day—at noon and midnight—due to the timing of his medication.

Fionn moved his hands in a circular motion, something resembling what the druids of the Church would do during sermons, though he wasn't quite sure what it was supposed to mean. The healer didn't notice, as she busied herself tending to the patient.

He stood there in silence for the next five minutes, pretending to pray while the healer worked. He dared not let his mind stray from his task, lest he insult the dead knight who was surely watching.

Once the healer was done, she shooed Fionn away, telling him that he'd have to finish his prayers through the door. Instead, he walked away with defeat, cursing himself for having even tried such a foolish endeavour.

I should have thought of something else. I could have given us more time, or picked a time when he was feeling more lucid, or—

No, came Sir Bearach's voice, more jarring than usual after its previous absence. *There was nothing more you could have done. And what you did was far more than I ever expected anyone to ever do for me.*

A strange sound echoed from the back of Fionn's mind. If he hadn't known any better, he would have thought Sir Bearach was crying.

I once believed my brother was the most honourable man in Alabach, continued the knight. *A man who would put the needs of the many before his own, and never expect anything in return. This was what I believed, until this very moment. If I still had knees, they would bend for you, Firemaster Fionn.*

The knight's words made Fionn stop in his tracks. A lump formed in his throat, and his mouth went dry. It was fortunate that he didn't need to use his tongue to say *you're welcome* to the knight. Although it was just a thought, he still stuttered over the words.

Before he could make his way back to his bedchambers on the first floor of the House of the Triad, a sharp cry rang out from somewhere down the hallway. It seemed to belong to a Simian, a female Simian perhaps, but the difference between the two was often hard to discern.

His feet began taking him towards the voice's source. The portraits of stern-looking men and gruff Simians rushed past either side. At the end of the hallway there were two doors, facing one another.

"Is everything alright?" called out Fionn, not sure where to direct his voice.

"Please, fetch the guards!" cried the hysterical voice. "Skies above, what have they done?"

For a moment Fionn considered leaving immediately to get help, but curiosity guided his hand to the door. When he pushed it open, Fionn cursed himself under his breath. But the dead knight in his head swore louder than the screaming Simian woman inside. A bloodied Simian corpse lay at her feet.

***

It took Farris more than a moment to gather his thoughts and figure out where he was. The summer sun had risen earlier that morning than it had all year, shining light into his weary eyes.

Nicole's cabin was tiny and sparse, furnished with as much as a hovel of the Dustworks would hold. The door was immediately adjacent to the bed, close enough to prevent it from opening all the way. Beside this was a dusty window, looking out into the hangar floor, and a squat iron-bound chest, large enough to contain everything one needed to live in such a squalid abode, but still quite smaller than what

Farris would have considered sufficient. The air was thick and musty, and carried a strange humming sound that seemed somewhat familiar to him.

The engineer herself stirred beside Farris. Although there had been little intimacy the previous night, the two Simians lay next to each other, partially naked, with arms and legs wrapped around one another so tightly that Farris had trouble discerning her limbs from his own.

Nicole grunted as she woke, turning to face Farris. Her eyes stared back into his and shone to through the dim light. In silence, the two looked at one another, as if neither wanted to ruin the moment with speech.

Don't let it end. By the Shadow of Sin, don't let it end.

Without any warning, Nicole leaned towards Farris and placed a gentle kiss upon his lips. She did it so deliberately, so naturally, that Farris had no idea how to respond. It was a kiss unlike anything he had felt before, as it didn't seem rooted in passion or formality. He certainly didn't instigate it, nor did he expect it. Nicole just did it, completely unprovoked, without meaning to imply anything further. It just...was.

"Good morning," she said, shuffling as she lay. She rested her head between Farris's shoulder and bicep; the rest of his arm stretched outwards and disappeared somewhere beneath Nicole's torso.

"Are you alright?" Farris asked, choosing his words carefully, daring not to ruin the moment by mentioning the mechanical abomination from the previous night.

"Yes," she muttered. "I was just in shock, that's all."

"Sure," replied Farris. He didn't quite believe it was as simple as that.

"But I'm pretty shocked at you, too," she said, looking up at him with a smile. "You're not nearly as bad as they made you out to be."

"Is that so?" laughed Farris. "What was it they said about me?"

"That you were the king's boot-kisser," she said, turning to snuggle her back into his chest. "That you were a follower of the Church now and grown far too comfortable living amongst the Humans of Cruachan."

"And you no longer believe this?"

Nicole hesitated. The strange sound of humming somewhere in the room seemed to grow louder than before. "Most of it," she said. "Your heart is in the right place, even if your brain isn't."

"Ha! And what's that supposed to mean?"

She considered him for a moment. When she spoke, she did so slowly, as if to a child. "What you said when we met, about Divine Penetrance and all that. Do you actually believe it?"

"It's not a matter of belief," he said, perhaps a little more harshly than he intended. "Humans believe King Diarmuid to be invincible just because they are told to. It's faith alone that brings them to this conclusion. But I've reached the same using rationality and evidence. There is no room for faith there."

"Tell me of this 'evidence,'" she said, turning to grin up at him.

Farris paused. "They call him King Diarmuid, Third of His Name, Nineteenth Incarnate. The 'third' is because there have been two King Diarmuids before him. And the 'nineteenth' represents the number of kings that have ruled Alabach since the Final Conquest."

"This is common knowledge."

"Yes," said Farris. "It is. Also common knowledge is the fact that not a single king of Alabach has died before first birthing a son."

"Coincidence does not constitute evidence," said Nicole. "If every coincidence in the world was considered magic, the Academy would be out of business."

"True. Yet nineteen is a number large enough to rule out coincidence. That, along with the minor Simian rebellions of the past and the secession and re-annexing of Dromán from the kingdom, gave plenty of opportunities for a king to be assassinated. Yet it has never happened."

"But that's because the Church's magic has never let it come to that. If the buds of past Simian uprisings had not been nipped before they began, or if there had been any kind of bloodshed during the Dromán incident, then yes, there would be an environment where one would expect a king to be murdered. The reason why none of Diarmuid's predecessors have been assassinated is because the Crown has never seen war before. Real war."

"Consider this then," said Farris, realising this line of argument was futile. "King Lionál the Fourth and Seventeenth—Diarmuid's grandfather—fathered a son at the age of eighty-four."

"Of course!" laughed Nicole. "That's because he had a sixteen-year-old wife to do the hard part for him!"

"But Lionál died moments after his son was born. The old king spent half his life in the sick bay, slowly dying of congestion. The healers had only given him weeks to live— thirty years before he died. Yet the moment a son was born to him, the ailment finally took him."

"An interesting interpretation, sure. But what is more likely—that this is just another coincidence, or that the Trinity exists and Seletoth channels his power through the current living king?"

"And what makes the latter so unlikely?" asked Farris. "In a world where a mage can bend the elements to his will, does the existence of a god seem all that far-fetched in comparison?"

"Maybe I'm wrong," said Nicole, gently patting Farris's cheek. "Perhaps they really were right about you. Farris Silvertongue: Lover of many women but married to one God."

Relax. She's only teasing you. He smiled at the thought. If some jeering was all it took to share the company of a Simian as wonderful as her, then so be it.

Still, her words brought back the image Farris had seen back in the Clifflands, down on the beach where he almost expired. For a fraction of a second, when he felt like he was supposed to die, he had seen the face of the Lady Meadhbh, as clear as if made from flesh and blood.

He brought his focus back to the present: the smell of smoke and fumes from outside, the beautiful female Simian in his arms, and that strange sound that swung through the air.

Farris closed his eyes and held Nicole closer. *No need to dwell on the past. There'll never be a time better than this.*

"Wait," said Nicole, abruptly. She lifted her head from the pillow. "Do you hear that?"

Farris didn't answer, knowing deep down that the correct response would cause this moment to end.

"Shit," she cursed under her breath, crawling out from her bed. She darted over to the chest on the other side of the room. "It's the Silverback's crystal. He must be sending a message."

She threw open the chest, and the sound grew louder. The half-crystal resonated with a distinct pattern: three long pulses, three short pulses, repeating. Whoever was in possession of the other half was sending a message, coded in a way that only a trained crystallographer could interpret.

"It's a distress call," said Nicole, panic setting into her voice. "Something's wrong."

"How can you tell?" Farris stepped out from the bed. "You're no mage."

"Argyll had us learn some simple patterns," she said, frantically dressing herself. "This one was to be saved for an emergency. We can't delay."

Farris smiled, remembering back to a morning just like this back in Cruachan.

"It's okay. I understand."

Once they were both ready, Farris and Nicole left the cabin and darted across the hangar, the empty frame of the Reaper standing abandoned in its centre. Nicole unlocked the front door and turned to lock it immediately after they stepped outside. It was Farris, then, who first noticed the state of the Steamworks outside.

"What's going on?" asked Farris, nudging Nicole's shoulder.

Nicole turned, glaring at the empty streets all around her. At this hour of the morning, the Steamworks would usually be crowded with workers.

"Where have they all gone?" she asked.

Footsteps rang through the silence, and the shape of a Simian child appeared around a nearby corner. He was running frantically, his hands and face covered with soot.

"Lad, what's the matter?" asked Farris as he approached.

The child didn't slow as he passed the two Simians. He called back, "It's Borris! He's been killed. The Silverback is taking his seat on the Triad right now!"

CHAPTER 17:
THE OPPRESSED

BORRIS BLACKHAND FOUND DEAD IN TRIAD HOME. SILVERBACK WILL SPEAK TO THE CITIZENS OF PENANCE AT NOON TODAY

Pamphlet distributed in place of the Daily Penance on the morning of the 15th Day under the Moon of Dana

***

The Tower of Sin loomed high over the crowd of Simians standing in its shadow, the noonday sun high overhead. All those gathered there faced the House of the Triad, waiting expectantly before its empty steps.

Farris and Nicole joined the crowd, shimmying past a male Simian with a child perched upon his shoulders. The thick horde of spectators stretched out from the Triad's steps like a funnel, spilling into the streets and alleys of the market district nearby.

"Does the whole city know?" asked Nicole as they pushed through the throng. "How could the news of Borris's death spread so quickly?"

"Argyll practically runs the Daily Penance," said Farris. "If he wanted the city's population to come together at the same time, it'd take little effort."

Nicole sighed, clutching the still-resonating crystal in her hand. "Except for me...."

Farris didn't respond. If Nicole's crystal really had been calling her all morning, it certainly meant Argyll wanted her at his side much earlier than now.

But not me.

"Look!" cried a lightly shaded Simian by Farris's side. "Someone's coming!"

Indeed, the distant figure of Argyll the Silverback had appeared on the Triad's steps. He was alone, standing before the people of Penance with both hands raised.

The muttering that ran through the spectators was immediately silenced as soon as Argyll spoke.

The Shadow of Sin district had been designed by Penance's best architects, built from scratch after the Fall of Sin. The House of the Triad was situated in the centre of a wide-open space, with tall buildings leaning inwards at its perimeter. Through feats of engineering Farris didn't quite understand, this shape meant that the Silverback's voice could be heard by every single person in the crowd, no matter how far away they might be.

"Simians of Penance," boomed Argyll. "I come before you with grave news. Borris Blackhand, the Simian seat of the Triad, was murdered last night."

A spattering of whispers responded to Argyll's words, but these trailed off when he spoke again.

"Borris was murdered in his bedroom as he slept, butchered in the place he should have been most safe. No Human or Simian was found to be trespassing, yet our kind leader still lies dead."

Argyll paused, glaring at the crowd expectantly. Those nearby Farris spoke in panicked voices, as if afraid of the conclusion Argyll seemed to be hinting at.

"Why is he telling us this?" asked Nicole, also apparently missing the point. "Why so much detail?"

Farris didn't respond. He stared up at the Silverback, barely noticing that Nicole's quivering hands were clutching his own.

"The building behind me," continued Argyll, "is the closest thing to a fortress that any Simian has ever built. We were a peaceful race before the Final Conquest of Man, for it was they who taught us the ways of violence. But in a place so well protected and so secure, many of you may be asking how could this have happened? How was it that someone, or *something,* was able to gain access to the Triad's private chambers?"

Argyll paused again, letting the Simians in the crowd speculate amongst themselves. After what felt like an eternity, he spoke again.

"Borris was murdered by a Wraith of Seletoth!" he roared. "For he wished to take power away from the Church and its vestigial role in this city, and this worried Arch-Canon Cathbad and his high-cardinals so much that they sent one of their holy monstrosities to dispose of our beloved leader."

The crowd erupted. Curses and profanities filled the air under raised fists of defiance. Anger tore through the Simian swarm, replacing the panic and fear that had brought them there. Nicole's grip on Farris's hand tightened.

"He's lying," said Farris, calmly. "This was no work of a Wraith."

"H-How do you know?" stuttered Nicole. Although typically of height with Farris, she seemed to shrink with fear as she looked up at the Silverback.

"They only answer to Seletoth Himself," said Farris. "They've never answered to the Church or the Arch-Canon before."

Nicole gave no response, which Farris found fortunate. In his phrasing, it almost sounded like he believed Seletoth existed.

Worse still, there could be some truth there.

"But the House of the Triad is not the most steadfast building in our fine city," boomed the Argyll. "In the Dustworks of Penance lies a gated district of incalculable wealth and affluence. As impoverished Simians struggle to survive in the neighbouring streets, as their infants starve and freeze during the harsh winters of Alabach, those that serve the Church dine in the Basilica on plates of silver and gold. The cost of the Arch-Canon's stole alone could feed a family of ten for a year, but the Church prefers to put its own image before the well-being of our people."

A furious cry rose up from the crowd—several hundred voices in unison. Together, their words were incomprehensible, but their tone was as distinct as the broken tower that stood above them: a maddening anger born of life-long frustration. Discontent bordering on rebellion.

"To say that Borris's death was the last straw would be an injustice to this great Simian's life work," continued the Silverback. "For he stood up to the injustice and prejudices of the Church long before Arch-Canon Cathbad first donned the stole. If only we had stood by Borris then. If only we had supported his cause to loosen the Church's grip on the throat of our city, then we might have saved him."

Farris shook his head. "Borris was no iconoclast," he muttered. "He and Cathbad were allies if anything." Nicole didn't seem to hear him, however. She too was caught in the frenzy that Argyll had whipped up, her jaw clenched tight, her nostrils flaring wildly.

Skies above, she can't have been won over that easily. She's far smarter than that. Surely, she can see what's going on.

"But it is not too late!" cried the Silverback. "Even in his death, we are not lost to Borris's cause. For the first time in the history of this city, we need to stand together! Our voices united are stronger than their prayers. Our strength in numbers is more powerful than their magic. Let them know that the people of Old Simia will not bend to the whims of a tradition that is not their own. The Basilica of Penance is less than a mile away from where we stand. If you feel wronged by the teachings of the Trinity, go there, and let your voices be heard!"

The crowd responded immediately. People rushed past Farris, almost knocking him off balance. With so many Simians present, they pushed and shoved against one another, even though they were all headed in the same direction. Misguided rage turned to action, and those passing Farris almost seemed gleeful, like young soldiers marching to their first battle.

"Aren't you coming?" asked Nicole, pulling Farris's arm with the flow of the crowd.

"I need to speak to Argyll," said Farris, sternly. "And you do too. That's why we came, remember?"

"Oh...of course," said Nicole, shaking her head. "The guards will recognise me. I'll take us there."

With Nicole leading the way, the pair shoved through the stampede of Simians. Many clutched impromptu weapons in their hands: loose rocks and glass bottles. One wielded a dagger, as if he had come prepared for such a turn of events. Some Humans were dotted through the crowd, and those who were bore the sigil of the Sons of Seletoth around their necks.

The crowd thinned as they approached the steps of the Triad. One guard immediately stepped aside on seeing Nicole, bowing as she went. Up on the steps, Argyll hadn't moved from his position, but stood there alone as he watched the Simians of Penance marching towards the Dustworks.

"Argyll!" yelled Farris once the old Simian was in earshot. "What the fuck are you doing?"

The Silverback's face returned to the stolid expression Farris was used to. When he spoke, the fury disappeared from his voice, and was replaced with his usual calm and commanding monotone.

"I'm fulfilling my side of an agreement," he said. "All while furthering our cause."

"How does starting a riot help us?" snapped Farris.

"The Sons of Seletoth will not aid in the coming war unless I give them reason to. I promised to restrict the

Church's influence over this city before we march on the Crown."

"And murdering Borris was the only way to achieve that?" The thought to hold his tongue came too late. Fortunately, there was nobody else nearby to hear.

"I did not kill Borris," said Argyll, his tone barely changing despite the weight of Farris's accusation. "There will be far more casualties before this day is out. If the riots turn to violence, the Churchguard will send its mages to quell the dissenters. Many may die, but all will be united under a new, common cause. It will not matter who lands the first blow, only who suffers the greatest wound."

He's gone too far. We've waited too long to act, and now he's dug us deeper than we ever intended to go.

"When do we march?" asked Nicole, after a pause. "If people die today, we want to make sure that something good comes of it."

Farris turned to Nicole, not bothering to hide his shock. *Sin's stones! She's gone mad too.*

"Garth has left Penance to scout the lands south of the Glenn one more time," replied Argyll. "When he returns, the Reapers will be ready, and the Sons of Seletoth will be armed and on our side. Then we march."

"And the Triad," asked Nicole. "Will there be an election for Borris's seat?"

"No," said Argyll. "The Triad no longer functions as it once did. Now there is just one seat, occupied by the leader Penance needs the most right now." A quick smile crossed Argyll's thin lips for a fraction of a second. "They'll need me even more than that when the war comes."

CHAPTER 18:
WHAT WE'RE CAPABLE OF

NINE KILLED AND DOZENS INJURED IN BASILICA MASSACRE

The Daily Penance

16th Day Under the Moon of Dana, AC404

A peaceful march through the Dustworks of Penance yesterday descended to violence, followed by tragedy, as mages of the Churchguard attempted to disperse the crowds.

One eyewitness told the Daily Penance that twelve Pyromancers surrounded the protesters once they reached the Basilica walls, threatening to open fire if they did not turn home. With no further warning, the mages unleashed their flames, burning both Human and Simian alive.

"There was so much smoke," said one survivor. "I couldn't tell which way was up. Then everyone was running and screaming. I didn't realise that I was on the ground until I felt their feet trampling over me."

"All we wanted was some answers," said a representative from the Sons of Seletoth: a new faith to the city. "We just wanted to see if what the Silverback said was true, about how it was the Wraiths that killed Borris. The mages didn't say a word, but their actions told us all we need to know."

Arch-Canon Cathbad declined to comment.

***

"And following the events from last week, seven more have died of their injuries," said Ruairí. "The rest are still in critical condition."

The Human spoke to the council of the Triad, though there were more empty chairs facing him than people. The Silverback sat in Borris's old seat, looking as comfortable as one born to sit there. The other two empty seats of the Triad flanked him, one for Cathal Carríga—who still lingered between life and death—and the other for King Diarmuid.

We'd be more likely to see Borris alive again than Diarmuid's arse on that cushion. Farris sat between Nicole and another empty seat, which typically would have been kept for Garth. But the scout had yet to return from his latest skirmish. He was already two days overdue.

He'll be fine. He knows those cliffs and caves better than anyone.

But reassuring himself did little to take away the empty feeling in the pit of his stomach. If Garth really was so well-versed in traversing the Glenn, then why would he be delayed at all?

Most of the other advisors to the Triad were missing, too. Some were off treating with the cardinals of the Basilica, while others were controlling the damage Argyll had done in their own way.

Fionn the Red was the only one of those left, still taking Earthmaster Seán's place. Farris had seen spoken to him little since the night Conleth died, but it was probably for the best. The last thing he needed was another reminder of what had happened back in the Glenn.

Almost a year ago now. Skies above, so much has changed since then.

"And the mages," said Argyll, abruptly. "How many of them were injured?"

"Three killed," said Ruairí. "They were shot right as the crowd approached. The..."

His voice trailed off, and he threw a glance at Fionn, sitting at the edge of the room, then back to Argyll. The Simian nodded deliberately, as if to tell Ruairí to continue regardless.

"The Sons in the crowd shot first, with...strange weapons none could recognise. The Churchguard retaliated, but some civilians were caught in the crossfire."

Caught in the crossfire? The numbness in Farris's belly turned to rage. *They were burned alive for listening to Argyll. This was no accident.*

But the Silverback nodded, as if unsurprised by the news. In fact, none reacted in a way that suggested they weren't expecting a report like that. None, bar Fionn sitting by the side.

"Excuse me," he said, his voice slightly stronger than Farris had last remembered. "But that's not how the Daily Penance put it. They said that—"

"The papers write what they wish," said Argyll. "Half of the city was present at the Basilica that day, and they'll give you the same news Ruairí here did. Don't pay any mind to any other truths you find."

This seemed to satisfy Fionn, but Farris would put money on Argyll being the one to have chosen the words that article had used. Argyll was a leader now and could no longer support the dissident movement as openly as he once did.

But for how long? Surely, it'll be clear whose side he's on once he starts leading the Reapers south.

According to Nicole, the Reapers were ready, as were the Simians who would pilot them. Ruairí claimed that the Sons of Seletoth were armed and ready to march, too. The only missing piece now was Garth.

But will it be as simple as that? Farris threw another glance towards the Silverback. *Argyll is doing such a poor job of handling this crisis. Is it wise to create another?*

"And what of the Arch-Canon?" asked Fionn, still seemingly unready to stand down. "Surely Cathbad will want some sort of...closure, from all of this."

"He may dress like a fool," interjected Ruairí. "But Cathbad is a shrewd and careful politician. For him to strike back in any way now would only incite the people further. To play this whole thing down as an isolated incident would be his best course of action."

"And the Triad?" asked Fionn. "What course is best for us?"

"To hold your tongue, boy," said Argyll. "You are here to advise us on matters of the arcane. This concerns neither that, nor you."

Fionn's gaze fell to the floor. "Yes, sir," he stammered. "Of course."

Farris frowned. Sure, the Silverback was almost always in the right when it came to political matters but shooting down the young Pyromancer won't pay off in the long run.

Argyll could take a leaf from the Arch-Canon's book. There's no need to go creating more enemies....

"That will be all," said Argyll, glancing at each of those present, one at a time. "The following few weeks will be more taxing than the last. Be ready for whatever comes."

The others nodded together, while Fionn said "yes," aloud, despite being the only one who had no idea what he really meant.

The rest stood and said their curt, polite goodbyes. Argyll was the first to leave, walking side-by-side with Ruairí, the Human gesturing wildly and whispering frantically as they went.

"What do the coming weeks entail for you?" Farris asked Nicole before she had a chance to leave. "Are you ready for what they have in store?"

"Work, and no," said Nicole, coldly. "There's so much left to do, and without Garth..."

"You're worried about him. He'll be fine. You know what he's like."

"He's taken too much responsibility for himself. This whole...plan rests on his shoulders now. If he's not here to lead the—"

"He'll be fine," interrupted Farris, nodding towards Fionn, who was awkwardly packing sheets of notes and documents into a leather shoulder-pack. "You have enough on your hands right now to be worrying."

"That's true," said Nicole. "Argyll needs me more than ever."

"You think so? He seems to be doing very well without our help for now."

Nicole gave a defeated sigh. "You're far from understanding what's going on inside that mind, Farris. All of us are. We need to trust him."

"Oh, and letting innocent civilians burn to death is the best course of action?"

"Yes," said Nicole, lowering her voice to a whisper. "It may very well be so."

She went to leave, and Farris stepped aside. She walked with the same resigned tone her voice had carried.

Does she really believe that? Would she really do the same if–

"Chester? Can I ask you something?"

Farris turned abruptly to see Fionn standing by him.

"I told you before, call me Farris," he said, making little effort to hide his frustration.

"But we're alone," said Fionn. "Since when does a Simian care what he's called?"

"Fine. Ask away."

"It's just after what happened at the Basilica, I can't fathom why Argyll –"

Farris stepped forward grabbed the collar of Fionn's shirt, bringing the Human's face close to his own. The lad shrank back with fear, a muffled groan escaping his lips.

"You listen here," said Farris. "You're wading through a pit of vipers here, lad, and it'll do no good checking which ones bite. Keep your head down, and your questions to yourself, and you won't get hurt."

He let go. Fionn immediately straightened himself, fixing his shirt with that grotesque, over-sized hand.

"I'm a fully-fledged Firemaster," he said, only letting his voice quiver a little. "I could burn you from the inside out. You threaten me with your strength, but I could kill you in an instant."

"You could, but you won't," said Farris, pushing past Fionn to leave. "You wouldn't dare do something like that."

"How do you know?" called Fionn.

"Because you're afraid," said Farris, without turning back. "Just like the rest of us, you're afraid of what you're really capable of."

CHAPTER 19:
THE MARCH OF THE DEAD

We'll build our numbers. We'll take the Seven Seachtú. We'll claim the power of the Academy. Then we'll march on the capital, and I'll take the king's power for myself.

They called my father Yarlaith the Black, but soon I shall be known as Morrigan the Godslayer.

***

Fionn sat alone at the bar of *The Squealing Pig*, a tavern in a far better state than implied by the gruesome sign outside. It was in the heart of Penance's market district, attracting a wide range of customers from Simian merchants in the city to Human travellers from the south.

But none from the Shadow of Sin, Fionn reminded himself, taking a deep drink of red ale. *People from that district prefer to keep to themselves.*

A moon and a half had passed since he has last spoken to the Simian now named Farris, who had practically threatened Fionn for questioning the Silverback.

So much secrecy. How am I supposed to council a Triad that won't let me be part of their work?

I've told you before, interjected Sir Bearach. *The Silverback no longer has the welfare of the city among his priorities. There is too much he keeps hidden from us.*

Us. That was the way Sir Bearach had been referring to them as of late. Stranger still, Fionn agreed with the knight.

It was true: the others of the Triad kept mainly to themselves. Even where their own was concerned. When the Simian named Garth—Farris's brother—had returned from the Glenn, he had barely acknowledged his tardiness. It was Nicole who had pushed for an explanation, but the scout dismissed her queries just as he had everyone else's. 'I was delayed,' was all he said. 'Nothing major. Nothing worth discussing. We have more important work to do.'

What this 'important work' was, Fionn had no idea. So many meetings were carried out without him, with only rare inquiries into the nature of Pyromancy or Crystallography enough to make Fionn's presence amongst the Triad even remotely relevant.

I wish Earthmaster Seán would return from Dromán, thought Fionn, taking another deep drink from his pint. *He'd know what was going on. He'd know what to do.*

Seeing Borris's corpse the night he died was what spurred most of Fionn's doubts. The scene itself had been a shock, with Borris's wife inconsolably hysterical by her husband's side, and Sir Bearach roaring commands at Fionn inside the mage's head. Apparently, it had been one of the Seletoth's Wraiths that killed the Simian, but how the City Guard came to that conclusion, Fionn didn't know. After all, they had spent little time investigating the scene.

Fionn stared out through a dusty window across the bar.

Could the Silverback be lying? Could it be some kind of bid for–

A quick shape darted across the tavern's front window, followed by another. Then another.

"Did you see that?" said the absent-minded bartender, looking up from his newspaper. "Some folk running?"

"Seems like it," said Fionn, as three more Simians sprinted past the window. "Headed in the direction of the Rustlake."

The bartender laughed. "Might be that they're late for the ferry. People are dying to leave the city ever since what happened down by the Basilica."

The other patrons of the bar took notice as more passed, some standing and craning their necks to see more. By the time Fionn stood too, scores of Simians had poured into the streets, all heading in the same direction.

"Hmm, maybe not," said the bartender. "This seems different."

Fionn darted toward the door to see for himself. When he reached the crowded street, a glance southward was enough to confirm his previous suspicion: they were headed to the waterfront.

"What's going on?" Fionn asked nobody in particular. A young Simian girl stopped to answer, looking up at the mage with wide, innocent eyes.

"Ships and boats just turned up in the Rustlake," she said. "Lots of 'em!"

Strange. What could bring so many people to Penance at once?

Leaving any concern for his half-finished pint at the door of *The Squealing Pig*, Fionn hurried out toward the docks. The narrow streets of the Goldworks eventually opened up to the Goldgate, with wide wharfs in docklands just beyond. The roads coming and going were thick with people: Simians and Humans with expressions of dread, while oblivious children climbed the walls to get a better look at the spectacle.

Vessels of all shapes and sizes filled the lake, and each was full of people. Humans crowded fishing ships that rocked to and fro, threatening to throw its passengers out with the moving tide. Rowboats and canoes not built for long distance joined them, their capacities well past their critical masses.

A wooden trade cog was the first to reach the shore. As soon as it landed, the doors opened, and dozens of Humans spilled out, many dressed in rags, others crippled and wounded. They looked up at the Simian crowd, fear and pain in their eyes. One man stepped forward, walking with a limp. He grimaced in pain with each movement. When he spoke, it was as if each syllable brought agony to his lips, cracked and dried with thirst and exhaustion.

"The dead," he croaked. "The dead marched on Point Grey. There's no stopping them."

***

"Four hundred people arrived from the Clifflands this morning. If what they say is true, more than that will be here by the turn of the moon."

Ruairí delivered the report to the Triad meeting room, which was far fuller than usual. Businessmen and landowners throughout the city had come to hear the news, along with the usual attendees of the Silverback's meetings.

Farris watched as Argyll reacted to the report. True, it had been Fionn who brought the news to the Triad first—an armada of ships from Point Grey carrying refugees from a battle Farris could have scarcely believed was possible—but it was Ruairí and the Sons of Seletoth who counted the new arrivals and began the insurmountable task of tending to their wounded.

"And what do they expect to find here?" growled Argyll, covering his eyes with a pale white hand. "What gives them the impression that they'll be safe from this...this..."

"It has been described as a horde," said Ruairí. "We know little about it now, but if there's a sliver of truth in this account, we'll be hearing about quite a lot more than we already have."

Argyll leapt from his chair and leaned over the oaken table. He raised an aggressive finger toward the Human.

"Do you find this amusing?" he roared. "Would you really prefer we wait around for more news to reach us, sitting here twiddling our thumbs while we do so?"

"No," muttered Ruairí, though he didn't seem perturbed by Argyll's outrage.

"We need to deal with this in whatever way necessary," said Argyll. "We'll put every other plan on hold in the meantime."

The Silverback emphasised the word *plan* in a way that immediately let Farris and the other dissidents present understand what he meant. The march south. The Reapers. *The Plan.*

And we were so close, thought Farris, watching as Garth tried hard not to react to this turn of events too. *With him back, and the Sons armed, it was only a matter of days before...*

"I can give a discount to any who wish to take refuge in any of my homes," said Wheaton the Wise, a Simian merchant who owned half the property of the Saltworks. "It's a modest proposal, but I'm still a businessman in—"

"You'll take them for no cost," snapped Argyll. "The Triad will provide some compensation, but you'll make no profit."

"Y-yes," said Wheaton, bowing slightly as he spoke. "That will do."

"Now," said Argyll, the fury from before completely removed from his tone. "Given the wide space provided by the Saltworks, we'll set up a camp there. All vacant buildings in the region must be filled to capacity before we start setting up tents. Ruairí, the Sons may attend to this, aided by the City Guard."

"Yes," said Ruairí. With a curt nod, he vanished from the room.

"We'll need to scout the Clifflands to gauge what exactly it is we're dealing with. Garth, take your best men and arm them for an expedition."

"Please," said Garth. "If I may make another suggestion."

The Silverback nodded.

"Reconnaissance is certainly the best course of action," Garth began. "I agree with that much, but right now we know nothing more than a few disjointed rumours from commoners struck dumb with fear. If they are wrong, you risk losing me and a score of scouts on a week-long goose-chase across the Clifflands. If they are right, we'll walk right into the path of an enemy greater than our ancestors have ever faced before. Either would be a blow to the Triad."

Those who could read between Garth's lines nodded furiously in agreement. Farris knew what he was really saying: 'I am invaluable to the Movement. Losing me would set us back considerably.'

Of course, most of those present didn't see things the same way. The merchants and landowners grumbled amongst themselves, possibly wondering how the loss of ten scouts could be a 'blow to the Triad.' Fionn the Pyromancer looked on with a furrowed brow.

Skies above. The lad has been in on dozens of these meetings, and he still has no clue what they're really about.

"What I propose instead," said Garth, "is to rigorously question Penance's newest citizens and try to piece together a coherent story of what exactly happened in Point Grey, and what kind of enemy we are facing, if indeed one does exist."

"You propose to take up this task?" said Argyll, raising an eyebrow.

"Of course. I'll bring some of my men along, and systematically question all of those who can provide helpful information."

"I'll come, too," said Farris. "I'd like to find out a little more about what's going on."

"You're not alone in that," said Argyll with a concerned frown. "You're not alone at all."

***

By the time Farris and Garth reached the Saltworks, the Sons of Seletoth were already at work tending to the crowds of refugees.

"They don't waste time," said Farris, watching as two Humans carried off a wounded man on a makeshift stretcher. "I know now what Argyll sees in them."

"Obedient, hard-working men who would do anything if they thought it the will of their Lord?" asked Garth. "I thought that much was already obvious."

"Though some things are less so," said Farris as he passed a family huddled beneath soiled rags at the side of the road, waiting for their turn to be housed. "Such as, why would the Silverback go to all this trouble to help Humans in need?"

"Because he has the power to do so? Because if he didn't act, they'd starve and rot outside our walls?"

"No." Farris dropped his voice to a whisper. "But these are from Point Grey. The same Humans Argyll was willing to trample over with a dozen Reapers and a few hundred-armed fanatics."

Garth shrugged. "Maybe he had a change of heart. Maybe he took one look at these poor people and decided that they shouldn't suffer more than they already have. Maybe he realised that our cause isn't worth the lives of thousands of innocent people." He leaned towards Farris and placed a hand on his shoulder. "Or maybe this is just part of the same plan as before. What appears to be a huge setback could just as easily be a tiny step in the right direction."

Farris glanced around the camp. Dozens of Sons were setting up tents, while others formed the crowds into ordered queues with promises of food and shelter.

"I don't quite follow that reasoning," said Farris.

"I didn't expect you to." Garth smiled and pointed toward a group of villagers huddled in front of a squalid tenement garden. "I'll start with these. You ask over where they're being fed. Maybe those with soup in their stomachs will be the first to talk."

The first hour of questioning didn't provide much help. Farris gently asked those around him what they saw that night in Point Grey, but he received no clear answers. An old man recounted in detail about how he fled from the town when the fires started, though he never caught a glimpse of the cause. Two young girls said that their father refused his neighbours use of his boat, but the mob overwhelmed him and took it. That was the last they saw of him.

Garth arrived for an update after that, but Farris had little to report. When the other scouts arrived to help with the task, they spread themselves out amongst the crowd, questioning only who that had seen the horde itself. This immediately provided more tangible answers.

"An army of skeletons," said a broad-chested farmhand. "They swept over the hills and descended on the town without making a sound."

"Undead," said another, stouter and drunker than his companion. "That's what the Church folk here called them. But they looked quite dead to me."

"Some had flesh," said a mother cuddling a new-born babe against her chest. "But it was rotting and stinking, hanging off their bodies like rags."

"I saw one," interjected a young man. "He didn't look like he was dead for long. Dressed in a green cloak, he was. Like a mage. But he didn't use magic, no. He fought with his teeth and his nails, like an animal."

"Animals?" asked a slim fellow. "There were animals, aye. Horses and ground sloths, undead like the rest of 'em. I was chased by a dog, and his brains was hanging from a wound in his skull. Gods, mine would have looked like that, too, if it wasn't for the boats."

On the minor details, the accounts differed wildly. One particular witness claimed he saw a Human with four arms, each wielding a weapon. Another apparently saw a bear with two heads, one of which was sewn to its shoulder with black rope.

The numbers varied, too. Some put them at a hundred, others as much as a thousand, and everything in between. Farris was just about to give up hope of gaining any kind of workable insight into this threat, when one consistent detail emerged.

All those who witnessed the horde claimed that it moved in a coordinated manner, as if led by single person. Some even went as far as to say they saw such a leader.

"A woman," said one witness. "A beautiful woman with tattered, black wings spread out from her shoulders. If death had a physical form, it would be that."

"No," said another. "I saw her, and she was half woman, half crow. Her body was covered in black feathers, but instead of a face, she had a crooked beak. And great talons instead of feet..."

"A wicked old crone! Her eyes lit up the night, and when she shrieked, the dead responded, like children would to a mother."

"She was ten feet tall, and darkness oozed from her skin."

"She was covered in blood, laughing manically as she ran through the massacre."

"She was a mage. A powerful one, and she walked through fire like it was nothing!"

"She was undead, with skin rotting off her bones."

"She was dressed all in black."

"She was as naked as the day she was born."

"She was my daughter."

Farris paused.

"Excuse me?" he asked. "Can you repeat that?"

The man who had spoken was in a miserable condition. A mud-clad beard consumed most of his face, revealing only a pair of dark eyes almost void of life. His teeth were broken and yellowed, packed into bloodied gums. He could barely stand up straight, slumping drunkenly against an improvised soup-stand.

"I said she was my daughter," he slurred. "She was my daughter, and I abandoned her." He fell forward, grasping Farris by both shoulders.

"Morrigan," he said. "Her name is Morrigan."

CHAPTER 20:
ANSWERS

To His Lordship, Earl Carríga of Rosca Umhir,

Point Grey has fallen, and the Clifflands lie in ruin. The enemy is descending on Ardh Sidhe, and I fear that the city won't hold.

King Diarmuid had it on good authority that the Simians of Penance were planning an attack, and I do not doubt His Grace's council. But this enemy is unlike anything we have faced before. Thousands of dead bodies, strung up and marching like puppets. If there is a way to defeat them, I am at a loss as to where to begin.

It is well known that Keep Carríga is an impenetrable fortress, but I beg of you to please meet this force with your own army. The soldiers of Rosca Umhir do not fall in battle easily, and their numbers will serve the kingdom far better in open combat than defending your gates.

My time is short. I do not expect us to hold out for the night. My city cannot be saved, and the Clifflands are already lost, but you can still fight. There is hope, as long as you fight.

Crystal wave sent from Earl Broin of Ardh Sidhe to Earl Carríga of Rosca Umhir.

***

The meagre council of the Triad looked on in awe at the vagrant whom Farris had plucked from the refugee camps. A rough sponge-bath and a clean shave made him presentable enough, but the man's eyes were still those of a madman, and the perfumes of the bathhouse did little to remove the stench of alcohol from his breath.

The Silverback cleared his throat, grabbing the attention of all who were present. Garth leaned casually against the back wall, while Nicole sat forward in her seat, staring at the man from the camps. Fionn stood with his arm forward, his lips pursed together in thought.

"After thoroughly questioning Penance's newest arrivals," said the Silverback, "we have learned little more than nothing. The dead descended on Point Grey three nights ago and massacred its people in a matter of minutes. Relatively few managed to escape. Those that did brought some information of the enemy to us, but nowhere near as much we would need to retaliate. As for where this army came from, all we know for sure is that they are led by a single individual. An individual this man claims to be his daughter."

Argyll threw an expectant glance at the newcomer. The man nodded curtly and spoke.

"M-my...name is Cormac Ó Branna," he said, stammering through each word as he went. His body was shaking, but from fear of what he'd seen or nerves over whom he was speaking to, Farris could not tell.

"I come from a small village near the cliffs called Roseán," he continued. "I had a wife and daughter there, but I left them a year ago...and I've lived in Point Grey ever since."

"Where were you on the night the dead came?" asked Argyll. The lack of emotion in his words made Farris wonder if he truly understood what this man had gone through.

"I was at the inn," he said. "I...my friend came into some money a while back, see, and he bought an inn in Point Grey. I was living there, at the time. I guess it was around midnight when I heard people screaming first. I didn't know what to expect. I've heard talk of the..."

His voice trailed off, and his gaze fell to the floor.

"You heard talk of what?" asked Argyll.

"S-simians," he stammered. "Not to offend, but the king was getting ready for a war with Penance. I assumed it was the Simians when the screaming started."

None had a response to this, but Nicole shifted uncomfortably in her seat. Farris pretended not to notice, though it was clear what she was thinking.

It could very well have been us.

"Anyway," Cormac continued. "I ran from the inn and went along with the crowd. They were headed to the waterfront. People were saying it was the only way we could escape, and I didn't question them.

"But the dead...they came pouring over us, from either side. The town...it was surrounded. Surrounded before they even attacked. People all around me were being butchered. Women and children too. I could have stopped, I could have helped someone, but I kept running. I just kept running.

"I don't know how, but I made it onto a ship. It was crowded, sure, but it was safe. The village was burning by the time the anchor was lifted. I could smell the flesh..."

"And your daughter," said Argyll. "When did you see her?"

Cormac was sobbing now, with tears visible on his cheeks. "Just as we were sailing away. She was there, on the pier. Watching us leave. I don't know if she saw me, but Gods above and below, I saw her."

The story ended there, and the room fell silent for a moment.

"You said you left your family a year ago," said Nicole, her voice cracking slightly as she spoke. "What happened?"

As if the horrors of the undead hadn't been enough, this question ignited a stronger reaction in Cormac than any Argyll had asked. Cormac almost shrieked in response, and he buried his face in his hands.

"It was harvest season," he said, sobbing wildly. "We were out in the field, and out of nowhere...there was a troll."

Farris's heart sank.

No. Not the same. It can't be the same.

He looked over to Fionn, whose face had turned a deathly pale, his mouth ajar.

"There were strangers," continued Cormac. "They tried to fight the troll off and—"

"That was us," said Fionn, an air of defiance in his voice. "Our ship crashed into the Glenn, and we escaped across the fields of the Clifflands. The troll followed us from the valley." He threw a glance at Farris. "Tell them, Chester. Tell them about Sláine, Sir Bearach and the others."

"Chester?" asked Nicole. "Farris, what's he talking about?"

Farris fumed with rage. Although more than twelve moons ago, the pressure and anxiety of that mission was still fresh in his mind. The lies, the effort, the charade of pretending to be the Simian he had killed...

"You know far less than you let on, boy," said Farris, trying hard to keep a straight face. "You're in deeper than you should ever be, and you still have no idea what's really going on."

"Enough," growled Argyll. "None of this has any bearing on our present situation. Cormac, you claim that your child led the undead horde. Tell me, what could have led her down this path?"

"I...I have no idea," said Cormac. "All I know is that she went to live with my brother, Yarlaith the White."

"He's the village healer," said Fionn, raising his oversized arm. "Yarlaith saved my life. The man knows his trade well."

A sudden shadow seemed to appear over Fionn's face. His eyes stared off into the distance. "No," he muttered, as if answering a question that was not asked. "That couldn't be, it..."

"Speak, lad," said Argyll. It wasn't a request.

"Necromancy," whispered Fionn. "I have reason to believe Yarlaith was involved with Necromancy: The manipulation of the flesh made dead."

"That's a grave accusation. What reason have you to believe this?"

Fionn paused for a moment, his lips quivering as he tried to find the words.

"There were some... things he said. While treating me. References to alchemy and healing that the Academy would consider unconventional. Though I do not have something more substantial than that."

Something in the cadence of Fionn's speech to the way he stared at the floor as he spoke made Farris narrow his eyes.

"Thank you, Fionn," said Argyll. "We now know what we must do next." He turned to face Garth. "How many scouts are at our disposal this instant?"

"Four," said Garth. "Most are out in the Glenn, but four remain in Penance right now."

"Good. Farris has informed me that Jacob the Blind has started smuggling again. Are you familiar with his operations?"

"Of course," said Garth with a slight smile. "Jacob and I have a significant history together. He owes me a fair share of favours too."

"Then you will call upon those tonight," said Argyll. "Gather your remaining scouts. Together, you and Fionn shall sail to Roseán. There, we can learn more about what we face."

"What?" cried Nicole. "What about the horde? Skies above, Argyll, he's only just returned!"

"I'll do it," said Garth. "I can start making preparations right away."

"Why me?" asked Fionn. "What good will I do?"

"You are the arcane advisor to the Triad," said Argyll. "You are by far the most knowledgeable among us when it comes to the ways of magic. If there is anybody who can figure out how to fight the dead, it's you."

Fionn paused, narrowing his eyes as if struggling with his own thoughts. "Yes," he said eventually. "I'll go to Roseán."

"Me too," said Cormac. "I'm no fighter, but I'll go. There are many debts I need to pay, and this may be the best time to start."

"Then it's settled," said Argyll. "The horde is said to be marching south on Ard Sidhe. We have some reports that there is no trace of the dead in the Clifflands."

Garth and Nicole were the first to exit the meeting room. Farris went to follow, but Cormac called out to him.

"Farris, is it?" said the man, reaching out for the Simian's arm. "I wanted to thank you. I would have been in a bad way if I stayed there, in the camps. The fog of my mind is starting to clear now."

"So, you're finally sobering up?" said Farris. Immediately after he spoke, he regretted the words.

"No," said Cormac. "I did not flee when the troll attacked my family. I was on our horse, and he dragged me away from my home. When I came to, I was too afraid to return, too afraid of what they would say. I've been blaming myself ever since. I still do, sometimes. But now I'll make amends, in whatever way I can. Even if I can't help, I'll at least try. If you had never found me, Farris, I would have never wanted to *try*."

"Thanks," muttered Farris, not quite sure what to say. He was more aware of Fionn's stare from across the room. The young mage stood with his arms crossed and had not moved since the beginning of the meeting. In an effort to avoid another confrontation, Farris promptly excused himself and walked out into the hallway.

"I won't let anything happen to me," said Garth. He and Nicole were both leaning against the marble banister of the Triad's landing. With a sudden shock, Farris saw that his hands were clasped together with hers.

"That's what you always say!" she snapped. "We both know what happened the last time you went to that damn village!"

Garth hushed her gently. "Yes, we both know, but nobody else does," he whispered. "And they don't need to."

With that, he placed a soft kiss on her lips. "I won't be long this time, I promise."

Farris stood dumbfounded as Garth departed. Nicole didn't move, seemingly unaware that Farris was there.

"What was that all about?" asked Farris, not trying to hide the anger in his voice.

"It was nothing," said Nicole. "He just ran into trouble the last time he went into the Clifflands, and he didn't want anyone to know about— "

"Not that," said Farris. "You were all...together, and..."

Farris's heart lunged in his chest. Each beat seemed like a strain on his whole body. He tried to speak, but no words came out. Fortunately, Nicole seemed to understand.

"Farris, Garth and I have been sharing a bed for the past year now. I thought you knew this."

"Of course not!" he said, caught with surprise at how easily the words came out now. "I thought I was the only one."

"Skies above," swore Nicole. "What do I look like to you, a Human? You are not the only one. Garth is not the only one. There are plenty of others, too. That's the way it's always been!"

"But I thought this was different."

"Oh, that's rich, coming from Farris Silvertongue. Is that what you tell your others, too?"

"No," said Farris. "There hasn't been anyone else but you—"

"Listen to yourself, Farris! The whole world is breaking, and your brother just went out to investigate the cracks. Tell me, are you really so unconcerned about him that you'd rather worry yourself with me?"

She turned and left before Farris could respond. As he stood there, he considered that it was probably for the best. It was clear that she wouldn't have liked the answer.

CHAPTER 21:
THE ROSE OF THE CLIFFS

Two nights ago, I received a wave from the Earl of Ardh Sidhe, pleading with me to take our war on the undead out into the open field. I did not listen, but now, as I hear the walking corpses butchering and burning right outside my walls, I wish I had.

Fear was what drove me to do what I did. Both of my sons were once brave warriors, and the Gods have shown mercy in that neither of them lived to see their father become a coward. Aislinn begged me to open the gates, to take the townsfolk in while I lead the charge on the dead, but I refused. I claimed I was in no fit state to fight, that we would be safer barricaded deep in the keep, but she would not see this coward's reason. Instead, she donned her brother's armour and rode out to meet the horde herself. I'm sure she'll meet her death, too. But she shall die a hero.

Let it be known that when the dead came charging over the land, Aislinn Carríga did not yield. Aislinn Carríga did not hide.

Last entry into the journal of Earl Carríga of Rosca Umhir.

***

Fionn stared up at the rising cliffs as the tiny skiff rocked gently towards the coast, influenced by the soft waves of the Eternal Sea. Like a great curtain of grey stone, the cliffs seemed to hang from an iron-coloured sky, draping into the foaming waters below. Fionn took in the view with awe, though the knight's voice in his head was a little less impressed.

Sure, you've seen them before, said Sir Bearach. *The Lord knows I'd be happier to never see them again.*

Fionn nodded, though it was fortunate that none of the others aboard the vessel noticed. Sir Bearach had a point. It was upon those cliffs that Sláine the White had died, along with an engineer from *The Glory of Penance*. Fionn had never learned his name, and as the moons had drifted by one by one, he even struggled to picture his face.

Fionn stole a glance at the newcomer. The only other Human aboard, he seemed to be a lot more lucid than before. With a freshly trimmed beard and a set of new clothes, he was hardly recognisable as the old vagrant Farris had pulled out from the camps.

But his eyes, noted Sir Bearach. *His eyes haven't changed.*

It was true. Both now, and on the day they first met, Cormac had the gaze of a man who had witnessed too much, and who regretted doing so little.

We owe him this, thought Fionn. *We were the ones who brought the troll to his home. His wife would still be alive if it wasn't for us.*

True, said Sir Bearach. *And perhaps the world wouldn't be in the state of ruin it is now.*

Fionn shuddered. It was a frightening thought, and perhaps one not worth dwelling on.

"There's a pathway through the cliffs a hundred or so yards ahead," said Garth, pointing at the rocks ahead. He rested his other hand on the shoulder of the boat's pilot: a Simian larger than any Fionn had ever seen.

"Are you tellin' me how to do my job now?" asked the Simian. Fionn had overheard the others call him Jacob the Blind, but he didn't seem very blind at all. Simian names never made much sense.

"Of course," said Garth. "I've been scouting this region for the past year now. Tell me, when was the last time the Humans of the Clifflands required your smuggled merchandise?"

"There could have been a market there," said Jacob, barely taking his eyes away from the cliffs as he manoeuvred the skiff toward the coast.

The wooden vessel glided gently past the rocks. Only when the great cliff wall approached, could Fionn make out the pathway Garth had mentioned. It was less a pathway and more of a fissure, struck down the face of the cliffs and creating a tiny passage gently sloping upwards.

"Alright lads!" cried Garth. The four other Simian scouts aboard the skiff grunted in response. "Single file now. We all won't fit through at once!"

***

A weathered dirt road took the company away from the cliffs, through the fields and into the old village. The walls of Roseán were worn down from the winds of the Eternal Sea, but the buildings within were ruined by an entirely different source.

Most of the roofs had been thatched once, but all that remained now were tangles of scorched straw atop crumbling wattle-and-daub structures.

"This used to be called the Sandy Road," said Cormac, as if to himself. He walked at the back of the group, glancing back and forth across every aspect of the ruin. "My house used to be over there."

He pointed toward a pile of rubble just beyond the path. From the tone in his voice, Fionn guessed that he didn't want to take a closer look.

The path eventually widened out into a huge cobblestone square. It was here that the extent of the damage could truly be seen. A well stood in the centre, but that was all that remained intact. Burnt-out buildings lined the perimeter of the square, with dozens of broken windows and torn roofs between them. A mass of charred bushes and trees stood at the other end of the path, and the smell of burnt wood still lingered in the air. Just beyond that was a small chapel, its modest steeple reduced to a pile of assorted stones on the ground beside it, leaving a gaping hole in the structure's roof.

"My brother's house is beyond the church," said Cormac, walking ahead of the others to lead the way. He raised a finger toward the opposite path, which winded around the chapel and disappeared behind a hill beyond. "They used to call this the High Road."

He's far calmer than I expected, whispered Sir Bearach. *One would expect the sight of your hometown destroyed to shatter a man's mind.*

Fionn considered the knight's words for a moment, as he followed Cormac through the wreckage. Indeed, the old farmhand did seem utterly unmoved by the scene.

Perhaps there is nothing left to shatter, said Fionn. *He'd left his family for dead, and spent a year living alone, dwelling on it.*

Cormac stopped abruptly at the gates of the chapel. His shoulders slumped slightly, and he cast his eyes to the ground.

"The house is further up there," he said. His voice seemed even more morose than before. "I'll follow you up in a moment."

Garth and the other Simians did not even question the request; they carried on up the hill as if there was no interruption. Fionn went to leave too but stopped in his tracks when he heard the squeak of the gate opening behind him.

What's he doing? The gate closed with a gentle clink, followed by the sound of Cormac's footsteps trekking through the rubble beyond.

When the footsteps disappeared, Fionn turned around. Cormac was nowhere to be seen.

Maybe I can catch him alone. Fionn took a step toward the gates. *I never told him I was sorry for what happened back then, out on the cliffs.*

Tell him I'm sorry, too, said Sir Bearach. *It was my idea to lead the troll out into the morning sun.*

Fionn pulled open the gate. Its rusted hinges protested, but his oversized arm proved more than strong enough to overcome them. He stepped inside and took a short, winding path toward the back of the chapel.

The yard beyond was full of upturned dirt and open holes, like a field ploughed by a drunkard. Fionn stepped over a mound but lost his balance as the dirt fell away under his weight. He caught himself as he stumbled, propping himself up against a slab-shaped stone structure behind him. As he regained his composure, he turned to examine the granite monument that had prevented him from falling.

It's a tombstone, realised Fionn with horror. *This...was a graveyard.*

Indeed, the clearing was riddled with mounds of dirt and deep holes, and here and there stood stone statues, some weather-worn and deteriorating, marking what once were graves.

Fionn promptly recovered and trudged through the cemetery. Every so often, he caught a glimpse of a coffin sitting at the bottom of an opened grave, but no corpses remained inside.

A sound of muffled sobbing became apparent as Fionn ventured deeper. Eventually, it was clear where the sounds were coming from, and Fionn took a stone pathway uphill, winding back around toward the High Road.

The full view of Roseán's devastation spanned out from the crest of the hill. The town's square had faced the brunt of the disaster, it seemed, with smouldering piles replacing what were once tall and proud commercial buildings. Although the residential outskirts appeared intact, a vast clearing in the dense forests out to the east indicated the direction the horde had travelled. The sun was high in the clear sky, but its light did nothing to illuminate the dead landscape.

Just off the path, Cormac sat kneeling before a grave, his hands buried in his hands. He seemed to be muttering something between his sobs, but Fionn couldn't catch the words.

Perhaps I should let him be alone, thought Fionn, squinting his eyes to read the text on the tombstone. It was only now that Fionn realised what was different about this grave.

It was undisturbed. Although the flowers were dying, they were still arranged in an intricate pattern across the base of the tombstone. White pebbles lined the grave's perimeter, dappled with blues and blacks.

"Cormac," said Fionn, feeling he should make his presence known, at least. "I just wanted to tell you that—"

"I'm sorry," said Cormac, seeming to finish Fionn's thought. "Gods above and below, I'm sorry!"

Fionn took a step closer to the grave. Its inscription read, *'Aoife Ní Branna. Beloved mother, wife, and friend. She lived and died in the Light of The Lady, AC 360–403, and shall now live forever in the plains of Tierna Meall.'*

"I'm sorry," repeated Cormac. "I was never worthy to be in your life, let alone to be your husband."

"Don't say that," said Fionn, though he regretted his choice of words. He took a second to reconsider. "I mean, it's like you said before. It wasn't your fault you weren't there that morning. You can't blame yourself, Cormac."

"It wasn't my decision to flee," said Cormac. "But it was my decision to not come back. I said before that I stayed away from Roseán because I was afraid. But that isn't true. I never came back, because..."

He threw his head back and howled even louder than before, like an animal maddened by pain.

"Because I was ashamed. Ashamed of how I treated them. Gods, I did things no man should even consider. I hurt them in ways no woman should ever know."

He raised a hand and placed it against the granite. "I stayed away for Morry's sake. She was better off without me." He hung his head down. "I knew. I knew the whole time that she wasn't my daughter. Gods, sometimes it seemed like Morry was the only person in the whole village who didn't know who her real father was."

"Cormac..." whispered Fionn, stepping forward. Although he barely knew the man, Fionn found it hard to fight back his own tears.

"The truth drove me to the drink," said Cormac. "Every day I was forced to live with it, and I coped with it the only way I knew how. I lashed out against them. I lashed out against the woman I swore to love, because I knew she never loved me."

The two stood there in silence. Cormac's rambling made little sense to Fionn, but the pain he understood all too well.

"My mother died when I was born," Fionn whispered. "She was living out in the streets of Dromán, and she came to the brothers of the Academy, deep in labour. They couldn't save her, and barely saved me. The brothers took me in, but out of duty, not love. That's only family I have ever known."

Cormac didn't respond, though Fionn didn't necessarily expect him to.

Gods, why did I even tell him that? Was my past supposed to make his seem better?

"Your mother loved you," said Cormac, eventually. "Even though she never met you. All mothers love their children, even when they're still in the womb."

A lump formed in Fionn's throat. "Maybe you're right," he managed to say, masking how close he was to tears. "If the gods are good, you're right."

He placed his oversized hand on Cormac's trembling shoulder.

"Come on. The others are probably waiting on us."

***

Fionn immediately recognised Yarlaith's house, sitting on a ledge overlooking the town square. Of all the ruins of Roseán, this one was the most intact. Indeed, on closer inspection, the house seemed to be completely untouched by the doom that had taken the town.

Fionn and Cormac walked through the house's tiny garden toward an open wooden door. As they stepped into the abode, the ruin of its interior was immediately apparent.

What was once a quaint little house had been ransacked from floor to ceiling. Furniture was overturned, paintings and pictures torn from the walls. Fionn stepped through the familiar hallway, back toward the white mage's clinic.

Gods, has it been only a year? he thought. Sometimes, it seemed like a lifetime ago when Yarlaith had sewn Sir Bearach's arm to Fionn's shoulder.

Feels like less to me, remarked Sir Bearach. *I still find myself forgetting that I no longer inhabit my own body.*

Whether the remark was meant in sarcasm or not, Fionn couldn't tell. Before he had a chance to consider it further, Garth stepped into the hallway.

"The dead haven't been through here," he said. He gestured into the clinic. "This mess was caused by the living."

The room beyond was in a worse state than the rest of the house. The screens and curtains that once gave the clinic's patients privacy lay torn and broken. The beds were turned over, with crumpled bedsheets strewn out across the floor.

Fionn stepped forward carefully, for the shelves that once housed Yarlaith's alchemical equipment were cleared, their contents and glass scattered to the ground.

"This was an act of passion," said Garth, speaking with the air of an expert. "Someone, or some people, did this in a fit of rage."

"A mob?" ventured Fionn. It was common knowledge that the country folk were fiercely loyal to the Church's teachings. If anyone had learned that Yarlaith was a Necromancer, then...

"Sir," called a voice. One of the other Simian scouts stepped out from a small study on the far end of the clinic. "I think you should come look at this."

Garth strode across the ruined clinic, Fionn and Cormac following cautiously behind him. As he approached the door to the study, Fionn felt a frigid draft sweep across the back of his neck.

"There's a trapdoor on the floor," reported the Simian scout. "Should we investigate further?"

"Yes," said Garth. "I'll go first. Ready your arms, lads. I don't know what we'll find down there."

The Simian scout crouched down to the ground and busied his fingers with the wooden floorboard. Fionn had no idea what he was doing, until a trapdoor seemed to materialise before them. The scout lifted the door deftly and barely flinched as a breeze washed through the study.

How on earth did he spot that? But Fionn didn't let himself consider the question. There, in the centre of the study, stood a yawning hole in the ground, with a rope ladder hanging down like a slender tongue.

Garth promptly swung his legs down into the hole and climbed down the ladder. The scout followed him, leaving Fionn and Cormac above.

"You stay here," said Fionn. "If the others come looking, tell them where we are."

"Sure," said Cormac with pride, as if he had been given the most important job of them all. In truth, Fionn was painfully aware that the man's mind was still slightly unhinged, considering all that had happened to him before.

And besides, thought Fionn, letting his feet dangle down, *I have my magic to keep me safe.*

He descended the ladder carefully, looking down over his shoulder between every other step. Squinting through the darkness, the ground was visible some thirty feet below.

A strange place to build a house. Assuming the tunnel was here first.

A strong, pungent odour struck Fionn as he turned around. He found himself standing on a cavern floor, with a wide tunnel spanning outwards, and curving off to the left. The faint sound of Simian voices echoed around the corner, and Fionn followed, trying hard to place the scent.

Like meat, he thought, the stench growing thicker with each step. *Bad meat, spoiled and warm.*

As he took the corner, the tunnel widened into a large chamber, with massive stalactites dripping from the ceiling. But his eyes were drawn from those to other hanging objects, lining the cavern walls.

Severed limbs of various shapes and sizes filled the wall. Some had clumps of blood dripping down onto a red-speckled floor. Beneath the limbs sat a wooden table, with an assortment of tools and sharp objects arranged in a tidy, clinical manner.

"What is this place?" asked Fionn. He walked through the laboratory, past rows of shelved potions and alchemical ingredients. Garth stood on the far end of the chamber, examining another workstation, this one with glass bottles and vials arranged across its surface. The chamber was lit by two tall torches in the centre of the room. They appeared to have been ignited by the Simian scout, who was tending to a third torch nearby.

"Fionn," said Garth, beckoning the mage over with a nod. "Tell me, do you recognise any of these oils?"

Fionn strode over. Of course, he recognised the name on the oil's label immediately. The brothers of the Academy used something similar to preserve their dead for burial. When he relayed this to Garth, the Simian snorted rudely.

"Smells like it hasn't been working. Take a look around and tell us if you find anything useful."

"Sure," said Fionn. He wasn't quite sure where to begin.

Another table stood on the far end of the laboratory, with stacks of papers and notes piled on top of one another. Fionn went to it and found a thick, leather-bound journal lying upon it. The page presented was written in an elegant script, though erratic and inconsistent, as if made by a hasty hand. Fionn began reading it frantically, his sense of dread growing with each line.

My previous fears have manifested in my work tonight. I feel as if the truth was just beyond reach all along, and it would have only taken a single rational look at the whole picture to realise it. I was reluctant to do anything else but push forward, and now I've paid dearly for it. Gods, even as I write this alone in my study, I can still hear her voice.

Necromancy is the manipulation of the soul. The flesh is never altered. The soul of the dead is bound to the user in the process, but control over the corpse is only a side effect. Because my first test subject was also a mage, and still breathing, he regained full control over the severed arm. This explains why he heard the voices even after he recovered from the operation.

I'm dismantling the workshop as soon as dawn breaks. The Church has outlawed this School of Magic not because of its desecration of the dead, but because of what manipulating one's soul can lead to. I will not elaborate here, however, lest this document falls into the wrong hands. I'll take the truth to the grave if I must.

Gods, forgive me. Please.

"No," muttered Fionn, scanning back through the passage after he had finished. His heart pounded with fear. *...First test subject was a mage.*

It's us, whispered Sir Bearach. *The bastard operated on us...here.*

Fionn flexed the fingers on his oversized hand. This was where it all began. Fionn's recovery, the molestation of Sir Bearach's soul, the horde of the undead...

Fionn reached for another pile of notes. He spotted the date on one, marked as falling under the Moon of Macha from the previous year. He flicked through the pages, past diagrams of severed cadavers and lists of ingredients. Wild scribblings appeared here and there in the margin, ranging from idle musings to elaborate conjectures on the nature of healing magic itself.

As he browsed, a glint of metal appeared in the corner of Fionn's vision. Beneath another pile of papers, there sat a strange brass object, about the size of a dagger. Fionn reached for it, gently pulling it out from under the notes. The brass was shaped into a pipe, of sorts, curving into a wooden handle with beautiful, intricate carvings. On the inside of the curve was a tiny trigger, like that of a crossbow. He held the object up before his face, examining each inch in minute detail. The craftsmanship was impeccable, with an elaborate mechanism of tiny switches and bolts at the centre of the device. Though he had no idea what it could be for,

Fionn found himself fascinated by its design. He held the opening of the brass end to his eye, peering down into the object's body, hoping to see more of its internal mechanism.

"No! Put it down!"

Before Fionn had a chance to turn, Garth grabbed him by the shoulder with one hand, and deftly discarded the object with the other.

"What is it?" asked Fionn, his eyes never leaving the contraption.

Garth hesitated. His lips pursed into a thin line, as if deep in thought.

"It once belonged to me," he said eventually. "I believe I met this Morrígan girl before."

"You did?" asked Fionn. The other Simian scout appeared by Garth's side. Although he appeared to have been drawn by the commotion, he didn't seem interested in the strange, brass object.

"Fionn, the Silverback has been hiding a great deal from you," said Garth. "Keeping the truth from outsiders has been our priority since he took his seat on the Triad, but I believe our priorities have changed, now that the kingdom is being chewed up by the dead."

Garth picked up the object, wrapping his fingers across the wooden portion. He seemed incredibly comfortable holding it, as if it was an extension of his own hand.

"We are not scouts," he began, "but spies. My skirmishes across the Clifflands did include cartography, but also involved gathering information on the Crown's battlemages, stationed in settlements like this. I got too close to the battalion here, however, and they captured me. While their prisoner, I was visited by a girl. She distracted the guards and set me free. I left this weapon with her so it could never be linked to me."

"Why did she free you?" Fionn asked with a frown.

Garth sighed. "Not a day goes by when I don't ask myself the same. She seemed like an innocent girl at first. Doe-eyed and curious. She didn't seem afraid to see me, bruised and chained. But... something changed. One moment she was like a kitten, then the next, there was fire in her eyes. I don't know if it was something she saw, or something I said, or—"

Garth's jaw fell open at that thought. "That's it," he whispered. He turned to look around at the room. "These caves...it all makes sense now."

"What?" asked Fionn. "How does—"

A guttural roar of fear echoed through the chamber. The other Simian did nothing to hide the sudden terror on his face as Garth and Fionn turned to face him. With eyes wide and white he raised a trembling hand and pointed at the far end of the laboratory.

There, stood a hunched figure, clad in grey robes. It shuffled slowly through the chamber, dragging one foot behind the other. Its head hung crookedly on a slouched neck, swinging this way and that with each step.

Garth responded immediately. He reached into his shoulder-pack and pulled out a brass item, identical to the one Fionn had just found. Except Garth wielded this one like a weapon, aiming the open barrel towards the stranger.

"Stop right there," he said, the strength of command in his voice. "Not one more step."

But the figure did not slow. As it came closer, the shadow over his face receded to reveal an aged man. The bottom of his robes was scorched and blackened. Two arms swung back and forth as he walked, but one looked far thinner than the other. Only when the figure reached the light of the torches, did Fionn realise that the arm was stripped of flesh, and consisted of burnt and broken bones.

In the following instant, Fionn recognised the face of the old healer who had saved him.

"Yarlaith?" he asked, but the old man did not respond.

"I won't warn you again," said Garth. "One more step, and I'll shoot."

Yarlaith shuffled forward again. With a deafening *bang*, smoke erupted from the weapon and something seemed to whiz through the air, too fast to be seen. Whatever it was, it struck Yarlaith right in the forehead, and the old man finally stood still.

"Is he dead?" asked the other Simian, after a moment. When the smoke cleared, it was evident that the man was still standing, yet he remained motionless.

Without a sound, Yarlaith sprang into a sprint. He bounded towards the Simians, both hands stretched outwards. Fionn flinched back with fright, until he saw the blank, dead gaze of the old man's eyes. Before another second could pass, Fionn flicked his flint rings together, grabbing hold of the spark as it appeared. He flared the fire in his soul, and engulfed the old man in flames, mere yards in front of where the Simians were standing.

The figure collapsed to the floor; his arms and legs folded over one another in a manner no living person's would. Garth gasped with fright, and the other Simian held a hand up to his face.

"He was already dead," muttered Fionn. The Simians didn't respond. They watched on as the old man burned in silence. Those lifeless eyes stared back at Fionn, unblinking behind the flames.

Fionn gestured back to the table. "Gather up the notes. There might be more, so we better leave at once."

"Of course," said Garth, tearing his gaze away from the burning corpse. "Is there anything else you think we should do?"

"Yes. You can start by telling me more about what the Silverback has been keeping from me."

CHAPTER 22:
THE COUNCIL OF THE
TRIAD

The Clifflands, Point Grey, Rosca Umhir, Ard Sidhe...all have fallen to the undead horde. Yet, I am confident that the mages of Dromán can fight back this threat. Why, if the mages are overwhelmed, and if they too join the dead, then the final light of our hope shall be snuffed out. They cannot fail. Gods above and below, don't let them fail.

Diary entry found in the remains of the Seachtú of Dromán.

***

Farris stood in the Hall of the Triad, shifting his weight from one foot to another as he waited. In these meetings, he'd typically have a seat to himself for the proceedings, but today, the chairs were reserved for those returned from the field, gathering information on this undead horde.

Gathering paper, too, apparently, thought Farris, noticing the huge stack of notes piled up before Fionn the Red. The young mage didn't seem at all perturbed by his expedition to the old village of Roseán, though Farris doubted they didn't at least run into *some* trouble down there.

Some of the Triad's scouts sat at the other end of the table. These had travelled further south, by the Seachtú of Ardh Sidhe and Dromán. Only half had returned, and those that did looked far more dishevelled than when they left. One sat with his face buried in his hands, shaking ever so slightly beneath his armour.

"If we may proceed," said the Silverback. He rested a thickly muscled forearm across the table, leaning over toward Fionn and his stacks of papers. "Firemaster Fionn. Tell us, what became of Roseán?"

"It's destroyed, sir. Ruined beyond repair. There was little we could learn of the horde from the state of the village itself, only that the undead are a force unlike anything we've witnessed before."

The mage gestured to the pages and books piled before him with his oversized arm.

"These are the notes and reports of Yarlaith the White," said Fionn. "He was the local healer in Roseán, and brother to Cormac." The other Human nodded solemnly at the mention of his name. "These notes indicate that Yarlaith was experimenting with the Nature of Death, endeavouring to bring the dead back to life."

"Necromancy," interjected Ruairí. "It wouldn't be the first time that magic has been turned to the dark arts."

"But this is the first time anyone has succeeded," said Fionn.

A panicked mutter ran through the hall at these words but was silenced at the raised hand of the Silverback.

"So," said Argyll. "Was it this Yarlaith the White who set the dead loose on Roseán?"

"I don't believe so," said Fionn. "It's not quite clear what transpired, but on the night he succeeded, Yarlaith reported that he discovered what he called 'the true Nature of Necromancy'. It was this revelation that caused him to halt his research. His writing indicates that his niece, Morrígan, would not take this news lightly, but that's all we know."

"And now she is the one leading the horde," said Garth. "We found Yarlaith's...corpse in Roseán."

The slight hesitation made Farris narrow his eyes.

He's hiding something.

Garth cleared his throat. "We hypothesise that Morrígan killed her uncle on hearing that he would not be continuing his research and finished the work herself. This would put her at the head of the horde, while leaving Yarlaith's corpse in the caves."

The Silverback turned to Fionn. "As a master or arcane knowledge," he said, "what do you suppose he meant by 'the true Nature of Necromancy'?"

Fionn's gaze fell to the floor. "I suppose nothing. I know for sure what he meant."

He stood from the seat, holding out his oversized arm to the others. "This is the arm of the late Sir Bearach Carríga of Rosca Umhir. Last year, after traversing through the Glenn, we were pursued and attacked by a troll. I lost my arm in the struggle, but Sir Bearach lost his life. Yarlaith of Roseán was able to remove this arm from Bearach's corpse and attach it to my body."

This was met with audible gasps scattered across the room. Farris shuddered at the thought.

Of course. The troll tore his arm off. Even the sound of the tearing flesh was fresh in Farris's ears.

"But there is more," continued Fionn. "Ever since that day, my magic has been stronger than it has ever been before. For the soul of one dead man has been bound to my own, and the soul is the fuel for magic. I have since learned that the Church has outlawed all practise of magic on corpses for this very reason. If one mage discovered how to harness the soul of another, for their own power, the outcome would be devastating."

A torrent of whispers ripped through the room. Farris recalled his experiences with Sir Bearach. Sure, he had been a typical high-born Human, condescending to the point of arrogance, but when the time called for it, he fought with courage and put the well-being of others before himself. To imagine his soul being used now as fuel for a mage was...unsettling.

"I believe your tale," came a voice from across the room. It belonged to a Simian, leaner than most who accompanied him. His cheeks were gaunt, and his complexion pale beneath lightly coloured hair. When he spoke, his voice quivered through the words, but he did not seem afraid. From the stern stare of his eyes to the blank expression on his face, it seemed like nothing could rattle this scout.

"I believe you," he repeated. "As I have seen her power first-hand." He turned to the Silverback. "But I must report that Dromán has fallen."

"No!"

Cries of fear and outrage met this revelation, but none seemed as disturbed by the news as Fionn was. The young mage collapsed back into his chair and buried his face in his hands.

The Academy of Dromán was his home...

"This news was not expected," said the Silverback, showing no remorse as usual. "How could so many mages fail to fight the dead?"

"It is true," said the Simian scout. "I saw the battle from afar with my own eyes. The horde poured through the woods, rolling towards the city gates like an unstoppable tide. The Pyromancers on the walls lit up the sky with their fire, and for a moment I believed this alone would be enough to throw the dead back into their graves, but it was not. As the flames fell, something else seemed to take hold of them. The next thing I knew, they were directed back at the city walls, and the Pyromancers burned to their own fire."

"So, there were red mages amongst the horde?" asked Garth.

"No," said the scout. "The flames of a hundred Pyromancers were being manipulated by one individual at the head of the horde. This girl. Morrígan."

Gasps rippled through the room in response. Argyll turned towards Fionn. "One mage fighting back the flames against a hundred Pyromancers. Is this possible?"

Fionn nodded slowly. "If she wields the souls of each corpse in the horde as if they were her own, then yes."

Silence fell on the hall.

"That is not all," continued the scout. "The walls of Dromán were torn from their foundations before the horde arrived. I watched the Academy building itself crumble before a single invader was inside the city. It seems she has full command over more than one School of Magic."

"And she's even more powerful now," muttered Fionn through his fingers. "If Dromán has truly fallen, then over a thousand mages have joined the horde too. Their souls have joined hers."

Nicole sat with her hand over her mouth. She didn't seem to have moved at all throughout the meeting. Ruairí's head nodded left and right, as if he was trying to convince himself that this wasn't happening. His lips were moving, too, perhaps in silent prayer.

Pray to your god. But I doubt it'll help. How could a god compete with power like this?

"Have you any more news, scout?" asked the Silverback. "If there are more ill tidings, don't leave us in the dark."

"No more than this," said the scout. "The horde is heading south towards the capital. It should have reached the king's walls by now."

"Well, let them be King Diarmuid's problem then," said Garth. "The further south they march, the safer we are up here."

"Aye, aye," called a few scattered voices.

"Wait," said Fionn. "If she already commands the power of every mage in Dromán, what could she possibly hope to gain by laying siege to Cruachan?"

None answered straight away. Farris could have bet that it was because none there cared why. Still, it was a question worth considering.

What power lies in Cruachan that could not be found in Dromán...

"No!"

Everyone turned to face Farris for the first time during this meeting.

"Is something the matter?" asked the Silverback.

"I know what she wants in Cruachan," said Farris. "The king's soul. He's one of the Trinity, after all. And that, along with Divine Penetrance means—"

"By Sin's stones, Farris," swore the Silverback. "Do you still wish to belabour this point, after all this time?"

"You don't believe me?" asked Farris. He tried hard to keep his voice from raising. "Skies above, Argyll, I've spent three years living by King Diarmuid's side. I've collected enough proof that Divine Penetrance exists to convince even the most hardened sceptics."

"Divine Penetrance is a myth," said Ruairí. "Even the Church says that the king does not possess immortality, and neither did those that came before him. Even the notion that the power of Seletoth can be passed on is—"

"Leave your faith out of this," spat Farris, pointing a trembling finger toward the Human. "Of the nineteen kings that came before Diarmuid, none died before birthing a son. I never did believe in the gods, or Seletoth, or any of that shit, but there's so much evidence! The capital's archives are full of accounts of young princes being mortally injured, only to recover miraculously afterwards. If Divine

Penetrance manifests in the soul of King Diarmuid, and Morrigan plans to take hold if it, then—"

"Then it will still not be our problem!" The Silverback stood now, trembling with rage. "If the capital falls, it falls. We will tend to our own needs as they arise. And that's all that will be spoken on the matter. Now, if there is nothing more to be said about the horde itself, you may leave."

Everyone tried to go at once, for it seemed that none wanted to be in the Silverback's presence longer than needed. The scouts left first, in unison. Ruairí strolled out after them, followed by Garth and some other members of the Sons of Seletoth that Farris didn't recognise. Then went Fionn, not acknowledging anyone else as he departed.

"Poor kid," said Nicole's voice behind Farris. "If he thought he was alone before, imagine how he feels now."

"Sure," said Farris. "But it won't be long until our home here is destroyed, too."

"Maybe. But as sure as Sin, we'll still fight."

Farris turned abruptly to face her. "You believe me. About Divine Penetrance, right?"

She hesitated for a second, but that was enough.

"I know you wouldn't lie to me," he said. "If you didn't believe me, you wouldn't think twice about being blunt."

"It doesn't matter what I think. Even if you're right about the king's power, what difference would it make?"

"If I'm right, then we can't let Morrígan take his soul and claim Divine Penetrance for herself. We need to travel south, and meet the horde head-on and—"

"Listen to yourself, Farris," said Nicole. Although their last meeting had ended with heated words, her tone now was soothing, like a mother's. "If I told you I believed you, it would mean nothing. The dead have already reached the capital. For all we know, King Diarmuid is already dead."

"Just tell me that you believe me, then," said Farris. "Everyone else in this city thinks that I softened up after working with the Crown. But there's proof, Nicole. Tell me that you see that!"

Nicole raised a hand to touch his face. "Truth be told, as crazy as it sounds, I do believe you."

"Then you agree that the king needs to be saved, if we're ever to have a hope in this war?"

"Well, yes," said Nicole, returning her hand to her side. "But like I said, it wouldn't make a difference."

Farris let his lips slide into a smile. "What if there was a way?" he said. "What if we could save him. Would you agree to help?"

"What? No. Farris, I'm not going to agree to something I know nothing about."

"What about *Skirmisher?*" asked Farris, excitement rising in his voice. "You said that it can make the journey across

Alabach in a day, and I know exactly where we could find the king."

"Farris! Are you out of your mind? We can't just swoop down into the horde and take the king to safety."

"But you just admitted how important this is. You said that if the king dies, then we'll have no hope fighting back the dead."

"Well, yes, but—"

"So, we should do everything in our power to prevent that from happening. Even if it costs us our lives."

Nicole paused again. Farris was sure she saw his reasoning but was searching for another excuse. Sure enough, it came to her.

"The Silverback would kill us if he found out. They'd hang us for treason, and—"

"Treason? We'd save the king, and they'd hang us for treason? That would be the day!"

"You know what I mean, Farris. They wouldn't be happy with us."

Farris smiled. "If you prefer, you can tell them I forced you to."

Nicole threw a quick glance around the empty Hall, assuring herself that there was indeed nobody else there. Then she smiled.

"Farris Silvertongue, as sure as Sin, you've earned that name, but this'll be the last time you draw blood from this stone. Grab what you need and meet me in the Steamworks in an hour."

CHAPTER 23:
RETURN TO THE GREY KEEP

"No, please! I don't want to die alone... She told me that I'd die alone."

King Diarmuid, Third of his Name, Nineteenth Incarnate, AC404.

***

"Ardh Sidhe," muttered Nicole, peering over the edge of *Skirmisher* as they flew over the ruined city. The northernmost side of its walls bore a massive puncture, and the buildings within were reduced to great piles of grey rubble.

"Skies above," said Farris. "Earl Broin was a renowned general and strategist, but what use is a lifetime of experience against an enemy as unnatural as this?"

They had been flying over the desolate wastes of Alabach for four hours now, but of all the ruins they passed, none hit Farris harder than the sight of what was once Ardh Sidhe.

"What would have been his final thoughts," asked Nicole, "as he saw the horde tear down his walls and spill into his city?"

Same thoughts he'd have if your Reapers did the same.

Farris shook his head. It was an unfair thought, one that didn't consider the regret Nicole had felt upon seeing the power of her own creation. But things were different now. Argyll's vision of marching south seemed a foreign concept when a new, more powerful enemy threatened to march north first.

So he held his tongue, and the two sat in silence as *Skirmisher's* engine whirred softly behind them.

The craft itself was built for function, rather than form. This was the first thing that had occurred to Farris when he had taken his seat behind Nicole. The ship's body was as long as Blind Jacob's skiff, but Farris remembered the old smuggler's vessel being far more comfortable than this. He was fastened tightly in his seat, with leather straps binding his waist to the chair and his feet to the floor. There was one more empty seat behind Farris, and very little room for much else.

It won't be a large rescue operation then. He couldn't help but think of those he had known back in the capital.

Derelith from the pawnbrokers, Ardal from the *Lamb's Head*...he even found himself smiling at the memory of that barmaid from the *Stained Glass* with whom he shared his penultimate night in Cruachan. He struggled to remember her name, though. Jana? Jade? The smile on his face quickly vanished when he considered that they were all probably dead already. Or dying.

Or undead...

After some time, *Skirmisher* took them over the valley of the Tulcha, the river of the same name meandering through the empty hills. The last time he had travelled this way, Farris had seen a plethora of life on the banks of that river, but now there was nothing. The more he thought about it, the more he realised that they had not seen a single animal since leaving Penance.

The sun was sinking over the Endless Sea to the west, illuminating the whole ocean with hues of amber and gold.

"Do you really believe the sea has no end?" asked Farris, hoping to take his mind of the dead landscape below.

"I believe in nothing until I see it," replied Nicole. "I did know an astronomer once who claimed there was only one ocean...and sailing west across the Endless Sea would bring you to the lands of the east."

"And those lands," Farris ventured. "I take it that you don't *believe* they are as inhabitable as the Church claims?"

Nicole snorted. "Whatever you do, don't mention the Grey Plague near Argyll. He could bore a hole in a stone with the stories he'd tell about that."

"Can you give me a summary, at least?"

She sighed. "Four hundred-odd years ago, Móráin the First led the Humans to conquer Alabach. This is common knowledge, of course, as is the reason why Móráin and his people were fleeing the lands of the east."

"The Grey Plague consumed them," muttered Farris. The memory of his final night in Cruachan suddenly surfaced. "I met a Simian once who claimed the Humans themselves brought the plague. He said something about more native Simians dying from illness than from the swords and spells of Man."

"Close enough to what Argyll believes," said Nicole. "but he goes one step further. He reckons there never was a plague. Móráin's people wanted to settle on our land, so they invented a story about a Grey Plague devouring their homes to give them a reason to come to our shores."

"And what do you think?" asked Farris.

"He has a point. Sin's stones! Even the Arch-Canon himself couldn't tell you what exactly the Grey Plague was. Tell me, why would such an important detail of such an important story be forgotten after a mere four centuries? The historians of the Basilica can tell you the colour of Móráin's smallclothes if you're enquiring. If such a plague did exist, surely those folks would know all about it."

"Maybe they do know," said Farris. "Maybe they're just keeping some truths to themselves."

"Aye. Not some truths, but *the Truth*. That's what the Sons believe, but that's an entirely different theory. If we make it back to Penance, I'll be sure to tell Argyll and Ruairí you want to know more."

***

Night had fallen by the time the fires of Cruachan could be seen, and it wasn't long after that when Farris could smell the acrid scent of the charring corpses.

The North Wall of Cruachan was ablaze, marked by a thick pillar of smoke spiralling into heavens. Here and there, flashes of fire illuminated the grounds surrounding the city. At first, Farris could have sworn that the ground itself was moving; writhing and pulsating like it were alive. Another flash came, and with blinding horror, Farris realised that the ground was far from alive. He was gazing at the horde itself.

"Gods," cried Nicole. The shock in her voice was evident, and it seemed she didn't notice her peculiar choice of expletive. Farris didn't comment. The more he looked down upon the teeming undead, the more the hope drained from his spirit.

"They...they just keep going," whispered Nicole, gesturing out to the east. It was true. As far as their eyes could see, the land was black with the dead.

Farris had never seen an army of any scale before, but he supposed he knew what one should look like. Nothing about the horde resembled what he imagined an army to be. None held torches, for he supposed they no longer had use for light, even as they marched through the darkness. There was no order to their movement, just wave upon wave of bodies, hurdling towards the last shore of mankind. Cruachan. The Grey Keep. The seat of King Diarmuid the Third.

"Focus, Farris," said Nicole. "We only have one shot at this, and I doubt that'll even be enough."

Farris tore his eyes away from the terror below and turned his attention to the task at hand. They were over the city walls now, and the cries of the battle beneath them were clearly audible. Plumes of smoke from burning buildings rose up to meet *Skirmisher*, but the little vessel ploughed through them as if they were mere clouds.

"That used to be Saint Lorcan's Cathedral," said Farris, gesturing to a collapsed and ruined structure to the south of the city. Like much else around them, it too was burning.

"Don't look down," said Nicole. "If we fail tonight, Penance might take this city's place. Keep your eyes on the Grey Keep."

"The Grey Keep," Farris reminded himself, squinting through the smoke. The great stone structure was still standing on the southern side of the city, but after seeing the extent of the horde, Farris supposed it wouldn't be standing for much longer.

"Do you think she's here?" asked Farris. "The girl. Morrígan. Do you think—"

"All that concerns you," cut in Nicole, "is whether or not Diarmuid is where you claim he'll be."

"He'll be there," said Farris. "His private quarters are just about the safest part of the keep. Any other king would have fled the city, but not Diarmuid. He has always blurred the line between stubbornness and strength."

Skirmisher glided over the Grey Keep. Despite his best efforts, Farris glanced down at the castle grounds, only for an instant. There, he saw men dressed in the reds and blacks of the city-guard struggling against the undead. The living corpses crawled across the moat, not slowing despite a heavy shower of arrows raining upon them. Two battlemages in green added salvos of rocks to the arrows, but these seemed to help even less. Beyond the moat, a group of four guards stood with their backs to one another, surrounded by a dozen skeletal soldiers. One wight lunged in first, only to be cut down by a living soldier...but the poor souls were unable to fight off the other skeletons that followed. Once the struggle was over, a moment of peace fell over the fallen guards before their fresh corpses spasmed abruptly. Farris looked away before they started to rise.

"This is as close as I can go," said Nicole. "Are you ready?"

"Yes."

"Are you sure? There's a lot riding on this, Farris. Clear your mind of all distractions and fears. All worries and—"

"Just give me the damn rope."

Nicole reached under the controls of the ship and fished out a thick loop of hempen rope. She passed it back to Farris without turning back to look.

"It's already bound to the stern," she said. "It'll be strong enough and long enough, provided you don't go wandering around the keep. Or gods forbid, attempt to fight the dead themselves."

"Again, with the gods," Farris said. "Has the sight of the horde turned you toward faith?"

"If we live to see the end of this, I'll take the damn cloth itself."

Farris went to work tying the rope around his body. Twice around the waist, around each leg at the waist, over his shoulders, criss-crossing at his back, then around his waist twice more. He leaned out from his seat and scanned the stained-glass windows of the Grey Keep.

"There," said Farris, pointing even though Nicole couldn't see him. "The window twice as large as the rest, in the centre.

Skirmisher glided closer to the keep. With each inch it gained, Farris's heart pounded and resounded throughout his body.

Gods, we're really going through with this. He cringed. *I may share her swears, but I'll never take the cloth. Even if the horde marches into the sea tomorrow.*

Now they hovered twenty feet over the roof of the Grey Keep, the window of the Royal Quarters immediately below.

"Whenever you're ready," said Nicole.

"Nobody could be ready for this. But I won't let that stop me."

With that, he leapt out over the side of the ship.

Everything seemed to slow as he fell. Each roar and shout from the battle below felt clear in his ear, as if he was standing in the fray itself. He fell face down, allowing himself a full view of the burning courtyards below. More undead were crossing the moat, and two had even started scaling the castle walls.

They might already be inside. He felt no fear, though. Weightless in mid-air, it seemed as if nothing could hurt him. As if there was nothing in the world even capable of hurting anyone. He felt at peace.

Then he ran out of slack. With a sickening crack, the rope went taut, jerking Farris's body and shaking every positive feeling from his mind. Jarred by the sudden change in velocity, Farris lost his sense of balance. He no longer knew which way was up, or which direction the castle walls were, but he knew he was spinning. And swinging.

As he soared through the rope's arc, Farris braced himself for an inevitable crash into the solid stone wall. Instead, the crash came with the sound of shattering glass. The shards cut against his hands and face, but Farris gritted his teeth and ignored the pain. Only when he felt the broken glass beneath his knees did he realise he had found solid ground. The next thing he noticed was the stench of thainol, thick in the air like mist.

"F-Farris?" called a stammering voice. "No...no, She said you were dead."

Farris looked up to see King Diarmuid Móráin, kneeling on the floor. His face was blemished, and his eyes were moist with tears. Next to him stood Padraig Tuathil, captain of the City Guard, with his sword drawn.

Farris sniffed the air again. "Have you been drinking?" He caught sight of a bottle of thainol, half empty, set upon a table with two cups.

Farris fought back a smile. *No...it couldn't be the same....*

"What are you doing here?" called Padraig. "The dead are inside the keep. There's no way out but through the horde!"

"I've come for the king," said Farris. He strode over to Diarmuid, letting the rope run along the ground behind him as he did. Farris held an outstretched hand. "There's a ship waiting for you. I'm taking you to Penance."

"No!" cried the king. "She showed me the truth! I am not to survive this night, and you should not be alive. Gods, at the time the signs were so unclear, but as each came to be, our fate became evident."

What is he rambling about? "We can discuss these matters further on the journey home."

Farris reached out an embraced the king tightly in both arms. To his surprise, the king did not object, but actually buried his face in Farris's shoulder, sobbing like a child.

Skies above, he thinks I'm consoling him.

"Unhand him at once," yelled Padraig, pointing his sword at Farris. "You turned your cloak on your brothers of the Guild before. How am I to believe you haven't turned it back on us?"

"Have some faith," said Farris, calmly reaching for the rope behind him. He gave it three sharp tugs in succession. "If you believe your own convictions, strike me down. I stand before you unarmed."

Padraig smiled. "Not a single day passes when I don't dream of this moment." He tightened his grip on his sword.

Before the captain could move, the rope suddenly went taut again, pulling Farris and the king back across the room. Farris held onto Diarmuid's body even more tightly, and the two went soaring out the window of the keep. Padraig roared and cursed as they went, but Farris didn't turn back to look.

"Hold on tight," said Farris, as the two swung through the air. "We'll be away soon."

Diarmuid didn't respond. Whether from the shock that they were both now flying over a burning city, or from whatever madness had manifested in his mind tonight, Farris couldn't tell.

"There's a clearing to the south," called Nicole from above, her voice barely audible. Still, the air of authority in her voice earlier had left. If the situation had been any different, Farris would have sworn that she was actually happy.

However, the sound of Padraig's roared objections still echoed in the back of Farris's mind. It was a strange feeling, knowing you left a man to his fate. To be consumed by the horde. Farris shook his head, but the sound of Padraig roaring and shouting didn't leave his ears.

"Let me down!" the king screamed, each syllable burning with rage. "Stop this madness! Stop it!"

Farris glanced down at the horde below. The mass of bodies wasn't what caught his eye this time. Some two dozen yards of rope had been left after Farris had made his knots, and it hung down beneath him as they glided over the city. But at the end of that slack was Padraig Tuathil himself, clutching to the rope with both hands, aware that his life depended on the tightness of his grip.

"Let go!" roared Farris. "Let go or you'll kill the four of us!"

"Gods take you," spat the captain. "If the world was still the way it was, I'd see you hanged for this!"

"The ship can't take your weight, fool!"

"It's alright!" shouted Nicole from above. "We'll be landing shortly. Just tell him to hold on."

"Great," muttered Farris. His muscles were starting to ache, for King Diarmuid was quite heavy for a Human. But despite the drunken, slobbering god-king clutched in his arms, and the raging captain sharing his lifeline, Farris smiled.

He drank it. He drank from the poisoned thainol, after all this time. King Diarmuid shall bear no children. The Móráin line has ended.

CHAPTER 24:
LADY CARRÍGA

During my time here in the capital, I have acquired a significant body of proof indicating that Divine Penetrance is indeed a true phenomenon. Amongst the many things I learned about the Crown and its intelligence network, this is the most disconcerting of them all. As much as I'd like to believe that King Diarmuid is a mortal man, the evidence here strongly suggests otherwise. I've enclosed a number of documents stolen from the Royal Archive that back up this outstanding claim. Amongst them, are the following:

Genealogy of the Móráin Line: Note the dates of deaths and births here; not a single king has died before bearing a son.

Healer's account of King Lionál IV's final days: When Good King Lionál was on his deathbed, he lived for far longer than those who treated his condition had predicted. According to Barra the White, Lionál died the very moment his wife gave birth to his son.

A letter from King Donal I describing how his son, then Prince Brian, survived after almost drowning. Here, the king himself notes that the child survived being under water for a full hour.

A translated crystal-wave sent from High Cardinal Conchobar to Arch-Canon Cathbad. Here, the High Cardinal alludes to something he calls 'The Divine Gift.' In the writings on the Apotheosis of the Trinity, Saint Mhórthos refers to Divine Penetrance in the very same manner.

I expect that this information will be sufficient to formulate a plan for moving forward. In the meantime, I'll continue to work close to King Diarmuid, and relay all pertinent information back to you in due course.

Coded letter sent from Farris Silvertongue to Argyll the Silverback in the year AC403.

***

Dawn had arrived by the time the Tower of Sin was visible from *Skirmisher*, but none on board gave any indication that they had reached their destination. Indeed, since leaving the capital, very little was said at all, bar the odd whisper and mumble from King Diarmuid to himself.

Barely a thanks, thought Farris. Sure, they managed to escape the horde, but Farris felt nothing but dread as the tiny aircraft glided towards the city of Penance.

Farris sat in the same seat he had taken on the outward journey to the capital, with Nicole in front of him, piloting the ship. Behind Farris sat King Diarmuid, whose incoherent rambling had only somewhat lessened since leaving the Grey Keep behind. Padraig Tuathil sat on the floor next to his king, his feet flat on the ground with his knees cradled between two gauntleted forearms. Farris considered how uncomfortable Padraig must have been down there, but the captain had barely said a word since boarding the ship.

I can thank the gods for that. The broken tower drifted past his view. *Well, if they're there to be thanked.*

"We'll be docking in the Steamworks," called Nicole over her shoulder, not taking her eyes off the controls. Farris nodded, and the other two seemed to have no objections to this.

Skies above. This is perhaps the king's first time in Penance. He probably couldn't tell the Dustworks from the Shadow of Sin.

Skirmisher glided through the smoke and smog of Penance's industrial district. Nicole's hangar stood out from the rest of the buildings. It was situated separately from the other factories, with a large clearing adjacent to it. Farris supposed it was for the taking off and landing of airships just like this one, but as they got closer to the ground, he noticed a group of Simians standing in its vicinity.

"Looks like someone's expecting us," said Nicole, letting only an ounce of worry enter her voice.

The ship descended horizontally, staying perfectly level as it went. Once they were close enough to the ground to step out, the figures waiting for them became clear.

"Argyll!" rasped Nicole, fussing with the controls as the ship's engines came to a halt. "What brings you here?"

The Silverback stepped forward. He was accompanied by six Humans dressed in scarlet robes over silver armour. Farris recognised them immediately as the Churchguard of the Basilica. What wasn't so clear, however, was why in Sin's name they'd be guarding Argyll.

"The capital has fallen," said Nicole, not waiting for a response. "The horde overwhelmed the Grey Keep. We barely managed to save the king, but he's with us now, as safe as ever."

Farris unbuckled the leather straps of his seat and moved to exit the ship. As soon as his feet felt solid ground once more, Argyll spoke.

"Farris Silvertongue of the Dustworks of Penance," he said, in a manner far more formal than normal. "Before witnesses representing the Church of Alabach, I hereby declare you under arrest."

"Arrest?" cried Farris. "Under what charge?"

"Theft," said the Silverback, gesturing to *Skirmisher*. "This prototype is owned by the Triad in conjunction with the Church. You are to be held in the Basilica until an appropriate sentence is decided."

"Elkshit!" spat Nicole. "This was my father's aircraft. He left it to me when he died."

"All airships are the property of the Church," said Argyll, sternly. "Your father, more than anyone, would have been well aware of this."

"Then why aren't I under arrest, too?" She stood by Farris's side. "It was my idea just as much as it was his."

"That won't be necessary," said Argyll. "You may pursue the formal appeal process if necessary." The Silverback looked up at King Diarmuid, who seemed to be having a difficult time exiting the ship.

"Your Highness," said Argyll, falling to one knee. "The gods are just to keep you in good health after all that has happened. I humbly welcome you to our fair city."

The sight of Argyll the Silverback kneeling before the king was enough to send Farris's mind reeling. *What manner of trickery is this? Has he really forgotten all that has happened? All that we've stood for?*

Farris's gaze fell on the tall poleaxes of the Churchguards. All care for why Argyll was acting so strangely vanished, for Farris had more pressing matters.

One of the guards stepped forward and grabbed him by the arm.

"You are to come with us," he said, the words barely comprehensible through his gruff voice. "Any action other than this may impact your sentencing."

Farris swore under his breath. It would have been easy to make a scene, between the dagger up his sleeve and the blades in his boots, but he decided against it.

I'd have a better chance figuring out what's going on without killing anyone. He let his arm go limp in the Churchguard's grip.

"Farris, no!" cried Nicole. She made a move as if about to step forward but seemed to reconsider it. "I'll fix this!"

"Don't worry about me," Farris called back as he went. "Just keep the king safe." Diarmuid had stepped out from the ship now and was frantically taking in his new surroundings. Immediately behind him, Captain Tuathil was stretching his limbs, having spent the majority of the trip folded over himself.

"But don't concern yourself too much with Padraig," added Farris. "That fool can look after himself."

***

Fionn shook his Simian inkpen and tried writing again, but no letters fell onto the page. He gritted his teeth and began shaking it once more. In the back of his mind, Sir Bearach was chuckling softly.

Isn't this Simian invention supposed to be an improvement on our inkwells and quills? Sir Bearach asked. The young mage ignored him and began scribbling away at the corner of the page once more. At last, the ink trickled forth, and the pen began writing smoothly.

Fionn paused to consider his words for the report. He had fastidiously studied Yarlaith's notes on Necromancy and compared them to some choice historical texts on the nature of magic, but whatever answer the Silverback seemed to believe he'd find was far out of reach.

Does he think this is like a bard's tale? thought Fionn. *That there's some long-lost secret to stopping the horde, and all it takes is some reading to uncover it?*

Well, said Sir Bearach. *You've made some progress, at least.*

Fionn considered the pages he had written already. It was true. One of the Triad's scouts who had witnessed the horde first-hand reported that the dead bodies began rising back up to join the others even when the girl, Morrígan, was nowhere to be seen. This observation, when cross-referenced to the account of Callaghan the Black—one of the first Necromancers to be tried and executed in Alabach—alluded to Necromancy having a significant range. It stood to reason, then, that if anyone in the vicinity of a Necromancer was to fall dead, even from natural causes, their soul could still be harvested.

That explains the graves, Fionn recalled, frantically writing as the memory from the day he returned to Roseán resurfaced. *She took the dead from their graves, even when buried under the ground long before.*

But what of their souls? asked Sir Bearach. *Surely the souls of the long dead would already have travelled to the Plains of Tierna Meall.*

"Yes..." mused Fionn out loud. He reached over across the desk and picked up the heavy logbook of Yarlaith the White. *In one of his final entries, the old healer described the soul being 'torn down' from the afterlife. The body, he claims, is just the vessel of the soul. Once one takes control of the vessel, they too can channel the soul, even if it had left the earth long ago.*

Fionn lifted up a stack of papers and grabbed an old religious textbook entitled *The Móráin Name*. On its cover was an illustration of Móráin the First, shortly after the conquest of Alabach. The male figure stood stark naked—bar a convenient loincloth—with rounded muscles covering every inch of his body. One would have claimed he was the perfect specimen of a man, if it wasn't for the two great, golden wings unfolding behind his back.

And to think, said Sir Bearach, *it was in this very city that Móráin Himself transcended to godhood, while his golden wings blinded the Simian natives.*

It's allegorical, dismissed Fionn. *The wings are just the artist's representation of the power of the Trinity. Móráin never grew wings like that. That would be absurd.*

Well, said Sir Bearach. *The chaplain back in Keep Carriga was adamant that the events leading to the capture of Penance unfolded just as that illustration depicts.*

It wasn't called Penance back then, said Fionn. He opened the large tome and ran a finger down the contents page. *That was before the Simians built the tower. It was before they committed their Sin.*

Fionn paused, and strange thought occurred to him. *If Simians are truly born without souls, as the Church insists, would that make them resistant to being risen by Necromancy.*

He shook his head. Sure, it would mean the Simians of Penance wouldn't add to the horde if they fell, but the horde was still a threat, nonetheless.

Somewhere down the hall, a door opened and shut violently, though Fionn didn't pay it much mind. In the House of the Triad, politicians and nobles were often ran the halls, arguing and slamming doors as if to make a point.

Although he tried to turn his attention back to his work, Fionn found his focus wavering. Two irate voices drifted in from somewhere down the hall: a feeble Simian voice flavoured with the flowery accent of those highborn in Penance, and a female Human. Fionn couldn't make out the latter's words, but there was such hatred and fury there that he thought it best to close the door to his chambers. Just in case.

Wait, said Sir Bearach. *I recognise that voice.*

Is that so? said Fionn, feigning interest as he reached for the door. There was much work to be done, and he didn't need to be distracted.

No! It can't be. It can't be her!

To Fionn's surprise, the old knight seemed excited, ecstatic, even, on hearing the woman's voice.

Should I go help her? he asked.

Yes! roared Sir Bearach. Fionn didn't need to be told twice.

The mage strode out from his chambers, down the corridor where the hall turned off to the left. As he turned the bend, the voices grew more audible, and even the words themselves could be made out.

"I'm not going to ask again!" barked the Human. "I will see him. Now!"

"I'm sorry, my lady," said the Simian. "The hour is not right, and—"

Fionn stopped dead when the two figures came into view. The first voice he had heard did indeed belong to a Simian. He was dressed like most other nobles in the city, with a light, loose gown draping low at the front, revealing a thick chest covered with dark, neatly trimmed hair. He seemed to be one used to a position of power, but his current stance certainly indicated the opposite, as he was almost cowering before the other figure.

She, of course, was a woman, but certainly didn't have the appearance one who would be referred to as 'my lady.' She was taller than the Simian, and seemed to be larger in bulk, too, but that could have just been her armour. A steel chestplate shimmered in the waning candlelight, scarred and stained from what might have been a long journey, or a great battle. Her thick black hair was tied back in an untidy bun, with loose, dirt-clumped strands sticking out here and there. The whites in her eyes shone like flames, beneath a heavy brow narrowed in rage.

"If you had seen a fraction of what I did on the way here," she rasped. "You wouldn't dare deny me from seeing my brother. Now, let me inside."

Brother? asked Fionn, surveying his surroundings. *We're outside Cathal Carríga's clinic. Is she...your...?*

Sir Bearach's silence was enough of an answer. The mage's heart plummeted. *Keep Carríga. Rosca Umhir. They said the horde ran over them all. How...?*

"There are healers tending to him as we speak," stammered the Simian, rubbing a nervous hand across his forehead. "Perhaps, if I kindly request...they could..." Without finishing a coherent sentence, the Simian backed into the door behind him, opened it, and vanished inside.

The woman stood in her armour, not moving, and not noticing Fionn, who slowly stepped towards her.

Do you want me to say anything? asked Fionn. *Should I tell her that—*

No! exclaimed Sir Bearach. *She can't know. Don't....*

The woman turned abruptly to face Fionn. She eyed him up and down, seeming to pay special attention to the ceremonial red gown the mage was wearing.

"Good evening, Firemaster," she said with a nod. "I didn't think there were any mages left. I heard what happened to Dromán and...." She trailed off, her gaze falling to the floor.

"And the rest of the kingdom?" Fionn ventured. "To my knowledge, Penance is the last bastion of Man—of life—in the wake of the horde."

For a moment, the woman's stern expression faltered a little. She closed her eyes and took a deep breath, exhaling it slowly between her teeth.

"I saw it," she whispered. "It...it was horrendous."

Fionn swallowed deeply. Surely Sir Bearach wanted to know more about how his house had fallen, but too direct a question may raise suspicion.

"I used to live in Rosca Umhir," Fionn lied, not quite sure if this was the correct route of questioning to take. "I believe I recognise you from the court. Lady...Carríga, am I correct?"

She lowered her head, but in a bow or in shame, Fionn couldn't tell. "Aislinn," she said, eventually. "Just Aislinn Carríga. I'm no lady. Nor a warrior either."

"But you are dressed as one," said Fionn, ignoring the feeling that he was overstepping. "And it seems like your amour has seen a fight or two."

"I fled," she said, raising her voice and letting the words echo through the hall. "My father wished to close the castle gates when the horde arrived. To keep us safe, he said. But I called him a coward. Gods, from the throne room, I could hear the civilians of the city being butchered. What good is surviving a little longer, I asked, only to die in the end as a coward?"

Fionn had no answer to this. Before he could reply, Aislinn continued. "I donned the armour of my late brother." She beat a fist against her chest-plate. "And I rode out into the horde. I fought some of the dead off, but they just kept on pouring into the city. I would have fought if I could—the Lady Herself can be my witness on that—but I was overwhelmed. I managed to escape the city, but I was pursued by a group of undead that had broken off from the rest. I ran and I ran, but the dead ones did not give up their chase. By the time I lost them, I had already reached the Clifflands. So, I continued on to Penance. To see my last living relative."

Fionn remained silent after she finished her tale, then shook himself from the stupor it left him in. *From Rosca Umhir to Penance. That's almost two hundred miles.*

"Lady Carríga," called a voice. The Simian from before had emerged from the clinic, although Fionn hadn't even heard the door open. "You may see your brother now."

"Will you join me?" said Aislinn, fumbling her hands as she spoke. "I never got your name…"

"Fionn," said the mage. "I'll join if my lady wishes it so."

As they stepped into the clinic, Fionn's attention was immediately drawn to the resting body of Cathal Carríga. Since Fionn had last visited, Cathal's state had deteriorated significantly. The thin tubes were still bound to his veins, but the man's complexion now resembled yellowed parchment. His cheekbones were protruding so much, it seemed as if they threatened to cut his skin. Indeed, the entirety of Cathal's skin was only barely bound to his face. Despite his decrepit state, the young man was still breathing. An aged female healer stood to the side with her arms folded, clearly unhappy with the unexpected visitors.

"Cathal," whispered Aislinn. She went beside the bed and fell to one knee. "Cathal, it's me. It's Ash. Can you hear me?"

The man gave no reply. Two hollow eyes stared up at the ceiling, unblinking, but they did not turn to look at his sister as she spoke.

"Bearach is dead," she said, trembling now. "Father and Mother too. The horde has taken Rosca Umhir, and they say the rest of the kingdom will fall soon. We're all that's left."

She took one of Cathal's hands in hers and placed a small kiss upon it. She closed her eyes and bowed her head, sobbing softly to herself.

Bearach, said Fionn. *Are you sure you don't want me to tell her?*

No, whispered the knight. But even from that single word, Fionn heard Sir Bearach's voice crack with grief.

Aislinn stood slowly, towering over Fionn and the old healer. She turned to the woman and gazed down at her like a judgemental father, or Lord Seletoth Himself.

"I was told he was alive. Have you forgotten your trade?"

"No, my lady," said the healer. Although her hands were trembling, there was strength in her voice. "He still breathes, and there is life in him yet. We are trying all we can to kill off the tumours, but every day they grow as he weakens."

"So, there is a chance he may never recover?"

"There is no chance, my lady. I am certain of that. The Simians are treating them with their own chemistry, rather than my alchemy, and that is keeping him alive. Though only barely."

"He was a warrior," said Aislinn. "He deserves a death on the battlefield, with pride and glory. Not to waste away in bed like this."

"I understand. But I took an oath to help the sick and wounded through whatever ailment may take them."

"I know of this oath," interjected Fionn. "It was written long before the Fall of Sin. If this kind of medical intervention existed back then, I doubt the oath would have taken the same form it does today."

"End his suffering," pleaded Aislinn. "Surely you can see that it's the right thing to do. What kind of life is this?"

"I understand," said the healer. "I will not stop caring for him, but perhaps the Simians can be convinced to forgo his treatment."

"Then who should I speak to?"

"Argyll the Silverback," whispered the healer, as if she was afraid the Simian himself would hear. "But he is not one to be easily swayed."

"I'll meet this Silverback, then." Aislinn straightened the chainmail beneath her armour. "As sure as the horde still marches, I'll convince him."

CHAPTER 25:
WHEN THE TIME COMES

Farris,

I have reviewed the documents you claim support the concept of Divine Penetrance, and I am convinced by your arguments. Instead of attempting to assassinate the unkillable king, we have devised another method for controlling the Crown. Enclosed with this package is a bottle of thainol, fresh from Penance's finest distillery. Present this as a gift to Diarmuid. His people will taste and test it for poison, of which they will find none. Continue to present gifts like this during your stay in the capital, until you gain the king's trust. Our chemists here in Penance have devised a compound to cause infertility in any man who ingests it. When the time is right, we will send a 'special reserve' of thainol to be given to the king. If King Diarmuid cannot be removed from his post, we can at least ensure that Alabach sees no monarch more capable than this drunken fool.

Coded message sent from Argyll the Silverback to Farris Silvertongue in AC403.

***

Fionn tentatively pushed open the door to the Triad meeting room. Its massive wooden body swung silently on its iron hinges—something he was all the more glad for, considering the Silverback and his men seemed to be deep in discussion. Fionn stepped into the room, followed closely by Aislinn Carríga. The woman seemed far more lady-like now, dressed in layers of skirts instead of battered armour. A yellow ribbon held up her dark hair, which seemed to be especially clean and smooth after having spent half a week buried beneath a helm. Although the inns and taverns of the city were overflowing with refugees from the south, Fionn had managed to arrange temporary living quarters for Aislinn in the House of the Triad. For this she had been very grateful but insisted that they visit the Silverback at the break of dawn.

The sun's morning rays filled the meeting room as Fionn and Aislinn made their way across the carpeted floors. The Silverback barely turned his head when they arrived, but the others seemed a little more anxious when the young mage approached the oaken table.

"Don't mind him," said the Silverback, his eyes glued to the map of Penance spread out on the table. "We may make use of his powers when the time comes."

"*If* it comes," corrected Garth. The Simian stood with his arms folded, eyeing Fionn with a narrowed gaze. "We have no reason to believe the horde will ever come this far north."

"Yet you never objected to arranging this plan," said Nicole. "There must be some fear in that barely beating heart of yours."

Garth snorted and leaned forward toward the map, placing both hands flat on the table. "So, dividing our forces in three should be enough?"

"Yes," said Ruairí, the only other Human present, bar Fionn and Aislinn. As always, he stood separate from the Simians. The pendant around Ruairí's neck marked him as one of the Sons of Seletoth, but why someone as staunchly atheistic as the Silverback would associate with someone from that cult, Fionn never knew.

"My men will take up arms at the Dustgate," continued Ruairí. "Our numbers alone will be enough to hold up against a force of any size. Nicole will take nine of the Reapers to the Saltgate." The Human threw Garth a quick glance. "I assume you'll be accompanying her there?"

Reapers? thought Fionn, watching as Garth nodded silently. *What in Meadhbh's name is a Reaper?*

"That leaves the Goldgate," said the Silverback. "The remaining Reapers will accompany the bulk of the Triad's army there. The geography of the Northern Reach will filter any forces to any one of these three sites, and we must be able to shift accordingly. Our mounted scouts will keep up constant surveillance over the outskirts of the city, giving us room to adjust."

Satisfied, the Silverback looked to Fionn for the first time. "Fionn, will you be willing to join the Triad's soldiers at the Goldgate?"

Fionn almost stepped back in response to the question. *Me? Fighting the dead? On the front line?*

You have nothing to worry about, whispered Sir Bearach. *You duelled a Firemaster and lived to tell the tale. A handful of corpses is nothing for you to fear.*

But I'm no Battlemage. I've never learned to fight before.

True, said Sir Bearach. *But you may very well be the last mage in Alabach. What a shame it would be for the most powerful man in Penance to not be able to help us!*

"I..." Fionn stammered aloud. *The most powerful man in Penance?* "I'll do it. I'll fight when the time comes."

"If," corrected Garth again, one hand pressed against the map. "The horde is still ravaging the capital, last we heard."

"Thank you, Fionn," said the Silverback, making it clear he was ignoring Garth's interjection. "If we survive this, the kingdom will thank you."

"I'll fight, too," said Aislinn, stepping forward. She raised her chin, revealing cuts and scars across the bottom of her jaw. She seemed to open her shoulders even wider, amplifying the presence her massive frame already granted her. Her voice boomed with pride. "I have faced the horde before, and I will not baulk when the time comes again."

The Silverback raised a single eyebrow. "My lady," he said, bowing ever so slightly. "We have not yet been introduced."

"My name is Aislinn Carríga," she said. "And I have been trained by the best swordsmen of Rosca Umhir. I escaped and fought the dead myself when Keep Carríga was overwhelmed. Although I am a stranger to this city, I will gladly give my life to help defend its citizens against this enemy."

"Its citizens shall live to thank you," said the Silverback. Across the table, Garth stared with an open mouth and wide eyes, as if he had never seen a woman before.

He's never seen one quite like Ash, that's for sure, said Sir Bearach.

"I ask but one thing in return," said Aislinn, bowing her head before the Silverback. "My brother, Cathal Carríga, was once a ruler of this city, yet today he lies wasting away slowly to an illness he shall never recover from. All I ask is to give him the gift of mercy. A man as strong as my brother does not deserve to waste away into nothingness, without dignity."

The Silverback did not respond straight away, but Fionn knew that beneath that strong brow and that stoic stare, the

Simian was deep in thought, quickly and rationally considering the implications of this request.

"I will speak to the healers," he said. "It is not up to them to deliver death where there is life, but as Cathal's next of kin, they may make an exception for you."

"Thank you," said Aislinn. "House Carríga will not forget this."

House Carríga is dead, moaned Sir Bearach at the back of Fionn's mind. *How does she not realise this?*

I'm sure she does, replied Fionn. *Perhaps it gives her courage to believe the house still stands. Perhaps her name is all she has left to fight for.*

The doors to the meeting room burst open, and two Humans entered. The first strode in with his head held high. Middle-aged, the man wore a broad chest-plate, yet it shimmered like one that had never seen battle. Insignias decorated his breast, but Fionn could not decipher their meaning.

City Guard of Cruachan, Sir Bearach noted. *This one is a captain.*

But what of the other? replied Fionn.

The second man did not walk with the same strength as the first. In tattered clothes that may have once been considered finery, he limped across the room, dragging his feet behind him. Dreary, bloodshot eyes stared blankly from a chubby unshaven face, pale with sickly skin. Whereas some men appeared ill when lacking sleep, this one looked like he had never known rest his entire life.

Kneel! roared Sir Bearach in the back of Fionn's skull. *Kneel, fool!*

Me? asked Fionn, glancing around the room. Indeed, everyone else had sunk to their knees when these two men entered the room. Fionn glanced at the armoured man once more.

But you said he was only a captain of–

Not him! barked sir Bearach. *The other! He's your king!*

Fionn fell to his knees without another thought, but as soon as he did, the dishevelled stranger made an upward motion, and everyone else in the room returned to their feet.

"Your Grace," said the Silverback. "You honour us with your presence. I hope you find the Triad is accommodating to your needs."

"Yes," muttered King Diarmuid, though the sound was barely audible through his dried, cracked lips.

"And Captain Tuathil," continued the Silverback. "I take it you are content with the state of our forces."

The armoured man nodded. "Content is as far as I'll go. They are ill-prepared for combat, but they do not fear the horde. Courage is a rare thing in this new world."

"Then we must set to our preparations at once," said the Silverback. "Garth, take your squad to Saltgate and start running through the usual drills. Nicole, if you could be so kind as to accompany our king to—"

"No," said Nicole, curtly. "I will not be held accountable for your king until Farris is released."

"How dare you?" said Captain Tuathil. He went to step forward but was stayed by a raised hand from the Silverback.

"Nicole," said Argyll, slowly. "Please listen and—"

"No, you listen to me." she interrupted again. "You imprisoned Farris for saving this fool, then you bow and grovel before his feet. I'll help you no more until I get some answers."

"What answers would you like?" said Argyll, so calmly that he may as well have been asking what she'd like for supper.

"My father," growled Nicole. She took a step toward King Diarmuid and pointed a trembling finger at him. "I saved you from the horde, so I deserve answers. One year ago, my father was murdered along with several more of your Royal Guard. You blamed the Silverback for their death, but I know this to be impossible."

"Nicole," said Argyll. "Please, His Grace is still in shock, there is no need to—"

"How can you not care?" she roared. Everyone else in the room seemed to shrink back in fear. Nobody had ever raised their voice to the Silverback before. "He blamed *you* for my father's death. He declared war on our people. How can you just stand there and not demand an answer? How can you expect us to accommodate this *fool* without question?"

"Because we have more important things to consider right now," said Argyll. "Despite our differences, we must stand together against the horde."

Nicole's head snapped back to face the king. "You killed him," she rasped. "Admit it, right here and now, that you killed him so you could declare war on the dissidents. You killed my father to further your own position of power."

King Diarmuid did not say a word since Nicole's tirade began, but now, his lips were quivering. He swallowed deeply, and a shiver ran through his body.

"I did not lay a finger on Santos," he whispered. "Your father and I were to unite Human and Simian alike with the railroad. But... She killed him."

"Who?" demanded Nicole.

"I...I promised myself I would never speak of it."

"Lies! Speak of it now, if you wish to clear your name!"

"No," said the trembling king. "I...I must not burden others with the truth I have seen. With the truth She has shown me."

"Sir," said another voice.

"What truth?" demanded Nicole. "Skies above, you better start making sense soon."

"Stand down, Nicole," said the Silverback. "This is not the time nor place to—"

"Sir!" said the voice again.

Nicole made a wide, waving gesture at Argyll. "How can we let him get away with this? How can you let him live in your city?"

"SIR!"

All went silent as they noticed a newcomer had entered the room. He wore the garb of a Triad scout, but his armour was chipped and worn, with bloodstains and mud spattered across his chest. The Simian was breathing heavily and sweat poured from his brow.

"Sir," he repeated. "Excuse my interruption, but I bring news from the south."

"You are excused," said the Silverback. "What news?"

"I was surveying the Floodlands when...when..." His voice cracked. All the air of formality that inhabited his words vanished when he spoke again. "I saw them cross the River Tulcha. I was barely a day's ride ahead of them when I reached the Glenn."

"Speak plainly, scout," said Padraig. "What did you see?"

"The horde!" Tears rolled down from the Simian's cheeks, and he let out a loud, wet sob. "They've made it to the Glenn. They'll be upon the city by nightfall."

A murmur of terror ran through the room, but it was Garth who spoke the loudest.

"Impossible! Your report must be mistaken. The dead were as far south as they possibly could be just one day ago."

"My eyes did not fool me," said the scout. "I saw them in all their might marching northwards."

"No," said Garth. "It can't be. An army could never cross the kingdom in a single day!"

Aislinn laughed.

"Army?" she said, throwing the Garth a jeering look. "This is no army. The horde does not have any scouts, or divisions, or supply lines. They do not rest. They do not feed. They do not move like any army our history has known, but like a single creature, crawling across the land and devouring all that stands in their way. If they take this city, they will not show mercy. If we put up a fight, none will break from their ranks and flee. We stand no chance of beating them if we continue to consider them as an *army*."

"Why did they change course so suddenly?" said Garth. "Why did they come here?"

"They came for me," said King Diarmuid, his voice a little stronger than before. Still, his unblinking eyes stared down at the floor. "I was not supposed to survive the attack on Cruachan. You may think you can fight the horde, but you cannot fight fate." His lips cracked into a defeated, joyless smile. "I once believed I could, and I did everything in my power to repel the coming tide. But She said there was no hope, and She was right. There never was."

CHAPTER 26: THE LAST BATTLEMAGE

The Triad's soldiers came into the camp and claimed that it was no longer safe there. They told us to grab our things and follow them into the heart of the city. People protested at first, but there were whispers among the crowd that the horde had finally caught up with us, and it would be only a matter of time before they took Penance, too.

As I write this, we're all huddled up in the Tower of Sin, with nothing left to do but wait for what's to come. I pray to the Lord to watch over us, and to the Lady to guide us through the night. But I don't believe we'll live to see the morning.

Diary kept by Cian Dranach, survivor of the attack on Point Grey, and asylum seeker in Penance.

***

By the time Fionn reached the Goldworks of Penance, the commercial district was already evacuated. Whereas typically the air was alive with scents of spices and the sounds of trade, now everything remained silent. A cold wind blew through the empty stalls, buffeting dust along the wide, stone streets.

The huge stone structure of the Goldgate loomed ahead of Fionn as he walked, but the mountains of the northernmost region of Alabach rose even higher. The Northern Reach was what the Firstborn had called the area when they came to conquer Alabach. It was said that the first Simians had fled through the rough mountainous terrain when the Humans came, and they made their last stand at the stronghold of Penance, though it wasn't called Penance back then. The Humans found it difficult to follow at first, but with the Lord Seletoth's gift of magic, the battlemages reached the Simian city with ease.

If only it was so easy today. Fionn took a corner past an abandoned warehouse. When he stepped into the area adjacent to the gate, Fionn recoiled with shock.

Rows upon rows of armoured soldiers stood at attention, facing the Goldgate. Most were clad in the grey and black colours of the triad, with blue-tinted armour beneath their surcoats. Both men and women, Humans and Simians alike, filled their ranks, while captains and lieutenants patrolled the perimeter.

"Firemaster!" called a voice Fionn didn't recognise. The red mage had come dressed in the traditional crimson robes of his station, so it was no surprise that even strangers would know him by title, if not by name. Still, there was none stranger than the Simian who approached him now.

In gilded armour that could have been set on display, the Simian held out a massive hand to greet Fionn. "I am General-Commander Plackart," he said, each word sounding like a cough. "I was told you'll be honouring us with your presence on the front-line."

"I..." stammered Fionn. It was almost too much for him. The General-Commander of the Triad's army was *honoured* to meet him?

Gods, I've never even seen a battle, let alone fought in one.

But he doesn't know that, whispered Sir Bearach. *And the dead don't know that, either.*

Fionn made a fist inside his sleeve and idly rubbed a thumb across the two flint-rings on his index and middle fingers.

General-Commander Plackart cleared his throat harshly, not bothering to cover his mouth as he did. He wore a heavy chainmail coif over his head, and most of his exposed face was thick with scars. One deep cut covered his left eye, leaving only a hollow, withered eyelid in its place.

"Yes, sir," said Fionn, trying to sound surer than he really was. "What news is there of the horde?"

Plackart nodded his head toward the gate. "Walk," he said, although it seemed more like a command. Fionn promptly joined the commander as Plackart marched past the ranks.

"It's possible that they've reached the Northern Reach by now," he said, not paying much mind to the many pairs of eyes that were drawn to them. "Though there's no telling how soon they'll be upon us. The horde has been anything but predictable over these past weeks."

Fionn nodded in vigorous agreement, noticing that a ripple of excitement was running through the crowd. Plackart grunted in response.

"Most of these are as green as the Glenn," he said. "Refugees who fled their homes and just want to fight. Some don't even know how to hold a spear, let alone wield one. But what they lack in discipline, they make up in mettle."

"And you think that'll be enough?"

The commander snorted. "I don't think anything will be enough. But Sin will be damned if we don't fight till our last breath."

They carried on toward the wall, when an audible cheer rose up from the front of the ranks. Amongst them, Fionn saw some fresh, young faces under their thick armour. One in particular grinned ear to ear like a fool and was even waving at Fionn.

"Cormac?" said Fionn to himself, squinting to get a better look. The farmhand looked as if he had cleaned himself up, or shaved at least, and enrolled in the very army that was about to clash with his daughter's. But despite this, he seemed completely oblivious of what waited for them beyond that gate.

Gods. What if she comes herself? Will he still be so eager then?

Plackart hurried onward, for which Fionn was eternally grateful. Now Cormac was no longer the only one smiling so strangely at him.

The commander grunted again, though this one seemed almost like a laugh. "That's why I'm bringing you to the front," he said. "The initiates have been talking about nothing else but 'The Last Battlemage of Alabach' ever since they learned you were fighting. Seeing you guard the gate will be a better morale boost than victory itself."

"Really? But...I'm no battlemage."

"Well, you won't be seeing much battle then," said Plackart. He pointed to the top of the wall. "You'll be with the marksmen, helping keep the undead from the walls. The infantry will see you light up the horde, and that'll give them strength when the time comes to open the gate."

"The gate?" asked Fionn. The wall stood before them now, thick with stone and twenty feet high. Dozens of archers and crossbowmen patrolled back and forth across the top, over a complex system of ropes and pulleys that looked like they operated the massive portcullis that made up most of the gate's width.

"We'll fight the at a distance as much as we can," said Plackart. "On the other side of the gate, the Silverback has left some 'surprises' for the undead. Whatever that's supposed to mean. If the horde get too close, I'll give the order to open the gate, and our infantry will charge forward."

Fionn gasped. "But won't that end in slaughter?"

"I was given the task of keeping the dead from entering the city, same as those at the Dustgate and the Saltgate. Only way to beat the horde is to put an arrow in the bitch that's leading them. All we can do until then is protect the civilians."

The commander led Fionn up the stone steps of the wall. Upwards they climbed, until the tingling fear in Fionn's stomach began to finally dissipate.

I have magic, he reminded himself. *I'll need to be brave, at least for the rest of them.*

All his reassurances failed him, however, when they emerged at the top of the wall. To his right, the soldiers of the Triad were visible in their ranks, a thousand faces eagerly looking upwards. To his left was the Rustlake, and the surrounding valley of the Northern Reach. It was this vast emptiness that filled Fionn with the most dread.

That's where they'll come from. The valley won't be vacant for much longer.

"Now," said Plackart. "I believe you've met Lady Carríga before."

Fionn barely recognised the armoured figure who stood before him. Her dark armour was glimmering in the waning light, topped with a huge great-helm fashioned into the shape of a swan's head. Only when this helm was removed, revealing the pale face of Aislinn Carríga, did Fionn offer his hand in greeting.

"Your armour," started Fionn. "It's..."

"It's been cleaned and repaired," she said, proudly beating her chest with a gauntleted fist. "It belonged to my brother, but Cathal would be proud to know that it's being used to fight our last stand against the horde."

And Bearach, too, said the dead knight in Fionn's mind. *The Black Swan of Carríga has never been more suited to anyone but you, sister.*

Fionn gritted his teeth. *Bearach, as you sure you don't want me to tell her?*

No! roared the knight. *Not when there is so much at stake right now. If we live to see the dawn, perhaps. But not now. Please.*

"Of course," said Fionn out loud, responding to both of the Carríga siblings at once. "Has Argyll spoken to the healers regarding Cathal's treatment yet?"

"No," said Aislinn. "Though I agree that my brother's fate can wait. We need to focus on defending the city first."

"Aye," said General-Commander Plackart. "And the Silverback has helped us do just that too, but he's left me in the dark regarding the details."

"What do you mean?" asked Fionn.

"Look down over the wall. Tell me what you see."

Fionn tentatively stepped towards the edge of the gate and peered down at the empty valley below. There wasn't much to see apart from the plain, dusty floor. But there, sitting right against the wall, were three strange azure shapes. Fionn squinted through the falling darkness, and made out their vague impressions, like huge suits of armour. Though instead of carrying weapons, the ends of their left arms formed pointed ends like lances. Their right arms, however, lacked anything resembling a weapon, and instead bore great holes where their hands should be.

Fionn tore his eyes away from the statues and faced Commander Packard. The Simian shrugged his shoulders in response.

"The Silverback tells me nothing," he said, as if the name itself was a curse. "He told me not to worry about them, and to stick to the plan. But something about them makes the hair on my brow stand on end."

"Me too," muttered Fionn, stealing one last glance down the valley. "Me too."

***

As darkness descended on the city, the troops at the Goldgate frantically made their final preparations. From atop the battlements, Fionn watched as colonels and captains hurried up and down the ranks below, shouting orders and running drills with their men.

Soldiers and couriers ran along the wall, bringing supplies and orders from the other gates in the city. From what Fionn could make out, there was still no sign of the horde yet. Every now and then, a Simian scout mounted upon a massive, armoured elk would arrive at the wall, deliver a message, and gallop away into the night.

"Firemaster," called a gruff voice, pulling Fionn's attention away from the troops on the ground. "A word, if you please."

"Yes, sir," said Fionn, bowing to General-Commander Plackart, though the young mage wasn't quite sure who should be bowing to whom.

"Tell me about your magic. Its limits, its uses, its weaknesses in battle."

Fionn hesitated, as the hundreds of dusty texts he had studied on Pyromancy back with Firemaster Conleth resurfaced in his memory. Complex calculations and equations on heat transfer across metal, through air, through flesh...

"I don't know where to start," said Fionn. "Is there anything in particular you'd like me to discuss?"

"Tell me about its range."

"Well," began Fionn, "the concentration of the heat dissipates with distance, but it can reach the same distance as a bolt fired from a crossbow, though with not quite the same power."

"What about energy? Will you be able to keep your magic up for the full battle?"

"Like the other schools of magic," Fionn recited, "Pyromancy uses the soul as its fuel source. I would need to rest after using a significant amount, but I have learned that I have more endurance than others."

One more soul than most others, more like, said Sir Bearach.

The commander didn't reply immediately but stared down at Fionn with his single eye. "I ask that you remain on the wall for the duration of the fighting," he said, eventually. "Given the range of your spells, you'll be just as effective up here as you are down there. Lacking close combat experience and armour, you'd be quite vulnerable in the fray. Accommodations can be made for the latter, but I believe you'll be more valuable up here, with respect to morale."

"Sure," said Fionn, trying to hide his relief. "I'll keep away from the fighting, if that's what's best."

The commander bowed curtly and left, weaving past a group of marksmen stationed on top of the wall and toward the stairs leading to the ground below.

"You seem glad," came a voice from behind Fionn. He turned to see Aislinn, her helm held under a thickly plated arm. "Most lads your age would kill to be on the frontline."

He nodded towards the ranks of soldiers below. "Most lads my age are fools. With so much death in the world these days, why are so many more willing to die?"

Aislinn sighed deeply. "My father believed it was part of Human nature," she said, lowering her gaze to the ground. "Humans conquered Alabach through force, and the sacrifice of their soldiers has paved the way for the peace our kingdom saw for the following four hundred years. But peace comes with a price. Many of the smallfolk live and die achieving next to nothing in their lives. Feeding one's family may be a man's only purpose, just so his sons and daughters can grow up to do the same. But if some earl or captain calls to your village, hands you a weapon, and tells you that for the first time in your family's history *you* can be part of something larger, what choice would you make?"

Fionn recalled the face of Cormac from amongst the ranks. He seemed so happy to be there, even awaiting certain death. Given his background, it was possible too that he lived a life not unlike what Aislinn had described. It was easy to understand why someone would want to make a mark on the world, and if running off to die was the only way to do that, then...

"Do you agree with your father?" asked Fionn. Aislinn didn't reply straight away, and instead stared out at the empty valley ahead of them. Flanked by huge, grey mountains, the land looked like a black and white painting, with bare trees and decaying plant-life staying perfectly still in the darkness.

"I didn't before," she said. "But on the night the dead came to Rosca Umhir, when my father refused to help, I felt the 'call,' as he had once named it. The urge to fight, even when there was no hope. I snuck away and donned my brother's armour, this armour, and rode out to meet the horde head on. It was such a powerful feeling, seeing all the other soldiers' spirits rise, believing Sir Cathal Carríga had returned from near-death to save them, and for the first time in my life, I felt that I finally understood my father. And my family.

"But as I crossed the drawbridge, I was thrown from my horse and disarmed. With no weapon, I found myself in the heart of the horde. Amongst the stench of decay and the guttural cries of the dead, all my sense of valour vanished. In that moment I ran, and I no longer felt like a Carríga."

"Aislinn..." said Fionn. "There's something I've been meaning to tell you."

"What's that?" Aislinn said suddenly.

"It's your brother, he's—"

"No," she said, grabbing Fionn by the shoulder and pointing down the valley. "What's *that?*"

Fionn had to squint to make out what she was referring to, but when he did, the hairs on the back of his neck stood to attention. A faint black cloud was rising above the mountains, amorphous in form, spreading inwards and outwards as it went. The darkness smothered the peaks, descending down the valley like a flood. A faint, screeching sound came with it, but only when Aislinn spoke did Fionn finally make sense of the shape.

"The crows," she muttered. "The crows always come first."

Other voices cried out below, and a maddening pandemonium came over the soldiers. If there was room to run, many would have, but instead a thousand cries and pleas for help resounded through the valley. Amongst the discord, Plackart's booming voice rose out, as stern and fearless as ever before.

"To arms!" he cried. "Marksmen, take aim!"

Immediately, the archers and crossbowmen all around Fionn raised their weapons, pointing up at the black mass overhead. The tiny details that made up the flock was visible now, and they were indeed crows. Thousands of them, like insects swarming the mountains.

"Fire!" called the commander, and a hundred arrows and bolts were loosed upon the crows. The swarm did not slow.

Fionn clicked his flint-rings together and tugged at the power of his soul. In a fraction of a second, his hands were alight. He raised both fists upwards, and a pillar of flames rose up to meet the crows. This time, the birds shrieked as they burned, and charred corpses littered the valley before them.

It's working, thought Fionn, gritting his teeth and adding more to his fire. *But I can't hold them off forever.*

Indeed, even as hundreds of their brethren fell, more and more crows poured down through the valley. The sky was alight with fire, but the new arrivals quickly outnumbered the dead.

"I can't hold them on my own!" Fionn cried. But the other marksmen had not stopped firing since the order was given, though their weapons remained useless against the horde.

The crows were right overhead now. Some individual birds broke away from the flock and descended upon the marksmen on the wall like arrows of their own. The men roared as they fell, but the cries of the crows covered their death-rattles. Above, more began to break away from the rest, and a harrowing sense of fear tore through Fionn's body.

It's over. It's over before it even began.

In a blinding flash of light, a tower of sapphire flames erupted from before the wall, consuming the crows overhead. These fires quickly outshone Fionn's own, and soon, the whole valley shimmered blue.

Gods, thought Fionn, looking up at the cobalt inferno. *What is this?*

By instinct, he reached out to control the fire himself, but it eluded his grasp. A familiar feeling came over him, like *this has happened before...*

Beggar's flames. Farris made them from thainol, back in the Glenn.

He sprinted to the edge of the gate to peer down at the source of the flames. The wall of fire flames stopped at the three strange steel statues from before, but now they were looking upward, the fires erupting from their arms.

"What sort of Simian... *magic* is this?" said Aislinn, shaking her head in awe.

"Reapers," Fionn muttered. "This must be what the Silverback was talking about before."

The blue flames extinguished suddenly, and the burnt bodies of a thousand crows fell from the sky. Cheers rose from the soldiers below.

"I better join the infantry," said Aislinn. "Stay safe up here, you hear me?"

"Sure," said Fionn, his attention still drawn to the three Reapers on the ground. *Though I'd rather just stay near those...*

Cries and shouts rose up from the men behind Fionn, some calling for supplies, others calling for help. A few had even begun singing war songs, as if victory were already at hand. But Fionn didn't turn.

The valley floor before him was littered charred bones and burnt carcasses of birds, but something else stirred the corner of Fionn's vision. There, in the distance, another cloud was rising from down the valley. But this one came from the ground, like dust kicked up by a thousand marching soldiers.

"They're coming," Fionn stammered, taking an involuntary step backwards. "The rest of them are coming."

CHAPTER 27: THE BASILICA

"As long as I am alive and breathing, as long as I am willing to fight, as long as my choices are mine and mine alone, there will always be hope."

King Diarmuid, Third of his Name, Nineteenth Incarnate, AC403.

***

Farris balled his hand into a fist, gritting his teeth as nails dug into skin. Hundreds of pounds of pressure seemed to be building up in his skull. He narrowed his eyes and swore under his breath. As useless as he felt before, working by the side of the Silverback, now, imprisoned in the bowels of the Penance Basilica, his worthlessness was even clearer.

He leaned his head against the cold stone wall behind him. *This is where I belong. I'm a criminal, not a politician.*

The cell was large enough to accommodate two prisoners, but Farris was fortunate that he was alone. He sat on a bench of rotted wood, which doubled as a bed, although he hadn't slept since being arrested the previous day.

Or was it two days ago? Farris thought. With no windows or natural light, it was difficult to tell.

Footsteps echoed down the hall, coming closer with each step. Farris stood to attention, like he always had whenever the guard approached on his regular patrol.

I won't let them see me defeated. I won't let them know they've gotten to me.

A Simian of the Churchguard eventually came into view, his brilliant red robes a startling contrast against the dank darkness of the prison cells. He didn't turn to look at the other prisoners as he passed, and when he was gone, Farris found his gaze land on the cell opposite his. It held a massive Human prisoner. As large as a Simian, a rigid scowl adorned his face, and faded tattoos encircled his eyes.

"What are you looking at, rat?" he growled, leaning forward against the bars, as if to give Farris a full view of his muscular forearms. "You're lucky these bars are solid steel, otherwise I'd come over and break your spine."

"Trust me," said Farris. "I'd consider myself far luckier if there was any way out."

The other prisoner looked like was about to respond but was cut short when the guard's footsteps came again. As he went by, Farris returned to his previous stance: tall and proud, as if he wasn't questioning his motives for even getting involved with the Silverback in the first place.

Did something change? he thought, recalling the way Argyll had spoken to him when the arrest was made. *Or was he always like this?*

When the guard vanished from sight once more, Farris returned to his seat on the cold, wooden bench.

It was possible, of course, that the Silverback had been hiding his true intentions all this time...but what in Sin's name could they be? First, he wanted to kill the king, then he agreed with Farris's assessment that the king could not in fact be killed. That was when they all agreed that poisoning the king and leaving him as the last of the Móráin line would be the next best thing. It would be far better, Argyll had argued, to have one fool of a ruler to manipulate, rather than a dozen lords and reagents acting on behalf of a child king. No, King Diarmuid was the Silverback's best bet in achieving his goals, and that was the last time he and Farris saw eye to eye.

Farris ignored the burning gaze of the human prisoner across the way. *Then what changed since then? Could it have been the Sons of Seletoth?*

It was plausible, of course, that Argyll's involvement with the cult had made him change his mind on the matter of Divine Penetrance. With the Sons believing that King Diarmuid held no real power, and that Seletoth was the One

True God, it would make sense that Divine Penetrance would clash with their ideals. And if Argyll had subscribed to those ideals, too, then....

Why do I bother? Farris pulled himself from that train of thought. *I'm no philosopher, nor a politician. I'm in no way equipped to be considering matters like these.*

He sighed deeply. It was true, of course, that he had no place in politics. That was a realm far better suited to his brother. Garth was always better at fitting in than Farris was.

Why can't things be the way they were? When all I had to worry about was the latest Guild job, or escaping the authorities...

He glanced around the cell, at the grubby walls and the rusted bars, and despite everything that had happened, a smile touched his lips.

"What's so funny?" called the prisoner across the way. "What are you laughing at?"

"Irony," sighed Farris. He leaned his head against the back wall again.

The old Farris would never had ended up in a cell...

A cry broke out somewhere overhead, causing Farris to jump out from his seat. It was followed by another, then another. Roars and shouts muffled by a hundred feet of solid stone. Farris pressed his ear against the wall. He heard them again, clearer than before, but he couldn't make out the words.

One thing was evident. These weren't cries for help, but cries of valour. Of men charging on their enemy. Of battle.

"What's that?" called the other prisoner. He stammered slightly through the words. "Did...did you hear it?"

"A street fight," said Farris, though he didn't believe his own words. "We're right in the middle of the Dustworks. You know how those gangs can be..."

More sounds of battle echoed through the ceiling, but Farris could do nothing but listen. Somewhere in the back of his mind, he knew what this was. But his logical sense knew it was impossible.

It couldn't be. The horde was at Cruachan not one day ago...or was it two?

The familiar footsteps of the Churchguard resounded through the corridor, though they seemed to be moving slightly faster than before.

"Hey! You!" called the other prisoner once the guard arrived. "What's going on up there?"

The Simian guard did not hesitate for a second. "The undead horde," he said, so calmly that Farris wondered if he even knew what those words meant. "The Triad is fighting them at the gates. They won't harm us down here."

"Oh, fuck that!" called Farris. For the first time since he had been put into the cell, the guard turned to look at him. "Do you honestly believe that? All the other Seachtú fell to the horde. What makes Penance any different?"

"It is not my place to question the Triad's authority," said the guard, turning again to leave. "And it is certainly not your place to question mine."

"No!" roared the other prisoner. "You listen to me. I'm not gonna sit on my arse and wait for the dead to come. Open up this damn cage or you'll regret it!"

The guard simply continued down the hall, as if he didn't hear the prisoner's request. But that didn't stop the Human from shouting obscenities as he walked away.

They'll never let us out. The dead will come down on top of us, and we'll be trapped. We don't stand a chance.

The cacophony of battle overhead grew louder, just as the anxiety ripping through Farris's body became more intense. He took a deep breath and closed his eyes.

This can't be happening. Not now. Not yet. Not when I can't even fight.

He leapt forward and grabbed the steel bars with both hands. He gripped them and pulled until his knuckles whitened, crying aloud as he did. He knew it was futile, he knew there was no point, but he had to try. Skies above and below, he had to at least *try*.

But even with all his strength and all his determination, the bars did not budge.

Breathless, and with aching muscles, Farris stepped away from the bars. *This is it. There's nothing left to do...*

The Churchguard appeared again, patrolling slowly back down the corridor. Something was different about his expression this time. As if he were no longer the cold-hearted soldier he was a moment ago. As if his mind was no longer in the prison with the others.

"Guard," called Farris, careful to keep his tone more diplomatic than before. "You said the Triad's army was sent to the frontline to hold the horde back. But what about the Churchguard?"

The guard stopped, and then took a moment to reply. "The Churchguard will remain within the Basilica. The Arch-Canon has ordered that the ancient relics and texts of the Church should be protected from whatever threat may enter the city."

"And you agree with this, that your place is to stay here and guard us, instead of protecting the citizens of Penance?"

"I have my orders," said the guard. "I will not abandon my post."

"I understand," said Farris, staring back at the Simian guard. "I grew up in the Dustworks, in poverty, and I know how important it is to make a living. I'd take the Faith and lick the Arch-Canon's boots if it meant my family would be clothed and fed."

The guard's stern gaze wavered for half a breath, but that was enough for Farris.

"If I was in your position," he continued, "I would not question anything, either. It's the Church you serve, not the people of Penance, and that is the life you have chosen. Some Simians may resent you for taking the faith, but not me. I know what it's like to go to sleep hungry, night after night. Thanks to your sacrifice, your family will never know that same pain."

"Whatever you say," said the guard. He went to leave, but Farris cleared his throat to speak again. When he saw that this caused the guard to stop where he was, Farris knew he had hit a nerve.

"But this night changes everything," he said, careful not to be too overbearing. "What good are you down here, when the dead are butchering the same people you've sworn to serve?" He paused for a moment, letting the silence add to the weight of his words. "Or do you serve the Arch-Canon first, and the people second?"

"You better watch your tongue, or—"

"Or what? You'll have me killed? Open your eyes. We're already dead! As long as we sit here waiting, there's no hope of surviving the night."

"You're wrong," said the guard. He took a step closer to Farris's cell. "The Basilica walls will hold. We are safe in here."

"Listen to yourself. Listen to the battle unfolding right outside your door. The walls of Penance couldn't hold them back, what makes you think these walls will do any better?"

"The Arch-Canon said—"

"The Arch-Canon doesn't give a fuck about you, or your family. If he did, he'd have you armed and outside protecting them. If he really did, he'd empty the cells and put all of us on the front line!"

"Now you listen here. There is no way in Sin's Shadow that the Church will let you lot out. I don't know about your crimes, but these cells are filled with the worst criminals the city has ever known. Many are petty thieves and blasphemers, but some are murderers and worse. No force on this earth will change the Arch-Canon's mind on that."

"He doesn't need to change his mind," said Farris, lowering his voice. "You hold the key. You hold the power to save this city. Arm us and send us into the battle. It's likely that these criminals will die, and no longer be a threat to society. At least they can help protect this city beforehand. Even the most hardened criminals have families to protect."

"Do you think I'm some sort of fool? Do you really think I'd just let you all...go?"

"I don't take you for a fool, nor do I take you as a coward. You want to join the others in the battle, but you're forced to waste away down here with the likes of us. When the dead come, would you rather die protecting your family, or die guarding the worst criminals the city has ever known?"

"You're...you're wrong. You—"

"You can join us," said Farris. "If by some miracle the city is saved, you can tell the Arch-Canon that we overwhelmed you. That we forced you to set us free. You'd be absolved of all blame. Or if you spin it right, you'll be hailed as a hero."

The guard shook his head. "I can't. I won't...it's just—"

A sudden shriek of terror rang out through the darkness. It was a woman's voice, far closer than the others from before.

"They're well inside the city walls now," said Farris. He paused and considered the guard for a moment. He was visibly shaken. A bead of sweat ran down his brow from under his half-helm.

"Tell me," said Farris. "Do you have any family living in the Dustworks?"

The guard's jaw dropped slightly, and panic flared in his eyes. Trembling, he reached for a small satchel tied to his waist and pulled out a large ring of keys.

"There's an armoury down the hall," he said, fumbling a key into the lock of Farris's cell. "Do you know how to use a sword?"

Farris nodded, trying hard not to smile. He caught the eye of the burly prisoner across the way, whose mouth was agape with awe.

"How many others are imprisoned here?" asked Farris, just as the lock clicked open. "Will there be enough arms and armour for them all?"

"There's a dozen," muttered the guard as he pulled open the cell door. "There should be enough, yes. Is it really wise to let them all out?"

Farris snorted. *Now he wants my advice?*

"There'll be no harm done," said Farris. "Some of these men would probably kill you if they got the chance under any other circumstance, but they'd be less likely to turn on their saviour."

The guard's lips moved silently, then formed a smile; Farris guessed he was musing over the word *saviour*.

"There's six held up on this floor," the guard said, handing Farris the ring of keys. "I'll get the rest, upstairs, and meet you outside the armoury down the hall."

"And the other guards?"

"I'll talk to them. I imagine most would want to join us."

A loud crash rang out from somewhere outside, joined by a cluster of scattered shouts. Even though he was so far away from the fight, Farris could swear he smelt the faint scent of burning wood outside.

"We best not delay." He gripped the keys in his hand and nodded curtly to the guard. And as if dismissed by a superior, the guard bowed slightly and went on his way down the dark corridor.

"Are you going to let me out or what?" asked the prisoner, both arms resting on the exterior of the cell, the bars pressing tight against his biceps.

Farris hesitated for a moment, then shook his head started sorting through the keys. "As long as you fight," he said, twisting one key into the lock, only to find that it didn't fit. "As long as you don't flee." The second key fitted in more smoothly but was unable to turn. "And only if you do as I say."

The third key proved successful, and the cell door opened without further hindrance. The prisoner stepped out slowly, his massive frame at height with Farris's.

"I'll give you my word on the first two," he said, squaring up to Farris. "But no more."

Farris left the prisoner and began working at the other cell doors. Some of the men and Simians inside asked questions, to which Farris repeated the same sentiment he had before.

"Fight, don't flee. Follow and do as I say, and you'll have your freedom."

Soon, four more prisoners filled the hallway. Two of were incredibly malnourished Humans. Farris could only guess how long they had spent down here. The other two were Simians. One was a head taller than Farris, with black fur speckled with white and grey, while the other stood hunched over and crooked, though this didn't seem to hinder his movement. When Farris had opened his door, the Simian assured him that despite his appearance, he was as capable of fighting as well as any other.

The company made their way down the hall, where a locked door met them, thick wood reinforced with massive slates of steel.

"Excuse me," came a voice from behind. Farris turned to see several more prisoners had joined the group, with expressions of bewilderment and glee upon their faces, and the red-robed guard pushing his way through the crowd.

"Let me through, thank you," he said, almost too politely. Farris stepped aside, and the guard began working on the armoury door.

"Any problems?" asked Farris, taking a moment to count the number of other prisoners.

"No," said the guard. "Not yet at least."

The door swung open, revealing racks upon racks of armour, chainmail and plates. Rows of heavy boots were arranged neatly on the floor, with all sorts of weapons hanging overhead, from polearms to daggers, and from longswords to maces.

"Arm yourselves," said the guard, stepping aside to let the prisoners through. He said some more words after this, but the sound of his voice was drowned out by the clamour of excitement that came with a dozen convicts looting the Basilica armoury.

Farris began assessing the armour. He took down a vest of chainmail that seemed large enough to be worn by a Simian and pulled it over his head. He shivered as the cold steel links grazed past his bare torso. It was a little tight around the chest, and the hood wasn't quite large enough to pull over his head, but it was well-suited otherwise.

Adjacent to the armour, Farris found a pair of short-swords, and a belt with two sheaths crossed over the back. Farris tried the belt on and found it fit perfectly around his waist. The two short swords slotted neatly into the sheaths, but Farris found it strange to wear a weapon on his back, of all places. He pulled on a pair of chainmail leggings, too, but decided against wearing boots. The soles of his feet were well conditioned against the stone roads of Penance, and ill-fitting boots would only slow him down.

"Sin's Stones! What's going on here?"

A rough voice cut through the excitement, and all those present immediately stopped what they were doing and turned to face the door. There stood three more Churchguards, all Simians, with three gold-tipped spears pointing forward.

"They're with me," said the guard from the cells. He pushed through the prisoners to face his brothers. "We're not going to sit here while the city falls. We're going out to fight."

"Ned! Have you lost your damn mind?" said one of the others. "The Arch-Canon will have you hanged as a deserter!"

"The Arch-Canon can fuck himself," said Ned. "If we survive this night, I'll gladly present my neck to the hangman in the morning."

"You're serious..." said one of the guards. "Gods, you're really going through with this."

"Gods?" Ned spat. "We've all made oaths to the Trinity for the sake of this job, but don't go pretending you really believe them."

He took a step back and gestured to the others. "We're going out to fight, and you're perfectly free to stop us. Help us fight for our home, rather than for the cardinals who've come in and built this monstrosity on our doorstep. They've never bothered themselves before with the well-being of our people, and as sure as Sin they'll happily lock themselves up while the dead overrun Penance. If you want to go join them, I won't stop you."

Ned turned without waiting for a response and marched on through the armoury. The other prisoners took this as their cue to leave and followed the Simian across the room.

Some had taken more than their fair share of equipment, but Farris paid them little mind. A deficit in inventory would be the least of the Church's worries after this night.

By the time Ned had the door on the far end of the armoury open, Farris noticed that the three other guards had vanished.

"You think they'd really go to the Arch-Canon about this?" he asked.

"It wouldn't surprise me if they did," said Ned. He opened the door to a spiral staircase twisting upwards. "As long as the gates are open, we'll be out before they can raise the alarm."

Gates, thought Farris, swearing under his breath. *All of this could be for nothing if we can't leave...*

They made their way up the thin staircase, with Ned and Farris both taking two at a time. The other prisoners were talking amongst themselves as they went, though Farris couldn't quite gauge what they were saying.

Eventually, the stairway ended with another locked door. Opening this revealed a wide courtyard, with the faint blur of red flames against the dark city skyline beyond.

Farris stepped out into the open air and took a deep breath. The scent of charred wood was clearer now, as was the faint stench of something Farris couldn't quite put his finger on.

"Burning flesh," said one of the prisoners. "I'd recognise that smell anywhere."

"Let's go!" cried Ned. He strode out across the open courtyard, towards the massive Basilica walls beyond. To Farris's horror, the gates were indeed closed. He jogged on ahead to catch up with Ned.

"Will this be a problem?"

Ned sighed. "There's a mechanism to open them in one of the adjacent watch-towers." He pointed. "If they're heavily guarded, we'll be in trouble."

They carried onwards, past a great golden fountain in the centre of the courtyard. Water trickled from three statues, built in the likeness of the Trinity, and splashed gently into a wide pool below. As its centrepiece, Lord Seletoth looked out into the city, his stern face half-hidden beneath a thick stone beard. The great domed House of the Basilica loomed overhead on the far side of the courtyard.

"I grew up right outside these gates," said Farris, keeping close to Ned. "But I never once saw what was contained within them."

"Do they meet your expectations?"

Farris smiled. "I was told the whole courtyard was paved with silver, with the statues of the fountain made from solid diamonds, spilling forth molten gold into its basin."

"Well, I'm sorry to disappoint."

As they reached the gate, a voice called out into the night. Farris turned, assuming it was one of the prisoners, but what he saw caused the last of his courage to abandon him.

A crowd of Churchguards marched across the courtyard, five dozen in their ranks. At the front, Farris recognised the three other guards from earlier.

"A fight?" roared one of the prisoners. He batted two hand-axes together. "I can handle that!"

"There's too many," said another. "This was a mistake; I knew this was a mistake!"

"They're not charging," said Ned. "If they wanted a fight, they'd be charging."

Farris pulled the two short-swords from his belt. "Well, we'll be prepared either way."

Once they approached, the column of Churchguards paused. A Simian guard stepped out from the ranks. Gold medals and emblems lined his collar, and his robes were even more extravagant than the others.

"Spearman Edward," he said. "Your brothers have brought it to my attention that you plan on abandoning your post to join the Triad in their fight against the undead. Is this true?"

"It is true," said Ned. "Have you come to arrest me and present me to the Arch-Canon?"

"No. We have come to join you, Arch-Canon be damned." He raised a hand to his mouth and roared "Gates!" up to the watchtower.

The prisoners cheered as the great Basilica portcullis creaked open. The Churchguards raised their weapons and joined the cacophony. For a moment, Farris felt that they actually stood a chance against the horde. That they may see the night through to the dawn.

But then the gates opened. Buildings burned with fires of red and blue all around, and scattered soldiers ran back and forth across the blood-stained cobblestones. A terrified cry rang somewhere nearby, cut short by a sickening crack.

With roar, the prisoners and the Churchguards charged into that Holy Hell. And Farris followed.

CHAPTER 28:
THOSE WHO FIGHT

It's been past an hour now since the soldiers ordered us all to sit and wait in the House of the Triad. Some of the Humans have taken to praying, but all I can do is write, and hope my words eventually find you. Those who are in charge are telling us little about what's going on outside, but I can tell from their demeanour that things are not going well. I've heard a few cries and shouts, but the fighting still seems to be kept away from the Shadow of Sin. As much as I hate to admit, I'm tempted to join the Humans in their prayers that the dead stay away for a little longer.

Unfinished letter found in the House of the Triad, Penance, AC404.

***

Volleys of arrows shot through the air, filling the night's sky with their burning tips. The roared commands of captains and lieutenants rang out all across the Goldgate, and the archers continued to notch and loose without hesitation. But none of these seemed to slow the approaching horde, charging through the valley.

Fionn flicked his wrist, pulling a ball of fire from the spark his rings produced. He idly moulded the fire between his fingertips, keeping his eyes locked on the coming army.

How can we stop them? He turned back to gauge the number of soldiers stationed behind him. *We're running out of time.*

The thundering roar of footsteps shook the entire wall, as hundreds of bodies emerged from the huge dust cloud on the far end of the valley, seemingly undeterred by the burning arrows that rained down upon them.

"Hold the gate!" roared a voice from somewhere behind Fionn. "Hold!"

What does he mean? thought Fionn, pulling the flames between both hands. The host was about three hundred feet away.

"Hold!" roared the voice again. Fionn quickly made note of the width of the valley. *Could I fill it with fire? Could I hold them back?*

The cries of the dead rose up over the clamour of their charge. Guttural, inhuman voices gurgling unintelligible sounds.

The individual faces of the dead were close enough to pick out. Men bearing crests and sigils of families Fionn didn't recognise. Faces half-obscured by decaying flesh.

Children clad in torn, bloody clothes. Some wielded weapons, fewer wore armour, and none showed any sign of slowing.

Children... Fionn shook his head in disbelief. *Why aren't we fighting them? Why is nothing being done?*

Once the front line of the horde was in stone-throwing distance of the wall, three strange figures leapt forward to meet them. For a frightening second, Fionn feared that some madmen had broken ranks to fight the horde alone, but when the valley lit up with blue flames again, Fionn understood what had happened.

The Reapers. They can move!

As the charging dead reached the blue inferno, their battle cries turned to blood-curdling wails unlike anything Fionn had heard before.

What kind of power is this? Fionn watched as the three figures paced back and forth, ensuring no wight made it through their wall of fire.

Blackened corpses started to pile up before the machinations. But even those that were charred to a crisp still writhed beneath the flames. Other undead soldiers climbed atop the stack of bodies to reach the Reapers, but the blue flames cast each back, and they too joined the others upon the smouldering heap.

They're holding them back! roared Sir Bearach from inside Fionn's head. *They're holding the whole damn lot of them back!*

From behind the pile, a single body leapt through the fire and collided with a Reaper. The metallic figure lost its balance for a second, then turned its cannon upon the corpse. As if taking advantage of this distraction, four more wights followed, leaping over the burning bodies and knocking against the Reaper.

A second Reaper took notice but continued to keep the rest of the horde at bay. The first swung its other arm in a wide arc, but more and more came pouring over the pile.

"No!" roared Fionn, watching on helplessly as the Reaper fell to the ground. More decaying corpses fell upon it, tearing at its armour. The other Reaper turned to look at its fallen comrade for a split second, but it too was overwhelmed by the coming dead. The rest of the wights climbed over the smoking pile and continued on their march towards the gate.

The last Fionn saw of the fallen Reapers was one of their heads being pulled off. Inside was a Simian soldier, alive and breathing as the undead pulled his bloody body from the wreckage.

No. They weren't statues. They weren't machines. They were....

"Now!" yelled the same voice from earlier. Beneath Fionn, the mechanisms of the Goldgate frantically churned into action, and the Triad's soldiers poured out to meet the horde. The two front lines crashed into each other amidst a cacophony of roaring voices and clashing steel.

"Fire!" came another voice from atop the wall, and another salvo of burning arrows rained down upon the tide of undead. More and more of the Triad's soldiers pushed against the horde, but their line still held. Inch by inch, the dead kept pressing forward, as more and more corpses joined them from further down the valley.

We can't fight them. There's just too many. There's—

Gods take you, lad! cried Sir Bearach. *Are you a Firemaster or not? Use your magic!*

Fionn glanced down at his flint-rings. After all that had happened, he had let the flames in his hand extinguish. He shook his head and produced another spark, turning it into a flame and cupping it between both hands.

He ran forward to the battlements and sent the flame soaring down into the fray below. He pulled on the power of his soul. Right as the fire landed on the side of the horde, it erupted into a spiralling cyclone of flames, consuming all it touched.

The side of the Triad took this opportunity to push forward again, this time making ground. Some soldiers split from the column and ran through the undead's ranks, only to be engulfed by their sheer numbers.

Quick! Do it again! roared Sir Bearach. Without question, Fionn reached for another ball of fire. But when it came to throw it amongst the undead, he hesitated.

I can't tell...I can't tell which side is ours anymore.

Indeed, the two frontlines below were blurred as one, and soldiers from either side were scattered into the other. But like the coming tide, another wave of undead surged through the valley, quickly overwhelming the living unfortunate enough to be on the wrong side.

"Retreat!" came the booming voice of Commander Plackart from somewhere amongst the chaos. "Retreat to the gate!"

There was some movement below as those capable of turning back did, but many more were still lost amongst the horde. Two Simian soldiers fought with their backs to one another, keeping the undead away in a wide circle around them. A Human tried to turn to make it back to the gate, but a skeletal soldier pursued him, running a spear into his back. A cluster of a dozen or so Humans and Simians had banded together beyond the frontline, keeping their backs against the valley wall as they fought against the undead. But the horde's numbers only swelled, the Triad's line no longer held, and the dead crept ever closer to the wall.

The churning of the closing gate beneath Fionn's feet caused every ounce of hope left in his heart to dissipate. It seemed only a fraction of those who fought had managed to safely retreat behind the portcullis.

"We've lost," he muttered, scanning through the horde. Those two Simian soldiers were nowhere to be seen and had more than likely joined the undead. But to the side of the valley, that small cluster of survivors by the valley wall was now three times its original size. They huddled together in a tight semicircle, those still capable of fighting on the outside.

They won't last much longer. The gate is closed. The call for retreat has been made. They–

Fionn froze as he spotted one figure amongst the others. A soldier of the Triad wearing no helm, pushing the undead back away from the column with a two-handed greatsword as tall as herself.

Aislinn! We have to do something. We need to tell the Commander.

No, whispered Sir Bearach. *There is nothing Plackart can do without risking the lives of the rest of his men. Her fate is already sealed...*

"Bollocks to that," said Fionn aloud, catching the attention of other marksmen along the wall. "I'm done with fate. I'm done with being afraid."

With that, he clicked both his flint-rings together, and conjured a stream of fire that encircled him. He climbed up atop the battlements and looked down at the valley beneath him, gauging his distance from the ground.

Fionn, what the fuck do you think you're doing? demanded Sir Bearach.

Instead of responding, Fionn leapt from the wall and joined the battle below.

***

Farris didn't realise that he had taken both short-swords into his hands, but they were there, moving in a flurry with little feedback from his brain.

Just like a normal bar fight, he thought, ducking under the wide swing of a great-axe and shoving a sword into the chest of its wielder. The undead soldier barely flinched as Farris twisted the blade and pushed further. The great-axe swung back again, but having anticipated this, Farris hopped back then struck forward again. This time he took soldier's head clean off, but the corpses did not fall in response.

Maybe not like one after all. He bounded back to join the others as the headless soldier stumbled around blindly.

The rest of the prisoners and the Churchguards were dispersed around the Basilica Market. Whereas once this was a regular meeting place for trade and commerce in the Dustworks, now its buildings burned with fires of crackling orange and bright blue.

A crossbow bolt whirred past Farris's head, but he did not turn to see where it had come from. Ned and several other Churchguards struggled against a group of skeletons pouring in from a nearby alley.

How can we possibly beat them? thought Farris, dodging to the side as a single undead villager swung at him with a broadsword. As the sword's weight knocked the villager off balance, Farris ducked under its arc and grabbed one of its arms. With a quick swing of his blade, Farris sliced it from the villager's shoulder. Before the broadsword hit the ground, Farris tore across the Market toward Ned and the others.

As he ran, booming footsteps echoed above the cacophony of battle. He turned to see a great, black shape bounding towards him, taking great leaps with each stride. The flames illuminated the shimmering fur of a black bear, its beady eyes fixed on Farris as it came. Flesh hung from its sides in strips, revealing greying, rotting bones beneath. The bear grunted and bore its teeth, shining white daggers protruding through bloody gums.

Farris held his ground, putting one foot back to augment his balance. He gripped both blades tight, lowering them beneath his hips.

"Come on!" he cried, bending his knees as the bear approached. "Come on!"

Just as the beast was mere feet away, Farris leapt to the side and ran both blades across its black body. But instead of reacting as he expected, the bear growled and shifted towards Farris. Its weight knocked him off balance, and the next thing he knew, he was lying on the bloodied ground, looking up at the bear's massive head. The beast opened its mouth and roared, blanketing Farris with the stench of decay. Something inside the bear's open mouth seemed to be moving, glistening, writhing...but Farris couldn't quite tell what it was. The bear's mouth opened even wider—more so than any living creature's should. Hundreds of maggots filled its corners, squirming with every movement of the bear's tongue. Some fell and trickled down upon Farris's face.

The Simian frantically pushed with his legs to get away, but a heavy claw came down upon him, pressing against his chest and pinning him to the ground.

"Do it," roared Farris, balling his hands into a fist. It certainly wasn't ideal, but he was not willing to go down without a struggle. "Do it!"

The bear raised his head back slightly, as if about to lunge forward, but before it could, a great blue hue filled Farris's vision. All he felt was heat—an unbearable, boiling heat—followed by something grabbing his shoulders. The next thing he knew, he was being pulled away from the burning bear, its shrieks of agony filling the sky like the blue flames that emitted from it.

"Farris, are you alright?" came a voice. Farris looked up to see a familiar pendant dangling before him. Three interlocking circles, each crooked in shape.

"Ruairí!" coughed Farris as he was pulled to his feet. The Human stood before him with a large breastplate covering his chest, the Son's pendant resting upon its surface. In his hands, he held what looked like one of Nicole's firearms, but much longer, to be wielded with two hands.

"Sweepers, to me!" Ruairí called over Farris's shoulder. There two other Humans stood, both holding weapons like Ruairí's, with blue flames pouring out of each. In an instant, the fires stopped, and both men left to return to Ruairí's side, leaving the smouldering body of the black bear behind them.

"The Dustgate has fallen," Ruairí said. "Our brothers were scattered, and our numbers are too few now."

"I brought men," said Farris, nodding towards Ned and the others, still fighting to keep the skeletal soldiers from entering the perimeter of the Market. But they wouldn't hold for much longer. "Can the Dustgate be taken back?"

Ruairí had started off towards the others. "Help these first!" he called back. "Then we'll see what can be retaken."

Farris sprinted up to join the three Sons. The two Ruairí had called sweepers held their weapons forward. They were of a slightly different shape to Ruairí's, with wider brims and what looked like a large container of liquid attached, built to be held under their arms.

Thainol. Beggar's flames. Nicole. The fires, they–

"You know how to use one of these?" asked Ruairí, shoving a small firearm into Farris's hands. He held it before him, taking a second to admire the complex mechanisms at its handle.

"Point and shoot?" guessed Farris, his finger finding the trigger. "Just like a crossbow?"

"Exactly," said Ruairí, raising his own weapon before him. "Aim for their heads."

"Help!" called Ned from the alley. "We can't hold them back much longer!"

"Everyone, move!" roared Ruairí, as he and the other two Sons pushed through the Churchguards and the prisoners. The others immediately stepped aside, though this left a wide gap in their defence. The alley was crowded with undead, all of which charged forward on seeing that the dozens that had once blocked their way were replaced by a mere three.

"Sweepers!" commanded Ruairí, and the other two Sons raised their weapons. With a crackling roar, blue flames flooded the alley, and the undead inside shrieked and burned.

"Push forward," cried Ruairí, and the two other Sons started moving slowly down the alley, one step at a time, and not letting their fires fail.

Ruairí turned to the other men who stood bewildered, staring at the brilliant blue flames that consumed the dead. "Guard our flank!"

The others nodded and fell into a protective formation, facing forward and following backward as the sweepers pushed through the alley.

Keeping behind them Ruairí raised his firearm and aimed it over one of the other Sons' shoulders.

"Make sure none reach us," he said lowering his eye to the surface of the weapon. "If either of the sweepers fall, the dead will overwhelm us."

Farris raised his own weapon in response. Some fifty feet beyond, the thin walls opened up to reveal the Dustgate. Its portcullis was opened, and some of the living were fighting the dead before it. Loud cracks rang out, and more blue flames filled the darkness.

"There's more Sons beyond," realised Ruairí. "I thought they were lost. I thought—"

A charging undead soldier leapt through the flames. Before it could reach the sweepers, Ruairí raised his weapon and fired. A huge bang echoed and resounded through the alley, and the wight fell to the ground, its head split in two. He burned along with the others. And the sweepers pressed forward.

A deafening buzz rang out through Farris's skull. "Skies above!" he roared, not quite sure how loud he was speaking. "What has it done to my ears?"

"You'll get used to it," said Ruairí, raising his weapon to fire again. "Focus on the dead. We're almost there."

Farris gritted his teeth and tried to ignore the buzzing. He pointed his own weapon forward. A skeletal soldier came running down the alley, showing no signs of slowing. Farris aimed for its head and pulled the trigger. The firearm kicked back with such power that it almost fell from Farris's hand.

He caught it with his other, and the skeletal soldier collapsed to the ground, a gaping hole left in its skull. It wriggled and squirmed as the azure flames consumed it.

Again and again, he fired at oncoming corpses, and the column pushed on. After shooting for the seventh time, Ruairí reached for his pack and handed something to Farris.

"You're out of ammunition," he said. "The compartment right above the handle clips out. Replace it with this, and you're good to go again. I'll cover you."

Farris took the object, and immediately went to work. The compartment slid out easily, and he discarded it on the ground. The second one slotted in with a satisfying click. When he went to return to Ruairí's side, however, Farris found that they had already left the alley and now reached the Dustgate.

"Split up," called Ruairí. "Disarm as many of the undead as you can. They won't fall until our sweepers burn them, but make sure they can't fight back!"

Farris stepped to the side and raised his weapon toward a coming wight—a woman wearing layers of folded skirts in the fashion of the countryside. He pulled the trigger and hit her right in the centre of the forehead. The impact knocked her to the ground, but she was still moving, struggling to find her feet again.

A sweeper suddenly appeared by Farris's side and set the undead woman alight.

"Go," he grunted. "I'll cover the alley. Take back the gate!"

Farris left made his way toward the gate. The other Sons who had been left now fought back against the oncoming undead tide, joining Ruairí and the others as they did.

Two Sons were tending to the pulleys of the portcullis as Farris arrived. One sighed in relief.

"Thank the Lord you came," he said, looking as if he wanted to hug Farris. "We've been trying to close the gate, but there's too many of them. We couldn't hold them off long enough to—"

"Say no more," said Farris, turning his back to the two men. "Lower the gate. I'll keep guard."

He raised his weapon and fired at another undead soldier, missing his head by mere inches. The pulley mechanism chugged into action behind him as more wights seemed to take notice. Three others broke away from the fighting and started towards Farris.

"Keep them away!" cried Farris. Frantically firing at each of the oncoming corpses. Some Sons and Churchguards chased down the dead before they could come any closer. Farris fired his weapon again and again, dropping two, three, four undead before pulling the trigger no longer produced a reaction. He swore under his breath and threw the weapon aside.

I'll keep them away. I'll fight them with my bare hands if I need to!

A loud crack came from behind Farris, followed by scattered cheers of joy. More and more voices joined them, and it took Farris a further second to realise that there were no more wights left. The survivors started making their way toward the gate, stepping over the charred corpses of the undead.

"We did it!" cried Ruairí. "We took back the gate. Now we stand a chance of holding them off!"

More cries rang out in response to this. The Sons started taking up their previous posts at the Dustgate, along its perimeter and among its battlements above. The prisoners and the Churchguard from the Basilica stayed where they were, panting for breath and tending to their wounded.

Not even half made it through. The horde has only arrived, but there's already so many dead....

"Look!" cried a voice from amongst the Churchguard. "It's a scout!"

Further down the wall, a huge elk trotted casually toward the gate. A figure lay slumped over its back, with two fists held tight to the great beast's reigns.

"He's still alive," said Farris, rushing to meet the scout with several others following. The elk stopped as they approached, its massive head held proudly above everyone else. Two antlers spread out either side, perhaps spanning a distance as long as the mount itself.

"Scout, can you hear me?" asked Farris, reaching to catch the fallen figure in his hands. The Simian scout pushed his weight against Farris, who gently let him down to the ground. His armour was stained deeply with blood, pouring out from a wound beneath his armpit.

"Too late for me," coughed the scout, his dark, bloodied lips all that was visible beneath his helm. "Still time to help, the others..."

"What happened?" asked Farris, ignoring the crowd of prisoners and Churchguards that had surrounded him. "What news from the other gates?"

"General-Commander Plackart sounded the retreat at the Goldgate," he rasped. "There's still hope for them, but...."

He coughed again, its sound more like a wheeze than before.

"But the Saltgate," he continued. "They won't last. Trolls. Mountain trolls from the Glenn are on the way to break through the walls. Like siege engines."

An audible gasp rose up, but Farris didn't respond.

"How are the defences there?" he asked. "Is there any chance of fighting them off?"

"R-Reapers," said the scout. "Most of the Reapers are still there. Some other scouts, too."

Garth. He could very well be there...

"Nicole!" said Farris, abruptly. "Is Nicole there?"

The scout hesitated for a moment. "The engineer? She is, aye. They must be warned. They—"

The scout trailed off with another salvo of sputtering coughs, then went silent. Farris swore under his breath and placed the Simian gently on the ground.

"Mountain trolls?" cried one of the prisoners. "I've seen one tear through solid rock before. The walls will never hold. They won't—"

"What good is this victory?" cried another. "What use is it to take back one gate, when the other two are about to fall?"

"What else can we do?" asked a Churchguard. "We stay here and guard this gate. We've won it back, we may as well hold it."

"No," said Farris. "If the other gates don't hold, it won't matter how well we guard this one. We'd be surrounded."

"So what are you going to do?" asked Ned.

Farris moved towards the elk and patted it on the head. The beast responded well, nodding and taking a stance of submission before Farris.

It's well trained, thought Farris, stepping to the beast's side and reaching up for its saddle. The sheer size of an elk meant that only Simians could ride them, but that didn't necessarily make it easier for Farris to climb atop of it.

Rather clumsily, he threw his other leg over the saddle, facing forward to see the rest of the host. Some of the Sons of Seletoth had joined the crowd, too, craning their necks up to get a better view.

Farris nudged the elk forward slightly, holding on tightly to its reigns. It responded without hesitation, taking several steps to stand amongst the crowd.

Just like riding a horse. Farris reached down and took a huge halberd bound to the elk's saddle into his own hands. He only had minimal practice riding horses, but he thought it best not to show his inexperience.

"I am going to ride out to the Saltgate," he shouted, his booming voice causing the elk to stir beneath him. "There are mountain trolls headed towards our allies there, and they must be warned. If I am too late, then they must be helped. I am not asking you to follow me..."

He swallowed deeply and closed his eyes. *Sins stones, what am I doing?*

"Because I am not a leader," he said. "I'm a criminal. I was arrested for theft and was held in the Basilica prison not two hours ago. I do not know how to lead, but I know how to fight. As far as I'm concerned, that's all that matters right now."

He lowered his gaze and gritted his teeth.

"If anyone wishes to fight," he continued. "You will not be following me but joining me as an equal. Churchguards, where was the Arch-Canon when the horde approached? Why is it that you left him in the Basilica to come fight the undead yourselves?"

A mutter ran through the soldiers, but Farris pressed on.

"Because this is not his fight. This is your fight, for your city! If you come with me, you won't be fighting for king, or country, or for the Lord, but for Mankind. For Simiankind. For life in the face of death. Our brothers and sisters, friends and relatives, are already giving their lives to save this city. Some already have. Do you want their sacrifices to be made in vain? Do you want the rest of our city's citizens to join them?"

"No," came a voice from the crowd. "But what hope have we got? We should stay here and guard the gate."

"Don't worry about the gate," chimed in Ruairí. He gave Farris a knowing nod. "The Silverback's plan was to spread our resources across the city as needs be. I'll stay here with the Sons."

Farris suppressed a smile and fought the urge to thank Ruairí there and then.

"This gate will hold now," continued Farris. "But the Saltgate will not. Not unless we help. You are all free men now. Some once imprisoned by the Church, others bound to their posts out of necessity. But now those shackles have been cast off. We are all equals in the face of death."

Farris raised the elk's reigns and turned the beast to face away from the Dustgate, northwards, towards the Saltworks. Towards Garth and Nicole.

"I'm riding out to meet the horde," Farris called behind him. He raised the halberd over his head. "Even if I must go alone, I will. You are free to join me, or free to stay. So, on your first night unbound by the Church, what will your choice be?"

Farris kicked the elk and the beast sprang into a sprint. He held the reigns tightly in one hand, lowering the halberd with the other. Careful to maintain his balance on the beast, Farris stole a quick peek under his arm. A great host of free men and Simians followed behind.

CHAPTER 29:
THOSE WE FIGHT FOR

This may very well be my final entry. Although, the weight of this statement is diminished by the fact I said the very same the night the horde came to Cruachan. But here, in the Simian City of Steam, I face the same threat once more. The dead have reached the city walls, but this time I am not on the frontline. My place is beside my king. Diarmuid still doesn't seem to have recovered from the fall of his capital, as even now he continues to babble beneath a thick haze of thainol. He offered me a glass, but I refused. Even the scent of the Simian drink brings back too many memories of that fateful night. The fires. The screams. Aideen...

I may have failed the ones I fought for back in Cruachan, but not tonight. Even if the dead storm the House of the Triad, I will stand my ground defending the king. Even if it means ultimately joining the horde myself.

- Diary of Padraig Tuathil, Captain of the Cruachan City Guard. AC404.

***

Fionn rolled as he hit the ground, the fires of his soul raging as bright as the flames that surrounded him. He jumped to his feet quickly, ignoring the dull ache that gripped his knees.

He stood with his back to the Goldgate and pulled the flames in toward his hands. A sea of black bodies waited before him, though none seemed to pay the young mage much mind. Some soldiers of the Triad still fought on in the depths of the horde, but with many of the wights now bearing the crests and armour of Penance's army, it was difficult to distinguish the living from the dead.

Fionn focused on the rising slopes of the valley beyond the horde. If the gods were good, Aislinn and the other survivors would still be making their last stand there, even if Fionn couldn't see them from where he stood.

Two skeletal soldiers broke away from the fighting to charge towards him, shields and swords grasped in hands of rotting bone. Fionn raised a burning fist before him, and with a tiny flare of his soul, the flames shot forward to consume the wights.

You can't take all of them, lad! roared Sir Bearach. *You'll burn yourself out. They'll swarm over and swallow you up. You can't—*

Ignoring the voice of the dead knight, Fionn clicked his flint-rings together, creating another spark. From this, he conjured two streams of fire, and sent them out into the undead horde.

The last battlemage, he thought, fanning the power of his soul to extend the flames out across the horde. *I'm the only hope they have.*

More wights broke away from their ranks, as if only realising now that this young lad was a threat. A living Simian soldier dropped his weapon in shock as the wight he had been locked in combat with turned away to fight the lone mage.

Fionn smirked. Isolating the dead from the living was exactly what he wanted. He tugged on the power of his own soul, augmented with that of Sir Bearach's, and set the valley alight. A thick ocean of flames flooded over the undead, giving those still fighting a chance to retreat.

"Get behind me," roared Fionn as a Human soldier fell to the ground mere inches away from the flames. The Human looked up at the inferno with awe, slowing turning his gaze to Fionn's hands.

Fionn took a step forward, channelling the flames towards the bulk of the horde. He didn't turn to look, but he felt the presence of several more soldiers leaving the battle to stand behind him.

"Keep guard of my back," he shouted over his shoulder. Indeed, far off to the right, a cluster of more undead broke away from the horde to attack from the side.

As the men behind him readied themselves, Fionn hesitated, dimming the flames that burned the horde for a moment. With just another second's thought, he pulled three streaks away from the bulk of the flames and sent them towards the coming undead. There was no use in risking more lives, he reckoned, given he was more than capable of taking on the horde alone.

You're wasting energy, said Sir Bearach. *If you tire yourself out too quickly, we'll have no way to make it back to the gate.*

I'm not going back, thought Fionn, clicking his flint-rings together again to add more flames to the horde. The thick scent of burning flesh washed over Fionn as he moved forward, but his attention was elsewhere. Narrowing his brow, he focused on the valley wall beyond the battle. *I'm not going back until the rest of them are burned to ash.*

Gods above and below, lad! swore the knight. *Can't you hear yourself? Don't you know how many more are out there? This is only a fraction!*

As they pushed further into the valley, a dozen or so more soldiers joined Fionn. Some limped with injuries, others were carried by their comrades, while a few seemed to be as near death as the wights themselves. Fionn produced another spark and set waves of fire to encircle the group.

As he tugged on the power of his soul, the familiar strain of fatigue crept over him.

There is still Bearach's... Fionn thought, switching his focus from his own soul to the knight's. Bearach didn't make a response, though, and for this Fionn was glad. He didn't need more interjections interrupting his focus.

"They're retreating!" cried a voice from behind him. "They're turning back!"

Fionn had barely noticed, but it was true. The dead no longer pushed against his flames. He picked up his pace, now giving the fleeing dead pursuit. With gallant cries of victory, the other soldiers followed.

"Aislinn!" Fionn cried, spotting the cluster of survivors on the far side of the valley. With the undead on the run, there was now nothing but scorched earth between his group and hers. Bewildered, Aislinn ran forward to meet Fionn, and the other soldiers cheered upon meeting one another.

Fionn extinguished his flames. With the thrill of the fight leaving him, the young mage fell to the ground, now only aware of how spent he really was.

"Fionn, are you alright?" Aislinn said, offering him a hand to stand up. "What's the situation back at the gate?"

"Plackart sounded the retreat," said Fionn. "He was forced to close the gate, locking the rest of you out. That's why I came."

"Firemaster Fionn," said Aislinn with a smile. "I thought you were smarter than that. But I am eternally grateful for your reckless stupidity."

"I learned from the most reckless of them all," said Fionn. "You set the bar much higher when you rode out to meet the horde in Rosca Umhir."

The two shared a laugh, but their joy was cut short when one of the soldiers let out a startled cry.

"The horde! They're coming back!"

All heads turned to look down the valley. Just like before, a huge cloud of kicked-up dust came first, followed by the dead's thundering footsteps.

"To me!" roared Fionn, quickly clicking his flint-rings together and pulling flames from the spark they produced. With a wide gesture, he created a massive wall of flames that swept from one side of the valley to the other.

They'll have a hard time getting through this! cried Sir Bearach.

"The gate!" came another cry. "It's opening! Plackart's sending out another vanguard!"

Fionn didn't turn to look, but a few startled cries indicated that the man's words were true. If the Triad's army was charging out to meet the dead again, the Commander must have seriously reconsidered his position in this battle.

It's me, Fionn realised, adding more power to the wall of flames. *The tide of this battle has changed because of me.*

He raised his hands again to mould the fire, stretching the flaming wall even higher while making it thicker at the base.

But something else suddenly tugged against the flames. Another force, far stronger than his own, sent the fires crashing down. All around him, the flames extinguished themselves.

No, he cried, fighting hard to reach the rest of the flames before they died. *It's happening. It's finally happening.*

He raised his hand to click his flint-rings together, but instead felt a sharp pain run through his fingers. Screaming with agony, he raised his hand to find his middle and fourth finger swelling, turning from raw red to deep purple. At the base of both fingers, the flint-rings pressed against his skin, tightening with every passing beath.

Fionn fell to his knees as the last of his fires died before him. The throbbing pain of his fingers took on another level of intensity as the rings cut through his skin. Steel met bone, and Fionn's voice went hoarse. The other soldiers could do nothing but watch as Fionn thrashed on the ground. With another searing pang, the flint-rings closed entirely, both falling to the ground as tight balls of steel, along with two bloodied, severed fingers.

As much as he tried to scream, no sound escaped Fionn's lips. He cradled his mutilated hand against his chest as streams of blood poured from the open wound. He paid no mind to the charging horde, nor to the Triad's army that was coming out to meet them. There was only one force capable of countering his Pyromancy like that. Only one force was capable of taking Fionn's flint-rings away from him through Geomancy.

She's here. Morrigan is here.

***

The elk's hoofs thundered beneath Farris as they entered the Saltworks of Penance. Past rows upon rows of deserted buildings, they rode, Farris leading the charge with a raised halberd, and dozens of Churchguards and prisoners from the Basilica following behind.

Don't let it be too late, prayed Farris. *Skies above, don't let me be too late.*

The faint cries of battle rang out through the night, joined by the scent of smoke from somewhere near the city wall. A faint hue of blue and red rose up from where Farris reckoned the Saltgate must be, which caused him to kick his mount harder, hoping they still had time.

The Reapers will protect them. They could very well be our last hope.

The road opened into a wide square, where a battle raged on. Men and Simians ran back and forth, fighting off undead soldiers and skeletons that came towards the wall. Those behind Farris roared with valour as they charged into the fight, but something else had taken his attention.

Further beyond the battle stood the Saltgate of Penance. But the wall adjacent to it bore a huge, gaping hole. Through it came more undead soldiers, some mounted on beasts from the Glenn.

Farris urged the elk forward and adjusted his grip on the halberd. An undead soldier ran out to meet him, but a quick swing of the polearm severed the wight in two at the chest.

Shocked by the strength of his weapon, Farris held onto the reins of the elk with both hands. The beast galloped directly towards a group of undead, showing no sign of slowing. Frantically, Farris pulled back on the reins, doing everything he could to halt the charge, but the elk did not slow. Instead, it lowered its head and accelerated, plunging its great antlers into the group of skeletons. In an explosion of splintered bones, the elk broke through, not losing a second's pace.

Only when they reached the wall, did the elk slow to a stop. All along the wall, tiny blue fires burned upon the adjacent wooden buildings. Right before the hole lay the broken body of a Reaper, blood spattered upon its thick armour.

I'm too late. They've already come. It's—

"Farris!"

A large figure emerged from the darkness, limping. Clad head to toe in Simian steel armour, the figure appeared larger than most soldiers. A thick great-helm covered their head, bearing no holes but two tiny slits for eyes and a square grill at the mouth. Although impossible to recognise by sight, Farris put a name to the figure on the sound of her voice alone.

"Nicole!" he cried, turning the elk to face her. "What happened here?"

"Trolls," she said, her voice muffled through the thick helm. "They came through the walls. We didn't stand a chance. I got separated from the others and...."

"Don't worry," said Farris. "I've come to save you."

"And what the Holy Hell is that supposed to mean?"

She was cut short by a low rumble somewhere in the distance. Although the cries of battle in the square before them filled the night, it was the faint *thud-thud* of footsteps that turned Nicole to shocked silence.

From an alley leading toward the gate stepped a mountain troll. Although near equal in size to the one Farris found in the Glenn, this one differed significantly in its form. A wide, round nose hung over a sneering face, scarred and cut with blood. From its massive belly hung shimmering ropes of entrails, emerging from a long gash from chest to waist. A thick, bloody bone protruded from a broken leg, though this only seemed to affect its stance slightly. It lumbered towards Farris and Nicole, leaving a trail of thick blood behind.

The elk balked, stepping back. The troll's mass took up most of the alley, leaving Farris and Nicole with no means of escape.

"Would you rather I left you?" asked Farris, offering a hand to Nicole. She didn't take it, but deftly climbed upon the elk, taking a place behind Farris. She wrapped two hands around his waist.

"Can we outrun it?" she whispered. But Farris didn't respond. Their only hope was to send the elk charging straight into the troll. Given how terrible a plan this was, Farris opted to keep it to himself.

The troll let out a horrible cry as it plodded forward, now faster than before. Farris held his halberd before him and urged the elk onward. The beast did not respond to his touch. A terrible fear gripped Farris.

There's no escape. There's no way out.

A crackling shot rang out from somewhere behind the troll, and the beast suddenly lost its footing. Its massive body fell to the ground with a crash. Behind it, stood a Reaper, a thin stream of smoke rising from its arm. The Reaper looked just like the others, though significantly damaged. Steel stained and torn by battle made up its body, and it had lost its helm. Indeed, the pilot's own head was only slightly visible over its two massive shoulders.

"Garth!" cried Nicole. "You're alive! I thought—"

"Run," said Garth, just as the troll began to stir once more. "There's not much time."

The troll forced itself upward with a roar. It swung for the Reaper, but Garth deftly jumped aside. He raised his great firearm and shot at the troll once more. A huge, black ball erupted from the Reaper with a crack of smoke, striking the troll's chest. The undead beast, however, barely stumbled.

"Get out of here!" cried Garth, as he plunged forward towards the troll. He raised the Reaper's other arm, shaped like a lance, and forced its tip through the troll's body.

"I'm not leaving you," said Farris, urging the elk forward. "We can outrun it. We can—"

"Skies above, Farris, listen to me for once in your life!" Garth pulled his lance from the troll's stomach, but even as more innards spilled to the ground, the troll still stood. "You were right about the king. I'm sorry I didn't believe you."

Farris gripped his halberd and went to dismount the elk. Only Nicole's hand on his shoulder made him hesitate.

"Listen to me," roared Garth again, readying himself for another strike. "The horde came here for a reason. This girl clearly wants to slay the king. You can't let that happen. Go to him. Protect him. Fly him across the fucking Eternal Sea if you need to."

The troll leapt forward, but this time Garth wasn't so quick. The massive beast fell on top of the Reaper, pinning Garth to the ground.

"What are you waiting for?" screamed Garth. "Go!"

Farris didn't remember sending the elk into a gallop. He didn't remember passing Garth, leaving him alone with the troll. In a daze, Farris rode out into the Saltworks, towards the centre of the city. It was only when he left the fighting behind, and the din of battle was replaced with the silence of the night, that Farris fully comprehend what he had done.

Chapter 30:
Apotheosis

The church teaches that Seletoth created the heavens and the earth, and all the life that dwell in both. But they do not elaborate on why He did this. The Church insists we worship not only Seletoth, but His wife Meadhbh, too, yet they provide no elaboration on why the Lord chose this particular mortal. The writings and teachings of the Church raise far more questions than answers. But when you fully embrace Seletoth in His purest form, He leaves no room for doubt. Some have learned of the true nature of God, but the blinding truth drove them mad. Maybe the Church is protecting us from this same fate, but perhaps they provide no answers because they too are afraid of what they could really mean.

Excerpt from *On the True Nature of God,* by Hamlan Caithin.

***

The elk's trot slowed to a stop as Farris and Nicole passed the Tower of Sin. Neither had said anything since leaving the Saltworks, but Farris's mind raced through the possibilities Garth's final words implied.

To take Diarmuid away from Alabach, he mused. *It'll keep him safe from Morrigan, perhaps, and they do say there are great lands to the south, but with the Grey Plague...*

This thought brought back the memory of the night Farris had killed Chester the Lucky. They had been drinking in a bar on the Cruachan waterfront beforehand. There, Chester had speculated that the Grey Plague was nothing more than a myth produced by the Church to prevent anyone from leaving Alabach.

Skies above, Chester. I hope you were right.

The great House of the Triad appeared ahead of them. The streets of the Shadow of Sin were deathly quiet, but there appeared to be more activity inside the Triad than usual. It seemed as if those who couldn't fight were sent to the House in response to the horde's arrival.

They won't be safe for long. Farris swallowed deeply on recalling the state of the Saltgate. The wall had been breached. The undead were inside. Farris had left dozens of soldiers behind when he fled.

They followed me. I fooled them into following me.

Gritting his teeth, Farris slowed the elk to a stop. Light from inside the building spilled out from the fanlight over the two iron-bound doors, illuminating the steps before him.

"Come on," he said, gesturing to Nicole as he climbed down from the elk. She was slow to move, but eventually pulled herself down from the mount. With the thick Simian-steel helm covering her face, Farris could only guess at what expression it hid.

They both sprinted up the stairs. Of course, the doors to the Triad were locked shut, but an answer came immediately after Farris pounded upon them.

"Are you seeking refuge?" came the loud, booming voice. "We've no more room, but Sin is still taking civilians."

"We have a message for the king," said Farris, keeping his voice as stern and official as the one he was responding to. "On the progress of the battle."

There was a pause. "Any word from the Goldgate?" he asked, less like a guard, and more like a concerned Simian.

"Last I heard, the retreat was sounded," said Farris. "But the gate still stands."

The door opened a crack, and the face of the Simian guard appeared. His eyes were wide, and his mouth slightly ajar.

"Plackart sounded the retreat?" he asked. "He's not one to turn his back on a fight."

Farris took a step forward. "Are you going to let us in, or would you rather wait for the horde?"

The guard promptly stepped aside, letting Farris and Nicole enter the Triad's hall. Hundreds of refugees, Humans and Simians alike, filled the floor. Mothers clutched babies, husbands held their wives, and young children ran back and forth around the encampment, blissfully ignorant of the terror that awaited them. A young Simian boy huddled with his family caught Farris's eyes. The lad threw him an amusing look, like one would make trying to stop an infant from crying.

Farris smiled back, despite everything. As he weaved through the crowd, he couldn't help but wonder where he would be tonight if he was a still a child.

I probably would have objected to coming here, he thought, taking the stairs two at a time while Nicole followed behind. *But Garth would have brought me.* Farris's throat went dry at the thought. *He always got his way in the end.*

They passed more guards, and they looked on with hope, perhaps expecting more news from the frontline. Farris averted their gaze. There was no point. The city was going to fall, and Farris's last hope was to escape. Even if they succeeded, it would mean leaving every person here to the horde.

Skies take me, I couldn't help the prisoners. I couldn't help my brother.

He attempted to compose himself as they reached the Triad's meeting room. Indeed, it was most likely that Argyll would be there, pouring over a map of Penance, carefully planning what was to happen next.

"I have a message for the king," said Farris to the Simian guard at the door. "He is not expecting me, but the news is urgent."

Without saying a word, the guard stepped aside. When the door swung open, Farris's prior convictions were proven partially true. The Silverback indeed was there, but he wasn't poring over a map of Penance. Instead, he stood with his back to the door, staring out the window at the fallen city. It was Padraig Tuathil who was studying the map of Penance, adjusting the wooden figurines scattered across it and mumbling to himself. King Diarmuid sat alone, his eyes far away, his body rocking back and forth. He too, was whispering to himself, but Farris guessed his words made less sense than the captain's.

"You escaped," said Argyll, as if he was barely surprised. "What brings you here?"

Farris stepped forward. "The city won't hold for much longer. If protecting the king is still your highest priority, then I recommend we escort him out from the city. *Skirmisher* can—"

Argyll raised a hand. "What authority do you have, to come in here and demand what our next actions are?"

"I have no authority," began Farris. "But we have no real hope of fighting the horde. If their leader really wants the king dead, we must ensure that doesn't happen." He gestured towards Nicole. "We are leaving Penance by airship. Anyone who would like to come too can join. The decision is yours, not mine. Will you come?"

"Let's ask the king himself," said Argyll, smiling as he bowed to Diarmuid. "What does His Grace think of this plan?"

King Diarmuid sat upright and threw Farris a peculiar glance. "This was not meant to happen," he muttered. "None of this was. We no longer walk in the Light of the Lady."

"See," said Argyll. "His mind is not sound. He is incapable of making a decision for himself."

Farris paused, considering his next move. He turned towards Padraig. "Captain Tuathil. You have taken responsibility before for the king's well-being. If anyone is able to answer for His Grace, it is you."

Padraig threw a peculiar glance from Farris to Argyll. He swallowed deeply. "If I leave, this will be the second time I've fled from the horde. But where are we to flee to? Is there any land left untouched by the dead?"

"To the south," said Farris. "Over the Sea of Storms. We'll keep flying until we find land."

Argyll let out a short, sharp laugh. "And then what? Settle? Make a new life for ourselves? Establish a new kingdom?"

A loud crash rang out from below, followed by several scattered screams.

Each strand of hair on Farris's body stood on end.

It's over. There's no escape.

Across the room, Argyll dashed to the window. "They're here!" he cried, his voice quivering with terror. "They're filling the streets. One of the gates must have fallen."

Nicole stepped forward and removed her helm. Her expression was stern and unmoving.

"There is no shame in running when your foe cannot be beaten," she said. "Come with us if you value your life over some archaic notion of valour. If you do not value your life, then do so for the king you have sworn to protect with it. Spending more lives now will only grow the horde. You can come with me or join the fight against us. Your choice." With that, she turned to leave without looking back. If she had, she would have seen that even King Diarmuid himself had risen to follow her.

***

"Get behind me!" cried Aislinn, positioning herself in front of Fionn.

The mage held his severed hand against his chest and could do nothing but look up at the great figure that protected him. Plates of steel covered her body, leaving nothing but her jaw and mouth exposed. In two hands, she gripped a massive greatsword, which she wielded as easily as if it were made of wood. Even with the horde approaching from down the valley, her stance did not waver.

Fionn gritted his teeth and slowly stood to his feet.

"I'll fight," he said, trying hard to ignore the blood dripping from his hand. "I can still fight."

"You need to retreat," said Aislinn, not turning back. "You're in no state to be here."

Fionn narrowed his eyes and focused on the wound. With all the time he had spent mastering Pyromancy, the other Schools of Magic had somewhat faded from his memory. He was still capable of boiling water with Hydromancy, and one occasion he'd use Aeromancy to turn the page of a book.

But can I still heal, he thought, reaching into his soul to pour power into the open wound. He felt the torn flesh resonate within his soul. He flared the fire in his heart and turned all his might into stopping the bleeding. His heartbeat began to slow, and a warm, soothing feeling enveloped his hand.

The ground rumbled beneath him, and Fionn found himself surrounded by hundreds of charging soldiers. Living soldiers. Those who had come from the gate didn't slow as they passed Aislinn and the others, but instead continued on to face the horde.

"Follow them," cried Aislinn to the others. "Let us take the fight to the dead this time!"

The others around her let out an uplifting cry and broke away from their position.

"Return to the gate," Aislinn said. "Your wound is too great. You'll only be putting yourself at—"

She paused on seeing Fionn's hand. He hadn't fully healed his fingers, but the bleeding had stopped, and a thin layer of skin covered the holes where they had once been.

"I'm not turning back," said Fionn. He could barely think straight over the agony in his hand, but he wasn't about to share that with Aislinn.

She sighed. "Mages," she muttered as she turned. "Don't fall behind. I'll do my best to protect you."

Fionn smiled. "As I will you."

Loud cries of battle rang out ahead, but by the time they reached the fray, it was difficult to tell who was fighting whom. Some men and Simians fought against those obviously undead, for it was easy to discern the skeletal and headless soldiers from those of the Triad. But some wights wore the armour of the Triad, and they fought against those clad in the same.

A crossbow bolt whizzed past Fionn's head, but he pressed on, keeping close to Aislinn. The mighty woman swung her greatsword in wide arcs, severing wights all around. A skeletal soldier mounted atop a horse galloped towards Aislinn, but she deftly dodged aside and plunged her sword into the beast's chest. The horse let out a harrowing cry and fell to the ground, crushing another corpse beneath its mighty weight.

Fionn turned to find an undead soldier behind him. With an ounce of Geomancy, he pushed the soldier's sword aside, letting it fall to the ground. Unarmed, the soldier still bounded towards him. The mage balked in response, but suddenly Aislinn stood between them. With little effort, she cut the wight down, barely acknowledging Fionn.

I'm little use without my fire. Fionn glanced around for an open flame to manipulate. Instead, his gaze fell on the sword dropped by the wight. He bent down to pick it up, holding it awkwardly with his oversized arm.

Do you even have any experience wielding a sword? asked Sir Bearach.

Fionn gripped the hilt tight and swung the sword to gauge its weight. The force of the swing caused him to stumble, almost dropping the weapon in the process.

Stay with Aislinn, urged the dead knight. *You are no fighter. You never should have followed!*

Shut up, said Fionn, looking around to find Aislinn again. *You're not helping. You're—*

The sight across the battlefield caused Fionn to pause. Mere throwing distance away, a short, black figure stood within the horde. At first, it appeared to be covered in feathers, but as Fionn stepped closer, the image resolved itself to that of a girl. Blood was clotted in her hair, as black and tangled as the feathers of her cloak.

She raised a dainty arm overhead, and something rumbled from across the battlefield. On the far side of the valley, a huge chunk of the surrounding mountains broke away, collapsing on top of the soldiers below. The girl smiled at this sight and turned her attention back to the battle.

Then her gaze fell upon Fionn. Her wicked smile widened, and she began moving towards him.

Put an arrow in the bitch that's leading them, echoed Plackart's words from Fionn's memory. *That's the only way to beat the horde.*

Ignoring all else going on around him, Fionn pressed on. He tightened his grip on the sword, but something stirred beneath his fingers. The blade began to bend inward, twisting under some invisible force. Fionn cast it aside. Instead of falling, the sword's hilt spun around and hit Fionn's leg, knocking him to the ground.

In a daze, Fionn tried to pull himself to his feet. But when he looked up, the face of Morrigan was all he could see. Lengths of knotted hair obscured her features, with dried blood speckled across her skin. Her cracked, dried lips revealed a smile, more terrible and mischievous than the last.

"You are the one who made the fire," she said, pressing a foot against Fionn's chest. "You're strong, but weak as a puppy without your rings."

Fionn stretched his arm to the side, hoping to grab another weapon, but his fingers only found dirt.

"There is power in your soul," rasped Morrigan, leaning in. She inhaled deeply, as if sniffing the air. "More power than most. There is something special about you. Something that sets you aside from the others."

"Aislinn!" cried Fionn, realising there was no other hope to be saved. "Aislinn!"

"There is nobody here to save you," said Morrigan. She reached out and pressed a finger against Fionn's lips. "Your power belongs to me now."

From beneath her cloak she pulled a dagger, its blade glinting silver in the moonlight.

Your magic, lad! cried Sir Bearach. *Cast it aside with your magic!*

It's no use, thought Fionn, powerless as Morrigan brought the blade down over him. *She has already won.*

***

Nicole led Farris down the stairs, Padraig, Diarmuid, and Argyll closely behind. Perhaps the sight of their king fleeing would be enough to cause the people in the hall to panic, but they seemed far more concerned with the undead horde right outside the door.

"There's an entrance at the back," said Nicole, leading the way as they fought through the crowds. "It'll take us right out to Sin's doorstep."

"And we can be sure that the dead won't be there?" asked Farris.

"We can't be sure of anything."

Armed guards ran past in the opposite direction, towards the main door. There, the other guards pressed their bodies against it, fighting back the force that thundered against its wood.

"This way," said Nicole, leading them away from the hall and down a dark corridor. Empty studies rushed by them as they went, along with portraits and busts of those who had served on the Triad in the past. Eventually they came to a door with a small window in its frame.

"It's clear," said Nicole, peering out through the window. She pulled across the various bolts and locks that held it shut. Once unlocked, Nicole swung the door open, revealing the great Tower of Sin, piercing an empty sky over vacant streets.

"Come on," urged Nicole, leading them out. Farris hastily glanced up and down the road as they went, half expecting the horde to turn the corner at any minute.

When they reached the tower, yet another locked door greeted them. Before Farris could try to consider what action they should take to get through it, Padraig Tuathil stepped forward.

"Your king demands entry!" he boomed, though Diarmuid didn't look like he was in a state to demand anything. "To deny him is to commit treason!"

The door immediately swung open, and the Simian guard behind it bowed aside to let them pass.

Like the House of the Triad, the hundreds of civilians from the city sought refuge in Sin. Except this time, they all looked on expectantly as King Diarmuid crossed the floor.

"Long live the king!" cried a single voice from amongst the crowd. "He walks in the Light of the Lady!"

"Glory to the Crown!" called another. "Blessed be His holy name!"

A buzz of excitement ran through them, though it seemed to dissipate slightly once they reached the stairs. Farris kept his gaze away from the crowd.

They must know. They must know he's here to leave them.

The hushed whispers of the townsfolk died as Farris and the others ascended the winding stairway of the broken tower. Eventually they came to the top, where more than a dozen airships hung silently along the tower's edge. Amongst them was *Skirmisher*, just as slight and elegant as ever.

"I'll get her ready," Nicole called, running ahead. "It'll be a tight squeeze, but she'll be strong enough to hold us all."

The Silverback walked to the edge of the tower. The Shadow of Sin district remained empty, but the cries of battle from the north echoed through the night.

"We were lucky to escape," Farris said, hoping to fill the silence that hung over them. "Maybe we walk in the Light of the Lady after all."

"No," said King Diarmuid. "The Light has forsaken us, for we have strayed far from the path She set out before us."

"What do you mean?" Farris asked. Even Diarmuid's ramblings would be helpful in taking his attention away from the fighting. From all the people they would leave behind.

"No, I cannot say. I cannot!" said the king. "My actions have already caused enough damage. I must not speak of it any further!"

Argyll turned around, abruptly. "What actions do you speak of?"

The king threw the Silverback a terrible glance, with something between sorrow and regret in his eyes.

"I blamed you. I...I'm just as responsible for this as the Godslayer herself. For I thought She was speaking about you..."

Argyll adapted a stance more defiant than ever. "You better start making sense, or we'll leave you to the undead. Is this about Santos's death?"

Nicole appeared by Argyll's side, the engine of *Skirmisher* rattling loudly behind her. "My father's death? What are you talking about?"

Padraig placed a hand on his sheathed sword. "His Grace's mind has been fragile ever since the horde came to Cruachan. It will do no good to interrogate him in this state."

"No," said Argyll. "He'll speak now. His actions almost threw the kingdom into civil war. He owes it to us to tell the truth."

"P-please," stammered the king. "I can't, I..." He closed his eyes. "I saw it!" he shouted. "We were inspecting the railway tunnel, and Lady Meadhbh appeared before us. She murdered Santos and my men. Then She showed me the horde, and I saw how they would march across the kingdom, consuming all they come upon."

Unmoved, Argyll asked, "What does this have to do with me?"

King Diarmuid shook his head. "She said they would be led by one named 'the Godslayer.' I thought...I thought it was you. So, I blamed Santos's death on the Simian dissidents, in order to prevent the future She showed me. But it was those very actions that brought this upon us. It was my own hubris, my own conviction that I could turn the tides of fate that thrust my kingdom into turmoil."

Something brushed past from behind Farris. He instinctively brought a hand to the two short swords held at the small of his back, but his fingers only found one.

The other was held by Argyll, who grabbed Diarmuid, pressing the steel against his neck.

Padraig was the first to respond. He unsheathed his sword, but stopped once he saw the position Argyll held his king in.

"Drop your weapon!" commanded Padraig. "In the name of the King, I command you to stand down!"

"Do it," whispered Diarmuid. "None of this was supposed to happen. I was supposed to die in Cruachan. We are too far from the Lady's Light. A quick death would be a mercy compared to life in this doomed world."

"Argyll, stop!" pleaded Nicole. "This is madness!"

"You heard him," rasped Argyll. "He lied about your father's death. He used it as a political gambit against the Movement. He deserves far more than death!"

A terrible cry cut through the tension, and a harrowing fear came over Farris once more. Leaving the others, he ran to the edge of the tower to see the horde, in all its might, pressing against Sin's walls.

"The undead," he cried. "They're here! We must leave, now!"

Argyll turned to Farris. "You claimed the king was invincible. You said he cannot be killed."

With that, he pulled the blade across Diarmuid's neck, and a crimson stream of blood followed it. Argyll let his grip loosen, and the king fell to the ground, grasping and spluttering at his throat. The king fell to the ground, eyes rolling into the back of his head. Then he went still.

"See," whispered Argyll, the bloodied sword in his hand. "Death comes to us all."

***

Fionn closed his eyes and braced himself as Morrígan's dagger came down upon him, but there was no impact. Cautiously, he opened an eye to see she was no longer paying the mage any mind. Instead, faced away from the battle, her focus now directed towards the centre of the city.

"He's dead," she whispered, rising to her feet. "The king is dead. The soul of Móráin is…"

She trailed off and closed her eyes. Slowly, she raised both of her hands.

"I can feel his power," she cried. "I can feel the strength of Móráin. Of Seletoth and Meadhbh, locked in the blood of the fool king. Their strength shall be my own."

All around her, the wights began collapsing, one by one.

"What's happening?" said Fionn, struggling to find his feet. The undead now littered the battlefield, unmoving as the dead that accompanied them.

"How?" said Fionn, turning to face Morrígan. "Why—"

But she was gone.

***

"No!"

Padraig Tuathil charged toward Argyll, leaping over the dead king on his way. But before he could reach the Simian, a blinding light burst out from before them.

Farris rubbed his eyes, and blinking frantically, refocused his gaze on the king's body. However, now there stood a dark figure over the corpse. Padraig stopped, dropping his sword in shock. But Argyll seemed unmoved.

Morrígan stood over Diarmuid's body. A black cloak of feathers covered her body, each twisted and bent out of shape.

"You!" cried Argyll. With the bloody short sword in his hand, he broke into a sprint towards the girl. "I'll gut you where you stand! I'll—"

He slid to a halt as Morrígan turned towards him. With a harrowing laugh, she let the cloak fall from her body. From her back emerged two great wings, black feathers spanning twice the length of her own body.

The power of Móráin. Farris recalled the images of King Móráin's ascent to godhood before the Simians during the Final Conquest. *She's claimed it for herself.*

Padraig fell to his knees before the terrible sight, and Nicole took a step closer to Farris.

The Silverback, however, was unmoved.

"Your power does not scare us!" he cried, raising the blade before him. "We Simians are a stronger people than you can imagine! I've already killed one god tonight. You don't know what I'm capable of!"

He leapt forward, but Morrígan did not flinch. She raised a hand and made a dismissive gesture. This knocked Argyll aside with great force. He hit the ground with a crash, then his momentum carried him over the side of the tower, into the horde below.

"Argyll!" cried Nicole. She went to run, but Farris grabbed her arm.

"Don't move," he whispered, watching Morrígan intently.

Slowly, Morrígan began to rise from the ground, her great wings folding and expanding as she did. With each beat, she soared above them, until she was high enough for the entire city to see her. With one last manic laugh, she took flight, disappearing into the distant darkness.

None responded at first, but Padraig slowly rose to his feet. Silently, he walked past Nicole and Farris, and peered over the edge of the tower, where Argyll had fallen.

"The horde," he said. "The undead. They're...dead. Unraised. How?"

Farris stepped forward to look, too. Hundreds upon hundreds of corpses still filled the streets, but none were moving.

"The horde was just a means to an end," said Farris. "All so she could claim the king's power for herself. What use is an army, compared to the power of a god?"

Beneath them, ecstatic cries echoed around the city. With each cheer, they grew louder and more elated. Here and there, pieces of song broke out, filling the night with joyful music.

Nicole appeared beside him. "What's going on?" she said. "Why are they singing? Why are they cheering?"

"Because they think it's over," said Farris. "Because they think we've won."

CHAPTER 31:
THE SEEDS OF CHAOS

Farris followed the others through the dark railroad tunnel. The air was warmer than he had anticipated, but every now and then he still shivered, unable to shake the feeling that they never should have come here.

Three days had passed since the Battle of Penance, but the memories of that night still replayed over and over in his mind, as if it had only occurred hours earlier. The image of Diarmuid's dying expression was still fresh, as was Argyll's body being thrown from the tower. The Silverback was in the care of the white mages of the Triad, now, but he barely clung to life.

Then there was Garth. Although Farris hadn't seen him die, leaving his own brother to the mercy of the horde hurt more than the rest of the images combined.

He gently patted the elk on the back. The great beast had managed to survive that terrible night unscathed and seemed almost happy to be reunited with Farris. It hadn't been difficult to find mounts for the others to take on this journey. There were more than a handful of horses left abandoned in the city after the horde fell.

Nicole rode by Farris's side. She seemed to be coping with the aftermath better than the others, though it was impossible to tell how she really felt. With a narrowed brow, her focus remained locked forward into the darkness of the tunnel that took them deep beneath the kingdom of Alabach.

Padraig Tuathil led the way, for this whole expedition was his idea. King Diarmuid's last words implied that the Lady Meadhbh was somewhere here, and if anyone knew what should be done next, it would be Her.

Assuming She's even here, thought Farris, although dismissing the existence of the gods was a lot more difficult now than before.

Back in Penance, all the corpses of the horde had been taken to the Saltgate to be burned, ensuring that none would rise again. Those that died during the battle were to be burned, too, including the king, though Padraig had objected to including the latter, claiming His Grace deserved a royal funeral. Given that no such arrangement had been made, this journey would be some form of middle ground.

But why did so many others insist on coming? Farris turned back to see Fionn following behind. The young lad held his arm in a sling. Apparently, he had lost two fingers in the fighting, though he didn't elaborate more on that.

Skies above, first an arm, then two fingers. He's lucky to still be alive.

Next to Fionn was Cormac, who had fought in the Triad's army at the Goldgate. He had narrowly escaped the battle with his life, and now walked with a limp.

Maybe he saw his own daughter there. Farris recalled the rumours that Morrígan herself was present at the Goldgate, before making her appearance atop the Tower of Sin.

None had seen her since she left the city that night. Much to Farris's frustration, the citizens had been celebrating their supposed victory over the dead for the past three days. Despite all they lost, the people of Penance were willing to grasp onto any thread of happiness, even though Morrígan was still out there, stronger and more powerful than before.

"Do you think She'll help us?" whispered Nicole. "What do you think we'll get out of this?"

Farris didn't respond. After all, Diarmuid had said it was Meadhbh who killed Santos. Surely Nicole should be worried a similar fate awaited them all.

The tunnel eventually widened out into a large clearing. This was one of the many outposts along the railway line, originally built to house the engineers who would maintain the line and the locomotives. Now it was nothing more than a desolate cave, with several derelict buildings scattered throughout.

Padraig stopped abruptly. "This is where Diarmuid claimed he was attacked. We should split up and search."

As they dismounted, Fionn stepped forward. "Wait, so we have no real proof that She's here? You're saying that we could have been travelling for a whole day just to find nothing?"

"What choice do we have?" asked Padraig, shrugging. "It's only a matter of time before Morrígan returns. Penance remains the last bastion of civilisation, and we certainly won't be able to hold it if it's attacked again. Now, search the area, and shout if you see anything strange."

They all split up, though Nicole stayed close to Farris. Slowly, the two of them paced around the perimeter of the outpost, examining the walls and floor for any indication of oddity.

"I never did thank you," said Nicole eventually, avoiding Farris's eyes. "As much as I hate to admit it, I'm glad you came back to...save me."

Farris swallowed deeply. His heartbeat quickened. "Why, wouldn't you have done the same for me?"

Nicole took his hand into her own. "That's another thing you'd never catch me admitting."

In that instant, all his fear left him. Fear for his people, fear for what Morrígan may do next. As much as it hurt, even the deaths those back in Penance no longer weighed upon Farris's shoulders.

"Nicole," he said carefully. "I've been meaning to say—"

"Hey!" came Fionn's panicked voice from across the clearing. "Come look at this!"

Dropping Farris's hand, Nicole turned and ran towards Fionn. Farris jogged on behind, cursing the lad's timing.

When they reached the other side, it was clear what Fionn had found. There, in the stone, was a large, crooked hole with irregular edges.

"What is it?" said Cormac breathlessly. "Another tunnel?"

"No," said Fionn. "There were circles drawn on the wall. Like the symbol of the Trinity. When I touched them, they opened."

"This must it," said Padraig, stepping forward. He unsheathed his sword. "There are stairs here, but they don't look very safe. You better watch your step."

The captain led the way, the others following closely behind. The stairs indeed were difficult to navigate, with each step larger or smaller than the last. Whereas they were once in a natural cave formation, this one seemed far less so. Oddly shaped columns held up the ceiling, as if conceived by a drunk architect. Or a madman.

The stairs eventually led down to a small opening in the darkness. Before them, stood an altar, with a strange, blue aura emanating from it.

"What is this place?" asked Padraig, looking around at the empty room.

In a brilliant flash, blue light engulfed the party. From the radiance came a terrible voice, each word drenched in spite.

"You have killed two kings," it said. Farris's hands cupped his ears. "And already you have strayed from the path set out before you. This day was destined to come since Creation, and I am ready for whatever force you have brought."

From the source of the light emerged a figure. A woman, slender and beautiful, who wore nothing but light as a gown. She stepped forward, and the blue aura began to dwindle, giving the party a full view of her grace.

Padraig was first to fall to his knees, followed by Cormac and Fionn. Nicole did the same, leaving Farris the only one standing.

"Holy Mother of Gods and Kings," whispered Padraig. "We are not worthy to witness your beauty. We humbly come before you for help."

The Lady Meadhbh paused and looked down at the group. A curious expression crossed her face, almost like confusion.

Is it possible for a god to even be confused?

"Who are you to come before me?" she demanded, her words echoing around the chamber. "None of you should be here. Where is the Godslayer?"

Farris stepped forward, his fingers curling into fists. "Her army was defeated at Penance. She left and hasn't been seen since."

Meadhbh frowned on hearing this. "No. The horde never made it to Penance. King Diarmuid died drunk and alone in Cruachan, and she claimed his power there. The army never travelled north."

Farris hesitated for a moment. None of the others seemed likely to respond, so he continued instead.

"This is not true. We took the king to Penance, and he died atop the Tower of Sin."

"Lies!" screamed Meadhbh. The shrill sound of her voice was worse than knives cutting glass. "What right does a heathen like you have to stand before me, and weave falsities in my presence? You—"

The Lady cut herself off. She looked down at each of the others and turned back to Farris.

"You..." She said, Her voice softer than before, almost like a whisper. "All of you. You are all dead."

Farris had no answer to this. Cormac gasped, and Fionn jumped to his feet. Nicole's eyes were as white and white as ever, but only Padraig was unmoved.

"How did we die, my Lady?" Padraig asked, perhaps more sardonically than he should have.

Meadhbh looked down at the captain. "Padraig Tuathil died in the Grey Keep, after bringing news to his king that the city had fallen. The dead stormed the building, and he died trying to protect the citizens of Cruachan."

"Cormac O'Branna," she said next. "He travelled to Penance after the fall of Point Grey and caught the bloody flux while living amongst the squalor of the refugee camp."

Cormac himself barely acknowledged his own name, but kept his gaze locked on the floor.

"Fionn the Red," she said next. "He was set upon by bandits on the way from Roseán to Point Grey. Chief Engineer Nicole was killed in an explosion that took down the Tower of Sin.

"And Farris Silvertongue," she said, turning to Farris. "He died after an encounter with a mountain troll and drowned on the shores of the Clifflands."

"You're wrong," said Farris. "None of these things have unfolded as you claim. I did not die on those cliffs. Padraig was rescued from Cruachan on the night the horde came, and the Tower of Sin still stands."

"The Tower still stands," echoed Nicole, rising to stand by Farris's side. "As do we."

"Impossible," mused Meadhbh. "This is not what was destined to happen. Your fates were determined before Creation. Before the Apotheosis. Before—"

A strange look crossed her face. Then the Lady smiled.

"Of course. I understand now. You no longer walk in my Light."

"What do you mean?" asked Farris. Even if She did, he certainly didn't understand what was going on.

"Most of what you have been told by the Church are half-truths," She began. "It is not my place to elaborate on them, but there is one thing you should know: Seletoth did not create the heavens and the earth. The land, the wildlife, and the animals that inhabit this world all predate Creation. It was only Humans that Seletoth created. Therefore, it is only Humans that are bound by destiny. By the fate I have seen."

Padraig shook his head slightly on hearing this. As unfamiliar with the faith as Farris was, this certainly seemed contrary to what the Church taught.

"But long before Seletoth's Humans made it to Alabach," Meadhbh continued, "something peculiar happened. The savage primates that once roamed the lands slowly changed over time, developing from generation to generation into what you today call Simians. The fate that binds Humans so tightly does not have as much strength over your people."

"So, we are free from your Light?" asked Farris, afraid of what the answer would be.

Meadhbh didn't respond to Farris directly. "Since the moment Humans were created, the fate of the land was sealed. A young girl named Morrígan was destined to find a means to usurp the gods, and even Seletoth would fall to her power. Every Human, from the highest earl to the lowest peasant, is bound to this destiny. King Diarmuid could not spurn the tides of fate, even when he saw what end awaited us all.

"But the Simian people are not bound by the same limitations. It happened once long ago, when the engineers of Penance began building their tower. Destiny dictated that it would not exceed Mount Selyth in height, but the tower kept on rising. This was the first and last time Seletoth would interfere with the Simians and their efforts to stray from my Light."

"The Fall of Sin," whispered Nicole.

The Lady gazed down at Farris. "But Seletoth is no longer as strong as He once was. Now the Simians' seeds of chaos have been left unchecked, and their roots have dug deep into the Tapestry of Fate, unravelling its threads one by one."

"I don't understand," said Farris, shaking his head. "How—"

A burst of blue light filled his vision, and Farris saw himself, more than a year ago, climbing the cliffs of Roseán. Then he saw himself fighting off the highwaymen that jumped him on the way to Point Grey. Next, he saw himself interrogating the false druid at Sin, the one who was supposed to carry out the Crown's attack on the tower. He saw himself picking Cormac from the crowd of the refugee camp, and then swinging through the window of the king's private quarters in Cruachan. Finally, saw himself and Nicole in an old hangar in the Steamworks of Penance, a blue fire burning amongst discarded papers at their feet.

"Do you see now?" asked Meadhbh "Farris Silvertongue, you are but one Simian, but your actions alone have caused ripples throughout the lives of those bound by fate. From the moment you choose not to die on the shores of the Clifflands, you walked outside of my Light. From there, your choices, though minor in themselves, have turned many from this path, even Morrígan. It was she who was supposed to stand before me today, not you. Even I did not think it was possible to fight fate in this manner, but it seems I have been proven wrong."

Farris's mind reeled at the revelation. *Me? I caused this?* He turned to the others, who looked expectantly at him. *I...saved them?*

"But what about Morrígan?" asked Padraig. "What is it she wants? Is she still a threat?"

The smile vanished from Meadhbh's face. "It was destined that she would seek to usurp the gods. First, she sought power, which she found in her undead horde. Now that she has claimed the king's power for her own, she no longer craves more."

The Lady closed her eyes, as if in pain.

"But she has caught a glimpse of the Truth, the same Truth the Church was established to conceal. She will come for me next, and on taking my power, she will learn what no mortal should ever know: What lies beyond the Eternal Sea, why poison flows through the Glenn, why Seletoth created Man.... These revelations will drive her mad. From there, destroying Seletoth and bringing an end to all life will be the only reasonable response."

The others stood in silence, but Meadhbh stepped down from the altar, towards Farris. The Simian did not flinch, even as the Lady's holy light strained his eyes.

"However, this destiny may not unfold as it was supposed to. I once said that we are all thralls of fate, and there is no hope in fighting what was meant to be. But through the fires of steel and steam, the Simian people have sewn chaos into this world." She raised a hand and placed it on Farris's shoulder.

"And where there is chaos, there is hope."

GUIDE TO ALABACH, HER PLACES, AND HER PEOPLE

AC: After Conquest. The Thralls of Fate begins in AC403.

Aislinn Carríga: Lady of Keep Carríga, Rosca Umhir, sister of Sir Bearach and Cathal Carríga.

Aldrich Canal: Simian-built canal connecting the Rustlake to Móráin Sea.

Aoife Ní Branna: Morrígan's deceased mother. *(Ee-fa Nee-Branna)*

Arch-Canon Cathbad: Head of the Church of the Trinity

Ard Sidhe: One of the Seven Seachtú of Alabach. *(Ard Sid-heh)*

Argyll the Silverback: Leader of the Simian dissident movement in Penance, formally the head of the Guild of Thieves.

Beadhbh: flightless bird of prey from the Glenn. *(Bayve)*

Borris Blackhand: One of the Triad, the governing body of Penance, along with Cathal Carríga and King Diarmuid Móráin III, XIX.

Cathal Carríga: One of the Triad, the governing body of Penance, along with Borris Blackhand and King Diarmuid Móráin III, XIX. (*Ca-hal Carry-ga*)

Col: Once was a settlement north of Penance, but long since abandoned.

Cormac O'Branna: Father of Morrígan.

Divine Penetrance: Also known as the Gift of Immortality, this is a power passed from father to son through the Móráin line, ensuring the royal bloodline stays intact.

Dromán: Capital of the Woodlands of Alabach, home to the Academy of Mages. (*Dro-mawn*)

Earthmaster Seán: Master of geomancy, based in Penance.

Elis Point: Northernmost point of Alabach, where the Simian Elis Highwind tested the world's first airship.

Eternal Sea: Sea to the west of Alabach, with no known land beyond it

Farris Silvertongue: A double agent infiltrating the Crown, relaying information back to the dissident Simian movement of Penance.

Fionn: A young Pyromancer. (*Fyun*)

Firemaster Conleth: Master of pyromancy, based in Penance.

Garth: Brother of Farris Silvertongue.

General-Commander Plackart: General of the Triad's Army in Penance.

Geomancer: Mage capable of manipulating the earth and Her fruits

Grey Keep: Residence of King Diarmuid Móráin, Third of His name, Nineteenth Incarnate of Seletoth

Grey Plague: Mysterious force that the Firstborn fled 400 years ago. Some speculate it was a sickness, others claim it was a supernatural blight on the earth.

Iron Concordant: Peace Treaty written up following the Fall of Sin. Promising Simians would not interfere with the workings of the Church and Crown.

Jacob the Blind: Simian smuggler based in Penance and Point Grey. Aligned with the Silverback.

King Diarmuid Móráin: Third of His Name, and Nineteenth Incarnate of Seletoth. Son of King Flaithrí IV, Diarmuid spent his reign attempting to bridge the gap between Man and Simian. *(King Dear-myid More-ain)*

Lady Meadhbh: One of the Trinity of Alabach. Called the Mother, the Lady, and the Weaver of Fate. Said to have determined the destiny of every living soul in Alabach. *(Lady Mayve)*

Lord Seletoth: One of the Trinity of Alabach. Called the Father, the Lord, and the Creator. Believed by some to be the One True God, rather than one of three as the Church teaches.

Móráin I: The First King of Alabach, also known as the Old, or the Great. Instead of accepting true divinity from the Lord, he chose to be with his wife. As a compromise, Seletoth bestowed upon him Divine Penetrance, in order to ensure that the Móráin line would never be broken.

Móráin Sea: Sea on the east coast of Alabach

Moray Head: Headland north of Point Grey

Morrígan Ní Branna: Daughter of Aoife Ní Branna, and niece to Yarlaith the White, Roseán. (*Morry-gan Nee Branna*)

Mount Selyth: A lone peak said to be the residence of Lord Seletoth, though no person has climbed the mountain and returned to confirm the myth.

Padraig Tuathil: Captain of the City Guard in Cruachan. (*Pad-rayg Twa-hill*)

Penance: The home city of the Simian people following the Final Conquest; named by Lord Seletoth following the Fall of Sin.

Plains of Tierna Meall: Human version of an afterlife, with rolling green hills and summers that last forever. (*Plains of Tear-na Myall*)

Point Grey: Capital of the Clifflands of Alabach.

Pyromancers: Mages who manipulate fire.

Pyromaster: An expert in all things pertaining to Pyromancy, recognised as such by the Academy of Dromán.

Resonance Crystal: Crystals that, when paired with another, can be manipulated by a crystallographer to relay messages over long distances.

Rosca Umhir: Capital of the Midlands of Alabach (*Ros-ka iv-er*)

Roseán: Small town in the Clifflands of Alabach, adjacent to the Teeth of the Glenn. (*Row-shawn*)

Ruairí Ó Críodáin: Member of the Sons of Seletoth in Penance.

Santos: Previous Chief Engineer of Penance – deceased.

Seven Seachtú: Provinces of Alabach. (*Seven Shock-two*)

Simian: Native people to Alabach, holding science and technology to a hire esteem than faith and magic.

Sin: The name given to the remnants of a once great tower in the centre of the city of Penance.

Sir Bearach: Knight of Keep Carríga – deceased. (*Sir Byar-ak*)

Sláine the White: Healer of Dromán – Deceased.

Tán: Once was a settlement north of Penance, but long since abandoned.

Terrían: Capital of the Godlands of Alabach. (*Terry-Ann*)

The Academy of Dromán: Educational and academic institute based in the Stronghold of Dromán. Thrives on research into the Nature of magic and training young mages. (*The Academy of Dro-mawn*)

The Black Sail: A smuggling group operating in Cruachan.

The Churchguard: Elite soldiers charged with guarding the Basilica of Penance

The Clifflands: One of the Seven Seachtú of Alabach, its capital city is Point Grey

The Dustgate: Entrance to Penance via one if its residential districts

The Dustworks: Residential district of Penance, home to the Basilica

The Fall of Sin: An event in the history of Alabach where a tower build by the Simians was cast down by Lord Seletoth for exceeding the height of Mount Selyth.

The Firstborn: Early Humans who conquered Alabach 400 years ago.

The Glenn: A valley separating the greater Penance region from the Alabach's Seven Seachtú. Uninhabitable as all flora are poisonous, and all fauna, carnivorous.

The Glory of Penance: Airship built for long-distance travel. Decommissioned and used as a trade vessel.

The Goldgate: Entrance to Penance via its commercial district

The Goldworks: Commercial district of Penance

The Kinglands: One of the Seven Seachtú of Alabach, its capital city Cruachan houses the seat of King Diarmuid III, XIX.

The Reardon Brothers: Twin brothers who work the forge of Roseán.

The Rustlake: Lake adjacent to Penance.

The Saltgate: Entrance to Penance via one if its residential districts

The Saltworks: Residential district of Penance

The Seven Seachtú of Alabach: The kingdom's seven provinces. They are (capital cities in parentheses): The Clifflands (Point Grey), The Godlands (Terrían), The Midlands (Ard Sidhe), The Woodlands (Dromán), The Wetlands (Rosca Umhir), The Floodlands (Tulcha), and The Kinglands (Cruachan).

The Steamgate: Entrance to Penance via its industrial district

The Steamworks: Industrial district of Penance

The Steel Mountains: Mountain range that surrounds Penance

The Stonegate: Entrance to Penance via one if its residential districts

The Stoneworks: Residential district of Penance

The Teeth of the Glenn: Mountain range north of Roseán separating the Clifflands from the Glenn.

The Triad: The governing body of Penance, comprising of Borris Blackhand, Cathal Carríga, and King Diarmuid III XIX.

The Trinity: The three Gods worshipped by Humans in Alabach, comprising of Lord Seletoth (The Father), Lady Meadhbh (The Mother) and King Móráin the First (The Son). The current ruler of Alabach is said to be an incarnation of King Móráin.

The Twelve Saints of the Trinity: Twelve men and women who accompanied Móráin I to Alabach.

Tulcha: Capital of the Floodlands, one of the Seven Seachtú of Alabach. Named after the river that runs through it. *(Tul-ka)*

Wraiths: Mysterious cloaked figures, agents for the Church, but rumoured to be affiliated with Lord Seletoth directly.

Yarlaith the White: Local healer in Roseán, and uncle to Morrígan Ní Branna. *(Yar-layth)*

ACKNOWLEDGEMENTS

As you can probably tell, I definitely in a better place writing this than I was with The Thralls of Fate. After dealing with the spaghetti-like narrative structure of Book One, this lovely and straightforward story was a dream to write.

But again, I cannot take full credit for the content you have just read. As before, I would like to thank all the writers from Scribophile's Ubergroup, and the Candied Sea Urchins who helped with this book just as much as the last. Also, thanks to anyone from real life who read an early draft of this. Again, thank you to my excellent editor Lauren Humphries-Brooks who helped turn this from a pile of pages to an actual, factual novel.

Big props to Cornelia Yoder for the updated map, and to MiblArt team for the excellent cover art. Your pieces have brought more life to this work than all the words I could write could!

Finally, I'd like to thank you, the reader, for picking up this book, and especially to everyone who read Book One. It was your incredible response and praise that helped motivated me to finishing this monster. Thank you.

About the Author

Alan was raised in the seaside village of Rush, County Dublin. He began writing fiction at the age of ten, starting with short stories about each of his classmates being eaten by dinosaurs. Fortunately, this behaviour was encouraged by both parents and teachers, allowing him to grow as an author.

The Thralls of Fate is Alan's first novel, written while studying for his PhD in Dublin City University. During that time, he also wrote a thesis on genetics and molecular biology.

Today, Alan works for the pharmaceutical industry, and spends most of his spare time playing Dungeons & Dragons and Magic the Gathering.

He has no pets.

Twitter: @AlanHarrison
Instagram: @TheRealAlanHarrison
Email: AlanHarrisonAuthor@gmail.com

CPSIA information can be obtained
at www.ICGtesting.com
Printed in the USA
BVHW040829300821
615580BV00015B/384